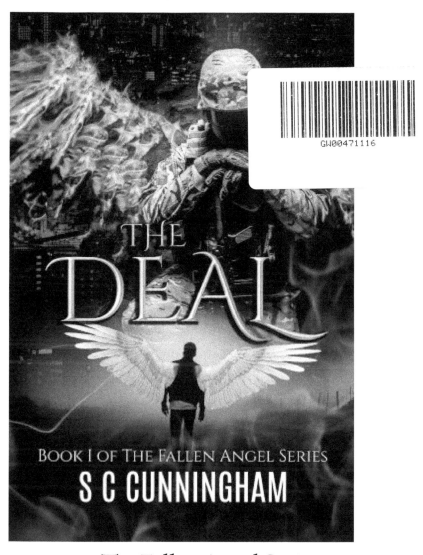

THE
DEAL

BOOK I OF THE FALLEN ANGEL SERIES
S C CUNNINGHAM

The Fallen Angel Series
Book I
The Deal

by
S C Cunningham

www.sccunningham.com @sccunningham8

Books by S C Cunningham

The Penance List
Book I of The David Trilogy
Unfinished Business
Book II of The David Trilogy
For My Sins tbc
Book III of The David Trilogy
The Deal
Book I of The Fallen Angel Series
Karma
Book II of The Fallen Angel Series
The Calling and *Criminal* tbc
Books III & IV of The Fallen Angel Series
The Ginormous Series (13 books, 3-9 yrs)
Empowering, Good-values, Children's Books
Write That Book
The How-to Series

Siobhán C Cunningham

Author of *The Penance List, Unfinished Busines, The Deal* and *Karma,* Cunningham creates psychological crime thrillers with a skilled mix of fuelled tension, dark humour, and pulsating passion. Her works offer a fresh level of sincerity and authority, rare in fiction.

An exmodel, British born of Irish roots, she married a rock musician and has worked in the exciting worlds of music, film, sports and celebrity management.

And as a Police Crime Investigator and Intel Analyst – CID, Wanted & Absconder Unit, Major Crime Team, Crime Investigations.

She is the proud mother to Artist Scarlett Raven and owned by a few cats and dogs, cast members of her empowering *Ginormous Series* children's books.

Thank You

A special note of thanks to all emergency and rescue service workers. The unsung heroes who live quietly among us, working tirelessly - in sometimes dire circumstances and with no thanks - helping keep us and our planet safe. I salute you. And in particular I thank the hard working men and women of Sussex Police.

Thank you to my supportive friends. You know who you are! To my hero of a mum, who keeps lighting the candles and saying the prayers - in the hope that one day I may settle down and get a sensible job. To the loving, soul-soothing pets who lie snoring at my feet as I write.

To my gorgeous proof-readers; DC Andrea Watts, Gigi Jessiman, Sue Robinson. To my supportive friends and work colleagues.

To my wonderful editor, Linda Kasten at *lindakasten.com*, who had the faith, patience and skills to turn my lump of coal into a diamond. To talented cover artist DesignRan at Fiverr.

To my uber talented daughter, Scarlett Raven, my reason, my life. Angel, thank you for the endless support, belief, courage, and idea-crunching. Two dyslexic blondes didn't do too badly! I am honoured to have you in my life.

The Deal

Dear Heavens, I was taken by a bad man, I got away,
but the next girl didn't.
If I promise to be a good girl, when I die,
can I sit on a cloud for a while,
be invisible, and get the baddies that
you and the Police don't get?
Amy Fox, age 4 yrs.

Dear Heavens, thank you for keeping our deal.
But WTF... really!
Haven't we got enough to deal with?
I get we're just physics Erthfolk don't understand yet,
but if criminals don't play by the rules,
then why the hell should we? ... (sigh!)
What'ya gonna do? Kill me?
I'm already dead.
Amy Fox, age 32 yrs.

Brompton south Police Station, London, UK

T he door to the custody interview suite burst open. The warm stench of cannabis, disinfectant, and rancid carpet hit Detective Constable Tony DeAngelo's face as he stepped into the dark, soundproofed box-room.

He flicked a switch. Harsh fluorescent light bounced off grey walls, worn flooring, and cheap brown office furniture. No windows, no pictures, no comfort in this room. It was a place to confess, to tell lies or remain silent. Soaked heavy in confession and deceit, it'd heard it all.

An empty desk sat tucked up against the wall on the left, flanked with four plastic bucket chairs, two either side. A wall-bracketed touchscreen computer protruded at head height over the desk. A CCTV player and screen sat on a cupboard against the opposing wall.

DeAngelo held the door open for the prisoner to enter. The waft of stale sweat, semen, and a night in the cells hit DeAngelo's nostrils as the slovenly male shuffled past him.

DeAngelo took shallow breaths, grateful for the strong-smelling nasal gel he wiped across his top lip prior to interview. The pine fresh vapours prevented retching when dealing with his less hygienic suspects. Especially when three or four bodies - Solicitors, Appropriate Others, Interpreters - squeezed into the airless room, got hot and bothered during questioning.

"Sit on the other side of the desk, please, sir. Your Legal Advisor, Mr. Maydew, will sit beside you."

DeAngelo pointed across the desk at the chair against the wall.

"Have you been here before, sir?"

The prisoner shuffled around the desk, pulled out the chair and manoeuvred his large frame into the seat. He grunted and shook his head; he wasn't used to being called 'sir.'

"No," he mumbled, his hooded gaze darting and scanning the space around him.

Above the table, a red plastic strip sat at shoulder height: a panic alarm. He would have to get passed his Legal Advisor and the Investigator to get to the door, and then tackle five or six Custody staff and three coded doors to get out of the station. No chance.

"Well, I'll explain it to you once we're seated. Are you comfortable? Do you want water?"

"No."

The prisoner closed his eyes and rocked his head back. For twenty years he'd managed to live undetected, below the radar. What the hell had gone wrong?

Immaculately suited and booted, Mr. Maydew flounced into the room, full of pomp and self-importance, his nose twitching at the sour odour emanating from his client. He plonked his shiny leather briefcase noisily on the table, dragged his chair away, as far as was polite, and sat beside the prisoner.

"My client would like to move cells," he announced. "It's disgusting. He's been kept awake by the occupant in the next cell all night, shouting, banging, and—"

"This is not a hotel, Mr. Maydew," interrupted DeAngelo with a sigh.

Maydew was a regular Legal Advisor in Brompton South Custody, a known complainer; he liked to show off in front of his clients and use whatever means possible to upset the rhythm of an interview, in an effort to change the power dynamics, but he just managed to piss everyone off. And DeAngelo sometimes wondered if his legal advice was sound.

"And now he has started a dirty protest. Excrement has been smeared everywhere. The stench is disgusting. My client needs to be moved...for his asthma." Maydew noisily banged the tip of his black ballpoint pen on the table between them. "I demand it."

DeAngelo calmly closed the door and seated himself opposite the prisoner. He placed a black file on the desk and reached up to the touchscreen. He tapped the start button and started to log into the interview system.

"Did you hear me, Officer?" The black pen tapped in time with his words. "I demand a move for my client."

DeAngelo carried on, entering information to the screen.

"Right, sir." He looked at the prisoner, ignoring Maydew. "You'll notice that on the wall and ceiling above us are microphones and cameras. This interview will be digitally recorded and given as evidence should the matter go to court. I can give you a copy of..."

"Will you talk to the Custody Sergeant about a move?" insisted Maydew, increasing the pressure on his drumming pen, not liking being ignored.

DeAngelo looked the prisoner in the eye, paying no attention to Maydew, and continued.

"After the interview, I can give you a form, which tells you how to get a copy of the interview, should you wish. You're entitled to free and independent legal advice—in person or via the telephone—throughout your stay in custody."

The prisoner wasn't paying attention. He dropped his hands to his lap and absent-mindedly scratched the skin of his forearms. DeAngelo wondered if he was suffering from drug withdrawal.

"I see you've taken legal advice. Are you happy with the advice you've been given?"

The prisoner's eyes shifted to the pompous man sitting beside him. He gave a resigned tilt of his head and nodded. The two men couldn't be more different.

"Are you happy to continue?" asked DeAngelo.

The prisoner nodded, staring into his lap, watching nails tear into skin.

"If you would like to stop the interview at any time and confer with your advisor, let me know, we can—"

"The stench is disgusting," interrupted Maydew. "Shit everywhere...I could smell it from the disclosure room." Incessantly tapping his pen, a spoilt little boy trying to get attention.

"I will see if the Honeymoon Suite is available after the interview, Mr. Maydew. Now, if you please, let us continue."

The prisoner sniggered.

DeAngelo punched the final setup details onto the screen.

"Very funny," tutted Maydew indignantly, reaching over the table and waving his pen at DeAngelo. "I will report you, DC DeAngelo."

DeAngelo ignored the threat, lined his file neatly in front of him, and focused on the prisoner.

"Once I start the recording, I'll introduce each of us in the room. I'll caution you, and then explain the caution. I'll then ask you why you are here today, giving you an opportunity to put your side of events forward."

The prisoner nodded, sweat gathering on his top lip.

"I ask that you speak up for the benefit of the recording, so that you can be heard. I also ask that you don't interrupt me when I'm talking, that you listen to my question, and in turn I'll listen to your answer and not interrupt you, do you understand?"

The prisoner squeezed his hands together, in an effort to stop the scratching, and nodded.

"Right, are you ready?"

The prisoner nodded again.

"Are you ready, Mr. Maydew?"

"Yes, yes, yes... Let's get this over with, and then I'll have words with the Custody Sergeant," grumbled Maydew with a wave of his pen.

"You know the protocol, Mr. Maydew. I assume your phone is turned off."

"Err...no...actually...err." Maydew blustered as he reached into his breast pocket and pulled out a phone. He fumbled clumsily with buttons, trying to turn it off. "Damn this bloody thing!"

DeAngelo caught the prisoner's eye; they gave each other a mutual look of annoyance at Maydew's antics.

Maydew finally succeeded in silencing his phone and slipped it back, out of sight, into his pocket. "Yes, yes...it's off. Now go ahead. Let's get on with it, for heaven's sake," he muttered, as if it were DeAngelo's fault.

"Thank you. I will now start the interview." DeAngelo pressed the recording button; the screen lit up with a timer.

"The time is now 10.18 hours. It is Sunday, the 18th of January, and we are in Brompton Custody Suite. I will introduce those present for the recording. I am DC DeAngelo, also present is…" DeAngelo waved his hand at Maydew.

"Allister Maydew, Legal Advisor for Winchestern Solicitors," mumbled Maydew in a jaded, I'm-way-too-important-to-be-here tone.

DeAngelo looked at the prisoner.

"Can you please give your name?"

"No comment."

"For heaven's sake, old boy," Maydew chided. "The no comment is for the questions. You can give your name; they know your name."

"No comment," repeated the prisoner, jaw set, eyes cast firmly down towards his lap.

DeAngelo continued.

"Can you please give your date of birth?"

"No comment."

"Ughh…" Maydew sighed, shaking his head, as if talking to a simpleton. "They know your date of birth. You can give—"

"Mr. Maydew," said DeAngelo, tired of the interruptions. "This is the prisoner's interview. You've been invited to give him legal advice, which it seems he is taking. May I ask you to stop interrupting? If you and your client wish to confer further, we can stop the interview and adjourn whilst you do so."

Maydew sat upright, tight lipped, quietly seething.

"Continue." He swept his pen at the room.

"Thank you." DeAngelo looked at the prisoner. "Are you happy to continue? Did you want to confer further with your Solicitor… sorry," looking to Maydew. "Could you confirm, are you a Solicitor or Legal Advisor?" knowing full well that the man didn't have the broader training of a Solicitor.

"Legal Advisor." Maydew spat, tightening his lips into a thin line.

"Thank you," DeAngelo turned back to the prisoner. "Are you happy to continue?"

The prisoner nodded.

"I am now going to *caution* you and then explain it's meaning. OK?"

The prisoner nodded again, head down, his gaze boring into his lap.

"You don't have to say anything, but it may harm your defence if you do not mention when questioned something which you later reply on in court. Anything you do say may be given in evidence." The prisoner shifted in his chair.

"To explain, you don't have to talk to me or answer my questions. Anything you do say will be given as evidence via this recording, but if you don't answer my questions today, and it does go to court, the court may wonder why you waited until then to answer my questions. They may also wonder if you're telling the truth. Do you understand the caution?"

The prisoner nodded.

"For the benefit of the recording, you are nodding your head. Is that correct?"

"No comment."

"Last night you were arrested for the offences of GBH, grievous bodily harm, and possession of indecent images of children, what can you tell me about this?"

"Bollocks."

Maydew sniggered.

DeAngelo didn't flinch.

Maydew held up a hand to stop DeAngelo's next question. He opened his briefcase with a smart double click of the locks and took out a piece of A4 lined paper.

"My client has written a prepared statement," he announced triumphantly, dropping the briefcase to the floor and placing the paper on the table in front of him.

The statement consisted of a handwritten short paragraph with Maydew's large black spidery letters scrawled across the page and the prisoner's tiny, meticulous signature along the bottom. DeAngelo noted that for a large, unkempt man, the prisoner had surprisingly small writing. Controlled, heavy pressured, narrow letters, all sloping to the left and making contact—suggested to him a highly cautious, intelligent, inhibited personality with authority issues.

"Would you like me to read it out to you, Officer?" Maydew tapped his pen on the table, smug that he was back in control.

"Yes, thank you." DeAngelo gave him his full attention.

Maydew swept up the statement with a theatrical sweep of his hand, and read to the gallery in a loud thespian voice. Enjoying the drama.

"I, the above-named person, categorically deny the offences against me. With reference to the GBH offence, I do not know of the victim, have never met the victim, and was at home, alone, watching football during the date and time disclosed. I know this because it was an important Chelsea V Manchester United match that day. With reference to the indecent images offence, my computer is shared by many friends and acquaintances, and is left alone when I am at the local library, acquiring coffee. If there are images on my laptop, I do not know who put them there."

Maydew triumphantly placed the paper in the middle of the table and slid it over to DeAngelo.

"Thank you, Mr. Maydew."

DeAngelo picked it up and quietly reread the text, taking his time as the two men waited in silence. He opened his file and placed the exhibit statement to the back, seemingly unbothered by its contents.

"I would first like to talk to you about the assault. I would like you to look at Exhibit Numbers AD06 to AD011, which are five images taken of the victim after the attack."

DeAngelo carefully pulled out five full-colour, A4 photographs and slowly placed them, one by one, in a line down the middle of the table, facing the two men. He took extra care to align each image, placing them equidistant between each other and the table's edges. Giving the two men time to absorb the horror. The colour red oozed before them.

Silence.

Maydew leaned forward to get a closer look, at first not understanding what he was seeing. When he realised he was looking at skin and muscle torn from a man's face and that the patches of bloody white were skull bone, he shot back in his chair in shock, swallowing back a retch.

"What the fuck!" He said dropping his pen to cover his mouth with disgust.

The pen rolled slowly across the table and settled between DiAngelo and the prisoner.

In less than three seconds, the prisoner picked up the pen, snatched Maydew's hand from his mouth, slammed it palm down onto the table, and stabbed the pen violently three times into skin, crunching through flesh and bone, the final stab given with such force it pinned the quivering hand to the wood. Blood spurted across the file and exhibit images.

Maydew screamed like a banshee. He scratched at the prisoner's face with his free hand, trying to make him stop. The prisoner's yellow, jagged teeth snapped at two of the flaying fingers, gripped hard and crunched down with a grunt. Maydew howled with pain as blood seeped from the corner of his client's sneering mouth and splattered the pristine white of his shirt cuff.

"For the benefit of the recording," sighed DeAngelo. "For no apparent reason, the suspect has stabbed his Legal Advisor in the hand with a pen and is now chewing his fingers."

DeAngelo hit the panic alarm.

All hell broke loose.

Chapter One

Eight years later, Kensington Apartments,
Knightsbridge, London, UK

He towered over the bed and watched with cold, narrow eyes, studying her face while she slept. In a few hours, she would be dead.

From the file he'd read, she was a healthy, hardworking, attractive young woman with a good soul and a clean record. They would determine no reason for her to move over. *This one'll be questioned, and they'll complain.*

Deep in thought, he brought a smouldering Cuban cigar to his lips, tilted his jaw to the ceiling, and drew long and hard on the Montecristo No. 2. *They'll fight for her. It's bound to get dirty.*

A burning sizzle cracked the silence as an orange orb hissed and glowed in the darkness, highlighting the lines of his battle-scarred face. *Erthfolk will ask why. They always do. Why her...why now...why so young...why's it always the good ones? Blah de blah...blah de bloody blah... whatever! When will they ever get it?*

He bent over the bed and leaned in close to her face; stale breath cooled her cheek. His body rattled as he took a deep rasping breath, inhaling her sweet smell. They all had a smell and he liked to smell them. *Erthfolk never understand death. It's always a shock. You'd think they'd learned by now they're only guests on this planet. I mean, it's not like they don't know it's coming, for fuck's sake. Death is the only certainty in life. Hmmm...you smell of lilies. I like lilies.*

He heaved himself up and stood over her; legs apart, arms crossed. His job required him to guard her until the morning sun eased through silk curtains and welcomed her to her last day on earth.

He loved his job, particularly this time of night: the silence, the calm, the world stopping to catch its breath. It was a time when Erthfolk slept, and were at their most vulnerable, enabling him to sneak into their lives and move about his business with ease.

He stared down at her. *It's time, young lady. Not gonna lie, you're not gonna like it. Nor will you feel ready. All those dreams you had, all the things you wanted to do, all those important possessions you coveted — your clock has run out, they're all gone, they have no value. No goodbyes, no nothing. It's gonna be a bit of a shock, and it will hurt...a lot...but it's time.*

He smoothed down his black tailored suit sleeves and glanced down to check out his gleaming patent shoes. To him, ever the dandy gentleman, looks were everything. Standards needed to be kept. The rancid smell of his body, he couldn't help, but the shine of his shoes he could.

She turned in her sleep. He sighed. *You see, dear, it doesn't pay to be special; you tend to piss off too many people. I hope someone sends lilies to your funeral. They suit you.*

Barely visible in the shadows, he stepped away from the bed and paced the room, getting itchy feet. Normally, he didn't mind waiting. He enjoyed the calm before the storm, but this one was different. He sensed a troubling aura and shook his head.

He gently pulled at the curtain to check on the night sky. The moonlight exposed his crabby war-torn face. His eyes squinted with the glare. He abruptly released the curtain and peered over at her. *Not long now, dear.*

He admired her face. He'd seen more than his fair share of faces and had taken thousands of lives in his time, but she was special. She had the beauty and intelligent, stubborn air of her mother.

He brought the cigar to his mouth and pulled on its bitter tip. Rocking his head back, he leisurely blew a torrent of thick grey smoke into the darkness. Its ethereal shadow percolated the air and gently tumbled around him, highlighting his body with a cloudy haze.

Maybe he shouldn't have taken this job. He still had time; he could let someone else handle her. But she was on his patch and they would ask why. He didn't like questions; he lived by his own rules. *They can fuck off.*

Pursing his lips, he gave a soft blow across the tip of his smouldering Cuban, its embers blazing anew as soft white ash fluttered to the ground. Skipping up onto his toes, he took a few nifty steps backwards, managing to avoid the snowy residue landing on his precious clothes.

THE DEAL

She groaned as she turned in her sleep. He watched quietly as her nightmares took hold. She was being warned. He sensed The Fallen were at work.

Used to it, he wasn't too concerned. Interfering Fallens flitted everywhere, Guardian angels, always trying to help Erthfolk, especially on their return journey -—if only the Erthfolk would listen.

They didn't realise they had choices, that fate could be altered or avoided. The power was in their own hands. The smallest tweak of circumstance or the gentlest ripple effect of the tiniest detail could realign it. Following gut instinct, a kind word, taking note of signs, delaying actions even by a nanosecond was enough to change life's pattern.

But luckily for him, Erthfolk seldom paid attention to the Fallen; they rarely looked at the bigger picture. Caught up in their small lives, their greed for objects and desire to be liked overshadowed reality. They hardly ever took time to listen to their own powerful sixth sense. The greatest tool in the box, the subconscious, stored in the brain's largest cortex remained unused. *What a waste, bloody idiots.*

The Fallen and their attempts to steer Erthfolk to safety were, in the main, fruitless. But every now and then, the Fallen managed to get through to a few, those who simply stood still and listened.

A Fallen tried to warn her now, visiting her dreams, but she wouldn't understand it. She was too hazy with alcohol and too busy with her hectic bubble-of-a-life to pay attention. She would forget her dreams the minute she woke up.

He watched as her head rocked from side to side and her skin glistened with fear. Her arms reached out with pleading hands, her breath quickening. Her cheek muscles twitched and jerked. Her eyes scrunched tightly shut. Her mouth opened wide in a silent scream. *Here we go. It's starting. Get ready to rumble.*

He waited patiently as her nightmares unfolded. He knew her fears, but would do nothing to help her— he was a Witness; it wasn't in his job description. As a Witness, it was his business to watch, to tot up her life, to account her good and bad deeds, the balance of which allowed the boss to decide where she went next—up or downstairs, above the skies or below the earth.

In a few hours, her soul would sift through her mouth in a final rasping breath. She wouldn't be alone during the ordeal; he'd be beside her, and possibly a few Fallens. He didn't feel sorry for her; she'd waited 28 years for this moment. *Careful what you wish for, dearie.*

He dragged another leisurely puff off his cigar, holding smoke in his mouth, savouring its flavours. He readily admitted he wasn't the best Witness to have in a soul's corner. He wasn't a very good boy; he didn't play by the rules. But hey, today, she was unlucky. *What can I say? Shit happens. Blah de blah...blah de bloody blah... bothered?*

Lifting his head, he slowly opened his mouth, releasing lethargic swirling smoke. Relishing the aroma, he allowed it to skulk about his tongue and amble through his nostrils. He stood still in the darkness, his majestic head smouldering as if on fire. *Today's the day. You made a deal and it's being kept.*

A distant police siren blared from the streets outside. He looked to the curtained window, then to the ceiling above him and winked. *No peace for the wicked...eh? You guys are busy tonight.*

Chapter Two

Kensington Apartments,
Knightsbridge, London, UK

Amy eased out of slumber and rolled onto her side, tucking her hand underneath the pillow and nuzzling her head into its cool, soft luxury. Her internal clock nudged her, reminding her it wasn't the weekend. With an irritated moan, she snuggled deeper under the duvet. How she hated weekday mornings.

Feeling hot, she thrust her leg into the open from beneath the duvet, letting her foot dangle off the mattress, enjoying the rush of cool morning air. It took a few seconds to realise her toes had brushed against something. Something warm and hairy...a leg. *What the hell was that? Shit.*

Her eyes flashed open and she stared into the dark room. When her eyes adjusted, she caught a glimpse of crisp blue and white striped bed linen. But she didn't have blue and white bed linen. She always dressed her bed in white—a thing she had. This meant she had been sleeping in someone else's bed. *Oh, no, I didn't!*

She held her breath, keeping very still as panic set in, her gaze searching unfamiliar surroundings. In the quiet room, she glanced at closed curtains and an ivory-upholstered chaise stretching across the opposite corner, a handbag perched on it. She peered into the dark, blinking rapidly to erase whatever dream fooled her. Was that her handbag? Her eyes scanned the floor. Were those her clothes strewn across the carpet? *Oh, fuck...I did.*

A black-faced digital alarm clock sat on the bedside table flashing large yellow numbers at her. Scrunching her nose and squinting her eyes, she pulled the shapes into focus: 08.19 hours. She was late for work. *Shit, shit, shit!*

She lay back, stared at the ceiling and concentrated on sounds surrounding her. She heard impatient traffic outside the window, possibly from morning rush hour. Which was a good thing; it meant she'd stayed in the city, and wasn't in the countryside somewhere, in the middle of nowhere.

Beyond the traffic, she detected the soft rise and fall of breathing, presuming it belonged to the leg. This was not a good thing. *Fuck, fuck, fuck! Who the hell? Think...think!*

She couldn't concentrate. Her heart pounded so loudly she feared the leg would hear it. Panic built in her chest. Now was not the time to have an anxiety attack. *Oh, no you don't, not now. Breathe...breathe.*

From experience, she knew if she didn't take control quickly, the attack would overwhelm her. She shut her eyes and took a deep breath, and then another, closing her mind to everything else, concentrating on the air filling her lungs and slowly releasing. She followed the techniques and mantras of self-help books and cognitive therapists who'd taught her over the years. It took all her might to silence and calm her body.

She hated the exhausting attacks descending upon her without warning but had learned to live with them. She'd become a master magician, hiding them from the rest of the world to keep up her Academy Award performance and to pretend everything was okay whilst she suffered in silence and clawed her way back from hell as life carried on around her. At least now she could control the dreaded curse and not freeze with fear as she once did. At least now she no longer begged for the only thing she believed would stop it...death

Many know-it-alls who professed to be experts on the subject were ignorant. Their naïve, insensitive commands of 'pull your socks up' or 'just get on with it' made her cringe. They didn't have a clue what a panic attack entailed. She'd read somewhere that geniuses were prone to depression, so fuck them.

Anxiety was a lonely place. She blamed *him* for her illness, the bastard who took her at the age of four. She believed that one day karma would make him pay...if she didn't get there first. Meanwhile, humour and planning her revenge, helped get her through.

THE DEAL

The attack subsided bit by bit as her breathing slowed to normal. Thankfully, the leg's owner hadn't noticed and still snored away. *Time to get out of here, the boss is going to kill me.*

She lifted her head off the pillow; a blistering headache hit home and pierced the back of her eyes. She dropped her head back down. She shouldn't drink on antidepressants. *Urrgh! How much did I drink?*

The office parties were renowned for their mayhem. She didn't remember hooking up with anyone. *So, where the hell am I, and who the hell is the leg? Gawd, I'm too old for this.*

Peering over the duvet to the end of the bed, she saw daylight seeping through a door frame, outlining her exit point. Her head continued to thump with pain, forcing her to lean back into the pillow.

She lay very still, trying not to wake whoever was attached to the leg, and sorted through the jumbled images of the previous night's proceedings.

The party had started with shots. *Always dangerous.*

Blotchy flashes of memory teased her brain. She'd been drinking, pub crawling, table-dancing, singing. *Urrgh! 'Mama Mia' again.*

A flash of being manhandled in the back of a black taxi flitted through her mind, a nice manhandle, not frightening manhandle. *But who?*

At least it was a man, the leg was hairy...unless it was Velma from Reception, who didn't shave. *Oh gawd, please don't let it be Velma and her obsessive crush issues.*

Velma, was their overenthusiastic office receptionist. Amy once ran across the reception area, rushing from one meeting to another. Velma caught her eye as she sat hawk-like behind her imposing desk. Being polite, Amy casually asked her how she was.

"Hello there. How are you?"

A quick, courteous, throwaway line. The kind of line everyone used but rarely meant.

Before she knew it, Velma had shared her life story, and because Amy had practiced good manners and listened, it somehow meant Velma had permission to report her every move to Amy, that they had formed a bond, a one-sided bond. Velma rarely asked how Amy was.

Ever since that fateful *'How are you?'* Velma had latched on to Amy. Taking every opportunity to phone, text, email and search Amy out, to detail the smallest day-to-day detritus of her existence. Regularly, she followed Amy to the loo, and would be waiting outside as Amy took her lunch hour or left to go home at the end of the day.

Amy didn't have the heart to stop her. She felt sorry for the lonely girl and simply accepted the missives and made 'ahhh,' 'ok,' 'how lovely,' 'sorry, I have to go' comments, hoping the zealous oversharing would eventually fizzle out. Possibly, when Velma acquired a boy or girlfriend—she wasn't sure which—and she'd have someone else to focus on. Setting Velma up on a date topped Amy's bucket list.

Amy tried again to lift her head off the pillow, but it pounded from dehydration. She needed water.

Slinking snakelike from under the duvet, she slid silently to the floor. Naked, on all fours, arse in the air, she crawled around the king-size bed, her knees burning on lush, thick-piled carpet. Praying the leg wouldn't wake and peer over the bed. *This is SO not a good look.*

Creeping towards the door, she gathered her belongings: underwear, dress, bag, and shoes.

Strangely, she could see only her clothes strewn across the floor with no sign of the leg owner's clothing. *Weird, unless they were very tidy, but who puts away clothes in the heat of passion? Has there been any passion?*

She couldn't feel any discomfort in her body, any sign of a passionate workout. She put her hand between her legs to check for tell-tale wetness. She was dry. *No sex...unless they wore a condom and I didn't come. How bloody selfish...effing typical.*

Sitting on her knees, she peered over the bed, trying to make out the leg owner's identity, but whoever the stranger was, they lay on their stomach, covered in the duvet's blue and white striped sea, their head tucked under pillows as if blocking out sound. *Was I snoring? Shit, I was snoring, wasn't I? Urrgh...embarrassing and I haven't waxed, cut my toenails, or worn matching underwear...bloody typical.*

Nervously, she braved getting to her feet and tiptoed the last few steps to her exit. Painstakingly, she quietly eased the door handle and heaved it ajar just enough to creep out. As she pulled the door shut behind her, she heard a loud fart blast unceremoniously from the bed. She giggled. *That must be a man...although...vegan Velma does have a penchant for beans.*

THE DEAL

As she turned away from the door, the apartment's bright light slapped her in the face, stinging her eyes. She recoiled behind her hand. *Urrgh...shit.*

The cheery morning sun shone through a wall of balcony windows. Squinting, toppling, and struggling to keep her balance, she held onto furniture and stepped into last night's clothing, which stank of stale perfume, acrid cigar smoke, and alcohol. *Why do I smell of smoke? Does the leg smoke? Yuck, ashtray-breath kisses...I must've been drunk.*

Her head throbbing, she braved the sun's glare and looked around the sumptuous open plan room, decked in creams and gold. They were up high, overlooking a glistening London skyline. She ran to the window, peered down, and gratefully recognised the bustling Knightsbridge street below. The sign for Brompton Court Train Station twinkled back at her. Checking her watch, she deduced she had 25 minutes to be sitting at her desk; no time to return home for freshening up or a wardrobe change.

Stilettos in hand and bag over her shoulder, she crept through the room in search of an exit, scanning the sideboard and coffee table, trying to work out who owned the apartment. But nothing, no pictures, no ornaments, no sign of life. The expensive, glamourous, tasteful, and very tidy pad was possibly a rental.

Her coat lay strewn across the floor, obviously dumped in a hurry. She snatched it up to pull it on, jamming her arms into the sleeves. As she tiptoed past a sideboard, she peered down and noticed a piece of paper sticking out from beneath it. She checked the bedroom door and found it still snuggly closed.

Curiosity getting the better of her, she popped her bare big toe onto the paper and dragged it out along the carpet into view.

A beautiful young woman's fresh face stared up at her with sparkling cheeky eyes, high cheekbones, and soft, pale pink hair curling about her shoulders. Her head tilted to the side, giving the camera a bright trusting smile.

She didn't recognise the girl. *Maybe it's the leg owner's girlfriend?...sister?.*

No time to delve further, she couldn't risk having the leg wake at any moment; she slid the image back under the sideboard and made her way to the front door.

Heaving it open with a quick, final glance over her shoulder, she exited and pulled it gently shut behind her.

Relieved to have escaped unnoticed, she snuck across the opulent communal hallway to an awaiting elevator, choosing it over using the large circular stairway. She stepped inside and pressed the ground floor button. The doors closed with a gentle chime. A shiny gold panel indicated she occupied the fifth floor, the arrow pointing down.

With a sigh of relief, she turned and fell back against the doors. Her dishevelled image stared back at her from mirrored walls. *Good God, I look rough!*

Licking fingers, she rapidly wiped tell-tale mascara smudges from beneath her eyes and across her cheeks. She smoothed down her dress and finger-combed her hair. Rummaging through her bag, she found a lipstick tube and skilfully covered her red-wine-stained lips. *Disgusting...I've got to stick to white.*

The elevator hit the ground with a soft thump, depositing her in a lobby where she stepped into her shoes and strode into the lavish silk, marble, and granite concierge area, sauntering as nonchalantly and carefree as possible. She held her head high and blagged it, as if born to be there.

Taking it all in, she gawked at the building that reeked of money, but whom did she know lived here. *Oh god, please don't let it be a client...or Velma.*

Her heart began to speed up again. *Not again! Shut up and breathe.*

Her heels clicked cheaply on the marble floor. The uniformed concierge looked up. She bet he'd grown accustomed to witnessing beautiful young women leaving the building in the early hours, his ready smile and slight nod confirming her suspicions.

She didn't have time, or the balls, to stop and talk to him, to find out who the hell she'd been with last night. Would he even know? She scampered on, giving him a weak smile and a hasty wave of her hand.

As she reached the entrance doorway, four burly men wearing police uniforms barged past her.

"Excuse me, miss." One of them turned to look over his shoulder, taking in the view of her long legs and tight-fitting dress.

She pulled her coat smartly around her body, hiding her thighs.

The officers hurried as their radios barked instructions and surrounded an alarmed concierge. The taller officer waved an official looking document at him.

Not waiting to see the fuss unfold, she pushed through the doors, skipped down the pillared entrance steps, skirted around the badly parked police cars with their flashing lights, and marched off into the London sunshine. *Coffee...now!*

Chapter Three

Brompton Court Train Station,
Knightsbridge, London, UK

He stood in the shadows, watching her fight her way through the barriers, one hand clutching the phone to her ear, the other balancing a tall iced latte and holding it aloft over commuters' heads.

Amy shouted into her mobile, competing with the station's hum.

"Urrgh! I've got the hangover from hell, Sal...sorry, what did you say?" She squinted her eyes from the pain, vowing never to drink again.

"What am I going to do, Ames? It's that bitch Dartagnia. She's been promoted, and she's driving me crazy. I swear I'm going to kill her." Sally's voice whined through the phone. When she was pissed off, her inflections picked up a faster pace and higher pitch.

"Don't let her get to you, hon. There's a little shit-stirrer in every office. Just suck it up. Life's too short. Leave it to karma." Amy hugged the phone tight into her ear, took a slurp of much needed coffee, and continued.

"What you need is a little protective Labradorite tumble stone in your pocket. That'll keep her at bay."

"You and your crystals. What a load of baloney," tutted Sally. "No, what I need is a little protective knuckle duster in my pocket and to chuck her into the bay. God help me, I'm gonna kill that woman."

"Revenge only gets you in trouble, Sal, and comes back threefold. She's not worth it." Amy bit her lip and crossed her fingers, justifying her own revenge plan because it was different; *he* was an evil, murdering, child abuser.

"I don't care. I'd gratefully do time for that woman."

"Just let karma do its stuff."

"Stuff karma. Who's got time to wait for blinking karma? I want her dead, now!" groaned Sally. "Do we know any hitmen?"

"No, I don't know any hitmen," Amy sighed.

Fellow commuters turned to look at her. She'd spoken a little too loudly. She gave them an apologetic shrug and turned away, whispering into her phone.

"Funny as it may seem, my contact list is fresh out of hitmen. You've got to calm down, hon. Maybe I should get you a Smithsonite stone. It's really pretty. You'll love it."

"Fuck off with the blinking crystals, for god's sake. What about some cyanide crystals, or ammunition? Can you get me some ammunition?" Sal had no time for the crystal hocus-pocus.

Amy sighed. "No, I can't get any cyanide or ammunition."

Her fellow commuters started to move away.

She carried on before Sal could continue.

"You need to calm down. Smithsonite is a stone of tranquillity. I know what you're like. You get all ugly-obsessive-revengey. Your neck goes red and steam comes out your ears. It's so not a good look, hon." A surge of nausea hit Amy. "God I feel ill. I think I'm going to faint. I forgot my crystal last night. Should've known I'd get into trouble."

As Amy squeezed through barriers, a wave of hurried, stressed commuters flowed in behind her. Well used to the rush hour chaos, she surfed the tide with ease. Tripping and bumping to the polite British murmur of 'sorry...ooops,' 'sorry...so sorry.'

The heaving travellers made their way across the forecourt, down the steps, and onto the busy platform. She strained to hear her friend's reply.

"You're a useless drinker, two drinks and you keel over...wish Dartagnia would, do us all a favour. Give me the biggest fucking stone you've got. I'm gonna fucking throw it at her."

"Now, that's not helpful."

"I'm gonna tie ten of them to her handcuffed body and throw her in the Thames."

"Sal..."

"I know, I know...you see the effect she has on me. I hate the way she brings out the bitch...grrrrrr! I can't help it. Nor can anyone else in the office. We all look forward to her days off or when she phones in sick. There's such a nice energy in the place when she's not there," Sally sighed. "Miss High-and-Fucking-Mighty is always belittling us, always having the last word, charming to our faces but stabbing knives in our backs as soon as we leave the room. We call her the smiling assassin."

Sally continued, barely coming up for air.

"She loves it when we fuck up, loves pointing it out and getting us in trouble, thinks she knows it all...and she generally does...grrrrrr! If we've done something, anything, you can bet she's done it bigger and better. I bet if I say I've had a morning shit, she's had two. She's all about one-upmanship. Why are some women such annoying dicks? Surely, we're all on the same side? Bitch, bitch...bitch, bitch...BITCH."

"You don't like her then."

"No, I bloody don't...and I'm gonna do something about it."

Silence.

"Like what?"

"Murder."

"Murder is not the answer, honey." Fellow commuters glanced over their shoulders. "God, I need some drugs." Amy rubbed her forehead as the throbbing became unbearable. She turned to notice the stares. "Headache tablets...I NEED HEADACHE TABLETS," she shouted, for their benefit.

"What?"

"Nothing. I've got a stinking headache."

"If murder isn't the answer, then what is?"

"Asking the Angels for help, then leaving it to karma...they'll sort it for you, but you have to ask. Otherwise they can't help."

"Yeah, like they'll listen to me. Fallen angels maybe, but I'm not sure they do hit requests. They're not the Mafia, Ames."

Silence. Amy could hear Sal's heavy breathing.

"Are you picking at your cuticles? Hands down, *now*," Amy barked, knowing exactly what her friend would be doing: sulking, slouching in a chair, cradling her phone against her neck, and pulling at the tags of skin around her fingernails.

Sally's cuticles took the brunt of her stress. Next would be the scrunch-eyed, microscopic scrutiny of split ends (that only she could see) in her long, beautiful, well-conditioned hair, followed by tearing the ends apart.

"Why can't blokes see her for who she is? See past the teeth, tits, short skirts, and promise of a cock suck?" Sally moaned. "Bet she's lousy at it, she has one of those skinny, small, thin-lipped mouths that so doesn't know how to enjoy a good meal...surely, blokes can stop thinking with their dicks once in a blue moon. Have you got a stone for dicks?"

"Well, there is one for impotence—Pink Beryl, I think it's called..."

"Ames...shut up!"

"Sal, calm down and don't even think about the hair. Drop it, *now!*" Amy barked before Sally could reach for her locks. "I'm so gonna get you a few stones to get rid of this negative energy. Maybe a nice bit of Smoky Quartz and a Sunstone. You can wear them in your bra."

"I don't need no bleedin' stones. I need a drink—a double gin and tonic would just about do it right now."

"It's 8.30 a.m., hon."

"Urrgh...so? It's blinking five o'clock somewhere."

Taking a leisurely drag of his cigar, he watched Amy's blonde head weave along the jam-packed platform, looking for a place to stand. She found it near the outer edge halfway down the tunnelled station. He flicked the smouldering stub to the floor, covered it with the tip of his shiny black patent shoe, and twisted firmly, left to right, grinding the smoking leaf into the ground. He flicked ash from the cuff of his suit, stepped out of the shadows, and followed her. He loved the 'click-click' sound of his shoes as he walked. It made him feel important.

"This is ridiculous. They need to put on more trains. Heaven knows we pay enough for our tickets," muttered Amy, squeezing into a gap between a little old lady and a suited city gent, ignoring the gent's tutting glare and impatient shake of his newspaper as he tried to read it.

"What?" asked Sal, barely hearing her over the noise.

"Nothing, hon. I'm at the station...chaos as usual. Another joyous journey of sardine-packed, stinky arm-pit, breath-holding hell. I'm soooo done with London. I wanna live by the sea, get a cuddly Saint Bernard dog, tend a vegetable patch, have good Wi-Fi, and work from a shed in the garden," she said, taking a sip of coffee. "No rush hour, no dirt, noise, congestion charge or the expensive costs of a city. Dartagnia—what kind of name is that anyway?"

"Her mum has a thing for The Musketeers, apparently," grumbled Sal.

"Ohhh...I love them in that TV show. Athos is delish, although Aramis is quite cute... and that theme tune always gets me tingly."

"It means leader or something. I call her plain old Tanya to piss her off. She hates it. And do you know, she shags on my desk when we're not in the office? I bleach my desk every morning and pick pubic hairs out of my keyboard. It's disgusting."

"Ewe...why don't you tell your boss, if she's so bad, hon?"

"Can't. He's the one she's shagging."

"What about his wife?"

"She's shagging her, too."

"What about her own husband?"

"He's invited."

"For god's sake, is anyone doing any work in that office?"

"Swingers...I ask you, how the hell can I compete? Have you got a little tumble stone for that?" Sal said, grumbling sarcastically.

"Nope, I don't think so, but Jasper may prolong sexual pleasure, and Rose Quartz is a great love stone."

"Oh, for eff's sake...shuuuuut uuup."

"*The next train on platform two is the Piccadilly line, eastbound train for Cockfosters.*" The tannoy screeched above commuter's heads while the platform bustled with anticipation.

"Talking of sexual pleasure, I think I fucked up last night, Sal."

"Good. Glad to hear it's not always me. What kind of fuck-up?"

"Waking-up-in-a-stranger's-bed kind of fuck-up...the walk-of-shame-from-an-address-I-don't-recognise kind of fuck-up...the what-the-hell-happened, and with-who kind of fuck-up. I left my protection stone at home. Should've known."

"Ooohh, who?" Sal said, cooing excitedly. "One of the guys from your internet dating site? The architect? The gardener? The scaffolder? The upholsterer? Oh my, not the priest?"

"No. Well I don't think so. I'm still trying to work it out. I didn't see who it was as I snuck out of the bedroom," Amy admitted with a prolonged sigh. "It was the office party last night; I don't even know if it was a guy. It could have been a client or Velma."

"Who's Velma?"

"You know—the one with yellow teeth and personal space issues who always stands too close when she's talking to you. Our receptionist."

"Oh yes, oh no. But she's not...and you're not...are you?"

"No, no. But she does get a little creepy, needy, in your face, especially when drunk. I'm sure I didn't go home with her. I think it was a man. Even paralytic, I would know the difference, surely." She shook her head, trying to get rid of the image of Velma's yellow teeth going in for a kiss. "It didn't smell like a woman."

"Ewe..."

"You know what I mean. It was a macho pad. A woman would've had nice perfumed smellies around the place. Oh, I don't know."

"You're such an old tart, Amy Fox," Sal giggled. "Never a dull moment."

Amy cringed. She could hear Sally's snorting laughter.

"Stop laughing. I've got to go straight into the orifice this morning, stinking of Beaujolais and vodka shots." She slurped her coffee. "If I see Velma later and she gives me a loving look, at least I'll know it was her last night and not a client. I can't ever walk through Reception again, I'll have to use the back door."

Sally's laughter got louder.

"Stop laughing," Amy shouted into the phone.

The stuffy newspaper gent gave Amy a raised eyebrow with a disdainful glint. She gave him a full-on, fake smile and shrugged. *Miserable twat, you need to get laid, mate.*

"She may be too mortified to turn up today." Sally's laughed.

"Will you stop laughing?"

"Sorry, Ames." Sally took a deep breath to calm herself. "At least you've put an end to your dry patch, hon. It's been a while."

"I'm not sure if I did...and if I did, it would be nice to be able to remember the moment, for god's sake." Amy sighed. A thought came to her.

"You don't think I was drugged, do you? My drink spiked? I'm never drinking again."

"I'll see you in the bar after work then."

"What if it's a client, Sal?"

"I hope not. You know what happened the last time. What did he...sorry she...sorry...*it* do when you left—" Sally's voice was drowned out as the tannoy screeched.

"*Mind the gap.*"

Amy cupped her phone closer, unable to hear.

"Hang on a minute, Sal. I can't hear you. I'll plug my headphones in. Hold on."

Placing her coffee cup safely on the ground between her feet, she fished around in her handbag for her headset. Something caught her attention.

She pulled out an old black and white photograph, torn and yellow with age. She turned it backwards and forwards in her hands, trying to understand where it had come from. She looked to the old lady and the grumpy gent, wondering if one of them had lost a treasured photo, but they ignored her, too busy preparing for the almighty charge to secure a place on the train.

The image portrayed a young boy and girl, no more than four or five years old, standing together and smiling for the camera. The blonde girl cupped a football in her short arms and the curly brown-headed boy cradled a toy machine gun. She couldn't make out their faces, the image too worn and blurry. She turned the photograph over and read the words 'I'm sorry' scrawled in black ink across the back.

"*Mind the gap.*"

Could the photo have found its way into her bag during her one-night-stand? She couldn't think now, her mind throbbing with hangover fog. She'd work it out later. She stuffed the photograph back into her bag and picked up her coffee. The distant train rumbled and churned in rolling rhythm, its vibration rocking the platform.

"Sal..." she shouted into her phone. No answer.

Leaning forward, she peered down the tracks into the black tunnel. Train headlights came screaming towards her while its thundering noise shook the air. Warm, soot-ridden wind sucked at her ankles, swirled around her body and lifted soft blonde hair from her shoulders. She scrunched her eyes tight from the percolating grime.

"*Mind the gap.*"

A grinding screech signalled the train's declining speed.

"Sal, I've gotta go. Speak later, OK...OK?" Amy shouted above the noise.

As the train neared, a breathy wisp of air blew across her body, unlike the train's stirring wind or an exhausted traveller gasping for air. Commuters jockeyed for position along the platform, knocking into each other, but this cool sensation delivered an eeriness she couldn't explain.

She shivered, glancing over her shoulder but saw nothing more than anxious people shoving their way to avoid being late for work.

They shuffled nearer to the platform's edge, ready to jump on board at the earliest possible moment. *Why are we always in such a rush?*

"Can you hear me, Sally? Sal?" She gave up. "I've gotta go. Love you," she shouted.

A large crashing sound could be heard over the noise of the train. Passengers turned to see where the noise had come from. In the entranceway to the platform, for no apparent reason, the station clock, hanging from the ceiling, had broken from one of its hinges and swung to hit a wall, shattering its casing. Commuters squealed to avoid the falling glass, then quickly carried on jostling for platform position. The train was almost at a standstill.

As it's cold shadow fell across her face, a powerful punch drilled into her lower back, delivered with such force it threw her body forward, and out onto the track.

Time stood still as she fell, flailing, hands grasping at her precious mobile, watching in slow motion as her coffee cup arced the air. She turned to see the stricken train driver's face, behind the pane of oncoming glass. *It's not your fault.*

With all his might, the driver mouthed a silent scream, "Nooooo..."

She closed her eyes and waited for the pain.

Black.

Silence.

"Hello, hello...what's happened?" The phone crackled, lying in the dirt beneath the platform's kerb.

"Amy...are you there? I can't hear you. Amy?"

Inquisitive tiny brown mice scurried to sniff the brightly lit screen and its surrounding droplets of blood. They scampered to safety as the train's brakes screeched to a final halt, blocking the sound of Sally's cries and commuter's screams.

"AMY.... AAAMMMYYY."

36

Chapter Four

One month later. The Prince's Estate,
East London, UK

S he stepped through the doorway and walked to the middle of the dimly
lit room. He didn't notice her or the cold, drafty air she brought with
her...*yesterday Monte Carlo, today London's East End...God I love my job,
never a dull moment.*

She glanced around, her eyes adjusting to the light. A grubby brown sofa
sat cowered against a wall; torn, stained, hidden beneath soiled clothes and
crumpled greying bed linen.

With its rusty chain hanging dejected to the floor, an upturned tandem
bicycle leaned against a bookshelf. Bulging black garbage bags huddled
together in a corner, supporting each other's weight. Takeaway cartons, beer
cans, and old newspapers scattered the floor, camouflaging the filthy,
thread-bare carpet. *Well, he's definitely not house-proud.*

A child's distant cry caught her attention. She spun her head towards
an open window and its partially drawn burgundy red curtains stifling the
bright sunny day and the chatter of children at play. A small gap in the heavy
material showed the bobbing blonde ponytail of a little girl standing outside
the apartment, giggling with her friends. Squeals and shouts danced along
the concrete walkway of their make-believe world.

They were four floors up in a damp, crumbling, council block—not an
ideal playground—but children possess the ability to create magical realms
wherever they are.

She turned to look at him and took a deep breath. An immediate
mistake. The stale pungent smell of sweat, semen, cigarettes, and old trainers
hit her senses. She covered her mouth in disgust and rasped at air through
her black suit jacket's cuff. *Urrgh, for god's sake, do you ever wash?*

Smells always get to her. As with music or old photos, smells conjured
up deep hidden memories, whether welcome or not. Tugs to the heart, or in

this case, bile to the back of the throat. She swallowed hard, forcing back the threatening retch.

The sooner she got out of there the better. It was time. Grabbing the lapels of her jacket, she gave a sharp tug on her collar. It stood up, framing her long neck, glossy blonde hair, and beautiful face.

Placing hands on her hips, chest out, and legs apart, she stood tall, squaring her athletic body to face him. She gave a discreet '*I'm here*' cough.

He didn't look up.

She coughed again, louder.

Nothing.

The little girl outside gave a shrill squeal of laughter, catching the man's attention. He looked over at the curtains with small beady eyes, listening, biting his lower lip, anxious to see what the children were up to. But a computer screen fought for his attention and won. He remained seated, scrolling through images and text.

She coughed again.

Nothing.

He didn't notice her; she was used to that by now. They hardly ever did, but it was always best to check since some were more in tune than others. Some of the people she had to deal with lived in their own selfish bubble with no thought for anyone but themselves. Being ignored was normal for her. He was no different.

Except, he was different. He was one of them, the reason she was there, the reason she did this job, the reason she'd been delayed in her journey.

A few feet away from her, he sat behind a cluttered desk and large screen. Busy fingers clicked across a keyboard. *He can type fast...hours spent surfing the deep dark web, no doubt.*

She cocked her head to one side, studying this chubby, diminutive man's outline. A lock of blonde hair untucked itself from behind her ear and fell over her face. Not caring, she didn't tidy it away like the old her would have, but she was no longer a slave to unruly hair, to looking good, to vanity. Such a relief.

She continued studying her man, her next job, staring at him through the wayward curl. *Do you know Dick, Richard Michael Parker? Is he a friend of yours?*

She sashayed over to his desk, taking her time, moving slowly into his space to get a closer look at his face. She peered down at him, examining his features like a plastic surgeon deciding what work to carry out.

He looked a bit like Dick Parker, and they would be around the same age, with the same stocky fat build, the same sweaty eagerness and glassy-eyed look, the excited stare of taking something that didn't belong to them, of taking something special, something out of bounds, something beyond their normal reach, and getting away with it.

She'd been only four years old. To a four-year-old, everyone towered like a giant.

He looked the same as Dick—dumpy, pallid, and pathetic. Why had she been frightened of a man like him? He was just flesh and bones, a cowardly bully, nothing special. *Ahh, but he is special. He's one of them.*

Dick had told her she was special, but she didn't want to be special. Special gets you noticed. Special gets you picked off from the herd. Special gets you attention you don't need. Special attracts bad people. Special fucks up your life.

He leaned leisurely back in his chair, legs apart, dressing gown falling open and exposing pink, sweaty skin and a flaccid sallow cock. His breath quickened as he stared at the screen. His right hand clutched at the mouse, gliding the flashing cursor from one image to the next. The monitor's flickering light dappled his eager, shiny face.

She watched his mouth open with concentration as his tongue absentmindedly licked the corner of his lips. His gaze darted through images, excited, squinting with smiles as something he liked popped up. His right hand dropped to his lap, giving his cock a quick squeeze, easing it into life.

She guessed Dick hadn't changed much over the years. He'd have gained weight and his thick dark curly hair would have thinned and greyed; and, like this man, his dark beady eyes would have shrunk, sinking deeper into his face, framed with age-crumpled skin, no longer full of the energetic youth she remembered.

She would recognise Dick again. She was confident she would, but memories could play tricks, especially when something that bad happens. Those memories never quite leave a person. The fundamental act remains intact, no matter how much protective, emotional scaffolding you put in place to forget it. *You smell the same as him, you bastard.*

She leaned over the desk to detect what engrossed the man so intently. His stench of sweaty feet and stale semen swirled in her nostrils. A memory flashed in her brain of a clammy hand clutching hers, guiding it, making tiny fingers do as they were told. She shook her head...*not now.*

Moving in closer, she focused on the man's computer and noticed a chat box open in the middle of the screen, lines of text rolling down it. His screen name, PrincessB07, shared comments with Sienna2006. His excited chubby fingers jogged across the keys, creating another line of text. He pressed enter, pinging the message up the line of conversation—*It will b r secret.*

Behind the chat box Amy witnessed images of young children, in various stages of undressing, scroll across the screen. Dirty gnarled hands pushed, pulled, and manipulated their innocent bodies. Child porn.

Amy's heart sank. A wave of tremors swept through her, ushering bile up her throat. She threw her hand over her mouth to tame her repulsion.

She closed her eyes as the scaffolding started to fall away. *Wait, wait, not yet!*

She edged nearer, holding the back of his chair. She bent close to his face and blew a long, cold breath across his cheek. He shook his head in annoyance, swiping his hand through the air as if chasing a pesky fly, but his eyes did not leave the screen. *He can feel me. Good!*

Ping. The noise excited him.

He had a reply to his message—*My mum told me not to do that.*

She moved in closer, eyeball to eyeball, daring him to acknowledge her. His rancid breath disgustingly warmed her cheek.

His fat fingers replied—*It will b r secret. Your mum won't know... ever.*

"Well, I'm here...just for you." Amy whispered.

He ignored her.

"I'm ready," she sighed.

He took no notice.

"What...don't you want me?" she cried in mock horror.

Tearing at her blouse, Amy unfastened the top buttons to reveal her braless cleavage.

He gave no reaction.

THE DEAL

"Don't you like what you see?"

She cupped her breasts and thrust them into his face.

Nothing.

"Too old, am I?"

Nothing.

"Good."

She could see him, but he couldn't see her. She was dead.

Chapter Five

A my Fox placed her hands around the soft folds of the man's plump neck and tightened her grip, her cold fingers sinking into his doughy flesh.

Her pressure made him feel uncomfortable, made his throat tighten, and cut off his oxygen. The man raised his hand to his neck and kneaded fatty skin. He swallowed hard, trying to loosen the constriction, but it didn't help. He opened a desk drawer and pulled out a bottle of heartburn medicine.

Amy whispered into his ear. "This ain't no heartburn, honey. This is karma. Meds aren't going to help you now."

She closed her eyes to concentrate, increasing the pressure. Her vice-like hold tightened.

He choked, crying out, his hands clawing at his throat.

"I can't breathe, agghhhhhhhhhhh..." He screamed long and loud, a pig in agony.

The children outside stopped to listen to the strange noise coming from the Stinky Man's flat. They looked to each other unsure what to do.

"Agghhhhhhh," he screamed again.

The children raced to the window, stood on tiptoes, and peeked through the gap in the curtain. They could see Stinky Man sitting in a dark room, at his desk, writhing in his chair, pulling at his neck. Alone.

They didn't see Amy standing over him, her blonde curls falling over her scrunched face, her arms ramrodded straight, her hands wrapped around his thick throat while she cursed at him and willed him to die.

"Jeez, for fuck's sake. Die, you bastard... die," she hissed.

Gripping with all her strength, she tried to strangle the life out of him, against his pathetic flailing struggle. Confident she had about succeeded, a disturbing slam jarred her concentration. Over her shoulder, she saw that the flat door had burst open. The one person she'd hoped to avoid long enough to complete the mission strolled into the room.

Her mentor and partner, Jack. All tall, dark, handsome, six-foot-four of him. His long black trench coat billowed from broad shoulders as his stride stirred up a recognisable wind.

He assessed the scene with a sweeping gaze from cheeky brown eyes, strutted over to the man's desk, swept papers and mess aside, and plopped down on the desktop, hands in his pockets, his face full of amusement as he observed her.

"Miss Fox," he said, greeting her with a calm nod of his head.

"What the fuck do you think you're doing here? Get out! I'm in a meeting." She panted, trying to keep a grip on her slippery, squealing prey.

Jack shook his head with a sigh and gave her a lethargic raised eyebrow.

"Really?" he twinkled. "What are you doing, Ames?" His brown eyes bore down on her through thick dark lashes.

"Killing him! What the bloody hell does it look like?" barked Amy, angry at being interrupted, tightening her hold on the wriggling man.

"But he's not on the list. You don't have authorisation." Jack shook his head. "Have you been working solo...again?"

Her silence answered him. Jack ran his hand through his long shaggy hair and sighed. He took a deep breath and with a sweep of his arm waved his hand through the air and flicked his finger towards the sofa. Amy's body abruptly rose in the air and flew through the air across the room. She landed in an undignified heap between the sofa and rubbish bags. She hated it when he did that.

The man, grateful for the sudden release on his throat, pulled himself up out of the chair, and scrambled out of the room, coughing and spluttering in search of a drink. The children at the window burst into giggles as his dressing gown wafted open, revealing his naked body. They ran down the walkway to tell their friends.

Amy eased herself into a sitting position, blowing her dishevelled hair from her face.

"I hate it when you do that. How come that magnetic shit works for you and not for me?" She dusted herself off, her black suit the lone article in her wardrobe.

"It takes practice," Jack said, flashing one of his famous grins. "You're a newbie."

"Hardly. I arrived only a few months after you," she muttered, brushing the dust from her legs.

"Yeah, well, I've got previous history in the body-throwing business. The Army taught me well."

"You make it look so easy."

"You can use the guns, can't you?"

She nodded.

"Well, use the same technique but cut out the grabbing. You're trying too hard. You don't really need to touch anything. Empty your mind, hover your hand over the object, feel the energy, let it build, and throw in the direction you want it to go. E-F-B-T: empty, feel, build, and throw...simple." He reached down to offer her his hand.

She reluctantly snatched it and pulled herself up, slapping the last of the dirt off her backside.

"Jeez, when did he last clean this place?"

For the zillionth time since they'd started working together, Jack tilted his head and studied her. She was beautiful. He could watch her all day.

"You went off grid again, Ames. You know you can't do that. We have to work as a team, or we'll be chucked out. Maggie will have our guts for garters," he chided.

"Yes, but the Unit doesn't get to enough of these people fast enough. All this permission-seeking takes up too much time." She gave him a long side look. "Besides, people like him are my reason."

"I know, I know...but rules are rules, Ames. You have to do this right or they'll get rid of us."

"Me, not us," she said, correcting him, staring up at his face.

Jack subconsciously ran a hand across his forehead, his fingers following the ugly scars that dragged around his eye socket and across his cheek. He turned away from her glare, frightened of seeing the distaste in her eyes.

"You're my partner. I am responsible for you. I'll get chucked out, too," he muttered.

With a frustrated sigh, she blew hair out of her eyes, the blonde strands momentarily lifted, then settled back down framing her face. He watched out of the corner of his eyes, he loved it when she did that.

"You need a haircut," he teased.

She ignored him, sulking, kicking at the corner of the man's desk.

Jack softened; he knew what Dick Parker had done to her, and understood her revenge more than anyone. He stepped closer and wrapped a protective arm around her shoulders.

"We have so much more work to do before our time is up. If we don't follow the rules, we're out, and I'm not ready to stop just yet. Are you?"

She shook her head. Not until she got to Dick Parker.

The man shuffled back into the room, clutching a steaming mug of coffee. Newly composed, the spluttering subsided; he sat back down at his computer and carried on surfing images of children. Jack and Amy watched him.

Unable to bear her revulsion, Amy pulled out of Jack's arms and rushed forward, reaching for the man's neck.

"The bastard," she spat. "Just let me..."

"No," snapped Jack, clicking his fingers over her hands. Her arms flailed up and out, swinging into a wide circle, as if warming up for a workout.

"OK, OK, grrrrrr...so many rules." She stamped her foot in anger. He also loved it when she did that; he loved everything about her.

"They don't play by the rules, so why the hell should we?" Amy sulked.

"Because if we don't, we're as bad as they are," he reminded her shrugging. "Karma sorts it, eventually."

She rolled her eyes, crossed her arms, and gave him a jaded look.

"We are karma, Jack. We are the ones that sort it. We've got to crack on with it. All this waiting for authorisation is getting on my tits. Do you know how many children get abused every day? Fear and shame keep them from speaking out. We have to do something."

He nodded. He understood her frustration, but she had to learn to look at the bigger picture.

"I know it grates. I don't like it either, but they have their reasons. Everything has a time, a place. Having said that, on my last shift the gloves will be off and I'll have a field day, but for now...come on. Let's get out of here. Maggie's authorised the next job. Pyke's waiting." Jack moved towards the door.

"I can't leave him like this." Amy looked toward the curtains. "There are children outside that window. God knows what he'll do. Well, actually, I do know." Her eyes hardened.

Jack spun around, grabbed her firmly by her arm, and pushed her towards the door.

"We're leaving, whether you like it or not. We'll sort him out legitimately when he's on the list, but not yet. Maybe Pyke needs more time to get into his computer, source his contacts, his victims, his sites, and then we can close in on him and his fellow pervs in one hit. You've gotta see the bigger picture...but, meanwhile..."

He waved his hand across the table top. The mug of hot coffee toppled into the man's bare lap.

"He's not going to be playing with his genitals, or anyone else's, any time soon."

The hot liquid burned into the man's skin. He jumped up out of his chair, screaming with pain.

"There are rules...and there are rules. Everyone spills their drink from time to time." Jack beamed his cheeky grin as he manhandled Amy out the door. "Come on, you."

She turned to face him in the hallway, giving a playful punch to his stomach, smiling up at him where they stared at each other for a moment. She wished he wouldn't treat her like a child. She wished she had the courage to take the risk and kiss him.

She knew any minute he would turn away from her, as he always did. Was he embarrassed about his face, or did he find her unattractive?

He was stunning in an ugly-handsome kind of way. His chiselled face was covered in scars she found beautiful, and she loved the way his generous mouth tilted up at the corners. She wanted to taste those lips. If she could just stretch up on tiptoes, she could reach his mouth with hers and smother his scarred skin with kisses.

What would he do? Would he recoil in disgust or take her in his arms? What would Mister 'always working by the rules' do? Did he like her or just see her as an annoying newbie he had to babysit?

Were they even allowed to have sex? Was it against the rules? Would the skies shake with rage and she and he explode in flames? She made a note to ask the boss.

He looked down at her, silent, his twinkling eyes momentarily serious. She considered reaching up to his mouth, just for a second, then lost her courage. His face had lost its playfulness. One thing she hadn't left behind was her fear of rejection. She put her hand on his chest and gently pushed him backwards. The moment vanished.

"Wait, I'd better just close the curtain. The children...they may see him," she said.

Before he could stop her, she squeezed past and scurried back into the room.

Jack, lost in the moment, confused as to why she'd pushed him away, didn't have the strength to argue. He let her go.

He couldn't blame her. He knew he was ugly. A beautiful woman like Amy wouldn't look at him twice, wouldn't be able to see behind the damage. He closed his eyes and lowered his head. If only she knew.

"I won't be a second," she shouted out to him through the doorway.

He sighed and waved an exasperated hand through the air after her. At least he got to spend time with her. Precious time he didn't want to lose by her being stupid, going vigilante and getting chucked out of the Unit. The boss only gave them so much leeway, and he had been pushing his luck.

"OK, OK, but hurry up! We're late. I'll call us in," he shouted. "And do those buttons up. It's hard enough working with you without your tits hanging out." He stepped through the front door and out into the stairwell.

He tapped his ear and waited to be connected.

"Bonjour." Pyke's cheeky voice picked up.

"We're on our way back to the office."

"Bon."

"Just checking in."

"Qui."

"Shut up, Pyke..."

"Non."

"Look, mate, could you quit the Franglais stuff? I barely speak English, never mind French, and you're an East End boy whose closest thing to France is a bottle of Kronenbourg."

"OK, OK. Touchy aren't we, mon petit chou. What's rocked your boat?"

"Nothing. That last job was a bit messy. That's all. I'm getting old...and I ain't your shoe."

"Non, Monsieur...chou, chou ...it means cabbage...or is it powder puff?"

"You're weird."

"It's a term of endearment in France. I'm learning French, widening my horizons," Pyke announced excitedly.

"And that's gonna be of use, why?"

"Pourquoi. It's pourquoi."

"Pour what?"

Amy could hear Jack busily talking to Pyke while he stood outside on the communal staircase. She quickly walked back into the man's flat, fumbling with her shirt, doing up the buttons. *He sounded angry. Shit! I've pissed him off again*!

She looked down at her chest. *But my tits are a distraction. That's a good sign, isn't it?*

Walking over to the curtains, she peeked outside the window, checked for children, and finding none present, took a deep breath. *Right, I can do this... empty, feel, build and throw.*

After a few false starts she managed to pull the drapes tightly shut. Decades of dust permeated the air. Waving it away from her face, she spluttered in disgust. *You sooo need a cleaner, mate.*

She looked back at the squealing man leaning against the wall, desperately dabbing his shrivelled penis's burning skin with his dressing gown's hem. She sauntered towards him; a smile crept across her face.

Checking the doorway, she eyed the coffee mug lying on the floor. *OK, here we go...empty, feel, build, and throw.*

She held her hand over the mug, closed her eyes, and tried to empty her brain of everything else but moving the mug. She cupped her hand and waved it forwards. Nothing happened. She did it again. The mug rolled forward on the ground. She took a deep breath, brought her mind back to her four-year-old state, felt the fear, the hatred, the disgust. Her hand tingled with heat, building until she couldn't stand it any longer.

With an almighty sweep of her arm, she threw her hand at the man. The mug flew at the wall above his head, smashing into pieces. Porcelain fragments fell around his feet. The anger rose within her. The heat in her hands built further. She leaned down, held her hand over the largest jagged piece, and with a gasp of air, lifted it off the floor.

The man stopped whimpering, staring in awe, eyes wide, mouth open. The mug seemed to have a life of its own. It raised itself off the floor and smashed against the wall, just missing his face. *What the fuck?*

He watched as chunks of china fell to the ground, then one piece swooped up into the air in front of him. *What the...?*

With an ascending sweep of her hand, Amy brought the serrated edge up under his chin, causing his wide-eyed head to slam back against the wall with a thud. Her second driving thrust slid the edge deeper into his neck with a quick left, then right, flicking motion. She sliced his throat wide open.

The porcelain remained wedged in his throat as she took a step back and watched his gurgling body slide to the floor. He sat slumped against the wall, his bemused wide eyes staring vacantly across the room. His legs splayed out in front of him. His arms wilted at his side and his head flopped forward over his rotund belly.

She leaned over and wiped her bloodied hands on his dressing gown.

"I haven't got time for rules. They're for sheep," she whispered into his ear. "Goodnight, kiddie fiddler. Hope you enjoy hell."

She slunk out of the room to join Jack.

In the hallway, a familiar smell hit her—a burning smell similar to a barn mixed with old grass, cinnamon, and stale, acrid tobacco. She instinctively looked back over her shoulder, but saw no one.

Why did it feel as if someone was watching her?

Chapter Six

Twenty-eight years earlier

Amy Fox, a four-year-old sweet little girl, loved to play in the street in front of her house with other kids from the housing estate where she lived. Back then, it was common for parents to encourage their children to play outside in the fresh air and enjoy the camaraderie in the neighbourhood they all deemed safe, and if a day went by without the sound of children's playful games, parents would peer out the window to see if rain had forced them back indoors.

But at the end of the estate's perimeter lay fields and thick woodland, dark and mysterious, the kind of setting found in bedtime stories. Everyone's read those frightening tales of bogeymen and scary monsters. And the children on the estate never ventured into those woods, those spooky fairy tales always in their minds.

They feared the bogeymen, witches, and wolves, and all manner of things that happened in the stories. So they remained just outside the boundary of the woods, as if an invisible magical perimeter kept them safe. They laughed and played all day... happy, carefree, and naive.

One sunny afternoon Dick Parker changed all of that. Amy and her friend, a little boy from next door, a few years older than she, played kick-about with a big red shiny ball Amy had received for her birthday.

The little boy accidently kicked the ball too hard, and with a skewed angle it sped away from them. The two of them stood and watched it roll cheerfully along a small winding path and disappear behind trees, landing in a clump of bluebells. Without thinking, Amy chased after it. She wouldn't normally go into the woods, but she loved that ball. It would only take a second.

At the age of nineteen, Dick Parker was a loner without friends. Abused by his step-father, ignored by his drug-addicted mother, he hadn't learned how to socialise, how to develop relationships, or what love even was.

Dick Parker liked the woods, how the trees kept him hidden in the shadows and made him feel safe. He didn't have to talk to anyone. He could just be himself. He liked to watch the children play. They had what he didn't: a childhood, a fantasy world of fun and games, parents to go home to and cuddle him at night. He had nothing.

Dick Parker had a plan to get close to these children, to feel them, to be a part of their cosy world. He would sit and wait for the right moment, the moment when he could pick off a straggler from the herd and initiate his plan. They had everything. Why couldn't he have a piece of it?

Today, little Amy fulfilled his fantasy; she was simply in the wrong place at the wrong time.

As Amy ran into the woodlands, chasing her ball, Dick snatched her. With his hand shushing her squealing mouth, he carried her to a wooden hut deep within the forest and 'played' with her. After a few hours, he brought her back to the edge of the woods and set her free, warning her to never tell a soul or he would come after her and give her to the bad bogeyman.

Amy ran home and obeyed, keeping quiet. She didn't understand what had happened, didn't have the words to explain, but instinctively knew something was wrong. She didn't understand why. It just felt bad. She vowed never to go into the woods again.

That night, nightmares about the bogeyman triggered her first panic attack. Her heart pounded as if it might burst. She thought she was dying. When she woke in the morning, she found herself in a wet bed. The carefree little girl in her had gone.

The following week the street bustled with Police and press. Amanda May, a little girl the same age as Amy, had disappeared. A dog walker had found her body three days later. She'd been raped and beaten. The police hunted for her murderer, for the evil bogeyman, for the sick monster who'd taken poor Amanda May from her grieving parents.

In the best way she could, with limited vocabulary, Amy told her parents about the strange man in the woods and what he'd done to her. They in turn informed the police. A very empathetic and consoling lady spoke to Amy, making her comfortable in a special cosy room with toys and sofas. With a pencil and paper, Amy drew a picture of the man in the woods. She sketched a stickman with dark curly hair, surrounded by trees. She held her nose and said, "Pooh!" He smelled bad. Soon after, her parents sold their house and moved to a new place, ready to let the incident bury itself and go away. They never mentioned it again.

But Amy did. She mentioned it every night in her prayers. She wanted God to stop the bad man and made a deal with Him. If she promised to be a good girl, when she died, she wanted Him to allow her to sit on a cloud for a while before going to heaven. She wanted to be invisible, to have special powers and stop all the bad people He and the Police didn't have time to arrest. She'd like to deliver justice to the ones that slipped through his fingers. She wanted to be like a Superhero and save lives.

Years passed. Amy grew up and went on with her life, forgetting all about her deal with God, and at times, forgot about God. But He didn't forget her. At the age of 32, on the way to work during a heavy rush hour, she fell on the underground tube train tracks, killed instantly, devastating her family and friends. She was way too young to die.

God had kept his promise.

She opened her eyes, dazed and shocked her life had been cut short, to find she'd not been the only one to ask for the same deal.

When Amy's spirit revived to the startling truth she no longer lay on the subway tracks, the echo of Sally's screams ringing in her ears, she sat dazed and shocked to realise her life had been cut short. Her hands reached out, passing right through a misty whiteness, an ethereal realm holding her up in some plane she didn't recognise. Once her eyes adjusted and her mind oriented to the new world surrounding her, she saw other spirits wander about the clouds. Out of curiosity, she waved one over.

"Err...excuse me...err...do you speak English?"

The cheery dark-headed woman giggled as she walked towards her.

"We speak a universal language here. We are all the same."

"Where's here?"

"This is the afterlife, the place all souls are destined. Don't you know?"

"No, I don't." Amy's face screwed up in question. "What am I doing here?"

"Did you make a deal?"

Amy rubbed the back of her head as if to nudge her memory. Then it flooded back to her.

"I may have...Yes, I think...when I was a child. Do you mean it worked?" she beamed. "Bloody hell...how effing fantastic...oops, sorry, I guess no swearing here."

The woman waved away her apology.

"Yes, it worked. He always keeps His promises. Everyone here made a deal with Him. This is the world network of the Fallen, of souls involved in the business of dishing out karma. You've got work to do."

The woman turned away and walked on, her words smacked Amy with such intensity she sat with her mouth wide open, staring into the mist, taking in the world around her.

"Oh my god."

It didn't take long for her to become acquainted with the other Fallen hovering the skies or learn the rules of the business, how they were to conduct themselves in serving comeuppance to evil, the ones who thought they'd escaped judgment.

Although excited to crack on and fight the good fight, Amy wasn't too happy with the list of rules. Bad people didn't play by the rules, so why the hell should she?

Chapter Seven

Present day, HQ,
UK Unit, Cloud 9

Jack and Amy walked into the light, airy office, clutching mugs of coffee and munching biscuits.

"I'm being watched."

"Nonsense. We're the ones doing the watching...don't be ridiculous," Jack scoffed.

"It's true. I felt it again just now back at the kiddie-fiddler's place. It's been going on for a while."

"The only one who's watching you is me...and Pyke, when he tunes in to see what we are up to," chided Jack.

"What! Why?"

"Cos you're a nightmare. Believe me, you need to be watched. You can't go around killing anyone you fancy. You can't go solo. You're a Fallen and must wait for orders."

"Where the hell do you get off acting like my keeper?" barked Amy, through a mouthful of biscuits. "So, I get in trouble." She shrugged. "What're they gonna do? Shoot me? I'm already dead."

"Touchy, aren't we?" teased Jack.

"Sorry." She took a breath and wiped crumbs from her mouth. "You know what? I also felt followed when I was down there, alive," she said, pointing to below her feet. "I was always looking over my shoulder. Maybe I'm paranoid."

"Maybe you sensed Fallens looking out for you."

"No. Most Erthfolk can't see Fallens. It wasn't a Fallen. It was more sinister."

Jack stared at her. His heart missed a beat.

She continued.

"I just get so frustrated with all this effing politically correct bullshit. I had enough of it down there. Don't do this, don't do that, don't upset this person, don't upset that religion...for fuck's sake. If someone is bad, whatever make they are, whatever God they worship...sort it, simple."

"Yeah, well, it's not that easy," Jack muttered, looking over his shoulder, checking to see if anyone was listening. "We have to play by the rules."

"Seriously, Jack? I repeat. I'm dead. What're they gonna do?" Amy shrugged her shoulders and held out her hands, palms up. But Jack wasn't listening. He was too busy scanning the room.

She followed his gaze.

"What?"

"I don't know," he said, waving her away. "Nothing."

"No, I mean what're they gonna do about me breaking the rules?"

"Chuck you out. Send you down. Who knows? But whatever happens, I'm responsible for you, and I'll get it in the ear as well. I don't fancy Hell, do you? We've sent too many of our clients down there. It won't be fun."

"Heaven, Hell...I'm not sure I believe there are such places. What if this is it? Up here is dead." She pointed down below her feet. "And down there is alive. We're just forever recycling. Living, then policing... living, then policing."

Maggie piped up from behind her enormous tank of a desk. Her designer reading glasses perched on the end of her nose.

"Where the bloody hell have you two been? This isn't a holiday camp you know. We've got Erthfolk to deactivate. Chop chop! Soho Sid is at it again. Pyke has the details. He's been given enough warnings. It's time to close him down."

Maggie, Margaret Delia Smithers, ran the office with a hand of steel. At 62 years of age, she died of a heart attack, a workaholic spinster; she'd given her life to a successful career in MI6 and was not ready to down tools just yet. On her hospital death bed, she'd asked for the deal.

Pyke, a lanky, cheerful, fun-loving internet whizz-kid had hacked multi-billion corporations with the best of them. A regular Robin Hood, he stole from the rich and gave to the poor—after funding his lavish lifestyle of surfing, fast cars, wine, women, and song. He didn't touch drugs, ever.

THE DEAL

Crack cocaine had taken his younger sister, so Pyke had a thing for destroying those in the industry by accidently ploughing their ill-gotten gains into drug rehabilitation projects or alerting authorities when deals were going down. Until, one day, at the age of 28, his luck ran out.

He found himself in the wrong place at the wrong time, looking down the barrel of a gun belonging to the minion of an angry wannabe drug baron. Whilst waiting for his sobbing mother to turn off his life-support machine, he'd asked for the deal. So much knowledge, surely he couldn't waste it, not yet...besides, hacking was fun.

"Mon petit, Chou, bonjour," greeted Pyke, happy to see Jack and Amy.

He waved them over to the middle of the room where an impressive Stonehenge-esque circle of eight rotating glass screens surrounded him; twelve-foot wide by five-foot high, each hovering three feet off the white marble floor.

Enclosed within his gladiatorial wall of glass monitors, he ran from one job to the next, from one screen to the other, putting out fires and causing chaos for offenders.

He preferred being on his feet, working on a large touchscreen, rather than being stuck to a chair and hunched over a desk. He worked best in visuals, like an artist, striding up and down, painting stories with his sweeping hands. He sometimes used a skateboard to add to the mix. The energetic workout kept his genius mind clear and agile...and it was *fun*, Pyke's favourite word.

Pyke liked being busy; he worked on all eight screens at once. Each contained the intelligence files of a current job Maggie had authorised; people or situations needing to be deactivated.

Running backwards and forwards between screens was his idea of heaven, like playing eight, life-size computer games. As each job finalised, Maggie would push forward the next, in order of high risk importance from a long list of awaiting targets.

The majority of jobs he could handle on his own, but some needed help on the ground. That's where Jack and Amy came in.

Screen three tracked the current file in his queue, displaying a collection of ten message boards, with chatroom conversations running on each. He darted to and fro between conversation threads, exchanging lines of dialogue. He was *'Cooldude888,'* flirting with each member.

"Oh, this is fun, like playing 10 games of chess at once. Love it! I won't be a minute...am just waiting for one of these wankers to get overexcited and sloppy and show an IP address. Then I'll be with you. I keep crashing their internet at sexually frustrating moments; one of them will get careless in a minute."

He pressed a button and *'PirateJack'* disappeared from a dialogue box.

"What is this case?" asked Amy, striding over to take a closer look. "These are children, aren't they?" Her eyes narrowed as she peered at the screen.

"Yes, but nothing for you to worry your pretty little head about. This is mine, all mine," he smiled, knowing she would jump at the chance to work on anything to do with children.

"What is it?" Insisted Amy, the hairs on the back of her neck standing up.

"Well, what we have here is a selection of nine to 13-year-olds talking to each other, but a few of them are paedophiles, dirty old men pretending to be kids, grooming, befriending, taking pictures, then blackmailing them into doing disgusting things. I just need one of these dirt bags to log on and join the conversation without taking precautions...and I don't mean a condom. Hello, here he comes," he beamed.

'PirateJack' re-joined the chat, his IP number identifying ownership of his hardware flashed onto the screen. In his eagerness to re-join a crucial part of the grooming conversation, he'd taken the risk of logging on without using a safe dark web server.

"Gotcha!" Pyke, fist punched the air with excitement. "Yesss! Come on my beauty. Come to daddy," he cheered.

Jack joined them, watching the screen, popping the last of a biscuit into his mouth.

"But with all your kit, you can easily see who it is? Why would *you* need an IP address?" he asked through a mouthful of crumbs.

"Because, my old friend, *'misslollypop2004'* here," he said, pointing to a name on a neighbouring chat screen, "is a member of the Child Abuse Crime

Team working undercover, pretending to be a 12-year-old, trying to close this sex ring down." He pointed to the floor.

"Down there, they still need the IP address to track offenders. They haven't quite caught up with tracking in the deep dark web yet. So, I've helped nudge her in the right direction. She'll have clocked this and be sending the cops in as we speak."

Jack caught Amy's eye and pointed at a one-sided chat that had been going on a while. '*Sienna2006*' asked '*PrincessB07*' if she was still there.

Amy grimaced. If she'd just waited ten minutes, the Police would have taken care of the man she'd just killed. Alive, he would have been interviewed and able to dish the dirt on others. She'd messed up. She shook her head with shame, she should have listened to Jack. She glanced over at Maggie. If the bosses ever found out it could cost her her place in the Unit. She wasn't ready to leave, she hadn't found *him* yet. Her eyes focused on the screen, ignoring Jack's scolding glare.

"My work here is done...finalised," smiled Pyke, high on success. He waved a hand over the screen and made the files disappear. "I soooo lurvvve my job. I'm playing with the best game apps ever."

Another file popped up on the screen, awaiting his attention.

Maggie shouted across the room. "Pyke, this is not a game. How many times do I have to tell you? We've got a change of plan. Check out eight."

Pyke obediently skipped to screen eight. "Now, what have we here?"

With the skilful hands of an orchestral conductor, he opened a dozen files. The screen lit up with maps, images, and lines of unfathomable text.

"Err...we haven't got time for Soho Sid right now." His tattooed fingers ran across a keyboard.

"A radical cell has just activated. You're off to Belgium. The Belgian Unit is a little stretched; they have six major incidents kicking off around the country, so they've asked for us, France and Ireland for backup. I've sent the intel for the job we're sorting, and you should be receiving it, just about..." He hit the keyboard with a flourish. "Maintenant...that's 'now' in French."

Jack raised an eye brow.

Pyke spun around and beamed at Jack. "This is high risk, so you have permission to TM8 all involved. Then you can give Soho Sid a visit afterwards. We have a short window of time before he starts. I'll delay his kick-off."

Pyke trotted to another screen and busied himself with lines of script, sliding effortlessly between websites, servers, and databases, the radical cell and child sex ring forgotten.

Jack and Amy closed their eyes for coordinates and images to light up in the back of their eyelids. Amy brushed crumbs from her suit lapel with a sigh.

"No peace for the wicked."

She spun around, walked towards the door, grabbed a handful of small white feathers from a bowl on her desk and stuffed them in her jacket pocket. She raised her fingers to her forehead and threw a salute in Maggie's direction. "See you later boss," she hollered as she strode out of the office.

Maggie shouted after her. "Report back to me later, Amy. I need to review your performance files."

"Will do, boss." Amy scrunched her face and shoulders with dread, as the pushed through the office door. No one enjoyed the boss's reviews. *Shit, what have I done now?*

Jack sneaked up beside Pyke, leaned in, and teasingly pointed a wriggling finger at a precious piece of screen text, pretending to touch it. Pyke froze in mock horror, tilted his head to the side, and gave Jack a Pyke-special death stare.

Jack grinned. "Just kiddin'...my little shoe." He backed off.

No one touched Pyke's stuff.

"In here you may be the boss, Pykey boy, but out there...we all know I am." Jack teased, giving Pyke a playful punch in the shoulder.

Pyke, not moving from his position, expertly flicked his leg out sideways, just missing Jack's kneecap. Jack leapt backwards in mock horror.

"Whoa! Careful, big boy," he teased.

"I'll come out with you one day, mon petit chou," grinned Pyke. "Then we'll see who's the man, who's the big bollocks, who's the mighty pair of shoes."

Maggie, watching the banter from behind her desk, smiled at them.

"Handbags down, gentlemen, please. Back to work! Chop chop!"

Jack nodded, sauntered towards the door, scrunched his biscuit wrapper into a ball, and aimed a throw into the wastepaper bin beside Maggie's desk. He punched the air with childlike glee as it hit its mark.

"Yes! Je suis un superstar. That's French for the dog's bollocks, mate."

Giving Maggie a winning smile, he sauntered past and blew a cheeky kiss.

"Later's, babe," he winked.

Maggie beamed up at him, proudly watching him walk out the door. She caught herself staring, blushed, and distractedly tucked a slither of hair behind her ear. Jack was too deliciously handsome for his own good.

"Cougar," teased Pyke, peering around a screen.

Maggie flushed rose pink.

"Don't be ridiculous. He's far too young. I don't do embryos. I haven't got time to teach." She smiled, waving him away with a dismissive hand.

"Later's, babe." She mimicked Jack's deep voice and swagger of hand on hips. "What the hell is that? Doesn't anyone speak good fucking English anymore? For goodness' sake, the place has gone to pot."

Giving Pyke a conspiratorial look, she tapped the side of her nose with a pencil. "Methinks our Jack has a big soft spot for Miss Fox. Romance is in the air and heaven help us, if the feeling is mutual." She shook her head with mock displeasure.

"Oh, its mutual all right. It's just that neither of them realises it. Both don't think they're good enough. Jack's got to grow some balls and get over his scars, and Amy's got to know her value and jump on him. Their pussy footing around is driving me nuts."

"As long as it doesn't interfere with their work."

"No, I think it enhances it. They show off to each other. She's trying to impress him, and he's trying to impress her, although he's a bit overprotective of her, which drives her mad."

"Mmmmm... we don't need any bleedin drama in this office," sighed Maggie.

Pyke adored Maggie; she was formidable and quaint in one package. She could kill a man with a glance; but show her some affection, and she'd fold into a coquettish, blushing puppy.

Pyke put it down to not having had enough affection in her life, which was understandable with her career history; there'd been no time for it.

Getting snapped up straight from the University at the tender age of 21 by MI6, she'd given her time, body, and soul to the wellbeing of her country. Dying at 62 years was way too soon for a matriarchal lioness such as Maggie. She didn't mention children; he guessed she didn't have any. Her caring for others went some way to making up for it.

Pyke understood her passion for the job, once a person had seen what humans were capable of doing to each other; it was all hands-on-deck to protect the innocents.

They were a strange mix; Pyke with his cheeky East London accent, hard knocks street education, skinhead haircut, body smothering tattoos, and cute little boy twinkle. And then there was Maggie, more than double his age with her crisp Queen's English, privileged education, immaculate mother of the bride suits, hairspray, and pearls. They couldn't have been more different.

On earth their paths would never have crossed. If so, they would have gone overboard to avoid each other. But here they were, a formidable team. Maggie loved his cheeky, speedy intellect, and he loved her ruthless sniffing out of bastards.

But what Pyke loved most, was that Maggie, with all her airs and graces, was totally non-politically correct. The word 'polite' was not in her vocabulary. She had no boundaries, said it as it was, and swore like a trooper.

When she said 'fuck' it sounded so posh, it made it difficult for him to stifle a giggle. You couldn't take offence; it was as if HM The Queen had blasphemed, so it must be OK, right?

Pyke loved his work. He'd nicknamed the office as Cloud 9 and it had stuck. His work colleagues were fun and feisty, and he and Maggie made a good supervisory team. They respected each other. Both loved the chase and the fight for righting wrongs or 'getting the shitty fucking bastard arseholes,' as Maggie had put it. And both had a penchant for a cup of tea and a custard cream biscuit.

"A cup of Rosie Lee before we start our next plan of attack, ma'am?" Pyke asked in his best Sergeant Major voice. Ever in a hurry, he ran to the kitchen galley and put the kettle on.

The fictitious taste of food and drink remained as one of the few pleasures Fallens were allowed to keep as they mid-surfed earth and the afterlife. A disease-free body, increased sensory input, and amplified perception had been offered as important pleasures.

Maggie smiled. "Yes, dear, an army can't run on an empty stomach, and we'll need a biscuit to go with that, don't you think?"

Maggie never used instant beverages. She insisted on a teapot, tea strainer, tea leaves, and porcelain cup. They could offer her all the hi-tech-fangled gadgetry in the world, but some things you don't meddle with. Tea was one of them.

Chapter Eight

Adini Square,
Brussels, Belgium

"I'm gonna get a grip on that moving object thing if it kills me," Amy declared as they marched down the centre of a quaint, cobbled, pedestrian street. "It's empty, feel, build and throw. Easy peasy."

"You didn't need to cut his throat. Pyke was on it." Jack shot her a dark look as he scanned their surroundings.

Busy café tables and chairs spilled onto the pavement, leaving a narrow channel of pathway for tourists and locals to meander through the beautiful Brussel's architecture.

"How could I have known? Anyway, I don't care. The shit bag had it coming," Amy snarled, her eyes scanning the sea of faces, searching for uneasy stares and anxious body behaviour.

Young, old, mothers, fathers, children, lovers, tourists and work colleagues made use of the cheerful morning sun. She saw chefs popping out for a gasp of cigarettes, waitresses clearing tables, beaming smiles, waving menus for clients to sit. Students debated while some read books. Elderly neighbours drank black coffee, played backgammon, and read newspapers. Depicting the cheerful, friendly bustle of city life.

"And he would have, if you'd been patient." Jack reached out and placed his fingers over the hand of a young man wearing blue jeans and a black hoody, just as he was pulling a silencer gun from his shoulder bag.

Jack wrenched the hand up under the man's chin and flicked the trigger. The guy seemingly shot himself. The bullet tore through his jaw and out the back of his head. Blood splattered those bustling around him. Unseen, Jack and Amy walked on.

Bystanders stood open mouthed with disbelief. No one screamed for a full 10 seconds.

"Patient," barked Amy, annoyed at being ticked off. "I haven't got time to be patient. Do you realise what those bastards do to kids' minds? How it affects them for life? How it has a ripple effect on everything they ever do from there on in? It doesn't matter whether they find success or suffer failure. Their life plans are altered, fractured. It sets them up for an exhausting battle of shame, fear, loneliness, and disgust. It takes away their childhood, any chance of throwing back their heads with innocent laughter, of trusting another, of loving another, of living carefree. It haunts and ruins any sweet moments, any simple pleasures. It sets them up for a lifelong battle of mental health issues, issues that should never have been triggered, issues that steal lives...all so that dirty people like him can get their rocks off, can have sexual pleasure for a few moments, can have a wank and ejaculate a bit of spunk. How ridiculous is that? All for a squirt of sperm! And you want me to be patient? Are you joking? I've waited 28 years already."

They walked in silence.

Jack bit his lower lip, angry at the thought of anyone touching her. "I'm sorry you had to go through that." Anger tensed his body.

"Hey, it's not your fault." She gave him a weak smile, realising she overreacted a little. "It's OK, now. We leave all our ailments behind when we get here. But being here, without the weight of all that anxiety, has made me realise what a waste of energy I put into living with it, what a waste of a life. I shouldn't have let his problem affect me in such a way, for so long. All for a fucking shot of spunk. He could've just had a wank...the selfish bastard. He didn't need to involve a little girl in his fantasies. I'm sorry to go on about it. I'll shut up."

"No, no, I understand. I wish I could have done something."

"Well, you are now. You and Pyke have my back whilst I stop a few of them ruining other kids' lives."

Jack looked over his shoulder, a crowd had formed around the shot male.

"Yes, but you have to have more trust in us, that they will be sorted, eventually. Pyke was on the job. If you'd trusted us and confided in us, you'd have known that."

"I know, but how can I trust that Miss Tinkerbelle would do her job right?"

"Miss Lollypop," corrected Jack.

"What?"

"Miss Lollypop04. That's her name."

"OK, Miss bloody Lollypop04, for fuck's sake, whatever…"

She stuck her leg out at a passing male; he tripped and fell to the floor, his face smashing against stone. "We need more time. Six months is not enough. It puts pressure on us. I wouldn't need to go it alone if I had time to wait for consent. Can we ask for an extension?"

She reached down and eased out a small handgun from the male's coat pocket. He writhed in pain as blood trickled from his forehead. Unaware, passers-by assumed he was a drunk and stepped over him.

The male slowly rolled over onto his back, panic stricken, frightened to move, his haunted eyes staring down at his stomach. Blood seeped from his face. His coat fell open, exposing rows of dynamite strapped to his waist. Someone gasped with horror and a circle opened around him. Fear whispered through the hushed crowd.

A voice shouted the words they didn't want to believe.

"BOMB… RUN!"

Bedlam erupted. Screams filled the air. People threw chairs and meal-laden tables crashed to the ground. Bodies scrambled over each other to the cries of, "Run…run!"

Throughout the crowd, people called out for their loved ones, searching for each other in the mayhem.

Jack and Amy remained calm, unflustered by the panic. Just another day at the office. They continued to move slowly through the street as frightened Erthfolk rushed past them, looking in doorways, scanning body language, checking skylines, turning in slow circles, hawk-like eyes searching out their prey.

"I don't know what the time policy is. Take it up with Maggie," suggested Jack. "Maybe she can extend it. I know for sure Pyke has been here for more than 12 months, but I guess he is a bit special, a formidable one-manned tracking, hacking, killing machine."

Peering over terrified civilians' heads, Jack's eyes locked on a third male striding into a café. The man produced an AK47 from his backpack. As he stood in the doorway, lifting the gun to fire at the faces of shocked diners,

Jack snuck up behind him, hooked an arm around his neck, and yanked him backwards, hard.

The thug tumbled back into the street. His gun spiralled over his head. As it flailed to the ground, Jack reached out and gently flicked the trigger. A round of shots filled the air, hitting a fourth gunman from across the cafe, his outstretched arm aiming a handgun at a group of hysterical teenagers huddled behind a billboard. His body flinched and jerked as he fell to the ground, writhing in agony.

"He doesn't do any hands-on deactivating. We do."

"But he sources who, how, and why, then tracks which stone they're under and sends us out to tidy up. We're lucky. He and Maggie are a good, fair, supervisory team. Apparently, our Unit's deactivation figures are above average."

While the street slowly emptied, Jack and Amy continued walking, chatting, and ignoring shouts and screams, nonchalantly stepping over falling runaways.

"I've got a review coming up. Shit," Amy grimaced, walking around a huddle of students helping an old man into a doorway.

"It may not be bad. She may be patting you on the back."

"No, it's bad. I think she's found out I've been moonlighting."

"You don't have to do the kiddie-fiddlers on your own, you know. Have a bit of patience," Jack sighed. "Why do you always have to steam ahead without thinking?"

"I'm Aries with Taurus rising. What can I say? We don't do patience," she twinkled at him.

He shook his head, ignoring her. "Besides, how would Maggie know? Pyke manages to cover for you, most of the time...for both of us."

"Why, what do you get up to?" she asked, raising an eyebrow.

He gave her a side on look. "As if I'd tell you," he smiled.

"Hey that's not fair. You can't slag me off for going solo when you're doing it."

"Yeah, but there's a difference. You get caught and I don't," he sighed. "Hopefully."

He stretched out his right arm and landed a punch to a bemused fifth gunman's face, who was staring at the scene, wondering what the hell had happened to his colleagues.

"Who do you go after? Are you going to tell me?"

"Nope."

"No worries. I'll work it out," she remarked, grinning, her eyes scanning the buildings around her, looking for movement. "Pyke has a thing for drug addicts, me, child abusers, you...I will work it out...and I wonder what Maggie's secret passion is, her reason for being here."

"She can't be seen to have any. She's one of the hierarchy. They have to be squeaky clean, whiter than white."

"Well, that counts me out ever getting a job as a Supervisor. I'm a sort of grey tinged," she giggled, looking over at Jack.

"A shade of grey," he said, the corners of his mouth turning upward. She loved his smile.

"Did you read the books?" she questioned, not able to imagine Jack reading a book, particularly a sexy one.

"What books?"

"Did you see the film?" She wasn't letting up.

"What film?" Nor was he.

"50 Shades."

Silence.

"Just asking," she teased. "Maybe you should, you might like it, learn something."

"You think I'm a prude," his voice turning cold.

"No...just saying."

"I like sex, just like anyone else. It's just not on my priority list at the moment." He turned to her. "And it's none of your business."

She'd touched a nerve, again. Why did she always manage to make him angry?

Silence.

Time to change the subject.

"I know you laugh, Jack, but I am being watched. I'm not making it up. Someone's following me. I'm sure of it."

"You're paranoid," Jack shook his head. "We'd know. Besides, we're invisible. No one knows we're here...except other Units, and why would they want to follow us? They have enough on their plate... unless..." He glanced back, over his shoulder.

"Unless what? Why are you looking over your shoulder?"

He shook his head. "Nah.. I would know."

"Know what?"

"Something that we don't get too involved in at our level, the bosses deal with them."

"Who?"

"The Witnesses."

"What would they want with me, us?"

"Exactly, we are small fry to them. Trust me Amy, you're not being followed."

They got to the end of the road and turned to study their handiwork. Tables, chairs, billboards, garbage cans, bodies lay in the once calm sunny street. People came out of hiding, scrambling from bars, cafes, and doorways and scurried down alleyways away from the terrorists.

Amy waited for the street to clear. Five gunmen lay strewn across the cobbles, two groaning in pain, three dead. No civilians were hurt. Police sirens rumbled in the distance.

"Forensics are gonna have fun sorting this lot out," grinned Jack.

Amy caught herself staring at him. She loved to see his smile.

"Yep. You're getting slack, Jack. How're they going to understand that broken neck?" She raised the handgun and aimed it at her sweating suicide bomber.

"What do you mean?"

"He... err... tripped... err... hard, very hard," Jack gave a sheepish grin.

"Tripped hard? Are you joking? It must have been bloody hard to snap a head clean off its spine." Amy steadied her outstretched arm. "Maybe this will help confuse them."

She squinted at her target and pumped three bullets into his stomach. The suicide belt exploded, shattering windows, spitting fireballs, and silencing the wailing gunmen. She javelined the gun high in the air to join the scorching mess. They turned and walked down a side street.

"And how do you think the forensic boys will understand today's death-by-coffee-mug?" teased Jack.

"He tripped... err... hard, very hard," giggled Amy, mimicking Jack. "We can't always give it to them on a plate. They have to have some unsolved mysteries."

"Yeah, but if they have good evidence, they can make things stick in court. Without it, the bad boys get off."

"Yeah, yeah, yeah...I know. Sometimes I'm not sure if I'm cut out for this job," she sighed. "I haven't got the patience." She looked across at Jack for comfort.

"Don't look at me, if you can't stand the heat, get out of the kitchen. You have to play by the rules...and if you don't," he chided. "Don't get caught."

She leaned her head to the side and studied him. *He is so fucking handsome.*

Jack, feeling uncomfortable with her gaze, ran his hand over his scarred cheek.

"Right," he barked, checking his watch and changing the subject "Where next?"

"Soho Sid, a whorehouse in Greek Street, London. We have such nice clientele, don't you think?"

She looked back over her shoulder at the plumes of black smoke, the sirens getting louder as they neared.

"Don't you just love the sound of a police car? It does it for me every time. Gives me goose-bumps."

Close by, a smouldering cigar dropped to the ground. The tip of a shiny black patent shoe stepped on the butt and slowly twisted left and right, scrunching it into the dirt. The shiny shoes calmly followed Jack and Amy into the side street, their smart 'click-click' resonating on the cobblestones.

Amy glanced over her shoulder, but couldn't see anything.

Chapter Nine
JACK

Six months earlier, Fulham Road,
Chelsea, London

Clutching a black briefcase and holding his raincoat tightly closed at the neck, Jack stood still in the cold, dark torrential rain outside his home. A streetlamp lit up his pained face as he stared into windows, watching the beautiful woman he felt nothing for excitedly preparing for his arrival. Becoming soaked, he felt numb. He simply didn't care. He wondered if he ever really had.

He watched Mara move from one room to the next, setting the table for supper. He knew what she would be doing; repeatedly realigning objects into perfect position. Knives, forks, flowers, candles, chairs: everything had to be just so. Everything had to be flawless. To the outside world, she mimicked the perfect wife.

His eyes closed with sadness. He didn't want to go home. He didn't love this woman. He lived a lie.

With a heavy heart, he trudged to the front door, inserted the key into the lock, and forced himself to cross the threshold. Perfect Mara rushed towards him: stunning, willowy, immaculate. Her long brown hair in a loose Rapunzel plait flowed down her back. She wrapped her tanned, jewel-laden arms around his neck and draped herself across his chest.

"Hey, I've missed you, lover boy." Her heady, cloying perfume hit the back of his throat. The scent used to turn him on, before he knew the truth, before the shedding of the first layer of snakelike skin.

Jack gently pushed her away; she smarted at his reaction, but pretended not to notice.

"I'm soaking wet. I don't want to ruin your outfit. let me go and change." He stepped away from her, avoiding eye contact.

He dropped his briefcase to the floor, slipped out of his raincoat, hung the damp garment over the banister, and lumbered up the stairs, his head low, his shoulders hunched with resigned acceptance.

With Cleopatra arrogance, Mara stood at the bottom of the stairs and held her head high. Eyes sly, she watched him ascend, knowing the truth but refusing to accept it. *He will love me...he will.*

She lifted his briefcase and placed it on the hallway table, exactly in the centre of its highly polished mahogany surface. She took time to nudge it backwards and forwards until all four sides sat equidistant to the table's edge.

It was important that everything she touched, everything she had control over, was always in its place, in an exact place for no particular reason. It was just so.

The obsession was exhausting and time-consuming, but for a few moments, whilst making things perfect, her fears took a back seat and the blissful escapism relaxed her.

Her peace was short-lived. Staring down at the shiny brown leather, she placed her hands either side of the briefcase, spreading her fingers wide across the glossy table top.

Slowly at first, then building in speed, she absentmindedly drummed her fingers, over and over, as if playing piano keys. Long red talons rhythmically rose and fell, repeatedly pounding the wood, getting louder and louder, until she abruptly stopped. She lifted her hands to the top of the case.

She gently stroked her fingertips across it, methodically and erotically, backwards and forwards, tracing the leather's cool softness, enticing it to open for her, to reveal its secrets.

Suddenly impatient, she gripped the sides of the case and ran her thumbs across the numbered locks, willing them to open, but she didn't know the combination.

Time stood still as she accepted defeat. She would have to wait.

Her glazed eyes wandered up the wall, to look at her reflection in the hallway mirror.

The briefcase forgotten, she tilted her head, admired her ethereal beauty and smiled.

"OK, darling," she trilled. "I'll pour you a drink."

Seeing the raincoat behind her in the mirror, she closed her eyes, lowered her head as if in prayer, and slammed the fingertips of both hands against her temples, pressing, kneading, and dragging the skin of her face to ease the anger building inside.

Then, with the flick of a switch, she stopped, dropped her hands to her side, straightened up, poised her head high, and feigned a fake smile. Mara, calm and in control.

She turned her attention to the raincoat and sauntered to the banister. Fussing with its material, she flicked rainwater from the lapels.

"And don't be too long, darling," she shouted up the stairs. "I have your favourite for supper. We don't want it to get ruined." The ever attentive, perfect housewife.

"Did you see her today?" she asked sweetly, slipping a searching hand into the raincoat's pockets. "Did you see the bitch today?"

Chapter Ten

Present Day, Cloud 9

Pyke and Maggie settled down to their tea and biscuits with the comfortable silence of age-old friends. Sharing the deep, leather-worn sofa, they kept their eyes on the screens of Pyke's Stonehenge storyboard world. He'd spun each screen to face the sofa. He liked to take a moment of free time, to stop and smell the roses every now and then, and to take a precious moment of mindfulness in his 24/7 work marathon.

Something he'd been unable to do when alive.

Like Amy, a brave soldier of depression, his mind had never let him stop, to relax and enjoy a moment. Destructive thoughts ruined any moments of quiet. Fear, shame, panic, self-loathing, and loneliness would rush to the surface whenever he stood still or relaxed his defences.

Beating the sadness was a daily battle, but he knew now it didn't need to be. He wished he'd reached out for help, had taken less meds and more therapy, learned a few mental tricks on how to manage the illness. But the thought of leaving his apartment and the safety of his computers to come face-to-face with those who didn't understand had kept him a prisoner.

Depression was one thing he didn't miss about his earth life, but he shouldn't knock it. Living his life through computers had made him what he was today; a genius and techno geek with the ability to multitask mercurial problems. Everything for a reason, he was a crucial member of the Unit.

Today, free from illness, he lived and relished every precious second to its fullest, especially intervals where he idly supped tea with Maggie. Today, he was all about enjoying his time, the now, making it count, having fun, mindfulness.

They sat quietly for a few minutes, happy in their solitude, lost in thought. With his cup of tea held mid-air, Pyke tilted his head this way and that way, viewing his work as if in an art gallery.

"We have some more help on the way for you. You can't keep up with all this on your own. I know you don't like help, but try...for me...will you?" Maggie nudged Pyke in the ribs.

He shrugged, gazing into his cup. "Maybe."

"Give this one a chance...OK? If nothing else they can make us tea."

Maggie smiled and shook her head, knowing the conversation didn't change his mind. Pyke hated sharing his precious walls. He preferred to work alone, but with their increasing workload he did need help.

A calm silence fell between them. Few people could sit together comfortably in silence, one or other would always try to fill the gaps with chatter. Maggie loved Pyke for that.

She sipped gently from her teacup, her little finger cocked as she raised the fine china to perfectly painted coral lips. The screen furthest away attracted her attention. She spied it with wolf-like eyes. Files and images were open across it, lighting it up with the face of a smiling young woman beaming at them.

"What are you working on, on number five? I don't remember authorising it," she asked.

Pyke followed her gaze.

"Oh...that," he said, giving a quick shrug. "It came in when you were at the departmental meeting. Thought I'd take a look for you. Alice Chambers has been missing for 31 days. Her family and friends have been searching for her. Her parents are frantic. It's hit the news headlines and is trending on social media...hashtag FindAlice."

Maggie nodded for him to continue.

"They have no body, no witnesses, no lines of inquiry. She could be alive, in need of help, or she could be dead in a ditch somewhere."

"We're overrun with misspers. Why are we...or more to the point...why are *you* interested in this one?" she asked with a wily smile.

"Well, she's cute," beamed Pyke.

Maggie raised an amused eyebrow. He shrugged and continued.

"Honestly, it's a strange one. Everyone likes her. She has no enemies we know of. She works with children's charities, loves saving lives, and has just returned home after a six-month stint in Africa. She has no previous criminal history, no charges, no reports, no intelligence anywhere on her. She lives with her mother. The day she went missing, as normal, she'd taken the bus into town to do a bit of shopping but didn't return. Her local Police force is overstretched with funding cuts and no men on the ground. After four weeks with no leads, their focus is moving on to other more pressing cases. She's drifted to the back of the pile."

He took a sip of tea before continuing.

"No CCTV, no witnesses, no forensics, no financial activity, no emails, or social media action. There is nothing to go on. She's grabbed the nation's heart and now mine. I want to find out where she is. It's only right to give a little special help to the good-uns down there, don't you think?"

"Who asked us to get involved?"

"Her mother has been praying night and day for a month. We are definitely invited."

"Has Alice asked us for our help?"

"No, but she could be drugged or something... not conscious."

Maggie eyed the beautiful young woman's picture and took another sip of tea.

"I'm not sure I like the pink hair or the nose piercing, but each to their own. At least she's memorable, from a witness's point of view. Where's she from?"

"Wales, on the coast, a tiny village."

"Where's the charity based?"

"Durban."

"Link up with African Units. They may have some Intel. Check out the Charity. Some are not what they seem." Maggie took another sip of tea. "I guess you've gone through her phone history, checked her love life, ex-boyfriends, family, and Doctor's files. There may be something there. Small villages can't keep secrets."

Pyke nodded. "Yep, her phone went missing with her, but I'm dissecting her phone records. She made a call to Brighton in West Sussex just before she went off the grid. I'm digging around down there."

"It's lucky I'm authorising it then, isn't it?" Maggie nudged him.

"I love you, Maggie," he beamed. "Thank you."

"But you know the rules. No solo jobs. Keep me updated. I can't protect you if you go off grid, and I can't abide lies, understand?"

"Understood. Would I ever?" he teased.

He rose from the comfortable sofa and skipped over to the screen. He liked the sound of Alice. She was a decent human being, who liked helping people. It didn't hurt that her image screamed with cuteness. If he'd been brave enough, and they'd met before his death, she would have been right up his strassa—perfect girlfriend material.

"I'm gonna find you, Miss Chambers," he sighed, staring up at her photograph. "You've got yourself an Angel."

Maggie shook her head with a concerned smile.

"Be careful, young man," she chided, knowing full well how dangerous it was to let the heart loose at work.

Chapter Eleven

Greek Street,
Soho, London, UK

Jack and Amy strode through the bustling traffic of Greek Street, a narrow road in the hub of London's colourful Soho where award-winning creatives and downtrodden sex peddlers managed to live comfortably side by side.

Opulent offices featuring film, fashion, music and advertising houses stood exquisitely lit with the glamorous and well-heeled Erthfolk running in and out of their chic entranceways.

Interspersed with dark alleyways and grubby doorways, the area housed all manner of services for the sins of the flesh, a Caligula melting pot. The creatives crafted beauty while the sex peddlers grubbed it up.

It was lunch time. Runners, secretaries, couriers, suited workers, and cool Fashionistas scurried about their business. Tourists, street walkers, and tramps politely danced around each other on narrow, uneven, chewing-gum-ridden pavements.

Jack watched a black Range Rover creep slowly past them, pull in a few yards ahead, and double park alongside a large white butcher's delivery truck; selfishly leaving only a narrow lane for two-way traffic to pass. Angry drivers waved fists and tooted horns as they skulked through the gap.

The delivery truck driver pried the heavy doors open, displaying bloodied slabs of meat hanging and swaying inside.

Three men, dressed in sunglasses, jumped out of the Range Rover wearing black hoodies, black jeans, and black trainers. A fourth man stayed in the driver's seat, playing with his phone, checking his reflection in the mirror.

The three men swaggered onto the pavement, pushed innocent pedestrians aside, and slid into a black, graffiti-covered doorway. The last one checked over his shoulder and closed the door behind him. A picture of a stripper with the numbers 727 had been scratched into the door's fading paintwork.

Jack strode up the middle of the street with Amy trotting along behind him.

The delivery van's driver slowly unloaded a tall, meat-laden trolley off the back of his truck, graduating it onto the road, carefully manoeuvring its four swivel castors to roll in the same direction. Jack stepped over to the van.

"Where is this place?" Amy asked, trying to keep up.

"Next corner on the right," Jack mumbled as he kicked one of the trolley's four brakes with his foot, slamming it shut against the wheel. With one castor locked, the trolley twisted sluggishly out of control. The delivery man stumbled, unable to take its weight.

Jack jaunted up to the driver's side of the Range Rover to find the driver busy adjusting his sunglasses in the mirror, preparing to take a selfie with his mobile. Jack reached through the window, pulled the car keys out of the ignition, and dropped them between the seat and car door.

He stepped away from the car, nonchalantly placed his hands in his pockets, and walked on with Amy trotting behind.

"What was all that about?" she asked, looking back over her shoulder.

"Just helping out Mr Plod."

"But..."

"But what? I tripped over that castor, it was an accident, it can happen to anyone... and the keys, they just fell out of the lock, so what? No big deal," he shrugged, striding on down the street, with Amy trying to keep up with him.

The meat trolley spun slow-motion in a semi-circle, rolled in front of the Range Rover, and toppled into oncoming traffic. Slabs of bloodied meat spewed across the tarmac, blocking the road and forcing drivers to screech their brakes. Angry Erthfolk laid on their horns, shouting and throwing their fists.

The black doorway burst open. Three men charged out with six bulging holdalls. They jumped into the Range Rover and barked at the driver to move.

"Move...*move*!"

The driver reached down to turn on the ignition – no key. Frantically, he scrambled to search around his seat. "Fuck, fuck, fuck!"

The owner of the strip joint and his two bouncers staggered out of the same black doorway with blood dripping from head wounds. They lunged towards the car, yelling obscenities.

On a nearby corner, two Policemen turned to see what the noise was about.

With traffic blocked, impatient car owners kept pressing their horns. The three powerless thugs stared out of the car window, their faces turning red and tense, watching the bouncers and police coming for them.

Amy laughed, shaking her head.

"How did you see that coming?"

"Oh, puhlease! If you're gonna be a thief, don't dress like one, drive a flash car, and walk about like the big-I-am. Jeez," he said. "Criminals of today... way too much ego... ego gets you caught."

Suddenly, a tone buzzed in Amy's head, she tapped her ear to answer the call. Pyke's voice resonated.

"If you're on Greek Street, there could be something kicking off at a strip club."

"Number 727? Three wannabe thugs robbing the place of something that fits into six holdall bags?"

"Yep. Drugs...how'd you know?"

"Jack's just sorted it. We came across it as an incident in progress. He's on it like a bonnet." She smiled, looking back at two running Policemen, shouting breathlessly into their radios. "Men in blue are at the scene, calling it in as we speak."

"Nice one, how...?"

"Don't ask. Slabs of meat were involved. Have a peek." A small green light clicked on to the right of her periphery. Pyke had tuned into the scene through her eyes to see what she saw. She stared at the chaos Jack left behind and heard Pyke chuckle.

"Next time, make him call it in for authorisation before he gets involved. I can't be watching over you guys all the time. But, hey, good job. Will chalk it up...the bosses are loving our stats."

"Yes, boss," she said, pleased. Pyke had a sensible, practical view of life; he didn't get too hung up on rules. "We're on route to Soho Sid. Will keep you updated. Do you know what the boss wants to talk to me about? I've got a review."

"She hasn't said anything. Maybe it's good news."

"Yeah. That's what Jack said, but I don't know." Ahead, Jack marched through the crowded street, and she didn't want to lose sight of him. "Gotta go. Trying to keep up with action man here. Speak later."

Pyke cut the call, severing the green light. Amy had to make a dash to catch up with quick-footed Jack.

They strolled in silence, side by side. Jack's eyes constantly darted this way and that; watching for signs, for body behaviour, for something out of the ordinary, for excessive, out-of-place energy.

Amy observed him, admiring his profile, his constant devotion to his job, wondering if he ever stopped working and what he was like on a day off. Were they allowed days off?

Catching her questioning look, he glanced across at her and turned away, avoiding her eyes. *She's staring at my scars again.*

Amy looked away.

"You never stop, do you? You're always working," she muttered.

"No." He subconsciously ran a hand across his face, feeling the grooves of skin reminding him why he was there.

"What drives you so hard? Do you ever take time out? Surely, we're entitled."

"No, we aren't here for long. There are too many bastards out there. I want to get as many as I can before my time is up."

He looked at her, questioning. "Besides, what else would I do?"

"Well, err...we could go to a movie...or something."

"What something?" he pushed.

Amy blushed; fearing he could read her mind. *Sitting in the back row of a cinema would be nice.*

She blurted. "Oh, I don't know, go to a shooting range..."

"What?" he laughed.

"You like shooting, don't you?" immediately wishing she'd said something else. *For fuck's sake...a shooting range? Why? I just wanna shag the guy. Urgh... duh!*

Just then, a young couple crossed their path. Jack stretched his hand out and gently brushed the female's wrist, causing a link in her bracelet to snap and fall to the ground. She heard it tinkle as it dropped and turned back to find it.

Jack and Amy walked on.

"Err...yeah. I like shooting, but not on my days off." He glanced at her.

Amy felt his scorching gaze. *Why do I always seem to make him angry?*

"We are here to do a job, Amy. We have a short window of time to work in. I'm just gonna get on with it and nail the baddies, OK?"

"Is that what you called them when you are a little boy, goodies and baddies?" she asked, wishing to lighten the mood.

"Yep, nothing much changed when I got older. I joined the army and was trained to kill the baddies, or they'd kill the goodies. Simple. They just wound me up and pointed me in the right direction. It's all I knew."

"Did you enjoy the army?"

"Yeah, it kept me out of trouble. The aftercare needs a bit of tweaking though. They don't know what to do with us when we we've burned out and it's time to leave."

"Is that how you died? On duty?"

He didn't answer.

"Is that how you got your scars?" she pressed.

"I don't discuss how I got here, Amy." He fidgeted about with her questions. "I just want to get on with it, OK?"

"Yeah, but you can't save everyone. There'll be others after us who'll eventually catch up with the shits that we don't get. Take some time out, Jack. Why are you so driven?" Amy said, tilting her head towards him, trying to understand this charming, funny, sexy, angry, achingly troubled man she just wanted to jump on. *If all these bloody criminals could just get out of the way for five minutes.*

She gave him a playful dig in the ribs.

"What have you done that you're paying penance for, Jack?"

He looked sheepish; his hand lifted to his face, hiding the scars on his jaw.

"Nothing. Shut up, Amy. Let's just get on with it, for god's sake." He marched on ahead of her. "You can talk about being driven, but you want to hang, draw, and quarter every paedophile in the country. You don't relax either."

She'd pissed him off. Amy scrunched her face. *Fuck, shit, bollocks. I've done it again.*

Behind them, a motorbike raced out of a side street at a high speed. The reckless rider noticed the couple, but too late. As the girl bent down to retrieve her bracelet, the male stepped ahead, straight into the bike's path. The bike smacked him, ricocheting his body high into the air. Where it flailed in slow motion before dropping and smashing down onto a parked car's bonnet, snapping his neck.

Amy heard the commotion and glanced over her shoulder. She turned and challenged Jack with a questioning what-the-fuck look on her face.

"He beat her," he said matter-of-factly. "He didn't deserve any help."

Additional Policemen, arriving at the robbery scene, changed course and scurried up the road to the crash site. The girl sat shocked on the pavement as onlookers fussed around her. She focused her gaze on the sky, then closed her eyes. Amy saw bruises, a black eye, and cuts to her lip. A small white feather floated to the ground beside her.

"How do you know he was responsible for the injuries?" she asked.

"I've been keeping an eye on him, gave him a few warnings, which he ignored. She just wasn't strong enough to leave. Fear kept her with him. His coercive behaviour has been building for a year. Sooner or later, he would take it too far and kill her, like he did with his previous girlfriend, it won't have been the first time, so..." he shrugged.

"You're playing God again, Jack?"

"You can talk. I didn't kill him. I just saved her."

Amy wasn't listening. As often happened when she accompanied him, her concentration would zone out as he spoke. Dreamily, she gazed at his lips, watching his mouth move, longing to reach out and kiss him.

Oblivious, lacking any ego or vanity, he couldn't imagine someone wanting him, least of all a woman as beautiful as Amy. He continued. "We're here to sort out the shits and protect the innocent."

She couldn't keep from staring at him. She found his scars attractive, especially the way they framed his face, underlined his cheek bones, gave him character and strength.

"I protected her," he added, as if he had to convince her.

"How did you get your scars?"

"I've told you. It's none of your business." He stroked the torn skin of his jaw as if rubbing them would make them disappear.

"Not telling me makes me want to know more."

"Well, tough."

"I think they're attractive. That's all. It's normal to wonder how you got them."

"You don't want to know."

"But—"

"Drop it. For fuck's sake," he barked. "What part of *no* don't you understand?"

She'd upset him again. She always pushed it too far. He hiked on, leaving her skipping behind.

Amy tried to appease him.

"Well, I'm pleased you saved her. You did good."

"I don't pretend to be God. I just help out. We all help out."

"Soooo pleased I'm not in the God business," she mused. "They have to make decisions like this all day long...who lives, who dies...pressure or what? No thanks."

"What do you mean *they*? Don't you believe in one God?"

"Not sure. There's something up there, but I don't know what, and I don't know how we, the Units, fit in."

They changed direction, taking a right on Thurloe Street and passing the oncoming ambulance. As the screeching siren subsided, Amy continued.

"When my dad died, a few nights after the funeral, his spirit visited my mum to say goodbye. She was sleeping. He sat on the edge of her bed and said, 'Honey, you're not gonna like this.' Mum, a staunch Irish Catholic, sat up, rubbed her eyes, and said 'What?' He said, 'There's three of them.' He blew her a kiss and left. My mum went back to sleep, muttering, 'There he goes again, still making trouble.'"

"Three of them? Father, Son, and Holy Ghost?" offered Jack.

"I don't know if it's three different religions or Tom, Dick, and Harry. All I know is there's good and bad. If there are a few Gods up there, as long as they get on, then great...and if there are no Gods up there, there's been a hell of a lot of waste over the centuries; wasted time, prayers, wars, and lives."

"Three Gods. I like that idea. But if there are three, working together, they'll be looking down on us, scratching their heads and wondering how the fuck their followers all ended up killing each other, asking where it all went wrong. But if there are no Gods, then who's running us?" asked Jack, looking up at the sky.

"Well, whoever, whatever it is, it'd better be good, or I want my money back." Amy let her lips turn up a bit.

They marched into the side of a building, the red brick wall giving them no resistance. In a nearby alleyway a smouldering cigar ash fell to the floor. A black patent shoe scrunched it into the ground and a black-gloved hand reached up and tapped an ear.

A gravelly voice whispered in the darkness.

"They're going vigilante and asking too many questions. It needs reporting."

Chapter Twelve

JACK

Six months earlier, Fulham Road,
Chelsea, London, UK

He had to get out, no matter the late hour, no matter the heavy downpour, or that her beautifully prepared supper would be cold.

When he had bound down the stairs in his jogging gear and muttered apologies about a hard day at the office, she'd said nothing. She just quietly watched him exit the front door into the howling wind and rain.

He knew she knew, that she searched his things, had found images, found the letter. He also knew she would never say anything about it, because that would mean facing an imperfection, and she didn't do imperfect. He had to grow some balls and put an end to the sham. If only he had the spirit left in him to do so.

He turned right at the end of his street, crossed the road, and headed for the gates of the Grade II listed Brompton Row Cemetery—his haven. The black, heavy, twelve-foot-high iron gate stood locked for the night, but he had a secret way of clambering over the back of a neighbouring wall to gain entrance. He had the place to himself, a magical oasis of stone, trees, and grass; his breathing space in the heart of London.

A beautiful tourist attraction by day, with its glorious trees, large black crows, pigeons, squirrels, and a cruising spot for gays (headphones on and eyes straight, he could happily leave them to it). At night, the cemetery became his private forty acres of magnificent solitude.

He plugged his earpieces in, pulled a few stretches, and started the hour slog of circuits around the graveyard's circumference. Dressed in black, with the half-moon in cloudy darkness, his figure took on an invisible aura.

Heavy rock music blasted in his ears, providing a base rhythm for his legs to keep a steady pace. His heart pumped as each step emptied his lungs and mind. Wind and rain stung his face as he weaved through tombstones, colonnades, and catacombs, pounding the ground of loved ones, buried and long forgotten. Wild flowers grew over graves where fresh ones had once decorated deceased souls' resting places, their memories having dwindled in friends' and families' hearts.

He never feared the dark of night. Occasionally, he'd come across a random homeless person huddled against lofty colonnade columns or hunched in catacomb doorways, but in the main they kept to themselves. If anyone ever did approach him, he'd rely on his ingrained training, the instinctive skills gleaned from his army days.

A complete circuit took 11 minutes. Each time he passed her home, he looked over the fence to check if her light pushed the darkness away. The willing and waiting egged him on to the next circuit, until he was dead on his feet, empty, drained of emotion, and time to go home.

About to pass her, he glimpsed up at her window, expectantly, longingly. But nothing. His face turned away in disappointment, the building bathed in darkness, indicating she wasn't home. He decided to jog around again, dragging his pace, just in case. He defied the icy rain despite his running trainers growing heavier with water.

When he'd discover her padding about her home, all cosy and alone, he'd covertly hide behind trees for hours, just admiring her and soaking in her beautiful face and smile. He'd anointed himself her secret guardian. He'd once shadowed her home from the tube station. He'd caught a pickpocket lining her up in his sights, and before the thief could strike, he'd wrapped his hands around his pathetic neck and dragged him into an alleyway. He promptly dealt with him, supplying a kicking that put him out of business for months.

When circumstances allowed, he would snap pictures of her, something to hold near when she wasn't around. He hadn't meant to, but he'd fallen in love with this girl. She consumed his thoughts, leaving room for nothing else. His relationship with Mara had deteriorated into a sad sham. Loving Amy added to his guilt.

His work offered him an escape; a stifling security consultancy office job, after years of frontline service. But it kept him away from home, until he figured out what to do. He didn't miss the killing of frontline work, but he did miss the comradery, the banter, the feeling of family, of belonging. He'd given his all to the army, but he'd been chucked out due to injury, a bullet lodged in his head, too dangerous to remove.

He hadn't meant to fall in love. He'd only meant to find her and make sure she was all right. Now, knowing she existed and wasn't his, made his life hollow. He didn't care if he lived or died. He sometimes willed that bullet to move and put him out of his misery.

Chapter Thirteen

Cloud 9

"We've had a complaint."

Maggie stood at the window, looking out over a stunning sea of white clouds, her eyes followed the dips and troughs of mountainous slopes. The deep monotone voice resonated in her head.

"And?"

"Your flock is asking questions."

Hands in her pockets, she closed her eyes and rolled her head back.

"What questions?"

"Questions."

"Bollocks."

"You are well aware of the consequences."

"It's a lie. Who reported it?" She snapped.

Looking over her shoulder, she saw a concerned Pyke peering around a screen, looking at her. He'd heard the anger in her voice. She waved him a quick reassuring smile, put her hand up, and mouthed 'it's OK.' He went back to work.

Calm and seemingly in control, she strutted elegantly across the office towards the exit, giving a quick wink to Pyke as she passed.

"A reliable source."

"They're wrong."

As she hit the hallway, she turned left into a door marked 'Washroom.'

"My team members are bloody good workers. We have the best figures in the northern hemisphere," she hissed.

"You are losing control. They're going it alone," the monotone voice continued.

She slammed the door behind her.

"For fuck's sake, this is bollocks. Who's telling you this shit? I demand to know," she bellowed, punching the nearest thing to her—a wall-mounted hand drier.

"Shepherd them in or lose them."

"Who's your source? They're lying to you, and you're falling for it." She stared at herself in the mirror, eyes ablaze, hands on hips, fuming. "It's jealousy."

"Consider this a warning."

"Who told you this crap?" she demanded. "*Tell me!* Is it Gregori? Gregori Duval?"

Click!

The voice drifted into oblivion.

She slapped her ear, trying to reconnect.

"*Tell me. Tell me.*" She slapped the side of her head again, hard, dishevelling her perfectly groomed hair.

Silence.

She picked up a heavy metal rubbish bin; with a howling growl, she flung it across the room. It crashed into the wall-mounted mirror hanging above the sterile line of white sinks with a loud *crack* before falling to the ground and rolling slowly back across the room to her stilettoed feet.

Taking a deep breath, she stood in front of the sinks and checked herself in the fractured mirror. She brushed down her suit, neatened her hair, and smoothed imaginary smudged lipstick from the corners of her mouth. Calm, sophisticated, butter wouldn't melt.

"I'm not going to let this happen again," she whispered.

Grabbing the sides of a sink, she leaned in close to her reflection, eyeball to eyeball. Her warm breath hazed the glass.

"No fucking way."

Chapter Fourteen

Alice

The Lanes,
Brighton, UK

She walked into the café, clutching her backpack. Dio said he would be there at 3.35 p.m., a pretty exact time. But from his text messages, she'd began to get the feeling he was a little anal about most things. His written word and punctuation were perfect: no short form or slang. Just beautiful perfect English. Although she had no idea what some of the words he used meant, she used a dictionary to look them up and learnt that 'pulchritudinous' meant beautiful, and 'don't absquatulate' meant don't do a runner. He was a little weird. She would have to be careful.

It was 3.28 p.m., and she had a few minutes to gather herself and work out what she would say to him. She wasn't sure how she'd found herself in the situation of meeting a stranger; this wasn't even her problem. She never could resist helping an underdog.

She scanned the cafe and settled on a corner table at the far side of the room. She placed her backpack on the chair beside her, her subtle way of forcing him to sit opposite her instead of directly next to her.

She ordered a coffee, took out a book, put on headphones, and positioned herself where she could clearly see the doorway and have the advantage of viewing the man before he joined her.

She would only have a few seconds to suss him out and decide whether she wanted to talk with him. If he looked dodgy, she would bury her head in the book, rock side to side to imaginary headset music, and pretend to be someone else. These days you had to be careful. Crazy people roamed everywhere out there.

At 3.35 p.m., the café door opened, issuing a blast of cold air against her ankles. She looked up to see who'd entered, but a waitress, shuffling towards her with a cup of steaming coffee, blocked her view. She rocked from side to side, trying to get a visual on the patron, but the waitress, a tad on the large side, took her time, balancing the full cup of brew, trying not to spill it as she travelled to Alice's table.

Alice cussed under her breath and forced a smile of thanks as the lady placed it in front of her.

"There you go, dearie, one cappuccino. Do you need sugar with that?"

"No thank you... thank you," she muttered, willing the waitress to get out of the way.

The waitress wandered on to the next table, collecting empty plates as she went. From behind her shadow, the man suddenly appeared directly in front of her. She had no time to calculate her next move.

She gauged him to be in his thirties, immaculately dressed in a navy pinstriped suite, white shirt, and coral silk tie. He pushed expensive sunglasses over his forehead onto a well-manicured mane of hair and beamed down at her with all the confidence of a wealthy, well-educated, spoilt rich kid.

"Hello. You must be Alice." His voice rang with perfect upper crust English, what she would describe as posh. His handsome eyes sparkled at her, as if pleased to see her.

"Err, yes," she replied, flummoxed, not expecting him to be so good-looking and feeling totalling unattractive in her cut-off jeans, baggy T-shirt, and travel-worn backpack "How do you do?"

What! Where did that come from? She never said, 'How do you do.' *Urrgh! She was trying too hard. What an idiot.*

"Do you mind if I join you?" he asked pulling out a chair opposite her, not giving her a chance to say no.

"No... err... go ahead."

He raised his hand at the departing waitress, catching her attention. Giving her a winning smile, he asked for a black coffee. The waitress blushed and scurried off. He came across as a man used to getting his way.

Alice pulled her headphones out of her ears and placed them with her book in her backpack, biding her time whilst gathering her thoughts. She took a deep breath in through her nose, enjoying his smell. It reminded her of soapy sage and lemons, of a freshly cut summer garden. He was pulchritudinous. She smiled.

She couldn't believe her luck.

Chapter Fifteen

Cloud 9

J ack and Amy landed in the office.

"Where's the Boss Lady?" asked Jack.

"In the loo, having one of her heated calls." Pyke poked his head out from behind a screen. "Not sure what's been said, but she's got that pink flush thing going on with her neck. You know...when she's trying to be a level-headed lady but oozes her inner pissed-off bitch. Stay outta her way for a while. That's my advice. How was Soho Sid? Did you upset his day?"

Pyke skipped over to the leather sofas and plonked himself down where Jack and Amy joined him. Amy sat beside him; Jack perched on the arm chair. All three stretched out their legs and propped their weary feet on the coffee table, enjoying a rare restful moment.

"Yep, he's not going to be popular. His stock was stacked up, ready for collection. We rearranged the trigger mechanisms. Whoever uses them will have their faces blown off. We passed his buyers on the way out. They will not be happy."

Pyke gave him a sideways look. "I just needed them to be out of action, not made lethal." He shook his head with a sigh. "You keep stretching the rules, Jack. Boss Lady won't like it."

"I figured if you're gonna buy a gun, you're up to no good and you deserve to have your face rearranged a little. That's 120 bad guys sorted for us in one hit...result." Jack grinned.

"How many?" gasped Pyke.

"At least 120 guns. I lost count after a while. I think we can assume in a week or so, he'll be out of business and on someone's hit list."

"I wanted him out of business, yes, but not with a pile of dead bodies."

"Dead criminal bodies...what's your problem? It's their choice to pull the trigger."

Pyke jumped up and walked over to a screen.

"What are you doing?"

"Sourcing the vehicle used to collect them and setting a Police stop. Let the cops discover the guns and seize them. They're safer in a property store than out on the streets." Pyke tapped at a keyboard with more of a flare than usual.

Angry, Jack jumped up off the sofa and stood menacingly behind him.

"If you can't stand the pace, you shouldn't be doing this job. We're dealing with bastards here...class A bastards. You can't be politically correct when dealing with bastards. We're doing the job because no one else will or can. Look, I'll take the blame." Jack slammed his fist on Pyke's screen, wiping out the command line he'd just inserted.

"When an innocent gets killed because you saved one of these arseholes, you're gonna feel like shit, Pyke."

"Yeah, but what happens if an innocent picks up one of these guns to defend himself and gets blasted to smithereens?"

"What if the criminals you're letting get away buy more guns and kill more innocents?"

"*For fuck's sake, boys, shut up,*" Amy shouted over their voices. "You sound like a couple of school kids."

Pyke and Jack stared each other out, teeth clenched tightly. Amy stood between them, and put an arm around each shoulder, pushing their heads together.

"Look, we can work this out. Aren't we on the same side?" She cuddled into them.

Jack pulled away. Amy noticed his awkwardness at her touch.

"For fuck's sake." Jack ran his hand through his hair and sighed. "OK, OK. Compromise... track each gun and I'll move in if needed, if one gets into the wrong hands."

"Deal." Pyke capitulated, punching Jack in the shoulder.

"We've just made a load more work for ourselves," moaned Jack. "Morals! Who fucking needs them?"

"It's why you're here," bellowed Maggie as she walked into the room, composed and regal, her episode in the washroom forgotten. "You were chosen because you wanted to do good, stop bad, help the underdog...commendable principles." She ambled to her desk and sat on its edge.

"I need to talk to you, all of you. Come here." She crossed her arms in front of her and waited for them to gather around her.

Jack, Amy, and Pyke silently obeyed and trudged over to her desk. They stood in a semi-circle in front of her, waiting nervously. She seemed tenser than normal, unnerving them. If she was worried about something, they seriously needed to worry about it. Not much fazed Maggie.

"I need you to trust me. I need you to stop asking questions about what we're doing here. Know that you're an important cog in a large wheel, that you're only here for a short period of time, that your work saves lives and corrects wrongs. I need you to trust and just get on with the work we're given. Stay within the rules. No going solo. No taking on jobs without authorisation." She looked each one in the eye.

Amy, Jack, and Pyke shuffled on their feet. Jack looked to the ground and Pyke shrugged his shoulders. Maggie pushed.

"Can you do that for me?"

Amy and Jack looked at each other. Amy took a deep breath. Jack could detect she was about to talk and piped up with a question to stop her putting her foot in it.

"OK, so sometimes there are moments when we walk into things on our way to a scene, situations requiring assistance, and I want to understand this. Are you saying that we have to turn away and not help?"

"Granted, there are the odd few moments when, if you call it in, we can catch up with the authority straight away, but that is not to become the norm. You cannot be seen taking matters into your own hands."

"That is not what I signed up for. If I waited for some unknown board of directors to give instruction, it may be too late."

"We can't all go around correcting life as we see fit. There has to be some order."

"Why not? We are all only here for the good."

"Not all."

"What do you mean?"

"Ying and yang. Where there is good, there is bad. Obviously, we try not to let it happen. We adhere to a pretty strict door policy, but we're not perfect. The rules are there to protect against the odd bad apple that sneaks in."

"So, if someone is in trouble, we have to walk on by and wait for paperwork...brilliant."

"Unless the person asks us directly for our help, then their request overrides the ruling, and we can attend immediately without waiting for permission."

"How the hell are they going to ask us? Being invisible, they don't exactly know we're standing right there to help. They don't believe. They don't know how to connect with us, and therefore, don't know they have to ask."

"Some do."

"A few do. We communicate with them, but not many. If we push them to do something that they haven't asked for, it is coercive behaviour."

"So we let them walk into dangerous situations."

"We have to be asked."

"Nuns and Priests etc pray for Erthfolk all the time, surely their prayers blanket everyone, everything," offered Amy.

"It helps, but the energy needs to be directed to a particular person or incident. We're part of the physics they haven't caught up with yet," Maggie shrugged. "We need rules, otherwise everyone would be playing God up here. And if Witnesses start infiltrating, we'll be in trouble."

Shaking his head with frustration, Jack ran his hand across his forehead and through his mane of dark hair. Amy watched him, wishing she could just reach out and touch him. Maggie noticed her longing, but said nothing.

"Why can't they just trust us to make the risk assessment and act autonomously?"

"They do. You're an excellent soldier, Jack. You all are, and that's why we have a strong Unit here. I'm proud of you and will support you all I can, but I've been asked to remind you of the rules."

"But...why if we're doing such a good job?" asked Amy, her eyes narrowing. "Is someone complaining?"

"Consider it like the army. A soldier doesn't go solo or question what, where, or why they're working on a mission. They just follow orders, trusting their superiors and the governments making decisions for them."

"Yeah, and look where that got us," scoffed Jack.

Maggie ignored him.

"You're doing a good job, but to do my job, I need you to trust me and keep quiet. Otherwise, I'll lose you and they'll close the Unit."

"Has someone said something about us?" Pyke asked.

Silence.

"OK. I admit. We stretch the rules a bit sometimes, but we get things done," Jack mumbled, hands stuffed low in his trouser pockets. He disliked authority, and this felt like the inflexible control of authority breathing down his neck.

"I understand you have to think on your feet out there. That's fine. But actively going on solo missions is not permitted. If you have a request, put it forward. Nine times out of ten, if ethical, we can help. Going solo ruins all we've achieved here; and if we are caught, it gives someone the opportunity to have us shut down. If you have questions ask now, and that will be the end of it."

Silence.

"I have a question." Amy summoned her courage.

"What?"

"How much time do we have here? I thought it was six months, but I'm not sure."

"It depends how much life you have in you when you die. Some die young, unexpectedly, not ready to go, still have things to do. Some are old, terminally ill, or commit suicide and are more than ready to move on, to rest. Some have the will to do more. The traits of life live in them for longer: hope, justice, love, anger, these are powerful energies. Once they are drained out of you, for some it takes six months, for others a year or so, you are of no further use here. You don't have the passion and are happy to leave the Unit."

"So, we are like batteries, just draining out." Jack muttered.

"In a way. You and Pyke are unusual, driven and dedicated. I'm guessing you'll have a longer stay here than most, and I'm lucky to have you on my team. Amy, you're new, and *sooo* not ready to go anywhere for a while. But be warned. You'll be asked to leave if you're not considered suitable, i.e., if you break the rules," she cautioned.

"When do we know it's time for us to leave?"

"You'll know."

"I've another question," Amy said, hesitantly but bravely.

"Go ahead."

"Where do we go from here? When we're finished, I mean. What happens next?"

"That's what everyone asks. I'm afraid I can't tell you. You'll be told nearer your time to leave. All I can say is you'll be dead, and this was just a stop-off point on the way out. I don't know any more than that, so don't ask me. You'll find out when your time comes."

"But..."

"But, nothing. I simply don't know." Through slit eyes, she shifted her gaze between them, daring one of them to respond. "Anything else?"

Amy looked to the two boys, hoping they would speak and carry on the discussion, but they remained silent. Intimidation had worked. They had no questions.

"Sorry, ma'am, but I have another quick question."

"OK. What is it? And then I really must go."

"Is..." Amy paused.

"Is what?"

"Is..."

Silence.

"Spit it out, for fuck's sake, Amy. I haven't got all day."

"Is someone following us?" she asked, softly under her breath for fear of being ridiculed. Jack rolled his eyes at her.

Maggie closed in on her. "Why do you ask?"

Amy saw the unease in her eyes and punched the air.

"I knew it," she squealed, nudging Jack. "See, I told you so. We're being followed, you never believe—"

"What makes you think you're being followed?" interrupted Maggie, her voice going up a notch.

"I don't know," Amy shrugged. "It's just a feeling."

Silence.

"Do you have a smell that goes with this feeling?"

"What?" Amy giggled. "What a strange question?" She looked nervously between the two boys, expecting them to laugh at her.

"Well, yes, actually I do. It's like pongy, acidy, cigarette smoke, like someone died, but it's not cigarettes, maybe a pipe, or a cigar. I don't know." She peered from one to the other. The boys and Maggie stared at her, making her feel hot under the spotlight.

"I know it sounds weird, but I get a waft of smoke sometimes. It feels like someone else is there...someone from this world, not down there. They don't say anything, they are just watching, witnessing everything we are doing, up here and down there."

Maggie gripped the edge of the desk for support. Her body weakened. Her legs buckled as fear washed over her, white knuckles squeezed tight. *It can't be. He no longer exists, or if he did, it would be down there, certainly not up here.*

"Many people smoke," quipped Jack.

"Not here. Not generally. Only if they request it on their privilege list," murmured Pyke, thoughtful. "I could run an HR profile search; see who's listed a pipe or cigars as a keeper."

"No...no, don't," barked Maggie, a little too loudly.

Pyke watched her, puzzled. He moved in close and put a concerned hand on her shoulder.

"Hey, are you OK?" he asked softly. "You look a little pale."

"I'm dead, Pyke," she grinned nervously. "I'm supposed to be pale."

Pyke didn't laugh. "Maggie?"

"Yes, yes, I'm fine," she squeezed his hand in thank you. "Sorry."

"Who was that call from earlier, the one you took outside?" Pyke questioned.

Maggie waved him off.

"Uh...of no importance," she turned to Amy. "Leave it with my Amy, I will look in to it." She walked unsteadily around the desk and pulled out her chair. "Now, unless there are any further questions, get back to work. Thank you."

"I have one more quick question, ma'am," cringed Amy. "Sorry."

"What?"

"Errr...well..."

"Spit it out girl, for fuck's sake," Maggie didn't have time for this.

"Ermm...are we allowed to..."

"What!"

"Oh, it doesn't matter." Embarrassed, she felt everyone's eyes on her, like lasers lining her up in target practice, impatient to end the meeting and get on with it.

"What?"

"Ermm..."

"For fuck's sake, spit it out, girl."

"Fuck...ma'am..."

"What?"

The two men stared, incredulous, looking from one woman to the other.

"*Fuck!*" blurted Amy. "You know, shag, make love, have sex, fornicate, hump the rhino, roger, do it...fuck, ma'am."

"I know what fucking fuck is," barked Maggie.

"Well...are we allowed to?" asked Amy

"You are joking, right?" muttered Pyke.

"It's a legitimate question. Are we allowed to have sex?"

Jack looked as if he would explode. "Why are you asking that?"

Maggie took a deep breath to answer, when her head beeped with an incoming call. She put her hand up to silence the three of them.

They were saved by the bell. Maggie hit the side of her ear and answered it.

"What?" she shouted at the caller.

Listening to the reply, she closed her eyes and took a deep breath.

"OK, OK, yes... wait one minute; I'm just leaving a meeting,"

She looked at the three of them.

"Amy, we will finish this conversation later. Meanwhile, all of you get on with the fucking job. We have work to do." She clapped her hands and waved them away.

"But..." Amy started to speak.

"No buts. You all bleedin' asked to be here," Maggie quipped. "Remember?"

She looked each of them in the eye, daring them to speak. Her cold glare ensured they got the message. The conversation had ended.

"So, get on with it," she instructed, walking out of the room.

As the door slammed shut, Pyke turned to Amy.

"What was all that about, Ames?"

"Nothing. I'm just curious about all the rules," replied Amy, waving it away as not important. She tried to change the subject. "Didn't you guys have any questions? I've got loads. What is it with you?"

Jack's gaze bored into hers.

"Who do you want to fuck? Is it that guy from the Rome Unit?"

"What guy from the Rome Unit?"

The double doors burst open again to a fuming Maggie halting in the doorway.

"… and why are you still standing there? Please, do tell. Get back to work."

They jumped away from her desk and skipped over to the screens. Pyke started to open the files for the next job.

Maggie spun out of the office, back to her call. Her voice echoed in the corridor, shouting at someone. And from the intonations and high pitches, she was not happy.

Chapter Sixteen

Jack

Two months earlier, Fulham Road,
Chelsea London, UK

As Jack walked up the street, he saw his home in darkness, no lights, no sign of life except for a soft, low glow teasing through the gap in their bedroom window curtains. Maybe she was reading. Good, he wouldn't have to sit through her excruciating small talk over supper.

After his last, particularly disturbing tour of duty in Syria, he had returned home to this beautiful, sexy, intelligent woman named Mara, a creature who had lured him into her lair. She sat with him whilst he repaired mentally from the pain, torture, and death. Grateful for her care he had agreed to marry her one crazy, heady weekend in Paris, where she had whisked him away for a Valentine's Day surprise. Mara always got what she wanted.

He knew little to nothing about her and never bothered to find out because the truth of the matter was, he didn't care. His heart and soul were consumed elsewhere. What he did in marrying her was wrong, a lie, cruel to her and him. He'd paid for it ever since. He had to find a way to escape, to spare them both.

Rain-drenched, he inserted his key into the lock and stepped into the quiet, dark hallway. The house's cuddly warmth stung his face. He kicked off his trainers and socks and placed them on the mat. He eased his body out of soggy, sodden clothes and left them in a pile beside his shoes to sort them out in the morning. Naked, he paraded into the kitchen and poured himself a large whiskey. Then another and another, anything to ease the pain of being without her.

He'd dallied long enough, hoping Mara had drifted off to asleep. With his cold skin now covered in goose-bumps, he poured a final tumbler of whiskey, hugged it to his shivering chest, and tiptoed quietly upstairs, taking two steps at a time to get to his warm bed.

The bedroom door, ajar, released the smell of perfumed candles, a pungent odour assaulting his nostrils. The candlewick flames danced and flickered, spreading a yellow glow and distorted shadows about the room. He lingered in the hallway, considered slipping into the spare room, but she may still be awake, waiting for him. He sipped the whiskey.

A voice cooed from behind the door.

"Jack, I'm waiting...come here...puhrrrrr, puhrrrr."

She always purred when she wanted sex, her signal for pleasure. Jack stood still, naked, shivering. He didn't answer.

"Jack, I need you."

He took another sip of his drink. Giddy from the alcoholic effects, he swayed in the darkness.

"I'm ready for you, Jack. You don't have to say anything. Just come in and take me. Just do it...just do it."

He wanted to. He wanted to so badly. He needed the sexual release, but he would just be prolonging the agony of leaving her. He needed to get her out of his life. He needed to tell her it was over. He needed to tell her now.

He pushed open the door, spilling his drink as he did so. Whisky splashed onto his chest and trickled down his stomach.

"Mara, we need to talk...."

She was laid out, on her stomach, naked, star-shaped across the bed. Her buttocks arched upwards, welcoming, willing. Her splayed legs showed him everything. Her lips curved slightly open, glistening wet.

She had been playing with herself in preparation for his arrival. She was ready, open, willing to get fucked.

He stood at the edge of the bed looking down on her. His cock leapt with anticipation. *The bitch.*

"Mara, please, I can't go on like this. We need to take time out from each other. We need to..."

She wasn't listening; she tilted her hips up and down, rhythmically grinding, as if being fucked, long and slow, enticing his burgeoning cock.

She groaned softly as she reached beneath her body and between her legs, fingering her cunt. Strands of juice stuck to her fingers as she eased in and out.

"Fuck me, Jack! Fuck me now."

His hard cock swayed proudly before him, just feet away from her body. He knocked back the last of his drink and threw the glass to the floor. He couldn't bear it; he would talk later. *If that's what she wants.*

He took a step forward and lunged into her open, gaping body, pushing deep inside her. His pent-up frustrations came to the fore as he pummelled hard and fast, over and over, not caring for her feelings.

In a final thrust he came, high up inside her. With arched back, clenched muscles, eyes closed and mouth wide, he cried out like a pained animal.

"*Amy...*"

The word struck hard, a slap to her face. *He said her name...her fucking name.*

Every sinew of Mara's body tensed with disgust. She eased her hips forward, off his still rigid cock as he tumbled exhausted onto her sweaty back, her eyes glazed with hatred.

Reaching beneath his pillow, she slipped a cold hand around a rubber handle. She heaved herself up and pushed his limp body aside. He rolled onto his back, stretched out beside her, breathing heavily and regulating his breaths.

With an almighty scream, Mara drew her arm up high above his torso and drove the knife hard into his chest, angled up and under the ribcage, deep into his heart.

"Don't you dare mention her name," she cried, dragging the blade out and thrusting it in again, harder, faster, just like his needy cock had thrust into her.

Jack's eyes burst open in shock. He jerked his head off the pillow, gagging against a soft groan gurgling in his throat.

"Don't you dare," she screamed, relishing the surprise in his eyes.

Still lost in the afterglow of sex, he stared back at her, confused, stark eyes, not understanding the mix of pain and orgasm.

He looked backward and forward from her angered face to his naked chest, trying to comprehend how his hunting knife had gotten there. He'd slept with the knife under his pillow out of habit, always alert, always ready for combat; it had lived with him for years, his faithful friend. But now, its familiar black handle stood proudly erect in his body, as the surrounding skin oozed pumping blood.

A few seconds of silence deafened as the realisation of what she'd done sank in. After the initial disbelief, his face seemed to relax and soften. For the first time since they'd met, his furrowed brow softened, his tight jaw loosened. He looked younger, happy, at peace.

Regretting her actions, tears welled in her wild eyes. For all the pain he caused her, she loved this beautiful, complex man.

"Take it out," he whispered, laying back, his head resting on the pillow. "Take it out...quickly."

She shivered with horror.

"Noooo, Jack, I'm sorry. Please don't move." Reaching for the side table, she hunted for her phone. "I'll call an ambulance...Oh my god, Jack, what have I done?"

"Pull it out of me...now...*now*," he begged, his soft voice impatient.

"I can't."

"You must."

"It will make it worse."

"No, it won't. Take it out, *now*."

She followed his command, believing it would help, but more blood gushed from the wound as the blade slipped out. He'd tricked her.

"No, no...*no!* I didn't mean for this," she cried, frantically trying to block the hole with a bed sheet, but the blood kept pumping, drenching her and the linen.

"Stop it, please! I can't stop it, Jack. It won't stop...*no...no.*"

He peered down at her blood-stained face and noticed rivets of tears track down her cheeks. He gave a contented smile and raised his finger to his lips to hush her.

"It's OK, Mara. It's OK. It's finally over. Thank you...thank you," he rasped, his voice failing. "I'm sorry."

His eyes glazed, his head rocked back, and a loud breath rasped his throat. His body lay still. He was dead...finally free.

Chapter Seventeen

Present day, Cloud 9

Pyke readied the screen for briefing.

"I need to go to the loo. Back in a min." Amy strode out of the room. Jack followed her. Maggie could be heard shouting at the end of the corridor. Someone had upset her; she was not having a good day.

Marching into the washroom, Amy walked into a cubicle and slammed the door shut. They didn't need bathrooms. They didn't eliminate waste. The food and drink they consumed worked as feel-good illusions, part of the privilege request list. Someone had once placed washrooms on their request list. They became popular and stayed. They served as a sanctuary.

Humans sometimes needed the undefinable solitude washrooms provided, the one place they could get away and be alone, take advantage of its privacy, even if only for a short while. Behind the washroom's closed doors, they could drop their masks and just be themselves, regroup, and walk out the door, ready to take on the rest of the day. A strange thing to keep in the skies, but an important one.

She heard the door slam as Jack entered.

"What is it with you?" he spat.

"Do you mind? I'm on the loo. Can I have some privacy, please?"

"No, you bloody can't."

"Charming. Ever the gentleman, I see."

"I repeat, what are you playing at? Don't you think Maggie has enough to deal with, without your childish, shallow chatter?" His inflection rang like a squeaky teenager. "Miss... can-we-have-sex-please."

"I can ask whatever I want. It's a free country...I mean sky, planet...wherever the fuck we are...shit, grrrrr," she growled. "I want to go to the loo. Leave me alone."

"Grow up, Amy. Stop being so selfish. Either get on with the job or get out. I'm not sure why you're here anyway. You're a fake," he spat, angry she wanted to be with someone else, angry it wasn't him.

Amy stormed out of the cubicle and ran at him across the washroom floor, hurling herself at his rigid body. They fell backwards onto the hand dryer wall. Jack laughed, raising his hands up against the wall in surrender.

"Hey! Careful."

"Don't you dare call me a fake. There's a reason I'm here. What's yours? Someone broke your toy car..."

With an open palm, she slapped him across the face. He stood stunned for a second and slapped her right back, not as hard, but the shock bewildered her.

"How fucking dare you hit a woman?" She grabbed his shoulders and pushed him back against the wall.

"You hit me. Why not?"

"You're supposed to be a gentleman."

"You behave like a lady and I'll be one."

"You wouldn't know what to do with a lady."

"Says the bird who wants to shag any Tom, Dick, or Harry she meets, puhlease..."

"I don't."

"Well, what was all that about with Maggie then?"

"I want to shag...yes, but..."

"Who? Pyke? That Italian schmoozer in his designer suits?"

"Can we shag up here? Is it possible? Is it illegal? I mean do we explode or disintegrate into dust or something?"

"How the hell would I know?"

"You mean you haven't thought about it all the time you've been up here?"

"No...yes...I mean...it hasn't come up."

She released her grip. They stood tantalisingly close. She could smell his maleness. If she could just lean in and kiss him.

"So, you've wanted to screw someone up here?" she questioned.

"Yes."

"Who."

"That's none of your business."

"Who is she?"

"Is she up here or down there?"

"For fuck's sake, Ames, this is ridiculous. We're not in kindergarten. That's my business."

"You wanted to know who I wanted to fuck, so why not let me know who you wanted to fuck?" She put her hands on her hips, waiting for his answer.

"Because you're a nightmare. You need protecting. You'll choose the wrong guy and jeopardise all of us."

"If I don't explode into thin air."

"If you don't explode...oh, I don't know! This is ridiculous."

"You know? You're right. I've chosen the wrong guy."

"Who?"

"You."

"Oh, fuck."

"Yes, oh fuck." She edged back from him. "You see...is that your answer? Oh fuck? I knew it. The wrong guy. You don't even fancy me, and now I've gone and laid it out there, and blown it...how embarrass—"

Before she could finish her tirade, he grabbed her face, pulled her mouth towards his, and kissed her hard, bruising her lips.

She backed off, trying to catch her breath. He spun her around and threw her against the wall, trapping her. Still holding her face, he pushed his body into her. She stared up at him open-mouthed.

He delved into her mouth with his searching tongue. He'd waited so long for this, he couldn't stop.

At first, she faltered, not knowing if he was real or playing with her.

Then...*fuck it.*

She joined in, pulling, grabbing, tearing at his clothing. She wanted him so badly it hurt. She kissed every part of his face, eating him up, taking as much of him as she possibly could. His smell and taste intoxicated her. The groans at the back of his throat gave her courage. He wouldn't let her face go. She could barely breathe.

She fumbled with her clothing, pushing her trousers to the floor, kicking her foot out of one of the legs, freeing her body to jump up onto his hips. He stood open legged, his body pinning her against the wall. He stopped kissing and looked hard into her eyes. Watching her, willing her, still holding her face.

A ringing tone sounded in Jack's head. It was Pyke... *shit*. He ignored the intrusion.

Keeping her gaze on his, following his lead, taking his look as a *yes*, Amy reached down and undid his trousers. The material slipped to his knees.

A ringtone sounded in her head. She pretended not to hear it.

Gazes still locked on each other, he moved his hands beneath her buttocks, cupping her, lifting her weight.

"Do you want this?" he asked. "Are you OK with the risk?"

"If you don't, I'll die anyway."

He eased her up over his bludgeoning cock and down onto him.

"Oh, my god! I've died and gone to heaven," she smiled, tentatively easing herself up and down on him.

He grinned back, "Well, so far so good. We haven't exploded yet."

She grabbed his face and kissed his mouth. "Shut up and fuck me."

He hadn't imagined it like this. In his dreams, he'd wanted to pleasure her for hours before he fucked her, watch her come over and over. And then take her long and slow. But this moment overpowered him. He couldn't hold it. All these years of waiting, of following her, of watching her every move, of standing so close but being so distant.

"OK, you asked for it."

He lifted her off the tip of his cock and bounced her up and down, just on the tip, just teasing her until she cried in his ear, then rammed her down hard on top of him, entering her deep. Making her cry out in pleasure, he repeated the teasing, again and again, with the tip of his cock rubbing her clit, then when she could take no more he drove her down on him, sinking into her, making her mouth open and eyes close in pleasure.

Until it was too much.

He started pumping hard, her back crashing into the wall. She didn't care. She asked for more and more.

The ringing tone in his head again; Pyke was persistent. Jack quickly answered it.

"Not now, Pyke," he gasped.

"What the hell are you doing?" Jack's green light popped on.

Pyke saw in glorious close-up what Jack could see, Amy's chest bouncing up and down, her legs wrapped around Jack's hips, the view of Jack's cock sliding in and out of her.

"Ooops...cor blimey, sorry mate...err," the call and light closed abruptly.

Jack didn't care; he couldn't have stopped if the Queen had walked into the room. He was on a roll. He pumped harder and harder against her cries, until the rush of ecstasy waved over him. He came hard, high up inside her. His body collapsed. His head sank onto her shoulder where her heavy breathing resonated in his ear.

They stayed, leaning against the wall, getting their breaths back, still panting, hearts pounding, sweat pouring.

She didn't want to move. She clung to him like a limpet and rested her head on his, giving tiny kisses to his forehead.

"I've got to put you down," he whispered.

"No," she sighed.

"Yes, my legs are about to go," he smiled.

He eased her gently off him. She wobbled as she hit the floor, her body in post climax jelly mode. They clung to each other, listening to each other's breathing.

"We didn't die then. I guess it's allowed," she managed to say, smiling up at him, wiping a droplet of sweat from his jaw.

Bang, bang, bang.

The washroom door shook.

They jumped.

Bang, bang, bang.

Pyke's voice, from the other side of the door, detonated in the room.

"Sorry to ruin the party, guys, but the boss is back. We have work to do," he thumped again.

Bang, bang, bang.

"Get out of here. Fast."

Amy giggled. They struggled to get into their clothes and ran out the door, running into a red-faced Pyke.

Chapter Eighteen

Alice

Brighton, UK

Dio lay his shiny black mobile phone on the small square table between them. Taking time to line it up in the centre of the table, equidistant from each edge. She watched, mesmerised as his long elegant hands deftly nudged the phone into place.

"How did you know it was me?" she asked, once the waitress had carefully placed his steaming black coffee in front of him.

"Well, I have to admit I googled you."

He slowly slid his coffee cup to his right, lining it up exactly midway between the edge of the table and his phone. She watched him, his movement languid and seductive.

"Oh," she muttered, blushing, flattered.

"I sourced your image through social media. It's a dangerous thing, you know, young lady. One can find anything one wants through the Web."

He scooped his hand across the table, and, without asking her, dragged her coffee cup to the other side of his phone. He stared down at the three items, happy with their perfect alignment.

Without looking up, he whispered.

"You should be careful," he mumbled, his voice too low for her to hear.

"Sorry? What did you say?" She leaned forward, trying to hear him. The smell of summer gardens explored her senses again.

"You need to be careful. The Internet is a dangerous place to play in for young girls like you." The slight reprimanding tone in his voice made her feel uncomfortable.

"Oh, well, I've got nothing to hide." She shrugged, pretending not to care.

"That's not the right attitude. It's a bad world out there. You should be vigilant," he chided, then whispered again, forcing her to lean closer.

"I wouldn't want any harm to come to you. You're way too special for that." He stared into her eyes, making her feel like she was the only person in the room. Her heartbeat accelerated.

He cocked his head to the side and trailed his fingers along his bottom lip. His eyes watched her reaction, happy she followed his every move, unable to look away. Her mouth eased open.

His fingers trailed off his lips onto his cheek, gently stroking his clean, soft skin, circling the length of his jaw, down his neck, and casually tugging at his shirt collar, as if feeling the heat.

She blushed. Was he flirting with her? He had to be at least twenty years older than she. Did he find her attractive? Flattered, she sat tall, puffed her chest out, and felt her confidence growing. She flicked her hair from her face and affected a grown-up sophistication.

Using the tip of his forefinger, he watched her closely as he absentmindedly traced the rim of his cup, his finger circling round and round, her eyes following his every move.

"It's a little hot," he whispered.

She couldn't talk.

With both hands, he gently wrapped his fingers around the cup and cautiously brought the scalding coffee to his waiting mouth. Holding the cup in front of his face, he looked over its rim and locked gazes with her. She stared back, silent, captivated, unable to turn away.

He pursed his generous lips and gently blew cool air across the liquid's surface with an overtly sexual innuendo.

Her mouth fell open. She wanted to feel those lips on hers, to taste them. As if reading her mind, the corners of his mouth curled upwards, forming the thinnest smile. Her gaze darted away. Embarrassed, she grabbed her coffee, causing it to spill on the table top.

Flushing with awkwardness, she looked around and snatched a few napkins from a holder on a nearby empty table. Frantically mopping up the spillage, she apologised profusely.

"Sorry, sorry, I'm so clumsy." She chased the droplets across the table. "I'm so sorry."

"Hey, it's OK." He rested his hand on hers to calm her. "Let me do that."

His hand lingered before he wheedled the napkin from her. An electric shock charged up her arm and prickled through her body. She reluctantly pulled her hand away, watching him tidy up the mess and deposit the soiled napkins on the next table.

"There you go. All is well again. No harm done," he replied, beaming.

She nodded a thanks, calming her nerves; she picked up her coffee and sipped quietly.

He smiled at her, safe in the knowledge that, as with most people, he captivated her, she was unable to resist his charm...*like lambs to the slaughter.*

Chapter Nineteen

Cloud 9

"He's a Brit, Zagan Black, Zigzag to his friends. The Italians want us to clean him up." Pyke talked Jack and Amy through the file. He pretended not to notice their disarray; he would tease them about it later.

Amy tried not to look at Jack. Whilst he couldn't keep his eyes off her.

"He works out of a relatively small casino in Porto Antonio, along the coast from San Remo, on the Italian Riviera. His modus operandi is to set up..."

The office door opened. Mara sashayed into the room.

"Well, hello, everyone," she said, taking them all in with one sweep of her fiery dark lash-laden eyes. All tits and teeth, her figure hugged a black dress leaving nothing to the imagination. Pyke's eyes lit up.

Maggie followed Mara in. The two women stood in front of Pyke. He looked at the two of them and smiled. They couldn't be any more different.

Maggie called Jack and Amy over. Jack was still staring at Amy, loving it that she couldn't look at him without blushing. It was cute.

"Everyone, this is our new recruit, Mara. She's joining the team for a while, helping Pyke out. Introduce yourselves." Maggie walked to her desk, leaving the team to get on with it. She looked over her shoulder and gave Pyke one of her warning glares.

"... and Pyke don't teach her any bad habits. Try to play nice."

But Pyke was the least of her worries.

Jack pulled his stare away from Amy and turned to meet the new recruit. His eyes hardened.

"What the fuck?" he cursed under his breath.

Amy gave him a quizzical look.

Pyke smiled at his lovely new assistant and stepped towards her with open arms. He was on his best behaviour; he'd promised Maggie he would give this one a chance, which was easy. The woman was sex on legs.

"Good to meet you, Mara. I'm in dire need of help. Welcome to the madhouse. How are your IT skills?" He embraced her, and then stood back, looking her up and down. "Wow, you're stunning. Not bad for a dead person," he grinned.

"Why, thank you, kind sir," she flirted. "My computer knowledge is good. Not as good as you, but good enough. My main talent is digging deep for dirt, profile analyst work. I'm a fast learner and here to help, so what do you need?"

"Well, let's get going. We've just started briefing on this new job. Come join us. This is Jack and Amy."

Pyke pulled Mara over to the screen they'd been working on. Amy shook her hand with a polite smile.

"Wow, Pyke, let her catch her breath. She's only just arrived. Mara, would you like a drink? Have you been shown around?"

Jack stood glued to the spot, his skin ashen.

"What the fuck are you doing here?" he demanded.

Amy and Pyke spun to look at him, feeling a tad awkward. It was not like him to be rude. Troubled, grumpy, and complex, yes; but not downright rude.

"You know each other?" asked Pyke.

"Oh, yes. Intimately," Mara purred.

She turned to Jack. "Why, honey, I thought you would be pleased to see me," she simpered; hand on hip, doe eyed.

"You know each other?" asked Maggie from her desk.

"Why, yes. He's my darling husband."

Jack grabbed Mara by her forearm and marched her toward the exit. She trotted along beside him, grimacing a smile to keep up appearances, but obviously in pain.

Pyke and Amy stood and stared, watching Jack push her out the door into the corridor.

Maggie turned to face the window, her back to the departing couple; she tapped her earpiece and waited for a voice to connect.

"I thought you said our new recruit had no previous history with any of our current team. I specifically requested no history," she barked.

A voice replied into her ear.

THE DEAL

"On whose authority?" she demanded.
The reply made her close her eyes.

Chapter Twenty

J ack slammed through the washroom door, forcing Mara to go with him. They stood a foot apart, hands on hips.

"I repeat. What the fuck are you doing here?"

Mara flicked her long locks over her shoulder and looked around the room in disgust.

"Well, you certainly know how to make a girl feel welcome. A washroom, thanks so much," she teased. "Very sexy."

As she picked up a fallen dustbin and stood it upright, she noticed the cracked mirror.

"What the hell happened in here?" She pointed at the glass with her manicured finger. "Is this where you come for all your fights?"

"Shut up and answer me." He was having none of her evasive, manipulative banter.

"I've been looking for you, Jack, and now I've found you. What can I say? I've missed you," she purred.

"You fucking killed me...remember?"

"Ah, yes. That was nothing." She waved it away with her typical dismissive attitude. "A little misunderstanding. I didn't mean to."

"How did you get in here? Surely there are protocols as to who can work here. I don't think murderers are allowed. Whose arm did you twist? Or more likely, who did you fuck?"

"I'm not a murderer, baby. You committed suicide, didn't you know? Well...that's what the Coroner reported." She played with her hair, twizzling it around her finger, something she used to do when they were together, when she was plotting to get her own way. The memory sickened him. He turned away.

"You have to leave. No way are we working together. Move it along and go find another Unit," he said, disgusted and fed up with her control.

"Ah, now, that's where you're wrong, I read your letter, Jack dear. I'm staying, or I will share your little secret with Miss Goody-Two-Shoes out there. I know what you did. I gather she doesn't."

Jack's eyes flickered with an underlying desire to strangle her. He bit his tongue before a vileness crossed his lips that he'd regret later.

Silence.

"No?"

Silence.

"Just as I expected. Well, let's just play along nicely, shall we?"

Losing it, Jack slammed into her, pushing her up against the sinks. She fell back against the mirror. Holding her by the throat, he snapped at her.

"There is no way I'm letting you anywhere near her, so help me...."

"I love it when you talk dirty, Jack." Mara leaned in to kiss him, her mouth touching his.

A polite knock interrupted her.

Amy peered apologetically around the door. Jack backed off from the wall, in disgust, letting Mara go.

Mara gave Amy a conspiratorial smile, leading her to believe she'd caught them in a romantic clinch. Mara neatened her hair, checked her bra straps, and brushed down her skirt.

Amy's heart sank. She and Jack had been in the same position only ten minutes ago. *What the hell?*

"Are you guys OK? Jack, what's happened?"

Jack opened his mouth to reply, but Mara interrupted him.

"Oh, nothing," she assured with a coy smile. "He just got a little too pleased to see me. We got carried away." The sexiness in her voice drooled with sappiness.

Amy grimaced. "You guys have a history. I thought that wasn't allowed up here."

"I have friends in high places, honey," Mara announced, winking with a tease. "I just couldn't keep away from my boy."

Jack gritted his teeth and stared at the floor, his fists clenched with anger.

Amy looked to Jack for support, but he didn't say anything. A flush of jealousy washed over her.

"So, you committed suicide, to be with him?"

"In a way...yes."

"But I thought suicide was not allowed here."

"Like I said...friends in high places."

"Great. Well, I'm sure Jack is pleased to see you. Now if you don't mind, I'd like to use the loo...in private." Amy walked into a cubicle and slammed the door shut for the second time that day.

Jack stood staring at the closed cubicle door, running his hands through his hair, not knowing what to do. Mara watched him, longing for him to touch her. She stepped towards him, standing close.

"I know you want me, Jack," she uttered, using her stage-whisper just loud enough for Amy to hear.

The arrow struck. Feeling a fool, Amy sat on the closed toilet seat and dropped her head in her hands.

Shaking with anger, Jack spun around, raising his hand, ready to hit Mara. Thinking better of it, he bit his tongue, turned, and marched out of the room. Mara chased after him, not about to let him go.

In the corridor, Jack lifted his fist and shook it in her face.

"You come near me, I will kill you. Do you understand? You are poison. I want nothing to do with you."

"Does Maggie know about your little naughtiness, your breaking of the rules?" she giggled, loving him when he lost his cool.

She stroked her crimson-nailed fingers gently along his jawline, tracing grooves in his scars.

"Poor little Jack. What are we going to do with him?"

He resisted grabbing her wrist and snapping her hand backwards, breaking every single one of her evil, pointy, taloned fingers. He wouldn't succumb to her games or fall for her tricks. She wanted him to touch her, but he denied her the satisfaction, the twisted pleasure. He snapped his head away from her grasp and stormed through the office doors to join Pyke.

Mara checked her makeup in a hand-mirror and followed him.

Chapter Twenty-One

Alice

Brighton, UK

"So, what can I do for you, young lady?" Dio beamed. "You said in your message you needed help finding someone."

"Yes, a friend of mine has a daughter. She's gone missing."

"Who is this friend?"

"Well, she's not actually a friend. She lives around the corner from me. We share the same bus and talk sometimes. Her 19-year-old daughter, Maria, has not come home for three days now. Eva, the mother, is very worried and asked me to help her. Eva is Polish and her English is not very good."

"Why doesn't she go to the Police?"

"She's not that comfortable with going to the police because her husband is always in and out of trouble with them."

"Where do you live?" He knew where she lived; he knew everything about her.

"In Wales, a small village on the coast."

"You've come a long way."

"Well, the lady asked for help...she begged me. I couldn't refuse. She is beside herself with worry...and it's exciting, seeing a new city."

"Why did you contact me?"

"Because Eva believes you may know where her daughter is. I have a picture of her. Look."

She pulled a worn photograph from a side pocket on her backpack and placed it on the table. The face of a beautiful young woman, taking a selfie in front of the Houses of Parliament, smiled for the camera.

He picked up the photograph and examined it, turning the image over, back and forth with strong, well-manicured fingers. Alice looked down to compare her own, nail-bitten, scruffy digits, and slipped her hands out of sight under her thighs.

"She is indeed lovely," he sighed.

Did she see recognition in his eyes?

"Do you know her?" Alice questioned, hopeful.

He placed the photograph back on the table between his phone and her cup. With acute concentration, and the tips of his fingers, he nudged the two cups, the phone, and the picture left and right until they lay exactly equidistant from each other. When he was satisfied the pieces had equal distance, he looked up at her and frowned.

"What did you say her name was?"

"Maria, Maria Iwanski."

He studied the image as if trying to recount something.

"Hmmmm." He shook his head, making up his mind. "No, I've never seen her. I'm sorry to have wasted your time, dear Alice. I don't know this girl." He sighed, as if genuinely sorry. "How sad it all is."

"Oh." She sat back in her chair, disillusioned with the wasted trip.

He glanced at his watch, took a few sips of coffee, and rose to leave. She didn't want him to go. Her heart sank further.

"If I can be of any further assistance, let me know." He smiled down at her, pulling the sleeves of his suit in line with his shirt cuffs, smoothing down his lapels.

As Alice glanced at him, she remembered something. She reached into her jean front pocket.

"If you don't know her, why was this piece of paper found on her bedside table?"

She produced a piece of lined paper, folded and crumpled. She meticulously smoothed it out on the table in front of her, being careful to line it up with his chess pieces, nudging everything backwards and forwards until the spaces appeared equal.

He smiled at her playing his game, but she hadn't quite achieved perfection. He deliberately leaned over and added a few nudges himself, then smiled, approvingly.

"Why?" She looked up at him, her arms crossed in front of her, waiting for him to answer.

He moved in closer, bending over to inspect the piece of paper, analysing the text scribbled in black ink. He shook his head with a bemused shrug.

"I don't know. I don't recognize the writing. It's certainly not mine."

"But it is your name, number, and address."

A small bead of sweat seeped from the pores along his top lip.

"That's not a Brighton address."

"I know. I've been there looking for you."

He sat back in his chair, eyes wide with innocence.

"Anyone could have given her that. But I certainly didn't."

Chapter Twenty-Two

Cloud 9

Amy sat with her head still dropped in her hands, feeling a fool.

Bang, bang, bang.

Pyke's voice echoed through the door. "Amy, come on. Maggie's on the war path. We've got to get going on this job. Zagan Black is on the move."

"OK, OK," she shouted, leaving the cubicle and staring at her face in the broken mirror, her heart mimicking the shattered pieces. "I'm coming. Keep your hair on." *For fuck's sake.*

Holding her head high, she plodded back into the office. Pyke manned his station in front of his screen, sandwiched between Jack and Mara. Both stood as stiff as cardboard cut-outs, their faces sober and strict, ignoring each other.

The room felt different, the energy no longer the same.

Maggie watched her return to the group and waved her hand for Pyke to get started. She was not happy. Tapping her ear, she waited for the call to be answered.

An assistant answered. She was out of luck.

"I don't care if he's busy. I want to speak to him now." She turned her back on her Unit and stared out over the clouds.

"OK, let's get on with it," exhaled Pyke. "I've been following this guy for a while now."

Feeling hot, Amy loosened her collar and took off her suit jacket. She focused more intently to concentrate on Pyke's yammering and the demonstrations he performed on his monitor, but his words droned off in a monotone without syllables. The screen's cursor streaked like a mindless doodle. She couldn't concentrate; she may as well have stayed in the washroom. She wondered if Jack were listening.

"You know what?" She rocked nervously, from one foot to the other. "I'm gonna take some time out for a moment. You guys carry on and I'll catch you up."

"But..." said Jack

"I need some air." She hurried out of the office.

"But what about the job?" Pyke called after her. Amy ignored him.

"How rude," whispered Mara, watching her walk out the door.

"Let her go," barked Maggie from across the room. "She'll be back."

"Oh, well. We'll start without her." Pyke tapped code onto the screen.

Jack shuffled uneasily on his toes, watching Amy leave and wanting to catch up with her, not feeling his chipper self. He looked to Maggie for guidance. She peered over her glasses and slowly shook her head with a do-not-dare glare. He obeyed and resumed his duty, listening to Pyke's briefing.

Mara placed a caring hand on his shoulder. He shrugged it off. She smiled and gave him one of her sexy pouts, the ones she used when trying to get her own way. He felt sick—her shit-stirring had started.

Pyke typed in a password and watched the screen burst alive with files, images, co-ordinates, and maps.

"Right, eyes down, here we go," he grinned with excitement, loving the chase.

"Zagan Black is a conman working out of the Mediterranean. He has a passion for Casinos and ripping off vulnerable punters."

"I've sent you the coordinates, Jack. I'll forward them to Amy as well. She can catch you up."

Turning to Mara he smiled. "I'll give you the next assignment to work on. You can get started over here." He escorted her to the hot desk area at the back of the room.

"This is your work station. You'll find files ready for you with action plans attached to each. You need to research, gather intelligence, and issue a target report for Amy and Jack's next briefing. Any questions, ask. Start reading. Meanwhile, I'll make us a cup of tea. You do like tea, don't you?"

"No, honey. I'm a coffee kind of girl...black, no sugar, please." Mara simpered, nervously eyeing the pile of files on her new workstation. She might actually have to do some work.

Jack shook his head and walked out. Mara disgusted him and Pyke disappointed him, the idiot was allowing himself to be suckered by a pro bull-shitter.

Maggie watched him leave. Tapping her ear, she waited for the call to be put through.

"We need to meet...now."

Chapter Twenty-Three
Alice

Brighton, UK

"Oh, well. I'm sorry to have bothered you." Alice ran a frustrated hand through her hair, and turned to stare out the café window. "You were our only lead," she said with resignation.

Dio followed her eyes, searching the street. Had she come alone?

"Is anyone else helping you with this search? Have you told anyone?"

"No, not yet, but I will when I get home. I think the police need to get involved."

"Yes, yes, you should. The poor young girl could be anywhere. As I mentioned, the world is a cruel place."

She stood up to leave, knocking back the rest of her coffee. He placed a ten-pound note on the table to cover their coffees.

"Thank you, but I can pay for mine." She liked to pay her own way.

"No, I insist. It's the least I can do. You've come all this way."

It seemed silly to squabble over the cost of a coffee, especially with someone who looked as if they could afford to buy the coffee shop. She backed down and nodded.

"Thank you."

They headed towards the door.

He put his hand to his head, remembering something.

"Wait a minute. I have an idea." He grabbed her arm in excitement.

"Maybe she was thinking of applying for the Charity project I'm setting up in Durban. My company supports schools over there. We've been recruiting and training up voluntary staff."

"Her mother didn't mention anything about charity work."

"Come with me. I have offices just around the corner. Let's check the files to see if she has applied. The training takes place here; the applicants are put up in a hostel. If her name is on file, we can find her."

"Well I don't know—"

"But it makes sense," he interrupted. "Why else would she have my name and office number?"

Chapter Twenty-Four

Soho, London, UK

"You know you have to be nice to me if you want to succeed here, Sal. I'm just sayin.'"

Amy sat on an empty desk in Sally's office. The time was 7.00 p.m., and the rest of her team had left for the day.

Amy missed her funny, cheeky, lovable friend and liked to visit from time to time, to check on her. She always liked to share her good and bad times with Sally, and she found it depressing not being able to talk to her now. Sally would know exactly what to do with the Jack situation, but it seemed Sally had acquired a pile of her own troubles. The office bitch, Dartagnia, caused Sal never-ending grief.

A large shiny stone sitting beside the telephone on Sally's desk caught Amy's eye. She smiled. Sal had succumbed to her crystal nagging after all. The stone was a colourful lump of Labradorite Crystal. *Good old protective energy...who'da thought? Go girl! You finally believe.*

When Amy had arrived at the Unit, she'd been instructed to forget about home and had been advised to say her last goodbye to loved ones and move on. Friends and family needed time to heal and come to terms with their shocking, devastating loss. To keep visiting loved ones would pick at the wound, not allowing it to heal. The bosses had reiterated how everyone benefited by the rule.

An only child, adopted at birth, she'd lost her adoptive parents in a car crash when she was 25 years old. She didn't think many would mourn her, only a few friends and work colleagues. But when she sat on the church roof and watched her funeral from the side lines—the large turnout, heartfelt speeches, and the tonne of white lilies—the whole sight touched her profoundly. *Who sent the lilies?*

The tear-jerking speeches astounded her. Who would've known people carried such sentiment for her? Why hadn't they expressed such thoughts when she was alive?

They played her favourite song as the coffin was taken away, 'Angel' by Robbie Williams, she held her arms high in the air and swayed side to side in time to the music, shouting all the lyrics out loud, pretending she was at Glastonbury; she missed music and the emotions it could evoke. There wasn't a dry eye in the house.

Causing such grief saddened her, but emotions people experienced on earth had no place where she lived now. She had to be tough. If only she could give them a slight understanding of what awaited them. "Please don't cry for me," she whispered, but no one heard her. "It's not so bad up here; no pain, no bills, no struggles, no stress. I'm just doing what I want for once. Please don't feel bad. I'm free, it's cool."

Death was worse for the ones left behind. The Irish had the right idea with a celebration, a wake.

Sally sat ramrod in her chair with Dartagnia holding court over her. The smug office bitch was modelled top-to-toe in tight-fitting, designer gear. Advertising her goods with bright coral talons and matching lipstick, prattling on, full of self-importance. *What a bore she is.* Amy yawned.

A mobile phone sat on a neighbouring desk. Bored, feeling a little mischievous, Amy reached over and gently pressed a few clicks to redial the last number called. The bitch's body language reeked with smugness. She needed to be taught a lesson. *Time for a bit of fun.*

"I can help you...just sayin'," Dartagnia rested a deceit-ridden hand on Sal's shoulder.

"But I don't want your help, Tania." Sally brushed Tania's hand away as if it were contaminated. "I just want you to leave us all alone. Stop bossing us around. OK. So you're shagging Simon. But hey, that doesn't mean you're suddenly our boss, we've all had enough."

"It's Dartagnia darhling, *D a r.t a g n ..i a*," she spoke slowly, condescending, as if explaining to a child, hiding her annoyance. "I think you're just a little bit jealous. You know I can make your life difficult if I want to, because I have Simple Simon's ear."

"His dick more like it. You don't seriously believe he promoted you for your marketing skills. He promoted you for your cock-sucking skills, and as soon as he tires of you, you'll be out. Lucky if you get a reference. And I will be promoted on merit, not dick work."

Amy dipped her hand into Dartagnia's open designer hand bag. Pulled out a bottle of bright coral nail varnish, unscrewed the lid and placed it back into the bag. Looking around making sure no one was looking.

"Tut-tut, Sally. Such language, so offensive."

"Quite honestly, Tania, with all the fucking, sucking, 'n' licking going on across these office desks, I'm surprised you find my language offensive. And can you not use my desk for fucks sake... I have to bleach it every morning, use your own desk Tania... such a slag."

"Dartagnia," she shouted, losing her patience. "You really ought to be nicer to me, Sal." Her long territorial nails rapped Sally's desk. "I can cause soooo much trouble."

"Are you threatening me?"

"No, just advising you. I know you want to keep your job."

"Does Simon know you're also shagging David in Accounts, and Olivia in Sales?"

"I can't help it if people find me attractive. Simon is a pussy, and he's led by my pussy... he has no balls... no way is he enough for me." She laughed with a grating voice. "He won't believe you. I've got him wrapped around my little finger, and that haggard wife of his." She clicked her fingers. "Her days are numbered. It's only a matter of time before I ditch my hubby and become the new improved version of Mrs. Simon Hogarth... Dartagnia Hogarth," she boasted, flicking high maintenance hair over her shoulder. "It has a nice ring to it, don't you think?"

"And then what?"

"And then you'll be out of a job, and as soon as is practical, I'll kick Simon into touch and take half his money. It's a win-win, darhling."

"Hello... hello?" A shrill voice hailed from the mobile phone.

The bitch looked back at her desk in horror, recognising her boss's number on the screen. "Fuck!"

"Hello...hello?" the voice continued, calling for attention.

"I think that's for you, Tania." Sally couldn't hold back the huge grin taking over her face.

Dartagnia grabbed the phone and with smooth, honeyed words, purred into its mouthpiece.

"Simon, darhling, I soooo miss you. Where..."

"In my office... *now*!" He barked so loudly Sally could hear. The bitch jumped with a squeal, not recognising the venom in his voice.

He'd heard everything.

As Dartagnia scampered down the corridor to Simon's office, Sal broke into hysterical laughter, shouting after her. "Karma, baby, karma." She hadn't laughed in ages, not since her best friend Amy had died.

She thought of Amy as she watched the bitch run. She reached for her own phone to call her, to tell her the gossip, but then recoiled, realising she couldn't.

Amy was dead. When would old habits break? She looked up to the heavens and smiled.

"Amy, you would've loved this. I love you and miss you terribly. You'll be pleased to know the witch is finally dead...and your stone stuff works." She leaned over and stroked the lump of crystal. "My secret weapon."

She punched the air with a "yes," and got back to shutting down her computer, ready for the journey home. She would leave the love birds to it.

As Sally packed up, Amy crept over to her chair, leaned over, and gently kissed her head.

"I miss you, too," she whispered, walking away with a tear in her eye.

As Sally stood up to leave, she picked up her bag and noticed a small white feather on the ground near her feet. *How did that get in here?*

She picked it up and smiled. "Is that you, Ames?"

Looking around the room, excitedly searching for a sign of her friend, she stuffed the feather into her handbag, then felt a little foolish.

A door flung open. Dartagnia stomped out of Simon's office and headed for the exit, grabbing her designer bag and jacket on the way, unaware of nail varnish bottle empting itself over the contents of her bag. With a toss of her mane, she flounced out of the office, shouting, "Your loss! You'll be hearing from my lawyers."

Sally watched, open mouthed.

"Bye, Tania," she shouted after her. *Good riddance.*

Simon popped his head sheepishly around the door of his office and summoned Sally to his office.

"I've been a plonker, Sal." He shrugged his shoulders in apology. "Get all the files from her desk and read up on them. They're now your clients...and you'll be happy to know, I won't expect any cock-sucking."

"Phew, thank god for that," she smiled. "Mixing business with pleasure is soooo not classy...and nine times out of ten, the bird ends up having to leave. Have I just been promoted?"

"Yep, and you deserve it. I should have dismissed that one months ago. All that frantic furtive sneaking around has affected sales figures. I vow never to shag anyone from the office ever again, or at least I'll try my best." His mouth tilted with a half-grin.

He picked up his phone and stared at it.

"How the hell did that happen? I must have turned it on somehow." He shrugged and popped the phone into his breast pocket. "I'd better get back to the wife. I'm sure Dartagnia is on the phone to her stirring trouble as we speak. She's not going to move on that easily. I suspect I'll have a fight on my hands. I can leave you to lock up, yeah?"

He threw her his keys and walked out of the office.

Sally dumped her bag back onto the floor and took a deep breath. Her promotion was unexpected, but just what she needed, and the rest of the office would be ecstatic. *The bully has left the building.*

She looked up to the ceiling and gave a quick wink.

"Thank you, Ames. You're a star," she whispered under breath, retrieving the white feather from her purse and tucking the memento into her pocket to have it much closer.

But Amy had already left.

Chapter Twenty-Five

Porto Antonio Piazza,
San Remo, Italy

Amy stepped between three young boys dressed in rags, huddling on the Casino's grand pillared entrance steps. The mix of poor and wealth pulled on her heartstrings, leaving a bad taste in her mouth. She shook her head in disgust.

She plodded up the steps, passed security personnel, and entered the Casino's large ballroom to scout around for Jack and Mr. Black. Pyke had sent her images of Zagan and his associates. She scanned the room, checking faces.

The ballroom bulged with hopeful gamblers, their overexcited chatter rumbling above slot machine noises, their pinging and whistles setting off shouts of joy from winners and gasps of sadness from losers. A large glitter ball hung over the tables, slowly turning, sending sparkles across the decadent room giving it a fake glamourous glimmer.

Casinos spread a gloominess she couldn't quite put her finger on, but she'd never felt comfortable in them. She'd tried her luck a few times, as her friends had, but an undercurrent one might experience in a funeral parlour kept her away. She found no comfort watching people's livelihoods, hopes, and dreams drain away with the roll of a dice, the turn of a card, or the spin of a wheel. It was depressing; she'd never quite understood the appeal.

She glanced about the decadent pillars, plush red carpets, shiny one-armed bandits, neatly dressed croupiers, and skimpily dressed waitresses; marketing tricks to encourage patrons to part with their money. Along with offering watered down drinks, salty food nibbles, and room upgrades. With not a clock anywhere inside the windowless premises—devoid of daylight or night shadows—the casino operators deceived punters, hoping the longer they stayed the more they'd lose.

ATM machines dotted the room for easy access to cash for purchasing additional chips. These tricksters understood the psychology behind handing over money, the emotional connection it instilled, and that using chips was less painful. When a punter hits a winning streak, the buzz creates so much excitement, he nearly always ploughs his winnings back into the pot. With every loss, the need and desire to win money back keeps the gambler playing.

In the old days, casinos could get away with sleight of hand dealing, removing cards from packs, selective reshuffling, altering the element of chance, and countering against card counting, which lost them money. But nowadays, strict conditions had been implemented. Authorities regulated and monitored casinos, enforcing them with diligence.

Some still cheated, but generally didn't need to. No matter what strategy gamblers tried, the casino always had the mathematical edge for guaranteed profits. Looking around the room at the desperate people, the waste made her feel sick.

She stood by a blackjack table and watched an old man, dressed in a suit that had seen better days, throw away his last bit of money. She guessed he was connected to the three boys sitting on the steps. He had the same proud jaw and huge brown eyes. His demeanour lacked pride now as he glanced toward the doorway, knowing they patiently waited for him, and that he had just spent all his money. He put his head to his hands and slid off his chair, leaving a space for the next eager player.

He shuffled towards the one-arm bandits and sat down, gathering his courage to face the boys.

Amy looked up and spotted Jack watching her from a balcony. Her heart fluttered at the sight of him.

Behind him stood double doors to a private gaming room, a very important room by the looks of it. Security guards lined the palatial steps leading up to it.

Jack's brooding eyes followed her as she flew up through the air and landed at his side.

"So, what do we have here?"

"Zagan Black is in the VIP area behind us. I was waiting until you got here. Where were you?"

"I popped down to see a friend who needed help, so I sorted it." She didn't make eye contact with him. Two could play at being moody.

Jack sighed. "Was it authorised?"

"No...but it was nothing. I just hit a redial button on a phone. No big deal. No one will notice."

"The smallest things have consequences. There's always a ripple effect. You know that."

She ignored him.

"Fuck it. I'm not your keeper. Do what the hell you wish." He turned away from her.

"I will."

They stood staring out over the Casino floor, watching the money men make money and the punters lose it. Amy saw the old man reach into his pocket and pull out four 100 euro chips. His eyes lit up. He glanced around to see if it was a joke, but no one noticed him. He stared at the chips in awe, turning them over and over with his fingers.

He had come in with 50 euros. He hadn't held this kind of money in a long time. He looked to the door where the boys still waited and then turned his gaze to a nearby roulette table, his eyes wide with anticipation. He should leave now, before someone discovered the mistake, or he could place it all on his lucky number.

Amy pondered hope, one of humans' strongest emotions, an unfathomable force that kept them alive. *You only live once, old man.*

"OK. So, what does Pyke want us to do with this guy?" Amy broke the icy silence. "It's not illegal to own a casino. Why are we here?"

"Mr. Black and his partners own this place. He makes a good living here, but the bulk of his money is made through online casinos, where gamblers are more vulnerable than these guys." Jack waved his hand across the room and continued.

"Mr. Black sets up online sites with rigged software, fake licences, hidden terms, and deceptive marketing tactics. Where punters place a lump sum into their account and place bets, he uses insider card readers and holds gamblers' progressive winnings by asking for notarised proof of the winner's identity, therefore delaying payments to winners for as long as possible, until he gets caught. Then he quickly siphons off the dosh, closes the site, and moves on to a new one, with a similar name and MO. It's big business."

"Why are we here?"

"Pyke is working on the software, but meanwhile, he has come across information that shows Mr. Black is planning an insurance scam. He's going to blow this place up, make it look like terrorists did it, and then claim on the insurance."

"Gosh, what a nice man."

"A gang of would-be-terrorists are due to come in through the back entrance in about 65 seconds, and we're going to stop them. It will put a dent in Mr. Black's business affairs."

"I'm just in the mood for a punch up," Amy said, rubbing her hands together.

The thumping of fireworks came from the piazza outside, a weekly occurrence for the Casino's clientele. The three boys nestled together, their hunger forgotten for the moment whilst they stared in awe at the display.

Jack and Amy walked down the staircase and passed the old man as he reached across a roulette table and put the 400 euro on number six.

They strode through the main kitchen to the back scullery just as five masked men stormed in through the supply store entrance. Jack took three. Amy took two.

Pots, pans, and hot fat flew everywhere. Later, kitchen staff couldn't report how it started, but it seemed like the men slipped on oil on the floor, knocking each other over in their haste, with pots and pans landing on them as they fell.

Shots rang out. The men were hit. A bloody mess turned the kitchen into a disaster. It had been unbelievably lucky none of the cowering kitchen staff suffered injuries or gunshot wounds. Someone had dialled for police and they descended upon the scene in moments. The fake terrorists sang like canaries, revealing the truth, that Zagan Black had hired them. Amid fireworks blasting in beautiful explosions over the piazza and the punters working in the main ballroom, Erthfolk went about their business totally oblivious.

Jack and Amy sauntered out of the kitchen towards the entrance. Jack insisted on viewing the fireworks. As Amy passed the old man's roulette table, she gave the ball a quick nudge. It landed on number six with a plop. The old chap gave a whooping, joyful holler loud enough for the boys outside to hear him over the fireworks. They sprang to their feet and peered through windows, trying to see into the room. Grandpa had hit a lucky streak. They would eat tonight.

Jack stood on the steps and stared up into the night sky. Amy joined him.

"Did you want to make a fool of me or were you just caught out?"

"You mean Mara?"

"For someone who doesn't do anything remotely fun, then to bed two women back to back in the same venue, probably up against the same wall, it was pretty cruel. What is it? A game? Are you bored or something? I know...let's fuck Amy up. She'd be easy."

Jack's gaze didn't deviate from the show in the sky, his face showing no emotion, the colourful glow of fireworks lighting up his face. Amy waited for a response.

Silence.

"You're screwed up, Jack. I don't want to work with you anymore; I'm asking to change Units."

"Mara is my ex. She means nothing," Jack finally answered, his voice cold and eerily monotone. "Whatever she tells you, or insinuates, don't believe her. She's a master manipulator; I don't know how she got here. There is not a good bone in her body. If I could, I'd kill her...again."

"You're a shit, Jack. Stop blaming your problems on everyone else."

Amy peered back into the Casino. The old boy still sat at his stool, staring at the numbers on the table. *For fuck's sake.*

She swooped in by his side, grabbed his hands, scooped up his winnings, and frogmarched him to the cashier's booth. He looked like a puppet without strings. Onlookers assumed he was drunk.

"Don't push Lady Luck, old boy. You're wise to know when your time is up. You've three kids out there who need feeding," Amy muttered into his ear.

Shaken, the old boy couldn't explain what was happening to him. He moved through thin air as if a ghost manhandled him. A strange force carried him out of the casino with such force and speed, he muttered frightful guttural noises, unable to form intelligible words. Amy deposited him out on the steps directly in front of the three boys, his hands full of money. They jumped up at him, wrapping their hands around his neck with joy.

He looked nervously over both shoulders, wondering if the weird feeling had gone. It had. He looked to the ground; a small white dove's feather lay at his feet. He looked at the sky and blessed himself; he'd been given another chance.

He vowed never to enter the casino again. This money would give him the step he needed to get a job and take care of the boys.

Amy walked off into the piazza. Jack followed a few feet behind. They soon lost themselves in the crowd of partygoers.

Chapter Twenty-Six
Alice

Brighton, UK

She should have walked away and not fallen for his persuasive invitation to accompany him to his offices. Why the hell did she think she could ever find this girl in a town she didn't know with a person she'd never met? It seemed so easy at the time—just go to Brighton, speak to the person mentioned on the piece of paper, and find the daughter Eva fretted about. Bingo, easy.

Using the designated number, she'd phoned him to ask for his assistance, but he'd claimed he was too busy to talk. He'd suggested a coffee the next day. She should have told him she lived miles away, that she just had a quick question, but with his soft voice and the opportunity to visit unfamiliar territory, it had all seemed like an adventure. Life could be so dull in her quaint coastal town.

When they exited the café, he held her by the elbow and guided her down a dozen backstreets until they arrived at a beautiful expanse of sea. It took her breath away. The sun shone, the sky sparkled with the clearest blue, and the sea shimmered a silver grey.

He chatted as they strolled along the walkway—kind, friendly chatter about the lovely shops in town, how she must visit the Lanes and walk on Brighton Pier. Before she'd realized, he'd escorted her through electric gates where she faced a massive block of apartments.

"Where are we?"

"This is my office...well my home and my office. I own the block and live on the top three floors.

"Wow...it's amazing."

She surveyed the luxurious building, gazing from side to side and up toward the rooftop, appreciating its beautiful architecture stretching high into the blue sky.

Pressing buttons, he entered a code to unlock the imposing double doors which swung ajar. Taking her elbow, he steered her toward the empty reception area and took her up in the lift.

"It's Saturday, so the place is empty, but how hard can it be to check a filing system? I can do it, I'm sure."

She shouldn't have come back with him.

Chapter Twenty-Seven

Porto Antonio Piazza,
San Remo, Italy

Crowds cooed with delight as the firework display crescendoed into a brilliant overlapping pattern of colours bursting across the night sky, lighting up the piazza with a palpable energy of sparkling excitement. Couples and families stood in awe, with their joyful, smiling faces tilted skywards, cheering at the heavens.

Amy was right. Jack should tell her everything, but losing her frightened him. As he followed her through the crowd, he sensed a strange presence nearby. An aromatic cigar wafted under his nose, or was it fumes from the fireworks? Sometimes his imagination got the better of him. He trotted along, trying to keep up with Amy, her head disappearing in the crowd.

Hidden in the dark shadows of a shop awning, a man watched Jack charge into the crowd. He kept a steady gaze on Jack's activities as he lit his cigar, a bright orange orb illuminating his face. A knowing smile pulled across his scars as he shook his head.

"Ahhh, Maggie, dear Maggie... you don't stand a chance. It's going to be so easy," he said as he threw the butt to the ground and scrunched it out with his black patent shoes, paying attention not to leave any sparks.

Out of nowhere, a rough hand pushed into his shoulder, backing him up against a shop window. Jack was in his face, large and powerful. The two men stared at each other; it took a moment for him to get his breath. He didn't normally get caught; he was famed for his stalking skills.

"Whoa...watch the suit," he barked, shifting his shoulder away from Jack's hand. "It's the only one I have."

"Who are you? Why are you following us?" Jack didn't have time for small talk.

"I'm just minding my own business, big boy. Now get off me, before I get angry."

Jack pushed harder, leaning his full weight into the intruder, eliciting a groan.

"Careful. You don't know who you're dealing with."

"I repeat. Who are you? You're obviously one of us, cos you can see me. Which Unit are you from, and why are you sneaking around?"

"You can ask your boss that."

"Maggie?"

"Yes, the darling Maggie."

"Let's ask her, shall we?" Jack smashed him harder against the window and closed his hand around the man's neck. He tapped his ear and Pyke answered.

"Bonjour mate, qu'est-ce que you want..." Pyke's cheerful voice filled his head.

"Put Maggie on," demanded Jack.

"Well, bonjour to you to, Pyke—"

"Get Maggie," interrupted Jack.

"She's busy, what's up?"

"I've got a friend who wants to talk to her. Now, Pyke, put her on," snarled Jack, not thrilled about containing the man this closely. He smelt bad; he smelt of death.

"Can I h...."

"Now!"

"OK, OK. Keep your knickers on." Pyke connected the link to Maggie, waving at her across the room to urgently pick up.

"Jack," she answered, curious as to why Jack would ask for her directly.

"I've a gentleman with me who says I'm to ask you why he's following Amy and me."

"You have?" Maggie faltered. "What's his name?"

Jack tightened his grip, pushing the man harder against the glass. "What's your name?"

"She'll know," he replied with a snickering smile.

Pyke, listening in, clicked Jack's camera on for a visual. The man's smug face filled the screen. Pyke swivelled the monitor for Maggie's benefit. She drew in a sharp breath.

"Let him go."

"What?"

"*Let him go.*"

"But..."

"Tell him to meet me in the usual place. I'll sort this out, Jack. Just back off."

"I don't tru—"

"*Now.*" A loud click told Jack Maggie had cut the call.

He grimaced. He didn't want to release this wanker, but orders were orders. He begrudgingly relaxed his grip.

"The boss says I am to release you. She wants to meet you in the usual place."

He released the stalker's neck.

"Told you." The man grinned, brushing down his lapels. "Now skip off, little boy, and do your duty. Chop-chop."

He walked off, looked back, and said with a sly voice. "And keep an eye on that girl of yours. She's a beauty. We wouldn't want to lose her again, now would we?"

"Fuck you."

"Blah de blah, Jack, blah de bloody blah, mate." His jeering laughter could be heard echoing across the square as he sauntered away.

Jack stared after him. *Who the hell?*

As the laughter continued, Jack couldn't keep his anger in check, he took it out on the nearest window with a forceful punch. With a loud crack, it shattered into a thousand small pieces and tumbled to the ground. The unexpected noise attracted the crowd's attention. Since no one witnessed a culprit anywhere close, they blamed it on a haywire firework.

Jack felt the tone buzz in his ear and punched his forefinger to his lobe.

"Yes?" he answered, expecting to get an icy blast from Maggie's tongue, telling him to control his temper.

Instead, he heard the soft, low, imposing voice of his Commander resonating in his head.

"Jack, it's Micael. We need to talk about your friend, David, David Howard."

Jack looked up to the skies. *Oh shit, what has he done now?*

Chapter Twenty-Eight

Porto Antonio Piazza,
San Remo, Italy

Amy walked on through the piazza while crowds of people enjoyed the fireworks. She recalled the childlike awe she used to feel for them—how she would stand with her mouth open, staring up into the sky, when time would stand still and nothing else mattered.

How little she knew then, how naive she was of the ways of the world, of the importance of the choices she'd make. She took way too much for granted, living in her own selfish bubble. Every moment, every person that crossed her path was special and had a reason for being there. Every action she took had a reaction, a consequence.

She shook her head. They should be able to warn Erthfolk about the value of their precious planet and their greedy destruction of it; how they should not be fighting each other for small pockets of land, but be fighting together to save their home, the planet. Why were Erthfolk so small-minded, unable to see the bigger picture? She was that small-minded person once. *What a fool.*

She peered over her shoulder, over heads in the crowd, and was pleased to see she'd managed to lose Jack, which was a blessing. She needed space.

A fat, elderly man strode across her path, dragging a little boy by the hand who struggled to keep up. He couldn't be much more than seven years old.

"Come on, little one. You know your mummy said you had to behave. And then you can have an ice cream."

"But I don't want an ice cream. I want my mum," he cried, fear in his eyes. Amy recognised that fear.

The man scurried down a side street, keeping the boy out of sight. He pressed a code into an entry phone and entered a dark building. Amy followed them in. A lift dropped them off in the basement. As doors opened, the smell of sweat, semen, and terror hit her nostrils.

They walked down a short corridor into a large black room with a low ceiling and dim lighting. It took a while for her eyes to adjust.

She stood at the doorway, taking in the sight. Six double mattresses lay pushed together in the middle of the floor. Sofas lined the walls, circling the mattresses. Near naked men lounged on the seating, watching the show in front of them.

Naked young boys huddled on the mattresses, some sitting, some crying, some lying face down into the floor, being taken by perspiring fat sloths, some kneeling in front of males, gagging with cocks in their mouths.

Amy stumbled back against the wall with shock, bile raised to her throat. She started to shake. Memories from her childhood flooded back, reinstating the fear and powerlessness she'd felt. She looked at the men's sick, smiling faces and saw Dick Parker in them.

Her first reaction was to go in all guns blazing, massacre the lot of them. But this was bigger than her. She would not get away with it. A room full of naked dead men with their cocks cut off would be difficult to explain away. And she had to think of the children.

She needed to keep calm, act like a grown up, and get help, which was hard for her to do. It took all her strength to remain composed and think clearly. Where was Jack when she needed him?

She put a call into Pyke.

"Bonjour, madam." Pyke's cheery voice gave her strength.

"Put your camera on now!" It was the second time within minutes Pyke had had a panic call. *What's going on this evening?*

"OK, OK. Please be nice." He flicked the camera on.

The room's image filled his screen. As the scene registered with all its darkness, he caught his breath. He could hear the panic in Amy's breathing.

He searched across the office for Maggie, but saw her exiting out the door. He would have to manage this alone.

"May I have authority to sort these guys out please, Pyke? *Now!*" Amy shouted, agitated.

"Amy, yes, OK. I know it's hard, but work with me on this, OK?"

Silence.

"Amy?" He could hear her breathing building, louder and faster.

"Amy, do as I say. We will sort this properly, OK?"

Silence.

"Amy, I need you to concentrate. Walk around the room close enough to capture the men's faces and let me scan their headshots. Flick through their pockets for any ID, car keys, anything. The more info we have, the more ripple effect we can cause in closing them down."

Silence.

Amy started to move forward, slowly controlled. Pyke didn't trust she was listening.

"Amy, I need you to forget about that jerk, Dick Parker, and work with me to get a few dozen men like him in jail. Are you listening?"

She walked toward the nearest male. He was holding a boy's face as he fucked it.

"I'll put an anonymous call into the local police station," Pyke shouted at her. "Is Jack with you?"

"I'm on my own. Can I shoot these guys in the balls, please?"

"No, Amy, you can't. I'll send help. We must do this properly. You can't be selfish here. You start hurting one, the others will run. We want to catch all of them."

"The fucking bastards," she spat.

"Amy," Pyke spoke low and slow, trying to get through to her. "If we are cool, we may be able to save many others, and these guys may lead us to Parker. Are you listening?"

Silence.

"Amy!" he shouted.

"OK, OK," she sighed, anxiously running her hand through her hair, taking deep breaths. *In and out, in and out.*

She leaned in close to the nearby male. "Get a good look at this bastard's face, Pyke." She pushed her face into the pervert's as he enjoyed the sex act. "I hope you like prison food, you dickhead, and taking it up the arse, cos you're so gonna get some where you're going, mate," she hissed. The man didn't feel the spittle from her lips, as he threw his head back with pleasure.

Amy obeyed Pyke's instructions, reluctantly. It killed her to watch what was happening to these poor children and do nothing. Her eyes pooled with tears, her teeth and fists clenched, as she walked slowly around the room. Her camera on, giving Pyke eyes. She carefully flicked through wallets in the clothes strewn across sofas, getting close-ups of the male's faces, resisting the urge to smash them in the face.

As she walked past the boys, she gently touched each of their heads, trying to send a small hint help was on its way, that they were not alone.

As she passed the vile rutting males, she nudged here and poked there, upsetting their libidos with subtle movements to ruin their pleasure. She slammed a boy's jaw, causing his teeth to tear into the abuser's cock. The fat bastard cried out in pain. She shunted another's body so his cock slid out of a boy's throat on a backward thrust, sending the aging pig toppling over on the forward thrust.

She looked up and saw Mara walking towards her.

"Looks like we're working together," Mara announced.

Unfazed by the cruelty around her, Mara picked up a few mobile phones and took pictures of the room. "Pyke says it'll make good evidence later."

"What the fuck are you doing here?"

"I sent her," Pyke's voice shouted into her ear. "Concentrate, Amy. Police are on their way."

"What do you want me to do?" Mara asked Amy.

"Take over; finish scanning faces and ID's."

"And what are you going to do?"

"Just do it, Mara, for fuck's sake."

"Amy?" Pyke questioned nervously.

"It's OK. I'm cool."

Amy protruded her arms out over the mess, over frightened, whimpering children being stripped of their innocence, to gently grip the hands of two naked young boys, leading them away from their abusers and slowly toward the back of the room where piles of children's clothes lay in rows. The men stood staring aghast. The boys started to pick up their clothes and get dressed. Amy returned to the mattresses and collected two more boys.

Their abusers stood with mouths open and hands on their hips, not understanding why the boys were leaving. They hadn't finished with them. They demanded the boys return.

Two more boys walked away. The men started shouting, waving hands in the air and lunging at the passing boys. The children ducked and dived out of reach, ignoring the men, warier of the unknown presence guiding them away from the mattresses than of the screaming, demanding men. They trusted the strange power and allowed themselves to be escorted to the back of the room.

Amy collected more and more children. The abusers became furious. Some ran over to the boys, trying to stop them. In their tussle to get to the children, Amy kicked over a bottle of baby oil to create a greasy liquid oozing all over the floor, but she wasn't satisfied. She stamped on the container, causing the oil to squirt out across the floor and onto the men's bare feet. The men slid and slipped, thwarting their attempt to claim the children.

Amy extended her foot to trip a few more of the bastards causing them to knock into each other. She elbowed their faces, kicked them in the balls, and slammed them to the ground. Mara leaned against a wall, arms crossed, amused.

The boys gawked at the scuffle, wondering why the men were beating each other up. One of the boys noticed the exit door stood ajar and hurried the other boys to get dressed.

Finally, the doors threw open and Police raided the den, rushing in but halting just before their shoes engaged the slick liquid.

Mara and Amy walked away, confident the children were in safe hands and the evil kiddie-fiddling bastards would soon find themselves in the hell they deserved, justice served.

"Nice work, girls. See you back at base." Pyke clicked off the link.

Chapter Twenty-Nine

As police and ambulance crews rushed passed, leaving flashing blue lights behind them, Amy and Mara walked back across the piazza. Mara's stiletto heels clicking on stone cobbles.

"You could've helped a bit more back there. What? You don't like to get your hands dirty?" spat Amy.

"You were handling it. No need for both of us to break a sweat."

"Why are you even here?"

"You know Jack cannot be trusted."

"Yeah, yeah... whatever."

"It's true."

"So why do you want him then?"

"I love him and always will."

"It's none of my business anyway. I'm leaving the Unit."

"He will only follow you. He has always followed you."

"What do you mean?"

"He has always wanted you, from the start. Don't you know?"

"How do you know?"

"I was his wife; I killed him because of it," Mara admitted.

Amy was stunned, especially to hear Mara speak as if she were talking about shopping.

"Does he know you killed him?"

"Oh yes. He wanted it, wanted to be able to be by your side always...watch you from afar."

"You are mad."

"Ask him."

"If you killed him, why are you here? You're a murderer, and I didn't think murderers could do the deal."

"I told you. I know people in the right circles. Blackmail is a powerful tool, in whatever world you're in."

"I don't believe you."

"How did you die?"

"I fell onto a train track during rush hour."

"Are you sure you weren't pushed?"

"Don't be stupid. Who would push me?"

"Jack pushed you."

"Good God, woman, you would say anything to get Jack in trouble." Amy shook her head with disgust.

"He wanted to be near you, watching you from the skies wasn't enough for lovelorn Jack." The sarcasm dripped in her voice.

"Shut up. You're lying."

"Ask him."

"What...and cause more arguments? You'd love that, wouldn't you?"

"Am just saying, don't trust him darhling."

Mara sashayed ahead, then flew up into the sky. Amy watched her leave. *What a bitch.*

Chapter Thirty

Alice

Brighton, UK

As the lift doors opened on the seventh floor of his apartment building, Dio gently guided her by the elbow, out into the dark passageway. The doors closed behind them. He stepped over to a panel of switches; she expected him to put the lights on, but no. He flicked a switch and classical music filled the air.

"Do you like music?"

"Errr... yes."

"Classical music?"

"Err... not really. It's not my thing."

He sighed. "Oh, you've so much to learn, Alice."

He walked down a long narrow corridor where doors lined either side; large black bolts kept them all closed while bright yellow luminous numbers shone on each.

"Is this your office?" she asked, running along behind him, her nerves beginning to rattle.

"Yes."

"Can you put the lights on, please? It's very dark here."

"Sorry, the electricity is out."

"But the lift works and the musi—"

"We've had power failure just in the corridor," he interrupted. "Now," he looked at the numbers on the doors. "Let's find the records office, and we'll be out of here in no time."

He roamed on down the corridor. Her eyes gradually adjusted to the dim light. The classical music crescendoed more dramatically. She stood still, straining her ears to listen. She thought she could hear other noises beneath the sound of stringed instruments and piano. It sounded like low cries, human cries.

"What was that? Did you hear it?"

"What?"

"It sounded like someone crying."

"No, there's nothing here. It must be the sound of those violins. Mozart is a legend, don't you think?."

She continued to follow him as he hummed to the music.

"I think I ought to leave now. I don't want to bother you." She stopped and looked back toward the lift, holding her bag tightly. "Maybe we can talk again on Monday when your office has had a chance to check their records. I've taken up enough of your time."

"Nonsense," he said. "It's my pleasure to help this poor girl and her mother."

He stopped at a door with the number 11 on it.

"Come on. Here we are. We'll have the information in a few seconds, and you'll go home a hero," he smiled, waving her to the door, his charming, friendly, handsome face seemingly excited about saving Maria. She believed him.

"OK, but quickly please. I've a train to catch. My mum will be worried about me."

He pulled the bolt across the door with a loud thud and pushed it open. He yanked her arm and pushed her inside.

Chapter Thirty-One

The River Thames,
London, UK

Maggie leaned on the wall and stood staring out over the River Thames at the MI6 offices, her old Secret Intelligence Services building. Memories of her time there flooded back. She smiled and shook her head at the worldly innocence she held in those days. They were fighting just the tip of the iceberg; they had no idea of the mammoth task to keep evil out.

She smelt him before she heard him.

"Looking good, girl. You haven't changed."

Maggie turned to see a dapper gentleman in an exquisitely tailored black suit, puffing on a cigar standing beside her. His handsome chiselled features were torn with scars, his greying mane swept back, not a hair out of place. The stump of a cigar lay wedged in the corner of his generous, grinning mouth. He had an intelligent air about him, commanding eyes, regal nose, strong dimpled chin, and stubborn jawline. He was pleased to see her.

"Gregori, I thought you were dead."

"I am."

"I mean dead, dead...you know."

"Thought or hoped?"

"Hoped."

"That's not a very nice thing to say to an old friend. We worked well together."

She looked down at his feet. His neatly laced spit-shine patent shoes glistened in the sun.

"Still sporting the Derby tie, I see."

"You know me, obsessed with the detail, can't let standards drop now, can we? Just because I'm deceased."

Maggie turned back to face the river, leaning with both elbows on the towpath wall. He stood beside her, close, their shoulders touching.

Drunken revellers trundled along the path behind them, oblivious to the invisible couple.

Maggie stared out at the water, biting her tongue, waiting to see what he wanted. It was hard to breathe. This man was the love of her life at one stage. She would've done anything for him. Standing so close was difficult.

She looked across the water; something caught her eye in an apartment block to the left of the MI6 building. Two silhouette figures stood in the penthouse apartment window; one held what looked like a knife, the other stood ramrod still, scared to move. She tapped her ear and spoke to Pyke.

"Send someone over to the penthouse at Vauxhall Towers, a male with a knife standing in the window, plus one other. Not sure what's going on."

"OK, boss. On it."

"And Pyke, I'm out of contact for the next twenty minutes," her voice sounded curt.

"Are you all right, boss?"

She cut the call.

Gregori smiled at her, titling his head to one side, as if inspecting her face.

"Maggie, Maggie, Maggie," he sighed. "You meet someone you haven't seen in decades, someone you thought you'd successfully put away, someone back from the dead and you keep on working, carrying on as if nothing has happened. You are an amazing woman. I've always said that about you."

"What do you want? Get on with it; I've got work to do."

He shook his head.

"Tut...tut. Nothing changes, Maggie. You always did put the job first. You never could relax or take time out. I don't even think you know what time out means."

Maggie stood still, staring out across the water.

"Twenty minutes...is that all you're giving me...after all we've been through?" he whispered in mock horror.

Silence.

"Oh, I think you'll give me more than that when you understand why I'm here."

A motorboat chugged up the river, stirring waves that rippled and slapped at the wall below. They stood in silence.

"What? No quick retort? No swearing? You've changed, Miss Smithers; you're not the brave, spunky, exciting girl I once knew."

Silence.

Maggie held her tongue. The best way to deal with Gregori, the manipulator, was to give his as little attention as possible. She'd learnt that trick too late.

"OK, you win. You never did waste words. It's what I admired about you, loved about you, until you grassed on me. Aren't you curious to know what happened, Maggie?"

Silence.

"Well, if you're not going to talk, I'm off." He doffed his forelock and started to walk away.

"For fuck's sake, Gregori, what do you want?"

He turned back to face her.

"I want us to talk."

"Well fucking get on with it then."

He laughed and stood back beside her.

"That's my girl, the girl I know."

"For fuck's sake, get on with it..."

He turned to face her, his smiling handsome face, cutting to hard solemnity. As he leaned in close, she could smell the death on him. His voice hoarse, he whispered in her ear.

"You know that I cannot let you carry on with the Unit, Maggie. I will have to tell."

"How did you get in?"

"That's not important."

"What do you want?"

"Oh, I think you know."

Chapter Thirty-Two

Porto Antonio Piazza,
San Remo, Italy

Amy sat on the steps of a church and people watched. The feeling of failure overwhelmed her. There was so much to do. Were they fighting a lost cause? Everywhere she looked, questionable behaviour demanded attention, people needed help. Everywhere.

Her conversation with Mara haunted her. Had someone pushed her?

She hadn't had time to think about it much. It had all happened so fast. Before she knew it, she'd been enlisted with the Unit and sent out to work. She had hit the ground running and hadn't given her death much thought.

Her gaze drifted to a man walking past, holding his wife's upper arm a little too harshly, marching her in step to his walk, tell-tale bruises poking out from her wrist as her cardigan rose through the force of his grip.

She looked past them, to a henpecked husband who trotted behind his wife, listening to her condescending remarks and belittling comments, just on the edge of snapping, wrapping his fingers around her throat.

She turned her attention to a gang of boys trailing behind a timid pipsqueak from class, waiting for an opportunity to beat him up.

She saw a businessman wandering home, drunk, in debt, in fear of giving the depressing news to his wife and five children, contemplating suicide.

Behind him, a drug addict spotted his dealer and his heavies coming towards him, with no money to pay his drug debt. He resignedly stood still, dropped his head, and prepared for a beating.

She watched a thug on his way to a dog fight, waving a stick and dragging his weather-worn, scarred dog across the road.

She closed her eyes, and dropped her head into her hands, feeling utterly hopeless, there was too much to do. Questions scrambled her thoughts.

Why was mankind so fucked up?

How could they ever help all these people?

Did Jack have real feelings for her?

Had she been pushed?

Mara had to go, but how?

Was it OK to kill a fellow Fallen?

A yelp caught her attention. She looked up to see the dog trying to escape his thug owner. The animal cowered, backing up, not wanting to go where he knew he would be torn to shreds in another fight, where men gambled and made money from the pain he and his opponent endured. Like Amy, he'd had enough. He sat on the ground, his owner beating him with a stick and dragging him by the neck. *What the fuck, you bastard?*

Amy's anger surfaced. She took a deep sigh, knowing she couldn't ignore the man's cruelty he dished out on his dog. She had to help. It was in her nature. No matter how daunting this world was, one small step at a time was all she could manage. Jack's encouraging words rang in her head. *The slightest ripples have a large effect.*

Jack, what the hell was going on there? How did he ever fall in love and marry that woman? She was something else. When they were in the child abuse den, she didn't flinch at the sight of young boys being raped. She was one cold fish.

Amy felt eyes on her. She looked to her right and saw a beautiful, large black German Shepherd dog standing, face on, looking straight at her. It can't be. She looked around and over her shoulder to see if the dog was interested in something else, but it wasn't. It was looking at her. *It can see me.*

The dog walked calmly over and sat down beside her. He watched the man and his dog. No one else noticed him. Maybe he was invisible, like her. Amy felt its soft coat stroke against her arm.

She tenderly reached out and stroked its back; the dog leaned into her, enjoying the touch. A tag on its collar said the name 'Connor'.

"Hello, Connor. What brings you here?"

She looked into his big beautiful eyes. He had one turquoise blue and one hazel. They stared right back at her, knowing, kind, calm, patiently waiting for her to understand what was happening. *How come animals seem so much more evolved than us?*

A short, sharp yelp disturbed the moment. Amy and Connor looked up to see the thug kicking the dog to make it walk. The dog finally gave in and let itself be led down an alleyway.

Amy stood up, anger boiling. *For fuck's sake, that bully needs sorting out.*

She started to follow the thug. To her surprise, Connor jumped up and joined her, trotting alongside, anxious to get to the pained animal. Amy put her hands on her hips and looked down at him. Should she tell him to sit, stay...but what harm could it do if he came with her? She smiled down at her new friend.

"OK, boy, let's go sort this bastard out. You bite his balls. I'll rearrange his face."

She called it in to Pyke as they walked, he gave her instant authority. Cruelty to animals was often fast tracked.

The two of them followed the thug down an alleyway.

A few seconds later, more yelps and squeals reverberated between the buildings flanking the alley, but this time, the cries didn't come from the dog but the owner. Concerned public called for help, leading the Police to uncovering a dog fighting ring.

Pyke was pleased to tally more successes for the statistic boys.

Once the police arrived, Connor gently licked Amy's hand goodbye and trotted calmly on, patrolling his streets.

Amy's heart leapt. He had given her courage. She hadn't thought about animals. Maybe there were more souls out there helping than she'd imagined. It didn't seem so overwhelming. Maybe the deactivating business wasn't fruitless after all.

Chapter Thirty-Three

Brighton, UK

Alice stumbled with shock as he pushed her into the dark space. What was he doing? Before she knew it, they both stood in a small black room, eight feet by six feet, with a single bed down one side and a bucket at its foot. She squinted her eyes to adapt to the dim light in the windowless interior.

He closed the door behind them and pushed her onto the bed.

"Now, this is how it's going to be, dear. No one knows you're here. The walls are soundproofed, so no one can hear you. You'll be mine to do with as I wish. If you do as I say, you'll survive. If you don't, you'll die."

"What... what the hell is happening?" She jumped up trying to get to the door.

With a brutish strength she didn't expect, he lunged at her, grabbed her, and threw her back across the bed. Her head smashed against the wall, sending her back onto the floor, lying on her back.

"Now please don't make me mess up my suit, dear. Please, just do as you're told. I'm in charge now. You don't need to think about anything."

He sat on the bed and stared down at her. Pulling his shirt cuffs in line with the sleeves of his jacket, he brushed down his lapels.

"You must know that I don't like to repeat anything, dear. So, you have to learn to listen."

"Why am I here? What's going on? Who are you?"

"Probably your worst nightmare. You are now mine, to do with as I wish. Do as you are told and life will be easier for you. You'll be given bread and water every morning. You'll use the bucket as a toilet."

"You can't do this."

He leaned over her and whipped the back of his hand across her face.

"Take off your clothes. You'll remain naked. The temperature is set to a comfortable warm setting. You'll not be cold."

"You are a nutter. You can't do this," she cried, grabbing for her backpack, trying to get her phone. He snatched the bag off her and threw it against the door.

"Give me my bag back. You can't do this."

He leaned towards her and smashed the knuckles of his right hand across her cheek bone. The pain seared through her body as she passed out.

She learned that he could.

Chapter Thirty-Four

Cloud 9

Mara sashayed into the office. Pyke had turned all the screens towards him, posed in the middle of his Stonehenge-esque circle, and rotated his gaze from one to the other. It was rare to find the uber-busy Pyke standing still. There was no one else in the office. Mara smiled and strode towards him.

"The Thames apartment block was a false alarm," she said. "The tenants are rehearsing and editing the script for a murder mystery weekend they're running...not sure why it was called in, but hey, maybe the boss's mind is on something else."

She squeezed between two screens and joined Pyke in the middle of his domain. He didn't answer her. He just stood staring, running his hand through his hair, tapping his foot nervously.

"You all right, Pyke?"

She followed his eyes to notice the blank screens and how the office lighting was out, shedding a semi-grey light throughout the room.

"Wow! What's happened? You had a power cut?" She kinked her head to the side, thinking. "Do you get those up here?"

Pyke ignored her, his eyes scrunched in concentration, his hand rubbing his jaw.

"No, I guess not. So, what's happened?" She tried to be helpful. "Try turning it all on and off to see what happens. That's what I used to do with my laptop."

Pyke gave her a disdainful look.

"Err, I guess not," she grimaced, apologetically.

Pyke tapped his ear, trying to get a call connection. Nothing happened. He tried again.

Jack sauntered into the office, walking across to the kitchen area where he started to make himself a coffee. "How's it going, Pykey boy?" he shouted across the room. Noticing Mara, his face hardened.

"We've had a power cut," announced Mara.

"Then why is the coffee machine still working?"

Pyke went to his desk, pulled out an old laptop covered in superman stickers, dusted it off, and fired it up. It burst into life, giving Pyke a reason to smile.

Maggie and Amy entered the station. Amy was filling Maggie in on the dog fighting ring. Maggie politely listened, but her mind was on other things. She took in the blank screens and darkness of the room.

"What's happening, Pyke?"

"Someone is trying to close us down," he replied, absentmindedly tapping away at his laptop. "But I'm getting back in the old-fashioned way. I'm so pleased I kept my old hacking mate. This laptop may be ancient, but it has all I need to fight back."

He sat scrunched over his laptop on the sofa, pummelling away on its tiny keyboard for five minutes whilst the others stood around him in silence. Maggie stared out at the sky, shaking her head. She had a clue about the problem and had a notion this was just the start unless she did as she was told.

Amy made herself and Maggie a cup of tea. She carried the teacups over as Maggie stared into the distance.

"Here, drink this."

"Thank you, Amy." Maggie gratefully took the teacup and sipped the soothing liquid. She looked across at Amy.

"You like it here, don't you, Amy?"

"Yes, I go through blips. When I feel overwhelmed by it all, I don't know if we manage to make a difference. There is so much evil out there. But then, we do a good job and I feel it is the greatest job on earth...sorry...in the skies."

"You're good, Amy. I'm proud of you. I'm proud of all my recruits. But you have it in you. Some don't." She turned her attention to Mara. "Some struggle, and I'm not sure how they got here."

"Thank you, ma'am. That means a lot to me."

"Sorry, if I bite your head off at times. If I give you shit, it means I like you. I know you can take it. It's when I am polite that you have to worry," Maggie replied, taking another sip of tea and watching the skies.

"Someone is trying to close us down, Amy. There are power struggles up here, as there are on earth. Please know any decisions I make are for the good of the Unit."

"Well, yes, but what kind of decisions? Are you leaving us?" Amy looked over at her, concerned. "Is it something to do with the man that's following us?"

"I would never leave willingly. This is my manor and I intend to protect it for as long as I am right for the job."

"I'm in," shouted Pyke from the sofa, punching the air. "Yes!"

The lights flickered on overhead, machines bleeped into action, and the eight screens flashed with colour as the office came back to life, stirring a rowdy cheer from the team. Jack slapped Pyke on the back.

"What was that all about, mate?"

"Not sure. Someone has tried to block our systems, but they didn't count for trusted Bessie here." He tapped his laptop fondly. "She and I ruled the world once. And now she's ruling the skies. I placed an added protective level to our system. They won't get in again." Pyke nodded with assuredness and looked around the room.

"Cup of char, ma'am," he shouted across at Maggie. But she was already walking out the door, making a call. Pyke returned to his duties, amused.

"Someone's gonna get an earful. Right, let's get back to work."

Chapter Thirty-Five

In the corridor outside the Unit office, Maggie paced, waiting for the call to connect, preparing for a battle.

"What the fuck do you think you're doing?"

"I don't know what you mean."

"I know that was you throwing your toys out of the pram. Back off."

"You are getting excited, woman, calm down."

"No...stop this now. You are jeopardising lives."

"Or what?"

"Or you have a fight on your hands."

"Oh, so you think good can beat evil, do you?"

"Abso-bloody-lutely," she said with more conviction than she felt.

He laughed. "Didn't have you down as naïve, Mags. Look around you. Greed, lust, and selfishness wins 'em over every time."

"For the weak maybe."

"For every one of them, Mags, and you know it."

"What happened to you, Greg? You used to believe in the fight. You were a good operative."

"Yeah, until politics and red tape got the better of me and I lost faith in who I was serving. Ya see, it gets us all."

"Bollocks, not me."

She heard a sigh at the end of the line.

"No, I guess not. You always were a stickler for right and wrong. But you did bend the rules once, and I know all about it. I know your weak spot. I know a gentleman shouldn't kiss and tell, but I want revenge. You will succumb. Meet me at our garden."

"Fuck off..."

"Oh well, I tried," his voice changed. His cold, hard resonance sent a chill through her. "So, we have a fight on our hands. Bring it on, Maggie...bring it on...then say goodbye."

"We don't need to do this," Maggie sighed.

But he was gone.

Maggie fell against the wall and held her face in her hands. She didn't like to, she'd been putting it off, but it was time to speak to the boss. She would have to come clean. Her heart beat rapidly as she tapped her ear and waited for the call to connect.

"I need to speak to the Commander, please."

"Yes, it's bloody urgent."

Chapter Thirty-Six

Brighton, UK

When Alice came around, her eyes opened to a dark empty room. He had gone.

Naked, stretched out on the bed, the coarse mattress scratching her skin, she lay very still, listening to the muffled noises around her. She could hear classical music in the corridor outside her room. Her heart started to race.

She recognized the signs and needed to stop the panic before it threatened to freeze her. She tried to relax, to gather her thoughts and work out what was happening, to figure out how to escape.

She took a deep breath, trying to still the thumping in her chest. She needed to move.

She got out of bed and stepped to the door. As she expected, it had been tightly shut. There was no handle, making it impossible to open. She banged on the door, crying for help.

"Help... help! Is anyone there? Help me!" She pounded on the door repeatedly until her knuckles bled. No answer.

Desperately, she turned to survey the dark, claustrophobic room and gently traced her sore hands along the walls, the floor, the length of the bed, and the bucket at the end of it.

The room seemed to be covered in soft foam tiles to deaden the sound. Her breathing and heartbeat felt muffled and her throat began to constrict with anxiety.

"Help... help... please," she screamed. "Help me."

But to no avail. No one answered.

The acoustically shielded room stifled any sound emanating from her throat and hid any trace of resonance. She lay on the bed and wept. She didn't recognise her own voice.

Chapter Thirty-Seven

Cloud 9

Amy walked into the office with a renewed bounce in her step. Meeting Connor had cheered her up, given her strength. She was in a light-hearted mood and ready to go. *Is it bad to prefer animals over humans?*

Occupying the sofa, Pyke and Mara chatted. Mara displaying way too much leg in short skirt and stilettos. Amy waved a cheerful "hello", prompting Pyke to hop up and attend his screen. Mara pouted, miffed with the interruption.

Amy had no sympathy for her and rather savoured her obvious discontent. *Fuck her.*

"Pyke," she smiled. "What's next on the agenda?"

"I'm working on a fraud scam where oldies are being conned out of their pensions. I may need you to follow a suspect when he collects a pensioner's payment."

"No worries. Hey, do animals do the same as us?"

"Yes, of course they do. They're awesome. They share the planet with us. It's so cool having them around. We could learn a lot from them. They have further advanced organisational skills than we do, and there are more of them. Our paths don't normally cross. They tend to sort out their own shit. That was cool you worked with Connor, it's a compliment. He's been around a while, he's a bit of a hero up here."

When Jack walked in, Mara stood up and brushed down her tight mini-skirt. She flashed dark coquettish eyes at him and finger-twizzled her long hair, trying out her best sexy moves. But he didn't notice as he was too busy scanning the office for Maggie. She skulked back into her seat.

Amy smiled to herself, chalking up another irritating moment for Mara and went about making tea, humming one of her favourite songs by the band 'Hot Chocolate'... *'I believe in miracles... you sexy thing'.*

"Where's Maggie?" Jack walked over to Pyke.

"Not sure, maybe talking to that guy."

"Who is he? Did you scan his face?"

"Yep, I've been running facial recognition software on him. I'll let you know what I find."

Pyke stepped in close to Jack, out of the women's earshot.

"She was rattled, Jack. What happened?"

"I think he's the guy Amy was talking about. I asked him why he was following us, and all he said was Maggie would know. Can you do some research on him? I don't like it. He's a cocky little fuck for an old boy, a snappy dresser, a suave old gent type. But, not being funny, he smells bad, real bad. He smells dead... I mean dead, dead... really long-term rancid dead."

"Shit, he might be one of them."

"What, one of them."

"One of those from below ground... a Witness. They use smoke to disguise their rancid smell. What the hell is he doing here? How did he get in?"

Chapter Thirty-Eight
Alice

Brighton, UK

The first time he came for her, Amy was grateful for the company. She had lain in her bed, naked, for what seemed like three or four days but difficult to be certain without windows. The hours tended to melt into one long fitful nightmare. The food delivered through the door served as the only measurable passage of time. Every few days or so, a panel at the bottom of the knobless door would slide open and someone pushed a tray of bread and bottled water into the room.

Whoever placed it there did not say a word and remained extremely quiet. Sometimes she would awaken to find the food waiting for her but hadn't heard it being delivered. Within minutes she would devour the bread, always hungry with such few offerings and miserly portions.

Whenever classical music played, she recognised it as a signal *he* had entered the corridor. If she listened carefully, she could hear him humming as he passed her door. She wanted to bang on the door and shout for help, but the fear of his fist in her face stopped her. Along with his humming she could hear a strange squeaking sound.

Then it was her turn. He opened the door and stood watching her. She'd been sleeping in the foetal position in her bed, curled up tight. She'd not heard him coming down the corridor, nor the thud of the bolt opening her door. The slam of the door banging against the wall broke her dream.

"Wakey, wakey. Rise and shine, dear. It's time to pay for your keep."

He waved his hand across his face, scrunching up his nose.

"Pooh, dearie, you smell!" He pinched his nostrils. "We will have to correct that."

Behind him stood a small Asian man dressed in pale blue scrubs, as if ready for surgical theatre. The Asian nodded at her and pulled a wheelchair into view, waving his hand for her to get into it.

"Don't worry. This is Jojo. He's deaf and dumb. He can't hear you and he can't speak to you. Just pretend he isn't there. He's my little helper."

"What's happening?" Her voice rumbled with a huskiness she found disturbing.

"Oh, you'll see. Because it's your first time, we will be lenient on you. But if you misbehave, we will be harsh on you. Your call."

"Who's we? First time for what?" she whimpered.

"You'll see...but first let's get you showered."

She sat on the edge of the bed, her hands covering her private parts. He laughed at her.

"Oh, don't worry about us, dearie. We've seen it all. No modesty here. I'll be naked in a minute, so you'll feel more comfortable. Now chop-chop."

Jojo skipped into the room and helped Alice walk to the wheelchair. He strapped her arms and legs snugly in position to prevent her from escaping during the journey.

Her captor walked ahead, humming to the music. Jojo and Alice trundled behind, the chair's wheels squeaking as they turned. She could now identify the squeaking sound she always heard.

They entered the lift, the same one she'd used when he'd tricked her into coming here. She had to shut her eyes as the bright light stung them and made them water. The lift descended one floor, and as they exited, her captor went off to the left, shouting instructions at Jojo to have her ready in twenty minutes.

Jojo turned right and pushed her into a large washroom with a row of showers. The light blinded her again. She winced through scrunched lids to analyse her surroundings.

Jojo put brakes on the wheelchair, undid her bindings and pulled her into the standing position. She stood shivering, her arms covering her nakedness.

He pushed her towards a shower head and lined her up beneath it. His hands were hard and sinewy. She sensed he had the strength of an Ox. There was no way she could fight him. She stood like a malleable child, obediently waiting to be bathed.

Jojo washed and prepared her. After her initial nerves of embarrassment in having another man touching her body, she got used to his attention and let him get on with it. The warm water felt good on her skin.

He showed no interest in her. He didn't say a word and didn't seem to notice when he scrubbed a sore part of her cheekbone and she cried out with pain.

He washed, brushed, and dried her hair. She stood quietly as he worked around her, eyeing the door to estimate an escape route, but a passcode pad accompanied each one. She spotted a pair of hair scissors in an open cupboard above the sink and thought about taking it, but had nowhere to hide it on her person.

Jojo spun her around, checking her overall appearance, smiled and waved for her to sit back in the wheelchair. She had no choice but to obey.

He strapped her in and pushed her out of the bathroom, down a long dark corridor to a large wooden door at the end. She could hear music coming from the other side of the door. Not classical, but soft gentle soulful measures like a ballad or love song.

Jojo stopped the chair a few feet from the door, undid her straps and motioned for her to stand up. She obeyed, her heart beating loudly. Jojo knocked loudly on the door. A voice shouted, "Enter."

Jojo tapped in the passcode and pushed the door open. Alice held her breath. A large plush red room spread out before her; soft lighting, cushions, sofa's, armchairs scattered the length of the walls. In the middle of the room lay a black plastic sheet.

As her eyes adjusted to the light, ten naked men stood up and paraded towards her, each smiling, each holding onto his cock, fumbling, rubbing it into life.

Her captor stepped between them, put out his hand, took hers, and led her onto the plastic sheet.

"Welcome, Alice, and come meet my friends," he said, his voice thick with sarcasm.

"They have been longing to meet you. I've told them so much about you."

Her heart raced, she couldn't speak. She looked back over her shoulder as Jojo closed the door behind her, tears staining his cheeks and glistening in his eyes.

Chapter Thirty-Nine

The Knightsbridge Club, Kensington Apartments, Knightsbridge, London, UK

Jack patrolled the back of the imposing block of flats, Kensington Apartments. The private Knightsbridge Club took over the ground floor and basement of the block. Taking two steps at a time as he ran up to the Club's grand entrance.

Standing guard at the front door, a burly, bald-shaven, square-jawed giant of a man spoke Russian into his headphone. His uniform aligned more with armed Police than that of a doorman.

He didn't see Jack run up the steps and through the closed door into the marbled reception hallway. Mara, following closely behind, teetering on stilettos and tugging on her short skirt, took a moment to appreciate the guard's rugged good looks. Not able to resist, she ran a teasing fingertip across the skin of his powerful neck, causing him to shiver, and not understand why. *Oh my, the things I could do to you.*

She sashayed on through the closed door and caught sight of Jack striding down a long dark corridor, talking to Pyke. She caught up to him. She hadn't seen him in action before. It made him even more attractive. She wanted him all the more. He was all action-man assertive, strutting his stuff, taking in his surroundings and assessing what needed to be done. *Very sexy.*

"What the hell is she doing here?" Jack shouted at Pyke, reaching the end of the corridor, passing through a locked door, and descending stairs to a basement.

"Well, since it seems you and Amy are having a 'moment,' we thought she should stand in for this one. Also, Amy can't be trusted to behave accordingly. This job will make her angry, whereas Mara doesn't seem to mind and remains calmer."

"That's because Mara couldn't give a toss. She's a selfish bitch with zero empathy. I don't need anyone with me on this. It's just one deactivation, isn't it? Simple."

"Maggie's orders, mate. Mara needs to learn."

"She's dressed like a tart, what the fuck..." Too late. Pyke had gone.

He entered a reception area furnished with black leather sofas, walls painted black, and lighting subdued. Seven men sat waiting. Scantily clad waitresses served drinks. A receptionist took the men, one at a time, down another set of stairs into a dark dungeon.

Jack paused in the doorway, taking in the scene unfolding at the bottom of the stairs. A wooden walled room stood in the centre of the basement. Spotlights circled the room, shining on the wood, highlighting large symmetrically spaced holes, placed at hip height running the length of each wall.

The four walls had different activities. One had naked women standing in a row, bent over, leaning into a hole. A black curtain hid their upper body, as men took them from behind. On the second wall, a row of two foot ledges stuck out, the lower part of a female body, lying on her back, hips resting on the ledge, legs flailing, her upper body also hidden behind a curtain, being taken by men. The third and fourth walls had smaller holes at hip height for clients to stick there penis into and have an unknown mouth suck on it.

With trousers wrapped around their ankles, men used the female parts to pleasure themselves, some fucking, some licking, some wanking over the skin on display. The women's faces could not be seen, but fake moans of pleasure could be heard coming from behind the walls. The men lined up, stroking their cocks, waiting their turn. Some sat on sofas, getting their breath back, for the next dip into pleasure.

Naked waitresses offered drinks, condoms, and tissues.

"Classy," Jack muttered, scouting the room for faces.

Mara came up behind him, wrapped her hands around his waist, and grabbed his cock.

"I've missed you," she whispered, her breath warm against his neck, her cloying perfume filling his nostrils.

He jerked forward, as if given an electric shock. "Don't touch me." He spat, spinning around to face her.

She laughed and stepped forward to press against his body, she lay one hand against his knife-scarred chest, as the other cupped between his legs.

"You're mine, Jack, and you know it. There's energy between us you can't resist."

Jack stared at her for a second, letting her hands remain on him. His cock lurched.

"Fuck off." He shoved her away.

She smiled at his hesitation, and the hardening of his beautiful cock, she still had *it*.

Jack jumped down the staircase, and walked along the line of fucking, sucking, wanking men, surveying their faces.

Mara strutted closely behind him, her voice in his ear, soft and sultry, just like she used to when they first got together. It reminded him of the snake in *The Jungle Book*. She'd always known how to get to him.

"She doesn't want you, you know. She told me."

"I know, thanks to you and your vicious tongue. Why are you so adamant in splitting us up? You want her sloppy seconds, eh?" he spat.

He spied another door under the staircase where a sexy blonde in a short white uniform entered, carrying towels. He sidled through right behind her.

Three massage beds filled the room. Three fat old bald men lay naked on top of them, each with two women and a man servicing them.

He clicked his phone. "Pyke, I'm in the basement. Help me out here. The man I am looking for..."

"Yep, Rudy Stonkavich."

"Well, I'm looking at three possibles. They're all naked, with no clothing or ID to scan, and the light's too dark for you to get a clear picture."

"Well, he's a big Russian," Pyke said.

"Yep."

"Bald."

"Yep."

"Sixtyish."

"Yep."

"Fat."

Jack scratched his head. "For god's sake, they all look like that."

"He's into boys."

Jack felt elated to spot the middle male who had a cock in his mouth as one female sucked *his* cock and another licked his balls. But his smile dropped as he saw one of the other males handling his masseur's genitals while a female rubbed her breasts in his face, and the other dropped hot wax on his cock. The third possible pulled the male masseur's face towards him and gave him a full-on tongues kiss.

"Shit, they all go both ways."

"He has a tattoo of a unicorn running out of his arse."

"Where?"

"On his back...duh. Where else would his arse be?"

"Very funny, wise guy."

"Have you seen any pink-haired girls with nose piercings there?" asked Pyke.

"Nope, not that I recall. Why?"

"Oh, nothing. She's on our missing list. I thought there might be a connection."

Jack couldn't concentrate with Mara whispering in his ear again, her hands pawing him.

"I'll get back to you, Pyke."

He clicked off his call, grabbed Mara by the arm, and shoved her across the room.

"Leave me alone, for fuck's sake."

"I'm bored," she muttered, grumpy, dusting herself down. "So, what do you want me to do?"

"Deactivate the one with the unicorn tattoo on his arse. I'll be back in a minute." Jack left the room. Leaving a confused Mara staring at the three men and wondering which had the unicorn.

He walked back upstairs and through the wooden sex wall to find a dark, humid box room, with twenty or so naked and drugged girls.

On two walls, the girls lay on raised beds with half their bodies protruding through a hole in the wall, some lying on their stomachs, some on their backs. Black plastic curtains drew across their bodies, giving the illusion of having been cut in half. The girls wriggled and cried out with pain, not enjoying whatever treatment the males on the other side of the wall enacted. A fake, pre-recorded soundtrack oozed groans and sighs from ceiling speakers, muffling the girls' cries.

The third and fourth walls had rows of hard, jiggling cocks of varying sizes and colours, sticking through smaller holes. Girls knelt on the floor in front of them, gagging as they sucked the men off. The room stank of semen and sweat.

Jack scanned the disgusting scene, noting the only exit was a door, bolted on the outside, with an overhead camera surveying the dazed women. He reached up and nudged the camera's angle away from the girls. He pushed his hand through the door and unbolted it, letting it fall slightly ajar.

He reached out to the nearest girl. She lay on her stomach, her lower body from the waist down was sticking out through a hole, hidden by a curtain. She drifted in and out of consciousness, her body rocked backwards and forwards on the bed, as she was being taken from behind.

He gently lifted her head and directed her face toward the door. He shook her shoulders, trying to stir her awake. He whispered in her ear. Through the hazy, mind-numbing drugs, she glimpsed at the open door and the shifted camera. The opportunity to escape slowly dawned on her. Frantically, she waved and whispered to her fellow girls, trying to get them to see it, too.

One by one, Jack helped them extricate their bodies from the holes and stagger to the door. Some started to cry, not understanding what strange force was surrounding them. Jack corralled the girls in a pack, giving each other support.

In the main room, unhappy clients shouted, furious the women had suddenly disappeared and were no longer providing them pleasure, but they fell silent when a single file of naked, dirty, drugged, sobbing girls staggered out of the sex wall door and shuffled barefoot through the room. Unseen, Jack guided them to the staircase, the way out.

The men hushed, staring in awe, some in shame at the painful state of their sex slaves. The greasy, bedraggled young girls, who they had just been intimate with, were ugly with lack of sleep, lack of nutrition and the haunting eyes of drug addiction.

Just as the girls walked to their freedom, a loud explosion blasted from the dungeon below, the whole building shook, as if an earthquake had split the ground. Dust and debris percolated the air. The men and girls clambered up the stairs, screaming to get out.

Mara was suddenly by Jack's side.

"What the fuck happened?"

"Err... I tried to get them to stand up to get a good look at their bums, but it failed."

"What failed?"

"Electrocution...I just wanted a short, sharp shock using the wires from the wax melting pot, but what with the water and everything, it went a bit wrong. They're all dead."

"What?"

"Except the masseurs. They're just under the rubble."

Sirens rang in the distance, someone had called it in.

Chapter Forty

Jack and Mara watched the commotion from the side lines. Television camera crews had arrived. A helicopter circled above while armed Police charged up the entrance steps.

Headlines and news spread like a fever, linking the incident to every outlet around the world: Russian oligarch's private club had been attacked during one of his sex parties.

Authorities escorted a cluster of crying girls, three dead bodies, and lines of shame-faced males from the building, including an MP, a Cardinal, a renowned Judge, a TV presenter and a premiership footballer, all under the glare of camera lights.

"You're not really cut out for this job, are you?" remarked Jack, arms crossed, leaning against a Police vehicle bonnet.

"What? It's not my fault," Mara said, stomping closer to the vehicle and leaning on the headlight to check her nails.

"We're meant to sneak in, do the job, and get out without anyone realising they'd been helped, subtle-like." He shook his head, watching the saga unfold around the planet. "Maggie is so not going to be happy."

"So, they had an electrical shortage. What's the problem? They may not understand the scorching around the base of their cocks, but hey... the target is deactivated, whichever one he was, they all looked the same to me... I never did find the bloody unicorn."

Jack, lay back against the bonnet and peered up at the sky. He closed his eyes, tucked his hands behind his head, and started to shake with laughter.

She hadn't seen him laugh in a long time. She stepped between his legs, leaned over his body, placed her face close to his, and gazed into his eyes.

He stopped laughing and stared back at her, wondering how someone so beautiful, could turn out so evil. Why had she been allowed to join their Unit? Had she changed?

"You know, if you'd been a good person, we may have stood a chance, Mara. What made you so evil?"

She could feel his breath on her lips as he spoke.

"My father," she whispered. "I don't want to talk about it. But he is the reason for everything in my life. He always has been." Tears welled in her eyes.

"I didn't know. Why didn't you ever talk about it?"

The concern in his voice surprised her. She hadn't expected his kindness.

"Do you believe we could have had a chance, Jack?" Her voice childlike.

She dropped her body onto him, and snuggled her head into his shoulder. It was too much. He gently pushed her off him and stepped away from the car.

"We best get back."

"How dare you!" She posed stiffly, hands on her hips. "Are you just shaking me off like a piece of dirt after all we've been through? After all I've done for you?"

"What? What have you done for me? You killed me. This is not happening, Mara. I'm not falling for your wiles. I know what you're like. You'll say anything to get what you want."

When he turned to go, she raised her arm and slapped his face.

He swung to hit her back but held his hand mid-air. If she thought she could elicit a reaction from him, she was mistaken. He walked away.

Red with anger, she chased after him and jumped on his back. Her legs wrapped around his hips. She pulled at his hair and slapped his head like a banshee, trying to hurt him with all her might.

He turned around, trying to shake her off, but she wouldn't let go. They spun up in the air, twisting tornado'esque in a blur, round and round, until they tumbled to the ground exhausted. She immediately rolled over and scrambled to sit on top of his prostrate body.

With strong legs astride his stomach, she pinned him down, held his hands up over his head and lowered her face close to his.

"You never did love me," she whispered. "I didn't stand a chance. You should never have given me hope. You should have left me alone. It wasn't fair." Tears streamed down her face.

He stared up at her in shame, knowing she was right. She never did stand a chance with Amy in his life. From the moment Amy didn't come out of the woods all those years ago, she'd stolen his heart. He'd wanted to protect her, to be with her and her alone. How did he ever get himself involved with Mara? He was as much to blame for her madness as she.

"I'm so sorry," he whispered.

"You killed me."

"I know."

She buried her head in his chest, her long hair falling over his face. Her cloying perfume filling his senses. He held her as she sobbed, waiting for her tears to stop. He had never seen her this vulnerable before, had never held her this way, and wondered if things could've been different.

Sensing his thoughtfulness, she raised her head, gazed into his eyes, put her mouth on his, and kissed him—a soft, loving, long sexy kiss. It caught him unawares. He didn't push her away; he couldn't, not again.

Knowing what he was doing, he kissed her back, in a fucked-up, apologetic way, giving her what she wanted, saying he was sorry.

Lying in the street outside the oligarch's house, surrounded with camera crew, police, ambulances, and rubberneckers, they had sex on the pavement.

He let her take what she wanted, what she needed, tears in both their eyes—his of guilt and pity; hers of knowing she'd never really have him, knowing he felt sorry for her, that this was goodbye.

Although in plain sight, no one in the crowd could see them. But Pyke did. He had them on surveillance, watching the incident through street cameras. He lowered his eyes, and shook his head.

Someone else had his eyes on the intimate moment, too. Gregori stood in the shadows, puffing on his cigar, glad at Jack's weakness, but sad at Mara's.

Chapter Forty-One
Alice

Brighton, UK

The trips to 'play' with *his* friends came every few days. Alice quickly learned to block her mind, to float off to someplace else as they manhandled her, grabbed at her, buggered her, raped her, gagged her, pissed on her, burned her, fucked her mouth and insulted her.

Her mind protected her, pretending the disgusting treatment was happening to someone else, not her. Sometimes, they would grip her neck so tightly, she thought she would suffocate, thought she might die. She soon longed for those moments, willing them to squeeze harder, to kill her, to let her die, to let her go. But they would always release their sweaty hands, just in time for her to gasp a breath.

Fat, ugly, rancid men piled on top of her, taking her body this way and that, with no feeling, no remorse, just for the fun of it.

She often studied her abusers, wondering if they were fathers, if they were brothers, how they would feel if their child, mother, or sister were mauled in such a way and forced to perform unspeakable acts. But she found it difficult to see them as human. They had the devil in them; she wanted them to burn in hell.

She learned she was not alone in the building. Although she never saw anyone else, he cleverly separated and isolated them. She guessed the other doors off the corridor housed numerous other victims he'd tricked into entering his lair. She surmised from their cries some were male, some female, some a lot younger than she. A few of the rooms held more than one person.

Whenever she heard the classical music and the squeaking wheelchair, she cringed to know he was on his rounds, choosing someone to entertain at his evil, twisted parties. Sometimes ten men waited in the room, sometimes just one, but he would always hover about the room, stand in the corner, top up drinks, and oversee events like a good host.

She noticed he was concerned about lighting, and often ushered people out of the way. She guessed the mirrors hid cameras, and that he was recording the sessions. Probably to blackmail his clients. A few of the faces, when she saw them, she recognised from newspapers and the television.

She wondered if Maria was there.

Chapter Forty-Two

Greystones,
Co Wicklow, Ireland

Amy sneaked off, desperate for some space, to be on her own.

She landed in Greystones, a beautiful coastal village in County Wicklow, just outside Dublin, Ireland—a reasonably quiet part of the world, where she could be left alone for a while.

She scoured the streets until she found a near-empty internet café. She wanted to sift through web browsers to answer a few questions.

She entered the café, wandered past the coffee counter, and followed the signs to a room full of desks and computers. She chose a desk in the back, a computer conveniently facing the wall and affording the right kind of privacy.

She could've worked in the Unit office to do her research, but Pyke would've inquired about her activity, and she would've been sent out on a job. Let Jack and Mara take the reins for a while.

Two students occupied desks on the other side of the room, their heads buried in books, their ears plugged into music, their demeanour appearing as if they were lost in their own worlds.

It took her a while to remember how to use the outdated keyboard, strangely old and clunky compared to the advanced resources in the skies. She would touch the screen to make a move, but failed to make it work.

She gripped the mouse and studied the instructions on the wall to log on and get started. Initially, she struggled to get the keys and mouse to move, but after a while, she perfected the right amount of force needed. The mouse rolled off the desk a few times, when she'd misjudged and swept it too far, but the students, plugged into their headphones, didn't notice her clumsiness.

Firstly, she wanted to read the news about her death. She inserted her name in the search bar and pressed enter. A short entry in a freebie evening newspaper popped up.

RUSH HOUR CHAOS
AS BODY FOUND ON TRACK

A woman died after being hit by a train on the Piccadilly Line during this morning's rush hour.

Emergency services were summoned to Brompton Court London Underground station shortly after 8.30 a.m., after reports of a person on the track.

Commuters faced rush hour delays while services on the line were severely delayed. Some station display boards were showing no trains for up to two hours, while crowds of people were forced to wait outside stations.

Two rescue crews from London Fire Brigade arrived first at the scene following reports a person had been struck by a train.

A British Transport Police Officer reported: "Officers from BTP and London Ambulance Service arrived on the scene a short time after; however, regrettably, a female was pronounced dead at the scene.

The female has been identified as Amy Fox, 32yrs, from Earls Court, London. The incident is being treated as non-suspicious and a file will be produced for the Coroner's Office."

A Transport for London spokesperson reported work had been done to restore a normal service to the Piccadilly Line, and that Brompton Court Station had resumed operations.

Amy stared at the screen. Is that what her life had come down to—how quickly the trains could get up and running again, how quickly they could clean up her body from the tracks?

The twitter messages that followed the incident were even more callous.

"What the fuck is going on?"

"Delays AGAIN on Piccadilly Line."

"Suicide, don't be so bloody selfish, go kill urself somewhere else."

Non-suspicious circumstances—what did that mean? That she'd accidentally fallen onto the track in the commuter rush, or that she'd committed suicide?

She didn't feel comfortable with people thinking she'd taken her own life. It wasn't her style, unless the day came when she couldn't wipe her own bottom or became a burden. Then she would want to pop her clogs.

Also, if she were going to commit suicide, it would be at a time and place where it would affect the least amount of people—no onlookers haunted by the image of a pulped body, no train driver guilt-scarred for life, no friends hearing it happen on a phone call, and no commuters late for work.

She searched again, locating nothing of note with respect to her death. An only child, with her adoptive parents dead, she didn't expect many would mourn her passing except her friends, a few work colleagues, and broken-hearted ex-boyfriends, but she shifted in her chair, pleasantly amazed. Her wake had a good turnout. A heartfelt emotion touched her in a way she didn't expect.

After her funeral, life had moved on. Her landlady re-let her apartment, her boss employed a new girl, and her cat had found a new owner. She seemed to have left the world with not much more than a blip... a commuter delay. Was that it?

The only sign she even existed appeared on social media. Sally's Facebook page had kindly celebrated her life. Sally had posted pictures of the two of them together with loving memories and quotes of the laughter they had shared. Tears streamed down her face as she scrolled through them. *I love you, Sal.*

Her own Facebook and Twitter pages still memorialized her existence, frozen just where she'd posted her last entries, which felt a bit weird. She would ask Pyke about deleting them. Each page had numerous entries from well-wishers, some she barely knew. RIP, rest in peace, well she certainly wasn't doing that. She'd never worked so hard in her life, certainly not in her previous life.

She wanted to reply to all the generous, kind comments, to tell a few how wonderful they were, a few how she wished she'd spent more time with them, and others a few home truths; to stop the fake bullshit, that they'd never really liked each other so fuck off, hashtag crocodile tears. But she thought better of scaring people. A dead person speaking through social media... *nah, Maggie would blow a gasket. There must be a rule against it, although no one has said anything... hmmm.*

Her search to clarify how or why she'd died bore no fruit. Maybe it was just one of those things, an accident. Mara was being a jealous arse.

Next, she wanted to search for Jack, but realised she didn't know anything about him; his surname, date of birth, school, Army regiment, place of birth, any titbit to launch a search. A zillion Jacks existed in the UK.

She sat staring at the screen. *Well this is a waste of time.*

She forfeited her googling to stare out the window and let her mind rest. Just beyond the landscape, the sea danced wildly under a blustery day. People walked their dogs, trudging along the sandy beach controlling leashes, holding on to hats, scarves, and poo bags, leaning into the wind.

She used to love the wind, the freeing feeling of blowing away cobwebs, of blasting through her hair and shaking life into her body. She sighed, and added it to the list of things she should have stopped and relished more, the many things she shouldn't have taken for granted.

A face appeared in her line of view through the window—a beautiful young woman in her twenties, wearing a black dress, with pale skin and long red flowing hair waving about her shoulders. The woman's gaze directly targeted her.

Amy glanced behind her; in case the woman had her sights on someone else, but no one else had entered the room. The two oblivious students and she had no other company. *Can she see me?*

Just as quickly as the woman came into view, she suddenly vanished from sight. Amy watched for a while, in case she came back.

A muffled sniffing noise caught her attention. She looked across at the students. One of them was sobbing, but she couldn't work out which one, as they huddled over their desks with hoodies covering their heads and headphones plugged in their ears.

She rose and walked over to the nearest desk. A young teenage boy was bent over his science books with heavy metal blasting from his headphones. Rocking in rhythm to the music, his eyes scanned images on the computer, checked chemical structures in his books, and made scratchy diagrams in his notebook. His eyes showed no signs of sadness.

She turned to the next desk. What initially looked like a young lad in a hoody, oversized jeans, and trainers wasn't a boy at all but a girl with short hair and geeky glasses. She yanked earplugs out of her ears and pushed study books aside. Tears rolled down her cheeks as her sad eyes stared at text on the computer. Amy stood behind her and read the screen.

THE DEAL

Someone trolled her on her Twitter account. For once, normally a tomboy, she'd courageously posted a picture of herself in a fashionable dress. She hardly ever braved wearing a dress and thought she'd looked good, well, better than she normally did.

She had a crush on a college boy and wanted him to see her feminine side, trying to attract his attention. But it had gone terribly wrong.

Vanity and beauty were not her strong points. Short and overweight, she had no skills in applying makeup, styling her hair, or showing her pretty features, like other girls her age. A caretaker for her sick, single mother and five younger siblings, she could barely afford College, never mind a beauty salon. With money so tight, she based her life around her and her family's survival, not on how good she looked.

Her name was Oonagh, and the cruel trolls were having a field day with cheap digs at her appearance. She didn't want to read the messages, but couldn't tear her eyes away from vicious comment after vicious comment, each one a knife in her heart.

As Oonagh clumsily flicked through pages, tears blurred her vision as she desperately tried to delete the image and stop the bullying. Amy surmised this was not the first time she had been attacked. The girl had been bullied for months.

Amy memorised Oonagh's Twitter name and returned to her desk. She pulled up the girl's account on Twitter, and using her own account, followed the troll conversation. Once she understood the gist of the situation, who commented what, who acted as the vilest culprits, she joined in the conversation, giving Oonagh compliments galore. *Maggie's not going to like this.*

Praising her, empowering her, complimenting her on how wonderful she looked, how beautifully the dress enhanced her eyes, asking where she'd found such a lovely design, she claimed her friend Jack also whistled, saying she was a stunner. Amy watched Oonagh's face light up as the tweets came through.

It amazed her how just a few kind words could have such power, change a person's mood, and give confidence. Oonagh smiled at the screen and typed back saying 'thank you.'

Amy sensed a presence beside her and twisted around to behold the red-headed woman who had lingered outside the window, solemn faced, hands on her hips, staring right at her.

"You can see me, right?"

"Yep."

"Hi. I'm Amy, UK Unit," Amy offered her hand.

"Yep." The woman didn't take it.

"I guess you're with an Irish Unit." Amy dropped her hand and shrugged.

"Yep."

"Sorry to be on your patch, but I'm playing hooky. I just needed to get away for a bit, sort my head out."

"Yep."

"You don't say much do you."

"Nope."

"Do you mind if I just help this girl out a little?"

The woman scrutinized Amy, taking her in, reading her energy. After a few seconds, her body language softened, as if she had come to a decision. She dropped her hands from her hips and stepped nearer.

"Nope, not at all," she smiled.

Her clever green eyes twinkled as her beautiful face lit up.

"Actually, I could do with some help," Amy said, apologetically.

"What kind of help."

"Dishing out a little karma."

The woman smiled, flicked her long red mane over her shoulder, sat down beside Amy, put out her hand, and said. "I'm Maeve. Good to meet you."

Amy shook it with glee, immediately liking this girl. She had a cheeky sparkle in her eye and a soft Irish accent to die for. It felt all the more fun working with a secret collaborator. They snuggled together at the computer, new partners in crime.

"Am happy to help," Maeve looked over at Oonagh. "That's Oonagh. She's on suicide watch. I like to keep a special eye on her. She's a good girl, a kind girl, but too soft for her own good," she informed Amy, shaking her head. "Oonagh's been bullied for years and has now had enough. She wants to go. She spends a lot of time in here, googling how to commit suicide. I've done all I can to help her."

"Well..." Amy leaned in close and whispered. "How do you feel about a little dirt digging? You know, the kind of stuff people don't want others to know about. It's easy for them to hide behind social media...'Look at me. I'm so wonderful' persona. I think these guys need a lesson or two, to be frightened off. I'm not sure if it's legal for us to do, but hey, they deserve it. I'll do it all on my Twitter account so the blame goes on me."

"Oh, I don't care. Hey, I'm dead already, whatta they gonna do?"

"Exactly, you and me both."

"I like it. What do you need?" Maeve grinned and rubbed her hands together with glee. "I love a good karma session."

"Well, I've just given Oonagh a load of compliments," Amy whispered, "which is gonna piss this lot off big time. They'll come back with a torrent of abuse. I need you to contact one of the intel boys at your Unit and get any juicy info you can on each of the viler offenders for me."

"Yep, easy," whispered Maeve. "Gabe in the office will love it. He lost his sister through this sort of bullying shite. He'll link us up on a call, and I'll pop out and visit their homes, be your eyes and ears on the ground. I'm guessing most will be from Ireland, so it won't take long."

"Why are we whispering?" questioned Amy, scrunching up her nose.

"Jeysus, I don't know. You started it." Maeve giggled. "*No one can feckin hear us*," she shouted.

They both laughed.

Oonagh's soft cry interrupted the merriment.

They glimpsed at Oonagh to find her head bowed, tears welling her eyes again. As expected, the exchange upset the trolls. They'd spent the day slagging her off, and here was someone building her up again. They came back with a vengeance, with a new onslaught of insults.

Maeve and Amy looked at each other. They were going to enjoy this. Maeve stood up, walked over behind Oonagh, and whispered closely into her ear.

"Don't worry little one. There are a few Angels here to dish out a little karma."

She gave Amy a wink and walked out the door, tapping her ear.

"Gabe, darlin', I've a little favour to ask ya..."

Amy smiled, watching her leave. *This is where the fun starts.*

Bent over the computer, Amy read the round of troll messages as they came in. Gabe connected her and Maeve up on a call. Amy recited the name and username of the targeted troll. Gabe searched a few databases and gave the name and address to Maeve. In a whirlwind dash, Maeve attended the troll's home, bedroom, schoolroom, and workplace; then reported each of her findings back to Amy. Amy then replied to the troll's message with uncomfortable snippets of information to unnerve the evilest of bullies.

The messaging went on for four hours. Every now and then, Amy checked up on Oonagh, who sat rigidly in her chair, aghast, staring at the screen. Sometimes she laughed out loud; other times cringed with embarrassment, and occasionally slammed her hand across her mouth in shock. But she'd stopped crying. She was growing in stature with every slaying of the dragon.

At first the trolls would fight right back and start slagging off Amy, revelling in the new kill. But Amy would gather the intel from Gabe and Maeve, edit the information to a short sharp deadly line of text, go in for the kill, and send it flying out there for all to see.

'Masturbating with a pink rubber glove is just silly, Patrick. Stop it, now #wanker.'

'Mark, sniffing ur finger after poking ur bum hole is gross. Just stop it #WashHands.'

'If ur gonna pull hair from ur butt crack, Christine, don't chew it... yuck!'

'Tim, peeing in the shower, watchin it swirl the plug hole isn't nice in Sonia's house.'

'Not sure ur co-worker Paul Hunter will like knowing u net-stalk him, Eva #crush.'

'Pls pop those blackheads in privacy of ur own home. A traffic jam is not the place.'

'U can grab thoz #LoveHandles all u want. They r not goin anywhere. #DietExercise'

'Those purple leggings u've got on don't do ur cellulite any favours, hon.'

'sorry u have to use a cock expander, Dick. Never mind. #ButtonMushroom.'

'Rick, does ur mum know about the bestiality porno mag under ur bedside rug?'

'Pete, does Sam know ur sexting his gf? #DodgyFriend.'

'Hilary, no worry. It's ok 2 fart in ur Gynaecologist's face. #GoesWithTheTerritory.'

'Oonagh may be an XXL, but Trisha, ur an XXXL. What's with u? #GlassHouses.'

'Stop picking ur nose n'eating it, Sheila. It's SO not a good look. #NastyHabit."

'Have u got the result of your HIV test back yet, Colin?'

'Sorry about the bankruptcy, Malcolm, such a nuisance when starting a nu company.'

'Does Harry no u've pinpricked holes in ur dutch cap, Anna? #UnwantedPregnancy.'

This is fun.

Oonagh sat transfixed as the verbal beatings assaulted each of her trolls. She punched the air when one of her more vehement enemies was hit with a bull's eye. Her following numbers grew by the second.

Finally, the trolls started to back off. The more they wrote, the more uncomfortable facts came out about them. One by one, they crawled back under their stones, hopefully to stay there.

They couldn't understand how Amy knew such private information. Some covered the cameras in their laptops. Some turned their phones off with fright. They particularly fretted when they realised the messages had been posted from a dead person's account.

Since the hour was late and the trolls had retreated and Oonagh had attracted thousands of new followers, Maeve popped back into the café for a rest. She and Amy high-fived as Amy chatted with Gabe.

"Thank you, Gabe. I'd better go. I've been AWOL a while now and I'm in serious trouble."

"No, it's my pleasure. I enjoyed it, and don't worry about the office. I had a quick word with Pyke. He and I have helped each other out in the past. He's cool with today's work."

Oonagh packed up her things and left the café. She carried a beaming smile on her face. Someone had stood up for her. She wasn't a worthless piece of shit. Amy and Maeve watched her as she walked down the street.

As she passed a hairdressing salon, she stopped to check the window for prices. She would come back tomorrow and book a hair appointment and maybe get her nails done. It was time she treated herself. She looked up and saw two white feathers float gently to the ground in front of her. She grabbed at them, giggling, caught them, and placed them in her pocket.

Today was the first day of the new Oonagh.

Amy stood on the street corner with her hands tucked in her pockets, watching the spirited girl continue down the street with a skip in her step. *I love my job. That was fun.*

She had come to Oonagh's aid, but in fact Oonagh had helped her. Bullies like Mara were not going to get to her. She possessed a newfound gumption to fight for what she wanted, and she wanted Jack.

Maeve gave her a heartfelt hug goodbye.

"See you around, Maeve. Thanks for helping me. We did good, changing that girl's life. If they come back again later, can you and Gabe continue the fight?"

"Course, it'll be my pleasure."

"Good. She deserves better. She's a nice girl."

"Of course, she is. She's my sister."

Amy stood open mouthed. "What?"

"Yep, I owe you, Amy. You need me anytime, let me know."

They hugged again and walked their separate ways. The sea wind blew through Amy's hair, tingling her body alive. She closed her eyes and cherished every single second of it.

Chapter Forty-Three

Cloud 9

Amy wandered into the office to find Pyke leaning over his desk fiddling with wiring encased in a large black box.

"What's up?"

"We've been hacked, but I'm sorting it. I hear from Gabe you've been a busy bee helping our Irish friends. Sorry I haven't been much help, but I've been tied up with this all day. Is it sorted?"

"Yeah, dishing out a little payback on a few bullies. They're a nice bunch, the Irish Unit."

"Gabe's a good boy. He's another ex-hacker. We have our uses. Not sure how I'm going to sort a dead person's Twitter account kicking butt, but hey, glad we were able to help. Now can you make me a cuppa? I've nearly got this sorted."

Amy smiled to herself with a feeling of accomplishment. If the systems were down, Pyke may not have witnessed what she'd actually posted to the trolls. She'd been a little cruel and had chucked a few people under the bus. But hey, they deserved it.

"Don't know how you understand all that stuff. Looks like spaghetti to me," she commented, tapping Pyke on the shoulder. "Cup of tea?"

"And a custard crème, please." He placed a screw in the box's back panel and closed it. "Nothing to it. Love this old fashioned stuff. I'm installing backup to counter any future failures. Didn't like being caught on the hop like that. Not good for my hacker image."

Amy wandered over to the kitchen, prepared two cups of tea, and noted how funny it was she'd become addicted to tea since her arrival on the Unit. On earth, she'd been a coffee drinker through and through. Something about tea calmed her and set her up for the next job. Mimicking and holding onto human habits had become a psychological pastime there, all make-believe, as they didn't really consume anything. A soul sometimes needed something soothing to hang on to.

She noticed how empty the office felt without Jack. His powerful energy ignited the room with so much drive, she loved being around him.

"Where are the others?" she asked, as she placed the steaming teacup on Pyke's table.

"Maggie's in a meeting. Jack and Mara tended to a job, but I haven't seen them." Pyke gave her a side look, debating whether to tell her or not? Jack and Amy were his friends.

"What are your thoughts on Mara?"

"Well, she's not someone I would normally hang out with. She's a little up herself for me, but we don't have much choice up here, do we?"

Pyke looked at Amy. She had a right to know. "She and Jack are married...were married...but you know that, don't you?"

"Yes, I know," Amy muttered, looking at the ground. "I just wish he'd told me he had a bird."

"Well, I'm not sure they're still together. She killed him, apparently."

"If that's the case, she's a murderer, so how come she is up here with us goody goodies?" Amy questioned.

"I'm not sure. The police report says suicide. Allegedly, she came home and found him, but from the angle of the knife, the fact he was having sex at the time, and the fact that the knife had been found outside his body, none of it rings true for me."

"She may have pulled it out when she found him."

"Yeah, I'm probably barking up the wrong tree. Jack will tell us the details if he wants to. Suicides don't normally make it here, not when their energy is spent. They just don't have the passion for it. But hey, you never know."

Amy sipped her hot tea, enjoying the warm feeling in her hands as she cupped the delicate china teacup. Pyke placed the black box on the floor and connected his laptop to it. Amy continued to drink as she watched his deft fingers scramble across the keyboard, typing lines of code to complete the setup.

"You're brilliant, Pyke. They can't ever let you go. You're too indispensable," she said.

"Oh, there'll be other geeks after me, much better ones, I'm sure."

She stared into her cup. She couldn't imagine the Unit would be the same minus Pyke. His humour and passion, his easy mood and attitude, and his willingness to go beyond the call of duty made the Unit a fun place to work.

"I'm a bit in love with Jack, you know."

"I know."

"Do you approve?"

"He's a nice guy...a little complex...but hey, aren't we all?" Pyke's diplomacy always diffused the mystery and added the fatherly touch.

"I realised something today. I spent so much time rushing around when I was alive, I didn't stop and smell the roses. I took everything for granted. A person always puts things off until tomorrow, never thinking there may not be a tomorrow. I don't want to do that up here, with whatever time I have left. I want to spend time with Jack. I want him, Pyke. I love him."

Pyke looked at her and nodded.

"I know. I get it."

"We had sex, and we didn't die...so I guess, the answer to my question is it's OK to fuck up here," she giggled.

"Yeah, I know. I was tuned in for a second and saw you...very traumatic," he said with a playful smile.

Amy blushed.

"I'm worried about Mara. She seems to have a hold over him."

"I know."

"How do you know?"

Pyke turned away, looking sheepish. "I just do."

"What's wrong? Tell me."

Pyke scrunched up his face, not wanting to reply.

"You're hiding something, what?"

"Nothing."

"What?"

"Urgh... I've just watched Jack and Mara at it in the street, down there, on a job." There, he'd told her. Lying didn't suit him, even if white lies served to protect feelings.

"What do you mean 'at it'?"

"At it, you know...fucking." He winced, knowing the truth would pain her like a blade slicing her heart.

Amy felt every muscle contract in a protective defence. Her gaze dropped, studying the golden liquid in her cup as if it offered solace. Deliberately and carefully, she lowered it to the table for fear of dropping it and making a mess. She dared to gaze up at Pyke, examining his features and creases for signs he was joking. His sad eyes and tight lined mouth indicated it was not a horrible joke.

"Are you sure?" she questioned, not willing to trust her impressions of his honesty, wanting it to be false, waiting for another punchline.

"Sorry, Amy, but there are no hidden truths here. I wouldn't do that to you."

The devastating news triggered waterworks. Tears spilled down Amy's face with convulsive sobs. Dizziness swept through her as her body swayed left then right. She pressed her hand against the table for support. Pyke opened his arms and let her gratefully fall into them. They didn't speak.

Amy rested her head on his shoulder as he rocked back and forth.

"Sorry, I forgot the biscuits," she mumbled, trying to stop the tears.

"No worries."

"I guess you don't have any remedy to harden a heart, do you, Pyke? Life would be so much easier without being able to feel all this emotional crap."

"No, and I wouldn't even if I could. Your heart is what keeps you here, keeps you kicking the shit out of the idiots down there. Keeps you looking out for the vulnerable ones."

"Why is he with her?"

"I'm not sure he knows. Sex is a weird one. It's one of those powerful energies that makes everything else disappear, a drug that reduces resolve and takes risks."

A clicking sound drew Pyke's gaze toward the door.

"Hey, we have a visitor. I think you're needed."

Amy lifted her head and turned around. Connor stood in the doorway, staring at her, stepping from one foot to the other, anxious to go somewhere. His claws clicking on the flooring. She smiled, wiping her tears.

"Whoa...Connor, what are you doing here?"

"Go, Amy go," Pyke ushered her out. "He wouldn't come here unless it was urgent. I'll follow on your eye camera, and we'll get whatever it is authorised as we go."

Amy wiped her eyes, gave Pyke a kiss on the cheek, knocked back the rest of her tea, and followed Connor out of the door.

Chapter Forty-Four
Alice

Brighton, UK

Alice lay very still in her prison, curled up on her bed with her back facing the door. Watching the locked barrier had driven her anxieties into overdrive, and she screamed in her head, wanting to get *out*. She played games in her mind, creating scenarios based on wishful thinking. If she didn't move, he might ignore her. He might walk past her door and move on to the next person. She prayed he would, prayed he and his friends had grown tired of her.

She buried her head in the mattress, trying to hold back the retch caused by the acrid stench of urine, vomit, sweat, and fear.

She had no one to hold on to, with whom to share her fear. Loneliness affected her, the isolation becoming unbearable. Initially, she'd felt relieved to be in a room on her own, but now she wished she had someone to share with, someone to talk to.

Depression in all its misery beat her down relentlessly as equally as the physical abuse. The windowless room suffocated her, locked her in darkness, filth, deafening silence, and hopelessness. Every day she battled anxiety attacks, sucking in putrid, heavy air, succumbing more and more to panicky breath and overwhelming fear.

She could hear others in adjacent rooms cry out at night, some calling for their mother, some for their god, and some in languages she didn't recognise. No other English voices apart from hers slipped through the corridor. She cried out the name Maria, but no one replied.

She stiffened, contracting every muscle in her body, even clamping her eyes solidly closed in rebellion, when the muffled classical music piped into the corridor with its ebbing announcement: He was coming. The squeaking wheelchair screeched, a dissonant contrast to the music. Her ears perked in high alert, listening to the noise seeping through the gaps in the doorframe. She could picture his controlled body sauntering down the corridor, humming to the music. His lemon fragrance wafted through the air. That smell of Summer she had so liked in the beginning now made her retch with disgust.

Holding her breath, she waited to see whom he would choose, if he would pass her door. He hadn't come for her in two days—two short days. Was it her turn?

Her fellow prisoners' whimpering told her each of them prayed as hard she did not to be chosen.

Whoever quietly returned after one of his sex parties took a strange comfort in knowing they would be free from sexual assault for at least a short reprieve. Some would return days later, crying, mumbling, going out of their minds.

Some would not return at all, their room left empty for a few days until he hunted and snared new prey. God only knew what had happened to them in this living hell. The energy of death was palpable. All of them begged for the end to come, for the living hell to be over: Alice included.

She jumped as a bolt slid and snapped, sighing in relief to realize he'd stopped at the room next to hers. Thank God it was not her turn today, but she cringed in empathy for the other poor victim.

She whispered a prayer for her safety, although it may be kinder to let her die.

She lay rocking on her bed, the squeaking springs giving her comfort. Silent tears rolled down her face. She now dreaded tomorrow. It may be her turn. She begged for God or someone to save her.

Chapter Forty-Five

Wye Valley,
Monmouth, South Wales

Connor darted across acres of lush green grazing fields with the speed of a hungry tiger, making it difficult to keep up. Pyke tuned into the scene via Amy's eyes; neither he nor Amy had a clue where Connor was leading them.

As they cleared the field and halted on a road in front of a farmer's property, they passed three teenage boys running, laughing, pointing at an old wooden barn at the end of the lane. Amy and Connor peered at black smoke billowing from the roof. Connor tore out, hurrying to reach it, Amy at his heels. As they neared, Amy heard horses neighing wildly. It was a stable.

The barn's four walls and roof sat ablaze with angry red flames reaching for the sky. Black smoke fogged the air, making it difficult to see or move around the monstrous bonfire. Connor and Amy stood in front of the imposing barn doors, untouched, but for how long?

Connor nudged Amy's leg, as if to say 'follow me,' and leapt through the doors. She followed, instinctively hiding her face behind her arm as she charged through, uncertain what awaited on the other side.

Inside, sixteen occupied stalls lined the walls, eight on each side. Frightened horses battered their stalls with bloodied hooves, trying to escape the heat, smoke, and flames. Neighing and whinnying with loud roars of fear. Amy spotted a young boy stretched across the entrance of the tack room. Amy tended to the boy while Connor ran to the stalls.

The boy's chest barely rose and fell with faint breaths. Amy noticed he had a bloody nose. His clothes had been torn and discoloured with blood. Amy rested a hand on his forehead and tried to give him energy, but she hadn't mastered this technique yet.

"Where's fucking Jack when you need him, Pyke?"

"I've let him know, and I've put in an anonymous call to the services. Can you get him up and out of there? It's going to blow any minute. I noticed gas cylinders at the back of the tack room."

She searched for Connor and found him running from one stall to the next, kicking his paws at the bolts, opening them. Skittish horses darted about the barn's central area, panicking with nowhere to run. She needed to open the barn doors.

After pulling the boy to the relative safety of the tack room, she raced to the doors, and realized they'd been locked from the outside. *Shit!* The teenage brats had obviously trapped the boy before they ran.

She stepped through the door and turned to face it, flames licked its sides. Summonsing all her strength, she pulled on the bolt, but it wouldn't budge. She kicked and swore, trying to get it open. *Empty, feel, build, and throw.*

"For fuck's sake." Tears streamed down her face as the horses cried in pain.

An arm reached over her. The bolt sprang out of its socket as if hit by lightning. She turned to find Jack standing behind her.

"You just have to remain calm. Put your hand on it and feel the heat go through you. No pressure, just thought. Empty your mind and feel...empty, feel, build, and throw. Got it?"

Amy spun round, punched him hard in the face, and rushed through the door to find Connor. Horses ran through her, galloping to safety.

She located Connor beside the boy, licking at his face and trying to wake him. The boy stirred and started coughing. Connor took hold of the boy's jacket with his teeth and tugged at him, coaxing him to stand. Amy quickly assisted him and eased the boy to his feet. He staggered to the barn doors and fell against them, pushing them wider open, allowing the horses to scramble out unharmed. They cantered to the fields for safety.

The boy tottered into the lane as far as he could before toppling to the ground, his body heaving, coughing and spluttering, his lungs fighting for air.

Connor rounded up the last of the horses, nosing a small pony trembling at the back of the barn, too frightened to move. Connor snapped at its heels, making the pony run out of the barn before the main beams started to fall.

A fire engine's siren reverberated through the countryside. Connor, Amy, and Jack stood watching the barn disintegrate to smouldering ashes. All were safe and unharmed. And the bullied boy would be hailed as a hero for saving the horses.

Connor gave a nudging lick to both Amy's and Jack's hands, a nod of his head, a toothy smile, and a swish of his tail before scampering off across the fields.

Jack rubbed his aching chin. "What the hell was that punch for?"

"Cos, you lied about your wife."

Jack closed his eyes, bit hard on his bottom lip and clenched his fists, fighting to hold back a tart retort. He spun away from her and walked off down the lane, towards the oncoming fire engine.

"Have you got nothing to say?" she shouted after him, aghast, hands pressed her hips.

"Nope."

"Where are you going?"

"To sort out the little shits. They can't get away with this."

She watched him trudge off and suddenly remembered the gas canisters. The fire crew would not know they were there; they would be walking into a trap. *Fuck!*

She ran around the back of the barn and stepped into the burning tack room. A door led to the rear of the barn.

"OK, I can do this." She followed Jack's instructions. She hovered her hands on the door bolt just as he had and channelled the heat through her hands. *Empty, feel, build, and throw.*

Nothing happened. She tried harder, willing and pushing it to work. *Empty, feel, build and fucking throw.*

Nothing.

"For fuck's sake." The more she tried and the more she failed, the more upset she became.

She needed to calm down, reduce her stress, but the flames built around her, and the gas canisters were heating up. She could barely see through the smoke.

She kicked the cylinder. "Come on you bastard!" she shouted.

Nothing.

"OK, calm," she chided. "For fuck's sake...deep breath and feel."

Using all her might to reduce the mounting panic, she closed her eyes and forced herself to relax, to empty her mind, to focus on the heat in her hands and build the energy. Black smoke swirled around her, flames licked her heels.

She scrunched her eyes tight, blocked out the noise, placed her hands on the lock, and just felt. *Empty, feel, build, and throw.*

The lock sprung open. The door burst ajar. Fresh oxygen gushed into the room, fuelling the flames. Elation hit her. She punched the air.

"Yes!" She could do it. Now to roll the canisters out of the barn.

She placed her hands on the first one, closed her eyes, and repeated the mantra. *Empty, feel, build, and throw*

It moved, falling on its side, allowing her to roll the heavy weight out onto the grass, a safe distance from the barn. She went back and did the same to the others.

By the time the firemen had reached the back of the barn, the canisters were safe. She sat on the ground and put her head in her hands.

"Fuck. This job is stressful."

As paramedics lifted the young boy into the back of their ambulance, the lad clutched a white feather in his soot covered hand.

Chapter Forty-Six

Cloud 9

"Another cuppa?" Pyke asked Amy as she arrived back to the Unit. "Well done. Excellent job."

"Yay, I'm getting the hang of this magnetic energy moving thingy, Pyke. Did you see me move those blinkin' canisters, every one of those pesky little buggers?" Amy didn't wait for an answer. "And I luuurve Connor. Can he be my new partner?"

"I wish. He's brilliant, and it's not like him to ask for help. We're honoured. And well done with the canisters. If we ever get to the next level, we won't have to worry about things like that. We'll have a lot more tricks up our sleeve."

"What level? There's another level?"

"Errr... yeah, I'm not supposed to talk about it. But I know it exists."

"What is it?"

"There is another more superior level of consciousness that exists above us. It'll mean we have more powers. I won't have to use this archaic equipment for one."

"Wow! Why don't I know about this?"

"Only a few get through. It's very hush-hush, secret squirrel stuff. I shouldn't have mentioned it. You didn't hear it from me. OK?"

"Does Jack know about it?"

"I guess he does. He deals directly with them from time to time. If he behaves himself, he'll move up for sure. But, I didn't say anything, OK?"

"Yeah, yeah. OK."

"Now, Amy," he said, taking on a more serious tone.

She grimaced, sinking her head into her shoulders. *What have I done now?*

"I need to talk to you about your Twitter account. I didn't realise you'd been quite so vitriolic. You've been freaking a few people out down there."

"Err...aren't we allowed to use our accounts then?" she asked sheepishly, knowing the answer.

"Absolutely not. How can you? You're dead. That would upset people way too much, although it would be nice, I know, to say hello to loved ones, but sorry...no. So, those were all your comments? You weren't hacked?"

"Umm..."

When the door smashed open, they both jumped. Jack strode into the room, shoving the door into the wall as he did so.

"Jack, for gawd's sake," moaned Pyke. "Why don't you just walk through walls like everyone else and quit with the dramatic noisy entrances?"

"Sorry, mon petite cabbage. Force of habit, mate." He gave one of his cheeky smiles and shrugged.

Amy pretended not to notice him. She wanted to rush over and tell him about moving the gas canisters but instead bit her lip and turned away, making excuses she needed to use the washroom.

Helpless, Jack pivoted to observe her departure from the room. He looked back at Pyke and shrugged his shoulders. Pyke wagged a finger and shook his head.

"You've got to sort this out, mate, if you two are going to work together. Or one of you will have to leave."

"Work it out? How? She's not talking to me. I well and truly fucked up."

"I know, and I didn't help. I told her about you and Mara. I was watching."

"Watching what?"

"You two at it like animals on the street."

"For fuck's sake, Pyke. Can you not do that? It was a private moment. I hate it when you watch. Your spying stuff is creepy. And why the hell did you tell her?"

"She's my friend...and I know, so are you...but you can't lie up here, mate. You get caught."

Pyke headed over to a screen and started setting up the next job. Jack followed him, forlorn, head bowed.

"What the hell are you doing with Mara anyway? Anyone can tell you're mad into Amy...everyone but her, that is."

"I don't know." Jack ran his hand through his hair. "I'm a dickhead. It was a goodbye, I guess."

Pyke sniggered. "Goodbye? Are you kidding me? She's toxic, Jack. Something not quite right there."

Mara stood in the doorway listening and gave a little 'I'm here' cough.

Jack and Pyke turned to look at her.

"Awkward," she sneered. "Don't mind me, boys."

Jack closed his eyes at being caught, but Pyke was unrepentant.

"I'm sorry, Mara, but it's true. You and he are toxic, and if you don't sort it out, one of you will have to leave."

"Everyone will be leaving at this rate," muttered Jack.

"It was all working fine until Mara came along. Now no one is talking to each other, Maggie is getting grief from above, and the systems are going down."

"You can't blame everything on me," gasped Mara. Jack and I are friends. No problem there."

"More than just friends," muttered Pyke, typing text into a code box.

"I don't know what you mean?" she said, raising her voice in protest.

"Mara, shut up. He saw us."

"Oh."

"Exactly, oh," repeated Pyke. "What's going on with you, Mara? Why are you hanging around him like a bad smell? Have some self-respect, woman? Surely you want more than a man who sees you as second best, a man who wants someone else. Move on, for heaven's sake. Have some pride. That's my advice."

"Mind your own business, Pyke," she spat. "He loves me and always has."

"No, Mara, I don't. I care, but I don't love you," Jack whispered. "I'm sorry."

Mara stared at him, shaking her head in disbelief. Her eyes pleaded with him to take his words back. "You don't mean that, you always come back to me, you don't mean it."

Jack stepped over to her, placed his hands on her shoulders, stared her in the eye, and said, "I do."

Mara looked up into his face. "You said that on our wedding day."

He dropped his hands to his sides. "I give up." He walked out of the room.

Chapter Forty-Seven

Pacing the corridor, Maggie closed her eyes and shook her head. The bastard had left her no choice. She had to come clean. She finally stood still, slumped back against a wall and looked up to the ceiling, waiting for her call to be put through to the Commander.

"Maggie, what can I do for you?" Micael's warm voice filled her senses.

"I need your help, sir."

"Don't call me sir. Makes me feel old." She could hear the smile in his voice.

"I am afraid I brought some unpleasant business with me when I came over."

"Hey, that's ok. It's what we do...sort the unpleasant stuff."

"This is a lie I kept hidden for decades, and now I've put my Unit in jeopardy."

"What is it?"

"I'd understand if you want me to resign."

"Don't be ridiculous. You have a good heart, Maggie. I'm sure it's nothing we can't sort out."

"A Witness has infiltrated us. He is here because of me, because of my lie. He is going to close my Unit."

"It can't be that bad."

"It is...he's a fucking wanker...oops, sorry."

Micael chuckled.

"I'm sorry," Maggie said, mortified. Swearing in front of the Commander came across as disrespectful.

"No worries, Maggie," he said with a forgiving chuckle. "I've heard worse, and I've certainly dealt with worse than that excuse of a man, Gregori."

"How did you know who I was talking about?"

"Well, I sort of get to hear everything in my position. And the vetting procedure at the gates is pretty thorough. Your 'lie,' as you call it, was highlighted on your arrival, but considered manageable."

"I'm sorry."

"OK, let's start at the beginning, what's happened?"

Chapter Forty-Eight

Alice

Brighton, UK

In the corner of the room, Alice sat with her legs pulled snugly against her chest and cowered with her face resting on her knees. She'd lost all track of time, uncertain if the sun shined brightly outside her room or the moon revealed its crater-like faces. The black-grey light kept her out of touch with what was happening in her normal world.

She tried to blank out the sound of music filtering through the doorframe. The prisoner next door had not been returned. Or had her sense of time deceived her? She could drive herself mad with the constant fretting and predictions of whether she'd be chosen next. She kept asking herself where the prisoner was. Had she been placed in another room? Or worse...had they killed her?

A slight sound broke her self-induced trance. A muffled humming droned faintly at her door. Perfume wafted over her...*his* cologne. Or had she imagined it? Was he wavering outside her door, contemplating whom he'd use as his next toy?

She heard him sing, "Eeny, meeny, miny, moe..."

She held her breath, buried her face, transported herself to another place, a happier place, at home in the kitchen with her mother. In that heart of her memories, a tender roast cooked in the pot and sent aromas swirling in the warm, homey room she'd long to see again. She desperately wanted to embrace her mother and hug her until she begged to be released, but she wouldn't. She'd never let her go. The pot roast smelled so much sweeter than that foul, sick, twisted excuse of a man's cologne stinking outside the door while he sang his taunting, childish tune.

He deserved worse than hell. She hoped he'd suffer in extreme pain and anguish someday the way he'd tormented so many innocent people.

A bolt thudded open.

Lost in her despair, she couldn't tell which one. Her door didn't budge. He'd chosen another. She sighed from relief, but her sigh transformed into a cry, then full-fledged sobbing. With each choice outside her room she knew her luck would run out, her turn was coming.

Soft cries filled the corridor, overshadowing the music. Alice thought it sounded like a young girl begging him not to take her. Or it could be a boy. She wasn't sure what preferences the filthy bastards had. Fear's high pitch transcended gender.

Alice gradually lifted herself off the floor and tiptoed to her door, listening more closely. She heard scuffles in the corridor. The child must have put up a frenzied fight. A pained wailing filled her ears.

"Please, sir...Noooo!"

A grunting sound told Alice the captor struggled to keep control.

She heard a loud slap followed by a heavy thud against her door. Alice jumped back in shock.

Silence. The victim was no longer making a sound.

She squeezed her ear closer to the door and listened, but could hear nothing from the child. Then came the familiar wheelchair's squeaking and humming, grating against the music. The sounds faded as he processed down the corridor, away from her.

Alice threw herself on her bed and screamed into the mattress, low enough so he could not hear her, loud enough to release her frustration. She didn't want to make him angry. She knew too well what would happen if she did that.

As the music stopped, the rest of the imprisoned residents in the corridor could be heard whimpering, begging, praying to their God for help. When would it stop?

Chapter Forty-Nine

Cloud 9

"Would you just piss off. I'm in a meeting."

"No."

Jack sat on the floor outside Amy's locked toilet door.

"You fucked her, Jack. You fucking fucked her."

"I know."

"So, what's that all about? What are you doing here? Shouldn't you be out there with her? The bitch from hell."

"No, I don't want her. I'm sorry. She pushes my buttons. I may have fucked her, but I was crazy stupid. I was thinking of you. I'm always thinking of you."

"Thinking of me... while you're entering another woman. Great. That makes me feel a whole lot better then."

"I know, it sounds bad, but it's not always that simple. Haven't you ever slept with someone and imagined it was someone else."

"Errr, no. Why the hell would I do that? If I'm thinking of someone else I will go with them. Why fuck someone you don't love? This is bollocks."

"In an ideal world, yes. But sometimes it doesn't work out like that. It's not love sex. Its survival sex. People do it all the time."

"What people?"

"Those stuck in unhappy marriages, those too frightened to leave for the sake of the children, money, fear, religion, many reasons. Some people end up having to sleep with people they don't want to. Fantasy helps make it bearable."

"Don't be ridiculous. If you don't fancy them, don't fuck them. Simple."

He raised his voice. "Life is not always that simple. Oh, it's OK for you to say, miss high and bloody mighty. Well aren't you the lucky one to have never been in that situation or been in a controlling relationship, or lived in fear of what your partner will do next, of not knowing how to get out of a bad situation? Sometimes giving them what they want buys you time."

"How do you know so much about it?"

"Because I lived it with Mara, and because I saw my mum go through it. She lived with a drunk. To keep me safe, she let him take what he wanted until we had a chance to get away. She always dreamed of getting away. But by the time I was big enough to help her, she was dead. So, don't give me that shit that fucking is all about love. Sometimes it's about survival."

Amy quietened. "I'm sorry about your mum. What happened?"

"It doesn't matter. I'm not gonna talk about her. We're talking about us. I fucked Mara for all the wrong reasons. I'm sorry, sorry, sorry, sorry...how many more times can I say it?"

"So, if I fucked Pyke, for all the wrong reasons, would that be all right?"

"No. Pyke's different. He wouldn't do that to a girl. He's a lover, not a control freak. And you're not weak enough to let anyone trap you into that sort of coercive behaviour in a relationship."

"And you are? Give me a break. You've killed people for a living. You're not weak."

"Apart from the first few occasions when I thought she was someone she wasn't, every time I fucked her, I dreaded it."

"Why didn't you just leave? I don't believe I'm hearing this. You're well over six foot, you know a hundred and one ways to kill someone. This is the worst excuse for being unfaithful I've ever heard, *'Sorry, she had a hold over me,'* bollocks."

"Cos, she had her talons in me. I got caught up in the guilt, she got me through the bad times, so I owed her. She knew I didn't love her, but I still married her. The one person I wanted, I couldn't have. Mara knew every time I fucked her I thought of that someone, imagined it was her." He ran his hand through his hair.

Amy shook her head. Her silence showed him she didn't understand or didn't want to understand his explanation.

"Look. She was good to me. She got me through a breakdown when I came out of the service. She was there for me, and I owed her. How did I repay her? I used her whilst I thought of you. She knew it, but we never talked about it. We were both in some sort of denial."

Amy put her head in her hands. This was crazy, and she was falling for it. She opened the cubicle door. Jack sat on the floor hunched over. She sat down beside him.

"How could you think of me? We didn't know each other then?"

He looked her in the eyes. "We've always known each other."

He pulled himself up off the ground. "I can't talk here. Let's go outside. I need to tell you something."

She looked up at him. "What you're saying is bullshit. I was weak once, with that arsehole Dick Parker. I was young, but never again would I let anyone do that to me. So, don't you dare say I don't get it, cos I do."

"OK, sorry." He leaned down and pulled her up.

He took her by the hand and led her out of the building. She went willingly, but as they passed the office, she saw Mara's angry face watching them.

He pulled her down to earth where they sat on a park bench in Hyde Park amidst tourists and families chatting and playing in the early evening sun. She forgot how beautiful it was. She'd never taken time to stop and enjoy the park. She'd run through it many a time when alive, her head full of busy, senseless thoughts: What would she wear? What would she eat? What would she say to her boss? Who was gossiping about whom? She mustn't forget to pick up her favourite skirt from the dry cleaners, she must call her mother, put out the rubbish, pay a bill, wax her legs, dye her roots, and place a cool image on social media.

Now it seemed her life had been wasted on worthless goals, selfish dreams, and egotistical desires. It was all much bigger than that, than her. It wasn't about her. It was about survival, and looking out for our home, the planet and everyone on it. She felt small and ashamed.

And she still hadn't learned. She still let a man get to her, let jealousy override her real mission.

They sat in silence, staring out across the lush green park, letting the evening sun warm their faces and the children's playful chatter fill their minds.

Jack reached out to hold her hand. She pulled away, muttering.

"You know what... I've got to go. What we're doing is bigger than us and our drama. It pisses me off that I let you get to me. It was all so easy when I made that deal with God. A little girl doesn't have all this drama, this ego of relationships, of wanting to own someone. To a little girl its black and white, her instincts are intact, she either trusts or she doesn't. Mara and you can have each other. I'm busy."

She stood up and walked away, shouting back over her shoulder.

"Do me a favour, Jack. Don't follow me."

He sat watching her, holding back the words he wanted to say, until she disappeared behind a bank of oak trees.

Chapter Fifty

Mara noticed Jack and Amy leave. Jack had dragged Amy out of the building by the hand. He had never taken Mara by the hand like that, and it pained her to realize it. Oh, he fucked her all right, but she knew it was only out of a sexual need to scratch and itch, out of guilt, of feeling sorry for her. If he closed his eyes, he would feel close to his beloved Amy.

If she could just keep the two of them apart, she could keep him for herself. A small part of him was better than nothing at all.

Pyke watched her from the other side of the room.

"You have to let him go, Mara. Anyone can see they were made for each other. You'll only put yourself through pain the more you wait for him. You are at the end of your life for god's sake. Enjoy what there is left."

"I've told you before, mind your own business, Pyke. He killed her. You know nothing."

"I doubt that, but if he did kill her, doesn't that just prove to you how he feels? Obviously, he did it to bring her here, to join him. He wants to be with her. Can't you see that?"

"Get back to work you two," shouted Maggie from the doorway. "We have more important things to worry about than your love life, Mara. Pyke, where are we on the hack job? Are we back on track?"

"Yep, and I have a backup. It won't cause a problem again. But whoever did it, knows our systems. It was an inside job."

They both looked at Mara.

"Oh, that's great. Blame it on me, why don't you? I don't know the first thing about computers. How would I know how to sabotage them?"

Silence.

Maggie and Pyke continued to stare at her, unbelieving.

She walked out.

Chapter Fifty-One

Kings Road, London, UK

Jack walked through the wall into the bedroom of the small terraced cottage in the Kings Road. Amy stood leaning against a chest of drawers, arms crossed, watching a naked male and female rolling across a double bed in a tight embrace, passionately kissing. Their cloths littered the bed, the floor, and corner armchair, strewn about as if in haste.

"Where the hell have you been? I've been looking everywhere. You've turned your tracker off?"

"I told you not to follow me."

"You cannot turn your tracker off."

"What is it to you?"

"Nothing."

"So why are you here? Shouldn't you be with Mara?"

The couple's passionate groans escalated. The male grabbed at the female's chest as he kissed her forcefully. She winced in pain, but tried not to show it. Instead, she carried on, responding to his kisses with matched fervour, turning her cry of pain into a groan of pleasure. He took the cry as a sign of enjoyment and continued to grind his hand into her chest.

Surreptitiously, the girl kicked her leg, trying to release her panties which had become caught on her ankle, but they stubbornly refused to budge. She kicked harder, but to no avail.

"Oh, for goodness' sake," Amy sighed, uncrossing her arms. She moved closer to the foot of the bed and flicked at the persistent lace, helping the girl out. The knickers flicked across the room, just missing Jack's face.

"Urgh...jeez, Amy." He ducked in time. The knickers landed at his feet.

Amy stepped back to the chest of drawers, leaned against it, crossed her arms and continued to observe the couple. Jack copied suit, lining up beside her, crossing his arms and watching the couple.

"What are we doing?" he asked, feeling awkward.

"Well, I'm just waiting for this guy to come. I don't know what you're doing."

"We have to try and sort this out, Amy. I can't go away." He looked down at the man, who knelt at the bottom of the bed, opened the girl's legs, and proceeded to give her private parts a lot of attention. The girl reached her arms up over her head and groaned with pleasure.

Jack gave Amy a sidelong look of disgust.

"Do we have to be here? This is weird."

"She's faking it," nodded Amy, as the girl's cries reached a crescendo.

Jack scrunched his eyebrows, turned his head to the side, and kept watching.

"I doubt that very much. She sounds as if she's in heaven."

"He's not hitting the spot. She's fed up with his tongue attack. It's getting painful, so she's pretending it's fine to hurry him up."

"You're joking. How are we guys supposed to know? She looks fine to me. I would be very happy if I were he. She's screaming in ecstasy."

"That's not ecstasy. That's excruciating pain. Our little panic buttons are very sensitive, you know."

"Panic button. Is that what you call it? I like it." He grinned. "Why isn't she telling him it hurts?"

"Because women are stupid like that. We don't want to hurt your ego, so we put up with it, and ever so gently move you on to another part of the job."

The girl gave a loud sigh of pleasure, raised her head to smile at the male, and flopped her body back down on the bed, exhausted.

"You see, she's come. She's good."

Amy looked at him and shook her head.

"Bollocks, she came. She just pretended."

The girl eased herself up on her elbows, looked down the beaming male between her legs, who was licking his lips with pride at his prowess. She smiled, and placing both hands on either side of his head, eased him up over her body to bring his mouth to hers in a passionate kiss.

"You would tell me if I wasn't hitting the spot, wouldn't you?" asked Jack, concerned. Nudging Amy gently, seeking reassurance. "You don't fake with me, do you?"

Amy looked at her watch.

"You would tell me, eh?"

Amy ignored him. He crossed his arms in a grump.

"OK, don't," he spat. "You know some women don't know how to suck cock. We boys just have to grin and bear it as well."

She looked sideways at him and smiled to herself. She loved him when he was angry.

"Well, that's not me."

"Huh, how do you know?"

"Cos, you can see it in his eyes. I know."

Jack, smiled and shook his head.

"Grrrr..." Amy growled. "For god's sake, hurry up... I'm bored."

"Bored? What the hell do you mean bored?" Jack raised his hands in exasperation, not enjoying the voyeurism. "This is none of our business. We shouldn't be here. Can we go now? Awkward!"

The girl opened her legs, wrapped them around the male's waist, looked down between them, lined up his cock, and eased herself onto him. Jack put his hands over his face.

"Great!" Amy applauded. "He will be done in a minute and we can go."

"What, dear God, are we waiting for?"

Pyke's voice clicked into Jack's ear. "Where are you Jack? Is Amy with you? I need to have a word with the two of you."

"Errr...not yet." replied Jack, "It's not a good time, mon amie."

Before Jack could warn him, his eye camera clicked on, and Pyke got a full view of their location. A naked couple hammering away on a bed.

"Ooops."

"Told you. Don't ask. Amy will explain later."

"Oooh, who are they?"

"Not now... go."

"OK." Pyke reluctantly switched off.

The couple rolled around the bed, pumping, puffing, sighing, and groaning, the sound of wet clammy skin slapping on wet skin.

"They look like a couple of sweating pigs. We're not as attractive as we think we are when we're doing it, are we?" pondered Amy.

"I guess it does look a little ridiculous." Jack grinned.

The male lover's face turned bright pink as he concentrated on reaching his goal. The girl stared up at him, encouraging..."yes... yes."

"Is he going to come?"

"How the hell do I know?"

"You're a guy. You know what it's like. When he does, we can go."

Jack shook his head, and tried to focus. He stepped closer for a clearer view of the situation. The man's eyes were scrunched shut with concentration, and he was holding his breath.

"Nope, not yet. He's doing the oh-fuck-I-can't-come look."

"What's that?"

"When his concentration is just off, he can't quite reach that place he needs to. Did they have a lot of alcohol beforehand?"

"Yep, a bottle of wine each... Dutch courage."

"That won't help."

The girl reached down and slipped her fingers around the base of her lover's cock as it slid in and out, gently tightening the circle of her grip as he eased in. His gasps became deeper, faster.

"Now is he coming?"

Jack peered in closer. "Well, maybe," he mused, scratching his head. "He's certainly trying."

Jack willed him on. "Come on, my son," he whispered, punching the air.

The male pumped and pumped, but after a few strives, he fell forward with exhaustion, not able to quite reach his climax. He lay his damp wet body over the girl, nuzzling his head into her neck, trying to get his breath. She reached her arms around him and gently patted his back.

"Oh, no... not the consolatory pat on the back. That's so condescending, so not good for the macho ego. He's gonna feel like shit now... a failure. Look, he can't even look at her." Jack, getting involved, ran his hands through his hair, feeling for the man.

"Well, to be honest. He is a failure, Jack. Jeez." Amy shrugged her shoulders. "She's gonna have to do something to get that mojo going again, and fast before it becomes too obvious."

As if hearing Amy, the girl whispered sweet nothings into the man's ear and eased herself from beneath him, off the bed. She walked around to the end of the bed and kneeled on its edge, her arse facing Jack and Amy. Jack shielded his eyes.

"For god's sake, do we have to watch this?" He kept his hand in place over his face.

Falling forward, on all fours, the girl let her knees slide outwards. Her bottom lowered, almost touching the bedcover, sticking up proudly into the air. She wriggled it, waiting for him to join her.

"She looks like a frog."

The male, gaining excitement again, scrambled off the bed and lined himself up behind her, grabbing her bottom with renewed excitement. As he eased his wet cock into her, she groaned with pleasure. He smiled, happy with her reaction. She slid herself up and down his cock, driving him crazy. He couldn't resist. He joined her, building up the rhythm.

"Yes," Jack got involved again. "Ya see? He's gonna be all right. Come on, my son," he cheered.

"About bloody time. I haven't got all day," moaned Amy.

"Err...I think he's gonna come. He likes this," cheered Jack. "I'm not bleeding surprised. She looks pretty hot from this angle."

Amy looked down at Jack's trousers. "Are you getting excited by this?" she asked, spotting a bulge rising beneath his zipper.

Jack snapped his hand to his groin. "No...just being helpful," he mumbled, winking.

Amy nudged him in his ribcage and stepped forward to get a closer look at the humping couple. Their moans built to a crescendo as the bedsprings creaked in unison, the bed's headboard hitting the bedroom wall.

"Oh, yes," cried Jack. "He's gonna come. That's my boy!" He punched the air.

The male bashed his cock hard into the girl, building up the speed.

The girl shouted. "Yes, yes."

Jack shouted, "Yes, yes."

The male couldn't bear it any longer; he pulled out ready for the final thrust. As he lined up mid-air for the final entry, Amy stepped in close, placed her hand between their bodies and gently nudged his penis upward.

His thrusting cock slid up over the crack of her bottom, just as he gave a loud cry of pleasure and came all over her back.

A doorbell rang in the background.

"Ohhhhh nooooo...What did you do that for?" Jack was mortified for the guy. "That is so unfair." Jack shook his head. "No, no, no... you can't do that, that was his moment."

Amy ignored him and wiped her hand on the duvet and straightened up her suit.

"OK, we can go now. Mission accomplished. Let's get out of here."

The doorbell rang again, longer and louder.

The male fell on top of his girl, hot and sweaty. They heaved sighs of relief whilst getting their breath back.

Amy walked out through the bedroom door and downstairs. Jack followed her.

"That was not fair...so not cricket," moaned Jack.

"She's trying for a baby."

"So?"

"She's in the right ovulation cycle."

"So?"

The doorbell went again, longer and louder than before.

"This lady here."

They walked through the front door. An irate female was now shouting and pounding at the door. Amy walked past her down the steps onto the street. Jack ran to catch up.

"She's his wife."

"Ohhh..."

"Yes, ohhh. Now that is not cricket."

"It's still none of our business what people do."

"It is mine. That's my mate, Sally, up there, trying for a baby with a man she thinks will marry her. Her world is about to come crashing down. She has no idea about the family he already has. Bringing an innocent new baby into the mix right now would not be helpful, for the child or her. She will have her baby, but later, with a father who deserves it. I'm just helping her out. Years from now she'll look back and say, 'Thank god I didn't get pregnant with him.'"

Jack scratched his head. "Great! We're in the contraception business now, are we? I'm so not doing that again. Watching people having sex is weird.

But... she *was* hot... not like you hot, but hot." He assumed a playful smile and prodded her in the ribs.

Amy laughed.

"I'm not leaving you, Amy. You can scowl all you like. We're going to work this out. You talk all the rubbish you want about our work here being holy and good, but hey, love is what we are trying to promote. Our bosses won't stop us being loved up. It's what makes the planet tick."

"You fucked someone else. What am I supposed to do with that? If I fucked someone else, it means you weren't enough for me, so I went sniffing elsewhere."

"I fucked someone goodbye. But I get it. So, can we split up over it, and then very quickly start again...like now?"

"What? Don't I even get my goodbye fuck?" She put her arm in his and walked. "Let's walk and talk. You're not getting away with this that easily. Pyke will have to wait."

Chapter Fifty-Two

Sloane Street, London, UK

Jack and Amy walked along a deserted street past shop fronts. It was late evening. Amy checked out the fashion in shop windows, amazed she no longer cared about clothes, handbags, jewellery, considering them all just things, stuff people put so much effort into acquiring, working hard to earn money, fall into debt, succumbing to peer pressure to fit in and be 'cool', trendy, acceptable.

What a waste. She shook her head at her own shallowness. What mattered was the person deep down; actions mattered, not whether you had the latest fashion, bigger boobs, or a drink-tray butt.

"What is it with Mara? What makes her the way she is?" asked Amy.

"Childhood, upbringing, dodgy parenting, and loving someone who doesn't love her back," answered Jack.

"With her airs and graces, I assumed she came from a wealthy family, that she had everything."

"You know as well as I do, not everything is as it seems behind closed doors. She told me once her father regularly abused her mother in front of her, and he encouraged her to watch. He adored his little princess of a child. She wanted for nothing, but he hated her mother, had no respect for her. I think he grew up with an abusive mother and turned into a woman hater because of it. Mara grew up mixing love with abuse, control... it's what she was programmed to be, the needy, controlling type."

"You're a protector type. What made you that way?"

Jack looked at her,

"My mother was hit a lot. I guess I always wanted to keep her safe. Our domestic violence jobs get to me the most. All this suffering in silence reminds me. She put up with it for me, until she could get into a position where we could run away, without my dad getting to us. She was a good woman. I was luckier than most."

"Did she instil that protective thing you have?"

"Yes, and knowing you."

"What is all this knowing me rubbish? I don't get it. We didn't know each other before here."

"Oh, yes we did. We played together as toddlers. Richard Parker...I was with you that day. We were playing football. I kicked the ball into the woods and you followed it in there. I stood waiting for you to come back, but you didn't."

"What?" Aghast, Amy stared at him. "You were that little boy?" She couldn't believe it.

"Yes. Can you forgive me?"

"Don't be ridiculous. We were young. What did we know?"

She stared at him. Was he really the little dark-headed friend with whom she played football, action figures, and cars? Their laughter from long ago filled her mind. Before Dick, they'd known happy days. She hadn't thought about him in all this time. She had always concentrated on Parker.

"I waited and waited, but you didn't come out. I walked home to my mum and tried to tell her what had happened, but she didn't understand. She thought I'd just lost my ball."

He ran his hand through his hair, nervous.

"Sorry I haven't talked about this before. I never saw you again. I would stand outside the woodland, for days afterwards, staring at it, wanting to run in and save you, but I couldn't. I vowed I would grow up and be big and strong, and one day I would come back and save you."

"Ahhhh... that's so sweet."

"Not really. A feeling of worthlessness stayed with me forever. I grew up fighting harder and stronger than anyone else, competitive, stubborn, fearless. I dared things to happen to me because I hadn't saved you. I thought you were dead. Then, in my twenties, I hired an investigator to find out what had happened to the little girl in the woods. He learned you survived, but a little girl the next week had died. I tracked you down, moved to London, lived near you. So, you see? You became my obsession. I followed you, watched over you, all the time."

"What?"

"I became your own little bodyguard. You really did take some risks, Amy. There were more times than I'd care to remember that you travelled home at night and were about to be attacked. You kept me busy."

"You are joking, right? You were stalking me?"

"Think more, a bodyguard that you didn't have to pay."

"Whitney Houston, ahhhh. I loved that movie," she beamed, bursting into song. "And I... will always love you..."

"Ames. I'm trying to be deep here. This is like open heart surgery for me. Do you mind? I've never spoken about this stuff, except to my therapist when I came out of the army."

"And what did your therapist say?"

"That I had to find out if you were dead or alive. If you were dead, he said to visit your grave and talk to you. If you were alive, to track you down and talk to you."

"So why didn't you... talk to me?"

"I couldn't. I tried so many times to pick up the courage but backed out at the last minute. I wrote a letter but never got to send it. I just satisfied my guilt by looking out for you."

She put her hand to her mouth and laughed out loud.

"What?"

"Sorry. But this is soooo sweet... my very own bodyguard watching over me, but," she said, grimacing, "you didn't always watch, did you? I mean, you didn't watch when I had boyfriends, did you?" She propped her hands on her hips, waiting for an answer.

"Yeah, well," he shrugged. "Those moments were difficult. I may have helped a few of your boys leave."

"What?"

"None of them were any good for you. You needed me, but I was too ashamed to contact you, and, unfortunately, I was tied up with Mara by then. She knew how I felt about you. That's how she ended up putting the knife in."

"What a bitch!"

"Yeah, well, I shouldn't have led her on. I used her..." Jack's head swung around, he'd seen something. "Wait here a minute."

He left Amy standing on the pavement as he skipped across the road and walked towards a line of recycle bins.

Amy watched him take something from his pocket and step in behind the bins, out of sight. He then reappeared at her side, continuing their walk. She ran along beside him, trying to keep up.

"What was that about? What's with the rubbish bins?"

"A Veteran," Jack grumbled. "I hate it."

"Hate what? Is he ok?" Amy looked back over her shoulder but couldn't see anyone.

"Well, he would be if our government pulled their socks up and looked after them when they'd done their bit for the country. He's ex SAS. That's a million pounds worth of training right there; leadership, planning, adaptability, loyalty, team building, mental strength, linguist, intelligence gathering, analysis, engineering... the list goes on. With a small amount of retraining and support in the job market, his skills can be adapted for the benefit of all of us, including his getting a roof over his head. It sucks. You risk your life for a country that chucks you out with the rubbish. Why bother?"

"What did you do with him?"

"I gave him dosh. He was out of it. He'll wake up in the morning and find a twenty in his top pocket. He'll eat a hot meal for the next few days, but what about the days after that? He's too proud to beg. It pisses me off. He's not a lazy git who thinks the world owes him. He hasn't sapped benefit monies from the country. On the contrary, he's worked darn hard protecting it for twenty, thirty years...for fuck's sake."

Amy hadn't heard Jack go into a verbal tirade before. She'd never heard him rattle on this much in one go.

"How can we help?" she asked.

"Apart from holding a government at gunpoint until they wake up? I don't know. I do what I can, but my work is just a blip. We'd better get back. Come on."

"Wait, what work?" she asked intrigued.

"Another time," he said, dismissively and hurried ahead of her. "Come on. Let's go."

"But I want to know. Can I help? What can I—"

THE DEAL

Shouts from a nearby alleyway interrupted her. Jack pivoted and followed the noise, Amy behind him. Rounding a corner, they witnessed three youths beating up a homeless man lying on a sheet of cardboard.

Jack stormed over to the youths with his hands planted on his hips, choosing who to work on first. The eldest youth had a can of petrol with him and poured the petrol over the cowering tramp while the three of them laughed and joked. The man begged for mercy. The petrol stung his eyes and spluttered on his mouth.

Amy joined Jack. "Sometimes I hate this job. All we see is evil stuff. Why do humans do this shit to each other. Now they're going to make me do something that's not very nice. And then I'll feel bad. The whole cycle sucks."

"Turn away, if you want. I love this shit."

"Is he a veteran?"

"Don't know. Nor do they. Whoever he is, he's hit hard times. Fuck 'em. They need a taste of their own medicine."

"OK, but..."

"No buts. Get out of here. This is mine."

He pushed Amy around the corner. She went freely.

"I'll call it in," she sighed. "But don't terminate any of them unless Pyke says so...OK? Jack? Give me a minute."

Amy walked around the corner to call Pyke.

The eldest youth placed the petrol can on the ground and dug around in his pockets for a lighter. The middle youth backed up down the alley, staring in part horror, part excitement. The youngest youth bottled it, realising the seriousness of what was about to happen. He shouted at his friend. "No, Dave, no. It's gone far enough, stop."

But Dave laughed him off, enjoying his 'big-I-am' moment.

"What's the matter boys? Scaredy-cats, are we? Get your phones out and start filming. This is gonna go viral."

Jack kicked over the can at Dave's feet, causing petrol to spill onto his shoes.

Dave was too hyped to notice. He'd flicked the lighter and waved it in front of the tramp's face, threatening, teasing, about to set him on fire.

The tramp started to pray, begging for Dave to stop.

253

"Look, mate. He's had enough. Leave him alone." The youngest youth tried to grab the lighter. He lunged at Dave's hand as he tiptoed around the petrol, trying to keep away from it.

"Nah, let's have some fun," Dave sneered, waving the flame in the air.

"This ain't fun no more. Let's go."

"Scaredy-cats, scaredy-cats...pussies the pair of you," spat Dave.

Amy returned to the alley, thankful the boys were still alive.

"We have authority, but not to TM8. Just teach a lesson."

Jack nodded, a little grieved. He was in the mood to terminate. He turned to Dave fending off the youngest youth's attempts to snatch the lighter and gave him a short sharp karate chop to the wrist. The lighter sprung from Dave's hand and fell to the floor.

The youngest youth jumped back. Dave watched in horror as the lighter hit the ground and a burst of flames ignited the petrol, engulfing his feet. He jumped in the air and stamped on the ground, trying to put out the flames, but splashing the petrol made it worse. Flames crept up his trouser legs.

Amy stepped around the chaos and seized the edges of the cardboard while the stunned tramp clung to it. Pulling hard, she dragged him away from the flames further down the alley to safety. The third youth screamed out in panic, running up and down the alley trying to be heard.

"Fire, fire! *Help*...please, someone... *help*."

Neighbouring buildings came alive with lights. Windows flew open with people grabbing their phones to call authorities.

Jack and Amy walked away, leaving two of the youths using their jackets to put out the flames on Dave's back as he crawled on all fours, screaming in agony.

"Who's the 'big-I-am' now, shithead, picking on a guy, three on one, a down and out, beggar in the street?" Jack spat vehement words over his shoulder. "Are you kidding me? What's so clever about that? Fucking bully, these idiots need to be rounded up and sent to war. Then we'll see how fucking big they are."

"Hey, calm down there, soldier. We're supposed to be spreading good karma," giggled Amy, not used to his being so verbal.

"Yeah, well, they can't hear me. I love good karma, and he just got a taste of it."

Chapter Fifty-Three

"Well, he won't be doing that again in a hurry," muttered Jack as that sat on a rooftop, watching the ambulance services wrap the screaming Dave in protective sheeting and place him on a stretcher. "Pussy. He can dish it out but can't take it."

"What is wrong with you tonight?"

"I'm on my period," he grumbled.

"Jeez." She punched him in the shoulder. "When I get Dick Parker, can you be on your period and come help me? He deserves some pissed-off-Jack treatment."

"Don't worry about Richard Parker."

Amy turned to him. "Why? What do you know about him?"

"I went after him not long after I found out about you. He's in jail. He's been there for eight years, but he'll be out soon."

"But he's mine. Why didn't you tell me?"

"Because, then I would have to explain who I was, and I didn't want to lose you. Besides, he's being well sorted in prison. They don't like kiddie-fiddlers in there. A friend of mine is keeping an eye on him for me. When he gets out, he's all yours."

"What friend?"

"A near lost cause I've been given by the boss to try and save. An innocent, a seven year old boy, who was abused by those in power trusted to look after him. A Priest and Headmaster, over a ten year period, systematically turned him into a monster, so I set a monster to babysit a monster. Call it penance."

"What's his name?"

"David, David Howard. You'll love him, everyone does, even though he's a killer, they all want a piece of him. He's a nightmare to watch over, with serious revenge issues, but he's my nightmare."

"You should have told me."

"It was never the right time. We're either at each other's throats or in a war zone. I did try to reach out once; I tried to give you a photograph."

"What photograph?"

"Nothing, you never got to see it. Richard Parker is all yours, but I think you'll see that karma has set in, you may not need to do anything."

They walked along rooftops, their heads down, deep in thought. It'd been a lot to take in.

Amy looked over at Jack. "And the scars on your face? Where did they come from?"

"Richard put up a bit of a fight. He had a blade on him and used it on my face. I underestimated him, ended up in intensive care, and he ended up in court for GBH. When my lawyers gave the police the files I'd sourced on him for child abuse and possession of child images, they sent him down. Add that to the fact he attacked his legal advisor during his interrogation interview, all recorded on tape. He got fifteen years...due out in ten. DC DeAngelo worked my case. He was good. I still keep an eye on him, and sometimes work through him."

He gazed over at Amy.

"These scars are worth it and remind me every day of my paying for doing nothing that day in the woods. I finally did something. They're ugly, but I wear them with pride."

Amy stopped him, wrapped her arms around his neck and kissed him long and hard on the mouth.

"I love you and I love your scars. They're sexy," she whispered, planting tens of kisses up and down his jaw. She'd finally said it. She'd finally told him what she really thought. Tears welled in her eyes. This complex, stubborn man had no idea how much he meant to her.

His outline black against the skyline, Gregori stood on a neighbouring rooftop, silently watching the couple embrace. *Blah de blah, blah de bloody blah.*

Chapter Fifty-Four

Alice

Brighton, UK

A haunting Mozart concerto piped through the corridor, disturbing Alice from her restless sleep. The squeaky wheelchair harmonised with the music. Music that Alice had now grown to despise, the sound had turned her life into a living hell. Once a lover of classical music, if she ever got out alive, she would never be able to listen to it again.

As the chair crawled down the hallway, getting nearer and nearer, panic rose in her belly, shortening her breath and bringing bile to her throat. She heard the squeak stop close by, but not at her door. *Thank God.* Her racing heart slowed.

Sickness tugged at her stomach as she recognized the familiar ritual of the evil bastard unlocking the bolt of his victim's door.

A sharp cry amplified through the corridor, enhancing the constant strident music echoing through the prison. Alice recognised the girl's begging voice as that of the girl they'd fetched earlier. Her pained moans from the abuse she'd endured were a sound Alice knew too well. She placed her hands over her ears to drive out the memory.

Even over her drugged state, the decibels in the girl's agony portrayed her hellish experience, reminding Alice of her time to come. The girl had been brought back alive, at least. Maybe being alive is why she cried. Maybe it was the sound of 'let me die.'

Alice pressed her ear to the door to hear the bastard cajoling the girl, trying to calm her in his charming, snakelike voice. High and excited, he was enjoying every minute. Whatever had occurred, it must have been special. He didn't normally hang around for a debriefing. Could she be one of his favourites?

Alice got back onto her bed and rolled against the wall. Hunger pains made her nauseous, but she'd gladly accept hunger pains over the toy room. Her head ached from dehydration. She willed herself to close her eyes and breathe her last breath.

Since the bastard had a new favourite, Alice wondered if she'd been left to die.

"Angels, if you can hear me, I need your help, please...please."

Chapter Fifty-Five

Cloud 9

Jack and Amy wandered into the office. From a quick visual scan of the room, Pyke appeared to be alone. He stood in concentration before his screen, evaluating the Unit's connections to endless missions. He was aware of their presence but kept his eyes on the screen.

"I'm not going to ask what you two have been up to," Pyke muttered between sweeps of hands across pages of text.

"Don't ask," grumbled Jack, striding over to the kitchen. "Tea anyone?"

"Jack's on his period. He's a little bit tetchy," teased Amy. "But you'll be happy to know we are friends again, Pyke, until the next time."

Pyke conducted a complicated manoeuvre on the screen, hardly listening.

"Oooops!" he cried in mock apology.

"What?" asked Amy, moving to his side.

"Oh dear, I've just pressed a wrong button and eight million Euros has been transferred from Mr. Baldwin's trust fund account to the Children in Need account. How silly of me."

"Who is Mr. Baldwin, and what has he ever done to you?" Jack asked, dunking teabags in three cups with a spoon. He placed the cups on a tray and joined Pyke.

"Oscar Baldwin makes his money selling drugs. Eight million won't make a difference to him, but you know how rich people are. The more they have, the more they want, and the tighter arsed they get about it. It'll do him good to share."

Jack offered the tray to Amy, giving her one of his sexy I'm-gonna-have-you-later grins. She picked up a steaming cup of tea and returned with an in-your-dreams raised brow.

Jack popped a cup of tea in Pyke's spare hand and stood sipping his own, watching Pyke tap a button that sent a scattering of messages across various social media accounts.

"And what are you up to now, Einstein?" he asked.

"Well, I'm trending #ThankYouOscar, before our drug dealing friend finds out about his generous donation. Half the world will have thanked him for his amazing kindness, and his ego won't allow him to chase it up and take it back. Boom!" He punched the air. "We have a double win."

"Is that legal? I mean, OK for us to do?" Asked Amy.

"S'ok, I got authority. But you can talk, little miss vigilante, we need a word," sighed Pyke, turning to face her.

"I don't know what you mean," Amy grimaced, a picture of innocence.

Pyke led her to another screen and ran his hand across its base. Ten windows came up, each with a different newspaper article.

"This," he pointed. "I've been watching a strange phenomenon of paedophiles dying off. It seems to be happening on a regular basis currently, multiple suicides, hangings, shootings, fires, car crashes, drowning, muggings, and the list goes on. Anything to do with you sweat pea?" He raised his eyes at Amy, who shrunk behind her teacup.

"Maybe, but they deserve it. I studied them all before I went in. If I waited for authority, more kids would be abused. Thought I'd take the risk. I didn't want to bother you."

Pyke shook his head.

"And what about you, Jack? Anything to tell me about?"

"Nope." Jack shook his head, another picture of innocence.

"Are you sure?"

"Yep, nothing to declare, Your Honour."

"Then what about this?" Pyke stepped over to the next screen and swiped across a line of icons. Jack gave Amy an '*oh fuck,*' bare-teethed grin behind Pyke's back.

The three of them watched twelve windows open with newspaper articles and headshots of various Erthfolk, beaten or disfigured.

"Well, I've been teaching a few bullies a lesson. Not enough to bother you with, you know, the odd wife beater, rapist, paedophile, drug dealer, pimp... a little touch of karma here and there."

"Don't forget the Presidents, Priests and MP's you've made contact with ..."

"They're the worst, abusing their power, becoming giddy on it... working for their own selfish greed. Besides, they're used to hushing up their embarrassing shit, no one will hear of it."

Pyke tilted his head, patiently waiting for further explanation.

Jack continued. "They're not dead or anything...although, admittedly a few will not look the same or be able to piss in a straight line again, but hey...they're alive."

"The Bosses aren't fools, we've been a little too proactive recently, and we may have been found out." Pyke shook his head. "This is not good. For some reason the Unit is being watched like a hawk at the moment. Someone tried to hack us. It seems they've gathered your files and may be planning to use them against Maggie. Our moonlighting could get us closed down."

"But we're here to dish out karma, protect the weak and all that. Sometimes you can't be all politically correct with these shits. They aren't. So why should we be?" moaned Amy.

"I'm so gonna scratch that onto your tomb stone, Miss Fox." Jack teased in a squeaky voice. "*They don't play by the rules, so why should we.*" Giving the mock-offended Amy a playful punch to the shoulder, she punched right back.

"This is not funny guys." Pyke put his hands on his hips and squared up to Jack. "I also know about your soldier saving mischief. The US, Iraq and Syrian Units are asking questions. You can't go around teleporting tanks away from land mines, or redirecting missiles into the sea. For fucks sake, when do you find the time, do you ever take a rest?"

Jack gave a little boy *'but I can't help it'* shrug.

Pyke shook his head. "I can't keep covering up for you guys. I'm gonna come clean with Maggie. I feel bad. She trusted me to keep an eye on stuff. It was all well and good, going rogue for a while. We got good shit done and our figures were good. But now that someone has the information, they may use it against us. Maggie will have a battle on her hands to keep this place open. If she's gonna win, she needs to know what she's up against. Sorry, guys. We may all be out of a job."

Chapter Fifty-Six

The office door slammed open to the sound of shouting. Jack, Amy, and Pyke all flipped around to determine the source. Pyke quickly closed his screens.

Maggie stormed into the office with Mara following her, yelling and arguing nonstop at each other.

"You're sick," Mara spat. "Why are you trying to blame everything on me? What about your blue-eyed boy? It's OK for Jack to kill Amy, but—"

Maggie lost her cool, spun round, and slapped Mara hard in the face.

Silence.

The room stood quiet, shocked at Maggie's loss of control.

"Jack didn't kill Amy," she whispered. "I did."

Maggie slumped, turned away from Mara, and walked slowly to her desk. Everyone stared in disbelief, the room so quiet one could hear a feather drop. They stared at her, dumbfounded, speechless. She kept her face downward, avoiding eye contact.

Mara rubbed her sore cheek and followed her with narrow eyes.

"What?" Pyke spoke first, shaking his head. "I don't believe you."

"Yes, Pyke, it's a long story." She took a deep breath. "When I was working undercover at MI6, I was tracking a rogue insider, a traitor. He was a manipulative man. I fell in love with him. God help me. I found myself with an unplanned pregnancy, and if caught, I could lose my job. He tried to blackmail me into working with him, using our relationship as a weapon to ruin my career and supply information to adversaries. I came clean to one of my bosses. I was a good recruit; everyone said I showed promise, so he was kind to me." She stepped around her desk and sat down, feeling the weight of what she was about to say.

The team moved slowly to join her. They surrounded her desk, standing in silence. She continued.

"Against the rules, my boss risked his job packing me off to a remote village in Scotland under the guise I was on another undercover job. He said I could give birth to my child, but no one must know... to keep it safe from the traitor. The child was adopted for her own protection. I was allowed to name her, but not know where she was. It nearly broke me to do it, but I had no choice. I feared for my child's life. The traitor was capable of doing anything; he had no soul, no empathy, no moral compass. He wouldn't think twice about killing, even his own child, to get what he wanted."

The four stood in silence, listening to her story, witnessing her pain in telling it. Maggie reached out for Pyke's cup of tea. He gave it gladly. "It's a teabag, I'm afraid, but you're welcome," he offered.

She grabbed it and knocked the soothing drink back on one slurp. Holding the warm cup with two hands, she stared into it, gathering her thoughts. Micael had advised her to be truthful with her Unit, that secrets would only weaken them and prevent strength as a team. Taking a deep breath, she continued.

"I then came back into the fold a year later and carried on with my career. The traitor seemed to have disappeared, but I lived in fear he would come back to haunt me, that he would find out about the child. I need not have worried. Years later, I heard the info I had given about him resulted in his execution. One of the gunrunning regimes he was involved in took him out."

Jack offered her the remnants of his tea. Maggie reached out accepted it with a grateful smile. She knocked it back with another slurp. They waited for her to carry on.

"Losing my child like that has burdened me my entire life. I never had a proper relationship after that. I threw myself into work, being a mother to the child from afar. I kept an eye on her from a distance, kept her safe. When I found out the traitor had died, I just couldn't upset the child's life. By then, she was an adult with great adoptive parents. I kept putting off making contact. Until it was too late."

"After I died, I regretted terribly not telling my child I loved her and was proud of her. When I arrived up here, I found I could still keep an eye out, so it was bearable."

Unable to look her team in the eye, she slowly spun her chair around and faced the window instead. Her eyes followed the swaying field of white clouds. Her voiced cracked as she said, "I was at the train station when Amy died. You were there too, Jack. So was he...the traitor," she whispered.

The boys looked at Amy. Amy's jaw dropped open.

"Are... are you... are you my mother?" she stuttered, pulling her hand to her mouth.

Silence.

"Yes." Tears welled in Maggie's eyes as she watched the white clouds swirl.

Amy took a sharp intake of breath.

"And you pushed me?"

"What a bitch," piped up Mara. "Some mother."

Jack and Pyke shut her down with a stare. The office doors slammed open, and the smell of cigar smoke wafted in as Gregori strode into the room.

"Do tell, Maggie...do tell. Did you push her?"

"Who the hell are you?" asked Amy.

"He's the one who's been following us," sneered Jack. "What are you doing here?"

Maggie turned her chair to face Mara.

"You were there, too, weren't you, Mara."

"No."

"Yes."

"I didn't even know Amy," Mara spluttered.

"Oh, yes you did! After Jack died, you took up a new obsession... following Amy."

Mara stepped back from the table, moving herself away from the other three. All gazes focused on her with suspicion.

Maggie spoke softly, controlled. "I'm the reason Amy died, because I didn't stop you. You stood behind her in the crowd, dressed as an old lady; you pushed her in the back. It all happened too fast for any of us to stop it."

"You bitch!" whispered Amy, glaring at Mara.

When Jack lunged towards her, Pyke grabbed his arm and held him back.

Maggie continued.

"You picked the wrong girl to kill, Mara. Oh yes, I'm happy she's here, but Gregori wants her to go back. He wants me punished. He wants to hurt me, to steal her away from me, cut my precious time with her. He wants her gone. She is in danger here."

Amy shook her head confused.

"So, the bitch is my killer? You are my mother? And the traitor is my father?"

She looked across at Gregori's burning cigar. "You've been following me, haven't you?"

"Yes, dear child. I'm your daddy," he said with a spiteful grin, eyeing her up and down as if appraising her. "I sent lilies to your funeral. Did you like them?"

Jack's strength outdid Pyke's. He broke loose and lunged at Gregori.

"A traitor! I might have known," he spat as Pyke regained his grip and yanked Jack back.

Amy stared, open mouthed, looking from one to the other, her new family. She felt dizzy. This was crazy. Jack shook free of Pyke and grabbed Amy's shoulders. Grateful, she let her weight fall into his body.

"Tell her, Maggie...tell her," sneered Gregori, enjoying the show.

Maggie stood up from her chair and leaned forward on her desk, tears in her eyes.

"You have to leave us, Amy. You can come up here again when I'm gone. But not now, or he will drag you down with him, below earth, and close the Unit. I have to give you up, again."

"She can't leave," offered Jack. "I'll take her place."

Mara gave out a dramatic sigh.

"Oh, for god's sake," she walked over to Gregori and stood beside him. "Daddy, get me out of here. I've had enough of this drivel."

"What?" asked Jack, horrified. "He's your father?"

"Yes, from another hussy I shagged," Gregori bragged. "Women are so easy. I've been the sperm donor for a few kids down there. But Mara is my favourite. It's a shame she had to fall in love with a loser like you, Jack, but for her bad taste in men, I would never have found Amy or Maggie. You brought me right to them. I thank you for that." He shifted to face Maggie.

"And once I discovered your obsessive interest in Amy, I put two and two together...sweet name choice by the way...Rod Stewart's *Maggie May* was one of our favourite songs, I used to sing it to you... remember? Amy is an anagram of May. How quaint. I'm touched. You always were an old romantic, Mags."

Maggie dropped her head. Their love had been heady and all-consuming. She winced at the memory. How could she have ever loved him? Gregori read her mind. He stepped closer. The others parted as he stood at the edge of her desk, looking across at her.

"We were good once, weren't we?" he said softly. "You were my angel for a while." He leaned forward, reaching out his hand to stroke the side of her face. She closed her eyes.

Jack stepped in. "Don't you dare touch her," he bellowed.

Gregori dropped his hand to his side, the moment gone.

"There has to be a way of sorting this out, of coming to an agreement," offered Pyke.

"No agreement. Are you kidding? I've waited for decades for this moment. You shouldn't have told on me, Maggie. I will never forgive you for that. They sliced my face. They did this to me." He thrust his scarred jaw at her.

"They had a lot of fun before they finished me off. Do you want to know what my last words were?" He jutted his head closer to hers, and when she didn't answer, he told her anyway. "I cursed your name. I will not rest until I repay you. Since death isn't an option, taking the things you love is. She's going back. You have two hours."

"You bastard," growled Jack.

"It's not my fault she's here," snapped Gregori. "I didn't know she did the deal. But I suppose she is her mother's daughter. A do-gooder, through and through."

"And what about being a good father? Being a man?" yelled Jack.

"Blah de blah, Jack, blah de bloody blah." Gregori gave a dismissive wave of his hand. "I'm bored now, goodbye."

Gregori grabbed Mara's hand and walked out of the office. A chill swept their ankles as father and daughter left the room.

It suddenly struck Maggie how alike the two were; both tall, striking, dark-haired creatures with piercing black eyes. How did she not see it?

Jack, Pyke, and Amy watched Maggie as she slumped back into her chair and leaned over her desk, her face hidden by her hands as she quietly sobbed.

"I'm so sorry," she whispered.

"What does he mean he'll take me below earth, what is that?" asked Amy.

She leaned on the desk, hovering over Maggie. She was shocked at finding her biological parents, learning that Mara was her stepsister, and that Mara had killed her. It was a lot to take in. Her world had just been tipped upside down.

"...and we're stepsisters... fuck!"

"You don't want to go below earth," muttered Pyke.

"Why, what is it?"

"Well, you know there is a yin and yang to everything. That place is the opposite to here. It's hell. Not good. Trust me."

"Amy, I'm sorry to put you through this. You have to go back."

"But I'm not done here yet. He can't make me go. Surely good wins over evil and all that crap. I can beat him. Isn't that how it goes?"

"No, not always that easy. You must go. You can come back later when it's your right time to die and re-join the Unit then."

"But I don't want to..." She looked at Jack for help. "I want to stay here. Hey, I've just found my mum and a bloke I fancy. Do you know how hard it is to find a good man?" She forced a weak smile, but they were having none of it.

"I'll be here when you come back," muttered Jack.

"I'll make sure his extension request gets accepted," Maggie nodded.

"But it could take years. I could be ninety!"

"I don't care. I'll wait, besides time is nothing here. It'll go in a flash. We'll be OK."

"But I'll be old and ugly by then, and you won't look at me twice."

"Don't be stupid Amy," Jack shook his head. "It's you, your laughter, your wild stubborn energy, the way you make me feel, that I love. I've always loved you. We fit. I like who I am with you. That's all there is to it."

"So, it's all about you," she said. A teasing smile cheered her face.

"I made a pact as a little boy, and I'm gonna keep it."

Amy moved forward to hold him, but he stepped back, placing an outstretched hand between them.

"Don't, don't make this any harder than it is already."

Amy retreated. "This is ridiculous, who the fuck does he think he is bossy us around?" She looked to Maggie.

Pyke saw a light flashing on one of his screens and rushed to check it out.

"And what about you, Maggie? If he gets his way, I won't be able to see you again, get to know my own mother."

"Exactly, that's what he wants."

"He can't do that."

"Look... I've spent precious time with you. I'm grateful for that. I will protect you. I love you. I'm proud of the woman you've become. It's a price I'm willing to pay. Thank you for not moaning about giving you up for adoption. You understand why, don't you?"

"Hey, I can't complain. I had a great life and you gave me that chance. To know you were protecting me from that little shit, and that you gave me the best you could...what's to moan about? Life's way too short...literally." She shrugged. Maggie smiled up at her.

"Hey, look at me being all grown up and philosophical," Amy teased as she walked around the desk and pulled Maggie to her feet. She wrapped her arms around her mother and held her tight.

"Thank you for being my mum. You rock. I'm proud of you. You do have lousy taste in men though. We're gonna have to talk about that... Gregori...I ask you."

She looked across at Pyke, her eyes pleading. "Are there any ways out of this Einstein?"

He shook his head. "I'll need to work on it. At the moment, you have no choice, so do as he asks. It will stall him whilst we find a way to get you back and keep everyone safe." He saw tears build in Amy's eyes. "It's shit, I know, but it may only be for a short time. We'll find a way. Promise."

Amy nodded. "The bastard! OK, but you'd better crack on with it. Don't forget about me stuck down there."

"How could I forget you? You're gonna keep us busy, I'm sure." He looked sheepishly at her. "I'm gonna miss you though...and Jack's gonna be a nightmare."

Lights began to flash on Pyke's screen. He reached over and converted files.

Amy took a deep breath.

"OK, I'll do it, on three provisos. One, you guys work your arses off to find a way to fight Gregori and get me back here ASAP. Two, the three of you will be here when I get back. And three, you let me win the lottery big time. I'm gonna set up child abuse and animal protection charities. It'll keep me busy until I get back. Oh, and four, Dick Parker is mine to deal with. I haven't finished with him yet."

"I haven't even started on him yet," muttered Maggie under her breath.

"What?" asked Amy, straining to hear her.

"It's a deal," agreed Maggie.

"A deal," Pyke seconded.

Jack couldn't stand it, he turned to walk out of the room.

"Hang on a minute, Jack," said Pyke, scanning through pages of text. "Before you go, I've got one last job for the pair of you. Jack, get back here." He tapped out some text and pressed send. "You've just been sent the coordinates. We don't have much time."

Chapter Fifty-Seven

Brighton, UK

With heavy hearts, Jack and Amy walked the length of the luxury penthouse balcony. Neither felt like working. They were too wound up in their own little worlds. This would be their last job together for God knows how long.

Amy couldn't get her head around what was happening. Father or not, she wanted to track Gregori down and kick the shit out of him. And Maggie was her mother, Amy smiled. *Awesome, the woman is uber cool.* And as for Mara...

But right now she had the rest of the team to think about. They needed to play the long game and work something out. For once it was not in her hands, not in her control, it felt uncomfortable. A gust of wind blew her hair off her shoulders and across her face, taking her mind off the madness. She turned to face the view below her.

Eight floors up, the stunning, exclusive apartment overlooked the much-coveted Brighton Beach. The holiday town's usual cheerful atmosphere had been interrupted by a flock of seagulls screeching abnormally loud, as if crying for attention, as they circled overhead.

"They're a little over the top, aren't they?" questioned Amy, staring up into the sky, watching the larger than usual, thug-like gulls as they bombarded the building.

Jack ignored her, lost in thought.

"What's going on with them Jack? They're enormous. What do they feed them on in this part of the world? Steroids?"

"Who?" muttered Jack.

"The seagulls. Look at them. There are zillions of them, with a serious attitude problem. And for some reason, they're concentrating on this building."

Jack looked skyward to see an angry Mike Tyson of-a-bird leave the circling flock, fly directly up high into the clear blue sky, turn and dive bomb the balcony from a great height, its powerful wings tucked tight into its side, its spearhead beak aimed sure and true at the ground near Jack's feet. As it plummeted towards the concrete, at the last minute, it swerved off, screaming abuse into Jack's ear.

"What the hell? Jeez!" Jack instinctively ducked out of the way. The bird couldn't hurt him, but it felt dangerously close. "They're a bit feisty, aren't they?"

"They're trying to get our attention. Something's going on here. At least we know we're in the right place." She surveyed the apartment.

Its wide balcony circled the length and breadth of the building. It had been adapted to form a synthetic running track that ran the circumference of the block. Amy wondered how long a lap would take. *For the man who has everything, an Olympic standard athletic track.*

"He's a doctor, right?" she asked.

"Yep, so his file says." Jack walked from one French window to the next, looking in each room. The apartment seemed empty.

"How can he afford something like this?" Amy peered through windows into the exquisite pristine living area, of state-of-the-art luxury.

White marble floors, white leather furniture, white-framed mirrors, white stone sculptures... everything was white. Even the paintings were white backdrops with a slight wash of pale grey shadows, outlining the form of male and female naked bodies. Something you would find in an art gallery.

"It's a little clinical, like a show house. It doesn't look like anyone lives here, or if they do, they've got serious cleanliness issues."

"Let's go around to the back," barked Jack, irritable. He didn't want to be there, and the kamikaze fighter birds were seriously pissing him off.

"OK, Mister Grumpy, but please cheer up. This is going to be our last job for a while. Let's enjoy it."

"I'm not grumpy. I'm thinking."

"Yeah, well, what'eves, I'm gonna miss you."

She trundled after him as he followed the balcony around a corner and strode the length of its side, his long legs making her run to keep up.

Each windowed wall showed one minimalist white room after another. Kitchen, dining room, three bedrooms, four bathrooms, laundry room, gymnasium, pool room, cinema. They walked the whole circuit. The apartment seemed empty. A pristine white world, unlived in, bleached, soulless, and empty.

Jack tapped his ear.

"Pyke, you sure you've given us the right address?" He stepped in through the glass wall leading to the swimming pool. "There's no one here, except for a bunch of suicidal birds on acid. It's totally empty."

"What birds?" questioned Pyke, confused. "Women? Is it a drugs den?"

"No, the feathered kind, seagulls."

"Seagulls?"

"Yes, seagulls."

"Seagulls?"

"YES FUCKING SEAGULLS!" Shouted Jack, losing his patience. "The kind you find at the beach, SEA... GULLS, for fuck's sake. Pyke, the place is empty."

"OK, OK," soothed Pyke, understanding why Jack would be hacked off. Amy's leaving could break him. "I'll check. Give me a minute."

Pyke could be heard tapping screens, talking to himself. "Now, what have we here?"

Amy trotted along behind Jack, trying to keep up, as he walked out of the pool house, and marched through the centre of the building; passing through walls, furniture, and cupboards, searching the apartment from the inside.

They scanned each room as they passed through. Nothing; no noise, no sign of life, nothing out of place.

Jack stopped in the central reception area by a lift entrance. A Bentley car key fob sat on a lobby side table.

"Yep, that's the right address." Pyke's voice echoed in their ears, confirming the mission.

"What kind of car does he have?"

"A few. His fav at the moment is a new Bentley."

"He's here."

Amy looked to the lift, then looked to the ground.

"Pyke, what's on the floor below? Is it his?" she asked.

Reading each other's minds, Jack and Amy nodded to each other and let their bodies slip down through the marble flooring into the apartment below.

The difference in atmosphere and surroundings shocked them.

The lower floor's temperature felt three or four degrees cooler, cold. Raven black paint coloured every surface. Smoky grey lighting barely illuminated a maze of narrow corridors, each littered with sinister doorways, all closed, bolted on the outside.

"Who owns the next few floors, Pyke?" pressed Jack, impatient.

"Hold on. I'm searching council documents. It seems the same chap does," muttered Pyke. "Yep, he owns the whole building. It's let out as luxury apartments. I'll check the architect's plans and see what's happening on the other floors."

Jack and Amy stepped through a wall into a small, cramped, dark, boxy room. Amy caught her breath. A young girl lay spread out, chained to all four corners of a bed. Her naked body, stretched star-shaped across a grubby excrement-stained mattress, was covered in bruises, small cuts, and what looked like cigarette burns. Amy cupped her hand over her mouth, blocking the stale stench of bodily fluids.

A red cloth protruded from the girl's mouth, gagged. Her head lolled, eyes rolling in a drug-induced stupor. The room was empty but for the bed and a trolley of gleaming hospital instruments. Various blades lay soldier-like in a row, prepped and ready for use. A black lampshade hung over a dull ceiling light bulb, giving the room a cold, grey light.

Jack stepped through the wall into the next room, the same image sickening them, but this time a naked, beaten, teenage boy lay strapped out on his front. Amy followed cautiously; again, she cupped her hand over her mouth.

"What is this place?" she managed to say, stunned.

Anger building, Jack ignored her and pushed through the wall into the next room, and the next, with Amy traipsing unwillingly behind him. A different person occupied each room, all drugged, all naked, all with cut marks on their bodies.

The final two larger rooms housed hospital beds. Four beds lined each wall with patients wired up to machines and solution bags. Barely alive, their bodies deathly still and heavily bandaged, exhibited missing body parts: limbs, eyes, ears. Some were scalped, red skull tissue oozing from gauze dressings.

Amy felt sick, dreading what they would find in the next room. Jack, anger building, kept on walking.

"Right," Pyke's voice chimed in their ears. "The apartments on floors one through five are rented out mainly to wealthy bankers, finance boys, or celebrities. Floors six and seven are empty, and floor eight is his. He wanted two floors below him to be empty for privacy and for noise reasons. I guess if you can afford it, why not?"

"Privacy and noise reduction is not what he's using it for," barked Jack.

He looked to his feet, then up at Amy.

"Are you ready for the sixth floor?"

"Are we capable of vomiting?"

"I don't know, but we're about to find out."

They held hands and fell through the floor together. The contrast again shocked them. They entered an enormous, brightly lit, open warehouse stretching the length and breadth of the block.

No windows offered light from the outside, just bright overhead lighting, white exterior walls, shiny white plastic flooring, glistening chrome shelving, and fittings. Large expanses of thick plastic sheeting hung from the ceiling, partitioning off chunks of floor space. A compact white metal box construction sat in the middle of the room, housing the lift.

Each space showcased its own workplace function, and could see through the plastic walls into the next.

"Jesus, you could fit a couple of small planes in here," muttered Jack.

They stood in the middle of the room and turned in circles, not knowing where to start. They split up and walked in opposite directions through the plastic sheeting, Jack towards a bright light at the southern, seafront end of the floor, Amy toward the back of the room.

Jack traipsed through a storage area lined with glistening chrome fridges, then a packaging area with stacks of plastic containers, bubble wrap, boxes, and tape. He stepped into a kitchen area with enormous melting pots and a pizza-like fire oven, large enough to take a body.

He kept moving through to an open shower area with piles of neatly folded white towels and surgical scrubs, then to a holding area lined with hospital trolleys. Picking up speed, he passed through the final plastic sheet where strong natural light dazed his eyes.

He strode into a large, bright, spectacular room with a panoramic view of the sea. He held his arm up to his face to shield his eyes from the sunlight. Through a wall of floor-to-ceiling windows he gazed out at a very private, magnificent view of the English Channel. No one could look in through the carefully angled windows, apart from a passing helicopter. But Jack assumed the glass had been adapted to see out, but not in.

Jack stood in the middle, spinning around, taking it all in. He clicked his ear.

"Pyke, what did you say he did for a living?"

"A Doctor, Diomedes Buchannan, Dio to his friends. Very good by all accounts, a generous philanthropist and celebrity hag. He has places in London, LA, New York, Durban, Warsaw, and Manila, and is a member of the old boy networks in the City."

"Who called this in?"

"Got a report from a reliable contact in the Polish Unit. Said we need to visit this guy. Why? What have you found?"

"You may want to take a look at this."

"Gawd, I get nervous when you say that, Jack. Tuning in to you is always a nightmare."

Pyke clicked his camera on.

"Fuck, what is it?"

"It's an operating theatre, except he's not saving lives. It appears he's torturing, raping, collecting body parts, killing them, and melting the evidence."

Jack walked around the operating table situated in the middle of the windowed wall. He looked up to see cameras hanging from the ceiling. "I'm guessing he's recording it and making snuff movies."

THE DEAL

The lift door chimed open. Jack turned to see a tall, dark, elegant male in hospital scrubs exit the lift. He clicked a switch panel on the wall and classical music filled the air. He walked away from Jack to the back of the apartment.

Amy entered the room, walking past him as she joined Jack.

"Is that him," she asked, nodding towards the male.

Pyke replied, "Yes, that's our landlord."

"Well, I've checked the north end of the floor. He has cages back there, imprisoning people. They've all been sedated. They're alive, but out of it. There's also a film editing suite and a storage unit with a collection of glass bottles displaying body parts: eyes, fingers, tongues, hearts, feet, genitals, brains, kidneys, foetuses, intestines...it's like a science museum. I haven't gotten sick...yet."

Amy couldn't believe what she was seeing. "What the fuck is all this?"

"He's operating on them. This is his operating theatre," snarled Jack, hands on his hips, surveying the room. "A great view, not something you get on the NHS."

A squeaking sound came from behind them. They turned to see Dio pushing a naked teenage boy strapped in a wheelchair. The skinny, malnourished youth's head slump to one side as his wild eyes jerked from left to right, taking in his surroundings. Conscious at some level, he'd not only been trapped in the chair, he'd been trapped in his own body, unable to move, unable to shout for help.

"It's some sort of date rape drug," suggested Pyke. "They know what's happening but can't react. This poor boy is panicking inside, unable to call out or move."

The Doctor effortlessly lifted the boy's light, emaciated body onto the operating table. He slowly straightened the limbs in readiness for an operation; tilted the head back, flattened the legs and tucked skinny arms against his skeletal hips.

"A lot of refugees, East Europeans, Africans, and Asians are going missing once they hit our shores. This may be where some of them end up," said Pyke. "They are easy pickings because no one knows who or where they are. No one asks any questions if they go missing. Families assume they are in hiding, avoiding authorities."

"OK, so, what do you want us to do? We need cops up here, pronto, before this boy gets cut up. I'd like to burn the whole lot down, but there are victims locked up in rooms on the seventh floor. Can we vacate the building, including those on the first five floors?"

"No, Jack."

"Fuck it. Let's just torch the place,"

"No, no, no...Jack...now calm down," Pyke said, using his soothing voice. "Step back from destruction mode, mate. We need as much evidence as possible for this to succeed in court. No drama here today, Jack, OK? No fires...OK?"

Silence.

"OK? Are you with me, Jack?"

Jack reluctantly nodded his head. He would love nothing more than to burn the rotten hellhole to the ground. He and Amy could get the innocent, tortured, dying victims out.

"Can you tell if there is anyone else involved? Is he working alone?" asked Pyke.

"We haven't seen anyone else. There seems to be a playroom on the seventh floor: beds, sofas, hot tub, the kind of place to hold a sex party. It would fit twenty or thirty people. There may be a lot of forensics to source in there," replied Amy, keeping an eye on Jack as he walked in slow circles around Dio and the boy.

"Have you per chance seen a girl with pink hair, nose piercings, about 25 years old? She's called Alice," asked Pyke, holding his breath.

"Nope. You asked about her before. Still not found her then?" Jack mumbled. "When can we start on this wanker?"

"Yes, actually," interrupted Amy, "there was a girl with pink hair in one of the rooms. She's chained to a bed, barely alive. Why? Do you know her?"

"Sort of," sighed Pyke with relief. "I've been looking for her."

The Doctor started to wash the boy's body, carefully stroking and cleaning every orifice, humming to the sounds of Mozart as he performed his ritual.

Amy walked over to a tray of utensils and eyed the scalpels.

"Well, he can't operate if he's cut his hand or something, can he?" She circled the methodically arranged tray, looking at Jack. "That would buy us time."

Jack nodded and turned away from the table, taking Pyke's eye view with him. He walked towards the lift to keep Pyke preoccupied.

"You can only access the place by lift. There will be passcodes for each floor. If you're going to put in an anonymous call, Pyke, you'll need to give them the info. Otherwise, it will take them an age to work out how to get in."

"Jack, Amy...don't kill him." Pyke's command crossed their ears with an emphatic tone. "We need him to be put under pressure and grass on any others he works with. With any luck, he'll expose international abusers. My guess is he is small game in a bigger picture. He won't want to carry the blame himself. He'll bring others down with him. I'll give the heads-up to the London MET, the US, the Polish, African, and Pilipino Units. Don't let him have access to his laptop, mobile phones, or computers. If he senses he's in trouble, he may trigger something and wipe them, OK, Jack?" asked Pyke. "Jack...Jack, are you listening? No drama, no burning the place down, OK? Just give us time to do this properly, Jack."

Jack stayed silent, his muscles tightening and throbbing. The man was a bastard.

"Did you hear me, Jack?" Pyke's persistence did little to engage Jack's cooperation. "No killing, no damaging evidence; we're on to a very big fish in a very big pond here, Jack...*Jack*?" Pyke screeched loudly in Jack's ear, turning up the volume.

"Yeah, OK, OK," Jack said, wincing in pain. "I get you. You crack on with the calling it in, and we'll protect the crime scene."

Pyke clicked off.

Jack turned to Amy.

"Well, possibly a major VIP abuse gang. Not bad for your last assignment," he smiled weakly.

They stood arms crossed, watching Dio as he finished cleaning the young body. The boy's eyes scanned the room, powerless, trying to work out what would happen next.

Amy walked to the table, leant down, and whispered in the boy's ear.

"Don't worry. It's gonna be OK."

The boy tried in vain to whip his head around. He thought he'd heard something, but no one was there.

Dio stepped over to his surgical trolley and eyed the gleaming array of scalpels, deciding which one to choose. His cock leapt with excitement. He lay his hand on it and gave an encouraging tug. He was so bloody horny.

"I love my life," he whispered to the scalpels. "Now which one of you is gonna be responsible for taking one with me?"

He picked up the largest one and held it to the window, taking a closer look at its blade; the sun shimmered on its gleaming metal.

"Ahhh...you will do, perfect."

"What a cock," ranted Amy, shaking her head. "Come on, Pyke."

Dio, happy with his choice, let his eyes wander to take in the beautiful blue sky and passionate sea glistening behind the scalpel. He stopped and stared at the view for which he'd paid so dearly. His little piece of heaven.

Seagulls circled above his building, squawking in the sunshine. As they caught his eye, he smiled, marvelling at their effortless dips and dives through the blustery sea air. They looked so beautiful with their white feathers glimmering in the sun.

More birds came, and more, circling outside the window. The young boy, lay terrified, watching them. Jack and Amy also stared, mesmerised as more and more birds came; circling, dipping, diving, screeching, shouting abuse at Dio through the window. It was as if they had been an audience to his vile actions before, that they knew the monster's deadly deeds.

Dio made the mistake of laughing at them.

A huge bird dived first, smashing his head into the window and bouncing off, his beak leaving a tiny spec of bloodied saliva on the gleaming glass. Then more and more came. Again and again, beaks smashed into the glass, covering it in red, slushy fluid.

Dio's laughter turned to anger. They'd dirtied his pristine place, ruining his view. He stared at the mess and cursed the birds.

"You bastards! Fuck off! Shoooo...shooo," he threatened, waving his scalpel at the window.

They ignored him. More birds joined in, so many that they blocked out the sky and darkened the room. The birds circled the building. Their calls climaxed into a deafening, screeching orchestra, drowning out the melodic notes of soothing classical music pumping through the apartment. Feathered bodies blocked the sun. The sky transformed into a black veil of thunder, clouds alive and moving. The room chilled.

Dio, incensed, stepped closer to the window, waving the scalpel, shouting, trying to frighten them off.

"Fuck off, you bastards, fuck off."

But the birds continued to swirl, round and round, scraping their bodies, beaks, and claws against the glass, shitting, spitting, hitting his window.

The boy on the table lay transfixed as Dio became angrier and angrier. The wild seagulls shat all over his beautiful balcony.

"Fuck off, you dirty, disgusting creatures."

He slammed his fist angrily against the window, attempting to frighten them off, scalpel still in hand.

"Shhooooo...shooooo, you dirty vermin. Get away from my building."

As he waved his arms in the air, lunging at the window, Amy put her foot out, catching his shoe. He fell to the ground, his full body weight slamming to the cold floor, landing on his right hand, the hand holding the scalpel.

Its slim blade struck deep into the base of his cock, wedged tightly between him and the cold floor. He screamed out in pain.

Amy laughed. "Now you know what it feels like, you bastard."

"Urgh...Amy, is that necessary?" moaned Jack, grabbing his cock in sympathy. "Did you have to cut him there?"

"It's not my fault. It's the birds. He fell."

The screeching abruptly stopped. Amy and Jack looked out the window, the seagulls had dispersed as fast as they had arrived, except for a few stragglers calmly circling as if nothing had happened, letting their agile bodies effortlessly lift and dip in the warm gusts of sea air.

"Mission accomplished, then. Thank you, boys," said Jack, saluting them.

Hearing the click-click of claws on marble, Amy turned to catch Connor standing in the doorway, smiling and panting, his tail slowly wagging from side to side. He gave her a long knowing stare, turned and padded out down the corridor. She watched him leave. *I love that dog.*

As if hearing her, Connor looked back over his shoulder and gave her a nod of the head before disappearing through a plastic wall. She smiled and shouted after him.

"Thank you Connor, the birds did good."

Jack turned to see his furry tail disappear.

"Hey, was that Connor? He's a legend. I've heard about him. You got yourself a new partner already, Ames," he teased.

"He is pretty cool, isn't he? I'll ask him to look after you 'til I get back," she said, leaning over to check on the boy. Jack winced with the jarring reminder of her leaving. Amy caught his flinch and bit her lip. *This is so fucking unfair.*

Turning her attention back to the young boy, she rested her hand on his forehead, instantly calming him. He closed his eyes and his face relaxed with relief. His breathing normalized for the first time in months. Tears filled the corners of his eyes.

"It's OK. You're safe now," whispered Amy. He gave a small smile.

Jack put a call into Pyke.

"Mate, you'd better get the boys in blue here quick if you want Dio to squeal. Amy's just sliced his dick off. He had a hard on at the time, and he's bleeding out."

"What? How the hell did that happen? I thought I told you not to do anything drastic, for god's sake. His balls? Amy!" Pyke sighed, grabbing his own balls in sympathy.

"I know," squirmed Jack. "A Bobbitt cut. She has no respect."

"OK, am on it. They're on their way."

Amy and Jack leaned against the wall, watching the police, ambulance, fire services, and forensic crews arrive. Paramedics patched Dio up in time to survive the deep laceration to his penis.

"He deserved it, hon. If he behaved like a dick, he gets karma via his dick, I say."

Jack smiled, watching a few coppers wincing at the sight of all the blood.

"OK, time to go back. I'm gonna miss you Amy Fox. I love you."

"What did you say?"

"You heard me."

Chapter Fifty-Eight

Cloud 9

"You have to let her go," Maggie followed Jack into the restroom; he was leaning over the sinks, staring into the mirror. She placed a gentle hand on his shoulder.

"I love her, Maggie."

"I know. We both do, and that is exactly why we need to protect her, keep her safe until we work out how to curtail Gregori's threat."

"Can I go with her?"

"Not when she's here under false pretences. A Witness had her killed before her time. There's a clause in our contracts that sends her back."

"That Witness killed me also."

"But Gregori didn't have you killed. Mara did that alone. He'll be able to slime out of blame. At that stage, he hadn't connected the dots to her being mine, but he did have Amy killed. There was intent. He used Mara to kill her, to bring her here before her time. Then he got Mara in here to cause trouble. I don't know how, or if he killed Mara, but she could be sent back also."

"Will Amy remember any of this? Remember us?"

"No, life will carry on as if nothing happened. She won't remember a thing."

"So, I have to watch her from afar and see her live a life without me."

"Yes... until we find a solution. Be strong, Jack, for her, for all of us."

"What about the jobs she's worked on, will they be cancelled?"

"Only the ones she worked on alone. I guess there are a few of those. Pyke will salvage what he can. She wasn't very good at being obedient."

With tears building in her eyes, Maggie turned him towards her, held his face in her hands, and whispered.

"Take her home, Jack."

Chapter Fifty-Nine

Kensington Apartments,
Knightsbridge, London, UK

S tricken with fear, covered in sweat, Amy shocked herself out of her troubled sleep and sat bolt upright in the bed, awakening as if she'd been asleep for weeks. Had she been that tired?

Taking a few deep breaths, she waited for her heart to still and flopped back down on the cool sheets. Relief replaced an underlying fear when she realized she'd only been dreaming, but it had seemed so real, even if she couldn't remember any details about the dream, or what subconscious message she'd conjured up in her sleep. She rolled onto her side, tucked her hand under the pillow, and nuzzled her head into its cool, soft, luxury. With a contented moan, she snuggled deeper under the duvet and dozed. *It was just a dream.*

The duvet's warmth began to stifle her. She extended her leg, poking her foot out from underneath the covers where it hung over the edge of the mattress and enjoyed the morning's scintillating rush of chilled air...until her toes brushed against something. *Shit, what was that?*

It felt like a leg, a hairy leg? *Fuck, I'm not alone.*

Her eyes flashed open. She held her breath; keeping very still as panicked senses searched her surroundings. Curtains sealed the room in darkness, shadowing a chaise lounge angled in front of the window. *Is that my handbag on the chaise lounge? Are those my clothes strewn across the floor?*

A black-faced digital alarm clock with large white flashing numbers beamed across at her from the bedside table, its bright light burning her eyes. 08.19 hours. *Shit, I should be on my way to the office.*

Closing her eyes, she listened for sounds, something to help her get her bearings. The way traffic buzzed outside the window, it had to be morning rush hour, which was good. That meant she was in the city, not in the middle of nowhere. Her ears then detected the soft rise and fall of deep breathing and presumed it came from the leg's owner, still in a state of slumber. Not good; that meant she'd been sleeping next to someone, sharing someone else's bed. *Fuck, fuck, fuck! I don't even remember... I'm too old for this.*

When she lifted her head off the pillow, a blistering headache hit home, piercing the back of her eyes. *Urrgh! How much did I have to drink?*

The office parties were renowned for their mayhem. She didn't recall hooking up with anyone, where she'd been, or how she'd arrived in this strange place. Peering over the duvet toward the end of the bed, she glimpsed at light seeping through a doorframe, outlining her exit point.

She remained very static, trying not to waken whoever lay next to her. Her head ached, as jumbled images shifted like puzzle pieces from the previous night's proceedings.

The party had started with shots. *Never a good start.*

Blotchy flashes from her memory and sound-bites teased her brain. She'd been drinking, pub crawling, singing, table-dancing, and manhandling someone in the back of a taxi. *But whom?*

Her head thudded with dehydration. She needed to find water and to get out of there.

Slinking under the duvet, she slid silently to the floor. Naked and on all fours, she crawled around the king-size bed, her knees burning on lush thick-piled carpet. Creeping towards the door, she gathered her belongings; underwear, clothes, bag, shoes.

She peered over the bed, trying to make out the leg owner's identity. But whoever the stranger was, the body lay prone, covered in a sea of blue and white striped duvet, the person's head tucked underneath pillows, as if trying to block out sound.

Nervously, she braved getting to her feet, and tiptoed to the door. With painstaking quiet, she eased open the handle.

"Sneaking off without saying goodbye?" came a deep husky voice from beneath the duvet.

"Errr, sorry, I didn't want to wake you. I've got to get to the office."

"That must have been some dream you had...tossing and turning all night."

"Errr...sorry," Amy paused in the open doorway, trying to cover her body with her bag and clothes. "I didn't mean to wake you."

A tussled blonde head peaked out from beneath the duvet, beaming at her. Her heart sank. She didn't recognise him. *Oh fuck, a stranger.*

"Errr... did we..."

"Yes," his blue eyes twinkled.

"Did anyone see us?"

"Yes, the whole office saw us leave together."

"Shit... sorry, I mean..."

"Don't worry, this won't affect work."

"What do you mean?"

"You don't remember?" he said, raising a cheeky eyebrow, grinning from ear to ear.

"Errr... no." She felt queasier by the second.

"Well, err, your boss introduced me to you last night. Remember? I'm a new client? You guys are running the marketing campaign for my new Jeans line. But I'll have a word with him, if you're worried about it."

"And then?"

"And then you took me home and ravaged me," he said, a smile taking the sleepy look off his face. "Now come to bed. We've got unfinished business." He pulled back the bed clothes exposing his naked, very excited, very toned, very beautiful body. *Oh fuck, he's gorgeous.*

Amy stood in the doorway, hovering between being good or being bad. How much did she want her job anyway?

He pulled a handful of condoms from beneath his pillow and held them out her.

"I've got chocolate flavour... what can go wrong?" He beamed up at her with his striking blue eyes and defining dimples. She could detect no wedding ring...and she could get another job. After the weird nightmare she'd just had, for some reason she decided life was for living and had newfound gratitude for being alive.

"Chocolate... well that seals the deal, coffee and I would've been outta here," she giggled, relenting. She stepped back into the room, dropped her clothing to the floor, and let the door close behind her.

Naked, she stood at the end of the bed, hands on her hips.

"But first I think I ought to know your name."

"Mr. Smythson."

"Mr. Smythson," she recited, mimicking his upper crust accent. "That's a little formal, don't you think?" She tilted her head. "Do you have a Christian name?"

"I'm not a Christian." His eyes glinted.

"A first name?"

"James... James Smythson...but you can call me Jim."

"Well, James," she purred, leaning onto the bed and crawling on all fours over his body. "I think I'll call you Jimbo. I like Jimbo. Is that OK?" She giggled as she straddled his hips and leaned in to kiss him.

"Oh, yes," he mumbled through smothering kisses. "But not in the office."

"Don't worry. I may well be out of a job."

Playfully, he threw her onto her side. Giggling, they rolled across the bed. *I love my life.*

Chapter Sixty

The apartment's front door swung open. Amy and James fell against the doorframe, wrapped around each other, snogging heavily. Amy could barely breathe and had to ease herself out of his grip to move into the hallway. He looked stunningly attractive with that tousled blonde hair and those sleepy blue eyes, a towel wrapped around his muscle-sculpted waist.

Apart from shoulders, her favourite muscles on a man were the ones that crawled seductively around the top of his hip bone, leading down to his privates. A directional sign post to heaven. He had those muscles, sneaking down into his towel. *What are they called, oblique's?*

She, dishevelled, quickly smoothed down last night's clothing, and gripped his shoulder for support as she stood flamingo-esque, trying to slip her feet into tight stilettos.

"Stay, I've run out of chocolate, but I still have banana." He snuggled against her ear, nibbling her lobe, licking her neck.

"Don't." His touch made her giggle. "Stop that. It drives me crazy when someone does that. I'm going to fall over. These shoes are killing me."

She swapped hands on his shoulder, and balancing as best she could, squeezed her foot into the other stiletto. He continued to stroke her neck. She couldn't concentrate.

"Stop," she pleaded, wobbling, stamping her feet to push them into her shoes.

"I want more." He grinned, his roguish dimples denting his cheeks with mischief. He pulled her to him and thrust his tongue into her mouth. His hands travelled her body, kneading her breasts and cupping her buttocks.

She gave an almighty push. "Stop," she shouted, holding him at arm's length, getting her breath back.

"Look, I promise I'll call you later. I have to go...before my boss has a hernia."

He put on a grumpy baby-face look, and peered up at her through knotted eyebrows, his arms held at his sides like the little boy who'd just been told off.

"Don't worry about your boss. I'll sort it. I told you," he simpered.

A newspaper had been left on the floor outside his door. When he bent to pick it up and slip it under his arm, his towel fell to the ground, exposing his proud hard cock. He grinned at her all innocent.

She put her hand to her forehead and giggled. "Oh, my god. Could you please put that thing away? This is hard enough as it is," she said, turning away from him, before she succumbed and ran back into the bedroom. *Urrgh! Why can't it be a Sunday?*

He smiled, pleased with her reaction, giving his cock a little manhandle, springing it more into life. He waited a few seconds before picking up his towel and hanging it on the end of his proud penis, as if on a coat hook. She laughed. He looked ridiculous.

"What if someone comes?" she looked nervously along the corridor, whilst ushering him into his apartment.

"Oh, I intend to."

She gave him a school ma'am raised eyebrow, and he relented.

"OK, OK. But later, yes?"

"Yes, yes, now go," she pointed into his apartment. Standing well back so he couldn't grab her.

"Call me." He mimicked holding a phone to his ear.

"Yes, yes... oh, my name is Amy by the way." She giggled again.

He moved forward to give her another kiss.

"No," she put her hand out, pressing two fingers against his lips, and scurried backwards, keeping him at arm's length. "No more."

She walked backwards down the corridor, watching him as she left, taking in the sights, enjoying his beautiful body and handsome smiling face. *Wow, good God, he's delish.*

She didn't see the tall dark shape standing behind him, didn't notice the shadow turn and place its head in its hands, didn't see the pain in Jack's face as James closed the door and let her go.

James chucked the newspaper on the hall table, flicked the television on to a news channel, and scurried to the bedroom, whistling as he went.

Chapter Sixty-One

A my walked down the corridor, hearing his door close behind her, and gave a little punch in the air. *Yes! Oh my god, oh my god, he's gorge.*

She had the choice of using the circular staircase spiralling around the central lift or taking the lift. With her shoes squeezing tight, she hobbled over to the lift and pressed the button. *Urrgh, must have done a lot of dancing last night. My feet are killing me.*

Stepping into the lift, she pressed the button for the ground floor and leaned back against one of the mirrored walls, her bedraggled image shone back at her from the opposite wall. As the lift descended, she quickly licked her fingers, and used them to wipe away mascara smears from her cheeks. She smoothed down her dishevelled hair and crumpled dress.

As the doors opened onto the reception area's opulent marble floor, she felt a faint vibration ringing in her bag. Her phone was on silent. She dipped into her bag and pulled it out. Sally's name lit up.

She answered the phone and squealed.

"Sal, I've just met the most amazing man. Oh, my god, oh my god, oh my god," she squealed again.

Sally's delightful squeal shrieked out of the phone as Amy performed a little stamp-foot rain dance in front of the lift's closing doors. The reception security guard looked over and smiled. She glanced up, saw him staring and mouthed a sheepish "sorry," as she sprinted past his reception desk to the front double doors, giving him a little wave. Four Policemen barged past her; she stood back, giving them the right-of-way.

"Excuse me, miss," an Officer said, glancing over his shoulder and giving her an appreciative grin of approval. Amy blushed. Was it that obvious she had been at it all night?

The Officer joined his colleagues pooling at to the reception desk. Amy saw one of the men pass the bemused guard a piece of paper.

"We have a warrant to search Dio Buchannan's apartment. Do you have a visitor's book? How long does your CCTV keep for? We need copies of whatever you have." Another Officer reached over and gave the guard a mobile phone, saying "DC DeAngelo would like to speak to you sir."

She didn't bother to wait and see what the fuss was about; her boss would be going crazy. She skipped out onto the street, skirted around the badly parked police cars, and speed walked towards the tube train station, ignoring her aching feet.

Watching her from the apartment window, Jack took a deep breath, closed his eyes, put his hands to the side of his forehead and massaged his temples. It broke him to see her with another man, he felt sick. With a heavy heart, he walked towards the door. James could be heard singing in the shower.

He couldn't bear it. This man would now be a part of her life, hold her the way he wanted, make love to her the way he had. And she didn't remember a thing about him, about their time together. She didn't know he existed.

"For fuck's sake." He threw a punch at the door with such force it threw him back across the room. Blood seeped from his knuckles. The pain made him feel alive.

He leaned on the hallway table to catch his breath. A newspaper lay open, showing the main storyline. With bloodied fingers, he wiped his hand against the front page to flatten out the creases. He bent to read it.

Their tramp-burning job had been reported. Demands for the government to increase the funding for shelter projects had been issued. He sighed. All this good work and she wouldn't remember a thing, and wouldn't have the slightest idea she'd played a key role in exposing the bastards they dealt with.

A female presenter shouted with animation from the television screen. He turned to look at what the commotion was about. He held his bloodied hand as he stood quietly and watched filmed images of Dio Buchannan being stretchered to an ambulance. The reporter talked loudly over noisy sirens and squawking seagulls.

"An international VIP abuse scandal has been discovered in the home of a doctor in Brighton, West Sussex. Twenty-five victims and twelve bodies have been removed from the property. It is reported that, at this stage, Officers are investigating his connections to eighteen MP's, three Crown Court Judges, a Bishop, and six Hollywood stars."

Outside Dio's apartment, a Police Liaison Officer, who had positioned himself on a stand behind a row of microphones, faced a barrage of sporadic flashing lights, cameras and questions.

"Investigations are ongoing. We are working with other forces, searching further premises in London, LA, New York, Durban, Warsaw, and Manila. We believe this is just the tip of the iceberg."

"We did good, Amy," Jack said, sighing, wishing he could talk to her.

He turned to hear raised voices outside the apartment. Police were shouting orders back and forth in the communal hallway. He walked through the wall and watched as armed Officers searched the corridor and ran up the stairway to the penthouse above, he heard the name Dio Buchanan mentioned. Pyke had obviously managed to forward intel. The relevant Authorities had been dispatched to ransack all Dio's addresses. Jack touched his ear to connect with Pyke.

"I'm at Amy's return point. Did you know before she came to us she'd spent her last night in an apartment block where Dio had a place?"

"No, but Gregori organised that death, so nothing surprises me."

"We should have dropped her back in another time layer. Weeks in the skies can be nanoseconds on earth. Or maybe we should have waited a bit until the Dio saga was over. I don't like it. She may have landed in a nightmare. She's hitching up with a guy who lives a few floors beneath Dio, James Smythson. Will you check him out for me?"

"On it, mon petit chou."

"Check out who her boss is as well, will you. They're connected."

"Are you OK, Jack?" Pyke asked, softly. "You know it's OK to take some time off if you need it."

"No, that's the last thing I need...time to think. That'd be worse. Besides, we've got a job on our hands getting Amy back with us."

"Maggie is a bit broken up. Can you give her one or your charm offensive cuddles when you get here?"

"Yes, as long as she doesn't start crying. I'm not good with the crying thing." Jack hesitated.

"Hey, in another world, she may have ended up being your mother in law," Pyke giggled. "I didn't see that one coming."

"Me neither, but that would've been cool. She's one special lady," Jack smiled, Pyke always had a way of calming him. "Pyke, are you allowed to extend your stay and wait with me for Amy? It could be a long haul, and as much as it pains me to admit it, I may need your help to get me through it."

"Sorted, my friend. Maggie's getting me an extension with you. Besides, I'm waiting for Alice. Now that you've saved her from Dio, she could up here one day, she's the type to have requested the deal."

"What are we like...a couple of old romantics?"

"Do you realise we talk more on these calls than in person."

"I guess it's a man thing."

"I love you, Jack."

Silence.

"Did you hear me? I love you," Pyke persisted.

Silence.

"I'm going now," Jack replied curtly. "This is getting awkward."

"But I love you."

"Stop with the Brokeback Mountain shit."

He could hear Pyke chuckle.

"But I lo..."

"Shut the fuck up, you moron, and put the kettle on," he grinned, clicking the call off, glad Pyke would be waiting with him. *The little shit will get me through this.*

Jack exited the building and trudged out onto the street, passing the mounting number of police cars and vans. He spotted Amy's blonde head amongst the scurrying pedestrians heading for the tube station. She suddenly stopped and turned. Something had caught her attention. Momentarily, he wondered if she could see him, if she remembered him and would come running into his arms. He caught his breath and waited, staring at her.

But no.

She was looking up into the air, watching a tiny white feather cascade to the ground, tumbling and twisting through the air. She reached out with a cupped hand and caught it. She looked up to the sky and smiled, popped it in her pocket, and stepped into the station entrance, becoming lost in the crowd.

He didn't follow her.

He let her go.

"Later's babe."

Chapter Sixty-Two

James stepped out of his invigorating shower and heard a disturbance coming from the corridor outside his apartment. He wrapped a towel around his waist, opened his front door, and peered into the hallway. *What the hell?*

Armed Police lined the hallway. Forensic teams scurried up and down the communal stairway. Those coming up were puffing with exhaustion. Those going down carried sealed forensics bags, boxes, and computer equipment. One Police Officer caught his eye, running down the stairs, clutching four bulging paper bags in each hand. The word Exhibit had been stamped across them in red ink.

"Please go back into your apartment, sir, until we are finished."

"What's going on?" asked James, eyeing the passing traffic.

"They closed down the lift. We have to walk."

"No, I mean, why are you here?"

"We have a warrant to search one of the premises above you, sir."

"Dio Buchannan's place?"

"Yes, do you know him?"

"I've seen him in the lobby a few times, but that's about it. What's happened? Is he all right?"

"We will be sending Officers to conduct house to house enquiries; they will be contacting you in a short while to ask a few questions. Please make yourself available to them, sir."

"Yes, yes, of course. But what's happened? Is he ok? Has he done something?"

"For the moment, we're not allowed to discuss details with you as we are conducting an ongoing investigation. But if you could be of help, it would be much appreciated. Even the smallest, seemingly insignificant piece of information can be valuable in an investigation. Meanwhile, it's best you stay inside your apartment for the time being. I'll be on my way. Thank you, sir."

"Yes, yes, of course. Thank you, Officer."

"One more thing. We may be asking for DNA swabs from residents in the block, to delete them from our enquiries. It's painless and shouldn't take long."

"OK, if it's necessary."

"And why did you know we were looking at Mr Buchanan's apartment?"

"Err... I... err... heard his name mentioned on the news channel."

"Thank you sir."

James closed his door and leaned back hard against it, thinking for a moment before he reached for his phone.

Chapter Sixty-Three

Foxtrot Union Bar,
Kensington, London, UK

"You're late," chided Sally as Amy plonked herself down on the bar stool.

Sally had already ordered. A large glass of cool white wine awaited Amy. She dumped her bag on the floor and grabbed at it hungrily.

"God, do I need this," she whispered, flashing Sally a look of gratitude.

The cool liquid filled her mouth and soothed her throat as she swallowed back the first sip. She let her body stop for a few seconds whilst she calmed. Sally waited patiently for her to relax.

"And breathe," she said softly, eager for her friend to fill her in on the night's excursions.

Being a couple of old romantics, they didn't shag around. Nights of naughtiness didn't happen often, and every delicious detail needed to be gone over and savoured. For Amy to have spent the night with a guy, he must have been uber gorgeous, uber charming, witty, and intelligent, with a cheeky touch of naughty rogue.

The two girls sat at the bar of their favourite Kensington drinking haunt, the 'Foxtrot Union Bar'. It was equidistant from their offices and a convenient meeting destination on their way home. Not too pretentious, it didn't have many hooray henrys lording it about. The staff were welcoming and the owner often treated them to a complimentary glass or two. They were beautiful women, and beautiful women attracted men who spent money.

"Well?"

"Oh, my god, Sal. He's gorgeous, tall, blonde, blue-eyed, and perfectly put together. And he's got those V shaped muscle things going on, that I like." She drew a large V in the air, with her two pointed index fingers falling and meeting at a point. "You know."

"Urrghhhh, I'm well, jel." Giggled Sally. "That's brilliant. About time you got laid, and out of your dry patch. It's good to see you all sparkly. Does he have any good-looking friends?" she asked with a hopeful glint in her eye.

"I've got to get you a Rose Quartz. It's your turn to get loved up," replied Amy. "You can pop it in your bra."

"Shuuuut upppp about the blinkin' stones, for god's sake. I'll sort myself out." Sally nudged Amy in the ribs.

"Sorry, I'm late. The boss was not that happy. I arrived two hours late this morning. But I think James—"

Sally interrupted. "Is that lover boy's name?"

"Yep, James."

"Very posh."

"James Smythson."

"Oh dear, Amy Smythson. You'll sound like a headmistress. Very la de da," mimicked Sally in her snootiest of accents.

"He's not anal like that. He's quite sweet, really. No airs and graces. I think he put it right with the boss for me. Cos whatever he said, it wasn't mentioned. I just cracked on with my work and the boss left me alone. The rest of the office grilled me, though. They saw me leave the party with him. Velma isn't talking to me."

"She always has been a bit funny, that girl," Sal replied, shaking her head. "Do you remember when she followed you home from the office, an hour out of her way, to give you a pen you'd dropped on your way out of reception? Weird."

The girls chatted for hours. They ordered a few dips, some olives, and pitta bread, and munched on the tasty snacks while dissecting the previous night's events. The bar owner sent them a free large glass of vino, which kept them there another spell. They agreed that Sally would do some stalking work on James, a bit of google research to check him out. Amy felt bad about doing it herself, but someone else doing it for her seemed less sordid, desperate, stalker-esque.

"So, how's you?" asked Amy. It was Sal's turn to have her life put to rights.

"Oh, same old, same old. Dartagnia's getting on my tits still. I'm seriously thinking of leaving. She has her nails well and truly into the boss. It's embarrassing."

"You can't leave, Sal. Speak to your boss about it."

"Can't. He's blinded to her and can't see her doing anything wrong. He's led by his cock."

"What about his wife?"

"She joins them."

"Ohhh! What about Dartagnia's husband?"

"He's invited."

"Bloody hell does anyone do any work in that office?" Amy took a sip of her drink.

"Maybe I should join in with them," pondered Sally. "I might get promotion." She shook her head and scrunched her face at the thought of it. "Nah. Second thoughts. I so couldn't go anywhere near the bitch. I'd gag."

"Have you been with a woman before?" asked Amy.

"No."

"Me neither."

"It's on my bucket list to try, though. Just not with Dartagnia. Urrgh! Surely the boss should just promote me for my good work, for my sales figures, not whether I give good head or not," whined Sally.

"What's her work like? Is she any good?"

"Well, she is good. Seems to know everything, but she doesn't have people skills. She thrusts her knowledge down people's throats, so they back off. She loves stirring up trouble and dumping people in the shit, so no one trusts her. And if we do a good job, she takes the credit. Fuck! Don't get me started."

At the end of the bar Jack nursed a tumbler of whiskey, watching them as they sat there oblivious to his presence. He nudged his half empty whiskey bottle aside to make room for his elbows, and cradled his face in his hands, watching his love carry on without him, enjoying life.

He'd followed Amy all day. He couldn't leave. Nor could he give her up. Hearing her talk about Smythson with giddiness and enchantment made his skin crawl. But she had done nothing wrong. She couldn't remember anything they'd done together or anything about her time in the sky on Cloud 9. How could she be unfaithful when he didn't exist?

Jack saw a dark figure standing at the other end of the long bar. He had unwanted company. Gregori beamed back at him.

"Fuck." Jack hissed under his breath.

The evil creature was spying on Amy and her friend. *How dare he, the bastard*? Jack would like nothing more than to dispose of the rancid knob-end once and for all.

"I thought I could smell something rotten. What the fuck are you doing here?" Jack shouted across the room. No one could hear him except Gregori.

"Just keeping an eye on my daughter, making sure Maggie keeps her promise."

"You can see she has, so you can fuck off. Crawl back under your rock, daddy dearest," he spat, knocking back his whiskey. "What kind of father are you anyway?" He slammed the empty glass on the bar.

"Well, at least I've fathered something. More than you can say, you dear barren boy."

Gregori hopped off his bar stool and sauntered along the bar, passing drinkers, walking slowly towards Amy and Sal while the bartender replenished their drinks. They were smiling and chatty, slightly tipsy, oblivious to the volcanic energy in the room.

"Get away from her." Jack snapped, flying off his stool to intercept Gregori face-to-face.

"What? You afraid I'm going to hurt her? Have her killed like last time?"

"You? Get your hands dirty? We all know you get others to do your dirty work. Men like you are cowards, traitors."

Jack looked around nervously, searching for Mara, wondering if Gregori had brought his evil daughter with him.

"I will kill her. But this time I'll take her straight down with me. There'll be no sitting on a cloud doing good shit."

"Except you conveniently forget one thing. She made the deal."

"Ahhh, but all I have to do is encourage her to do something really bad. And poof! The deal will be void."

"Bollocks. Shows you don't know a damn thing about your daughter. She's not that kind of girl."

"Don't bet on it. She is my daughter after all."

Gregori continued to strut along the bar, smelling the air as he neared Amy, enjoying her presence.

"She smells of lilies, and I love lilies."

When he'd reached her, he put his hand on her chair, leaned between the two tipsy women, and listened to their chitter-chatter. He pulled his cigar up to his mouth and drew in. "You might as well forget her, Romeo. She's got a new lover now. She's no longer yours. I've made sure of that."

"You're delusional." Jack smirked with disgust.

Gregori leaned in close to the back of Amy's neck and blew a line of cigar smoke across her skin.

"She's mine, get over it Jack." He started to sing the Rolling Stones track... *'you can't always get what you want...'*

"Shut the fuck up." Spat Jack.

Amy gazed up into the long mirror behind the bar, to see if someone was lingering close behind her, but she saw no one, just a group of patrons a few feet away, engaged in a heated conversation. She was sure she felt a breeze across her neck. She rubbed the hairline at her collar, maybe the alcohol had made her skin tingle.

She shivered and giggled. "Ohhhh, someone just walked over my grave."

Jack clocked her reaction, just for a split second, or had he imagined it? Had she sensed Gregori's presence? Had she felt something? No, surely not. How could she have sensed Gregori, yet not him?

Gregori stepped away from Amy and returned to his end of the bar. Calmly, he sipped his drink, never taking his gaze off his daughter.

"Be assured, Jack. She belongs to me. I will kill her when the time's right."

Jack stomped back to his empty glass, topped it up from the bottle, and knocked back another drink.

"Drinking's not going to help," Gregori scoffed.

"You know it's fictional. It has no effect."

"On the contrary. You're relying on old habits to numb your feelings. It affects you. Mark my words. Poor Jack, no one to play with," he spat sarcastically.

Jack had had enough. He jumped onto the bar and launched himself across the room, flying over the barman's head and landing in front of a shocked Gregori.

Gregori backed up, knocking over a nearby bar stool. A heart-stopping blast reverberated as it crashed to the floor, drawing people's attention to a stool rolling on the floor for no apparent reason. Someone rescued it and placed it upright. The crowd resumed their drinking and chattering, unaware of the antics occurring around them.

Jack hopped off the bar and landed on Gregori. The two men rolled around the floor, punching, kicking, strangling, throwing each other across tables, chairs, and people. They fought with unrelenting force, neither willing to surrender.

Amy, giggling at Sally's comment about finally getting through her dry patch, lost her amusement for a moment, as she felt the room's energy shift. As Jack and Gregori smashed each other against a far wall, she sensed something out of kilter. She gave the room a once-over, but she didn't see anything unusual, just a group of revellers having fun. She shook her head and turned back to Sally. She was tipsy. It was time to go home.

The two men rolled through the bar window and out onto the street. Their fight continued as traffic drove through them.

Jack grabbed Gregori, lifted him high above his head and threw him back into the bar. He rolled and landed at Amy's feet. Pained and exhausted, he looked up at her, realizing he wasn't as young as he used to be, his youthful army physique fading.

Jack stood over him. "Stay away from her, or you'll regret it. You'll burn in hell for eternity."

Gregori staggered to his feet, bloodied, bruised, and in pain.

"I'm already in hell, you plonker. I have nothing to lose and everything to gain. She's mine, Jack...when will you understand that? Get over yourself and piss off."

"I'm watching you, old man." Jack hissed after him.

Gregori staggered out of the bar muttering, waving his hand away at Jack. "Blah de blah, blah de bloody blah...like I give a toss." Hobbling, puffing on a beaten-up, shredded cigar butt, he disappeared.

Jack stood still, so close to Amy, but yet so far away. He reached out and stroked her cheek with his bloodied hand.

"I love you, Amy. I'm gonna bring you back to us."

He leaned in and kissed her lips, hovering for a minute, hoping for a reaction. But nothing.

Suddenly feeling a fool, he roughly swiped away a rogue tear from his eye and strode out. Not looking back.

THE DEAL

Amy touched her mouth.

She turned to Sally.

"Can you smell cigar smoke?"

Chapter Sixty-Four

Jack strutted down the Kensington Street, prodding his earlobe with an angry forefinger. He leapt on a nearby car's bonnet, climbed onto its roof, and jumped up onto an apartment block. He studied the street below while waiting for Pyke to pick up.

"Bonjour, mon petite plonker. What's up?"

"We have a problem." Jack paced the roof, backwards and forwards, anger building inside him.

"Don't we always? What's going on? Where are you?"

"I'm with Amy."

"Jack, you can't spend all your time baby-sitting Amy, not when we need you here."

"Gregori is stalking her. He's working out how to take her down. We must come up with a plan before it's too late. Is Maggie there?"

"She's out, in a meeting with the boss. I'll let her know about Gregori. She may want to add it to her agenda."

"Where's Mara?"

"I haven't seen her. Are you coming back now?"

"Not until Amy is safe. I'm sticking to her like glue. The bastard is not going to get her."

"You can keep an eye on her from up here...."

"What does someone have to do to be sent down?" Jack interrupted.

"Depends. A severe crime...murder, child abuse, rape...why? Are you thinking he may try to get her to do something that'll get her sent down? She wouldn't fall for that. She's too much of a goody-goody."

"I don't know how else he can trap her."

"Return to the Unit. You can't stay down there. You're needed up here. We'll keep an eye from afar. That's what we do."

"Yeah, but sometimes, in dire circumstances, a person can get the full attention of a guardian until they're safe. That's what I'm doing with Amy."

"Maggie's not going to like it."

"She's Amy's mother for god's sake. She'll love it. Besides, the boss has given me permission."

"How? Why? When do you get to see the boss? Only Maggie gets to see him."

"We've worked together on a few things in the past. We have an understanding. It's a long story. Get the message to Maggie. Let her know I'm here. And so is Gregori. I'm staying. The sooner you guys sort it, the sooner I, sorry, *we*, can come back."

"OK, OK. I'll tell her, but stay out of trouble, Jack...if that's possible. I'll get back to you. Oh, one more thing."

"What?"

"Check out Alice for me, will you?"

"If you check out James Smythson and set up a dating profile for me."

"What?"

"You heard me," Jack prodded his ear to disconnect the call.

He leapt across to the next building and jogged the length of the street. He chucked his body over a turret wall and disappeared into an alleyway below. His long black trench coat, outstretched, soaring wing-like behind him.

Chapter Sixty-Five

Foxtrot Union Bar,
Kensington, London, UK

Jack returned to the Foxtrot Union Bar and waited outside until a tipsy Amy and Sally surfaced, hugging each other in the street, taking an age to say goodbye.

He followed Amy home. He helped her stumble in and out of a taxi and navigate her apartment building's entrance and stairway. He knew her home well. Her tiny one-bedroom flat stretched its small square footage on the rear side of the second floor, backing up to the graveyard where he used to jog. With her nest's limited space, he could barely swing his arms in it. He sat on the floor, trying to stay out of the way as she stumbled around the room, giggling and singing.

When she finally crashed out in a drunken stupor, he helped her undress and pulled the duvet over her sleeping body. He left a pint-sized glass of water and two headache tablets on her nightstand for the hangover she was bound to experience after ethanol dehydration set in.

He checked through her phone and saw James had left several text messages asking her to meet him the following night. He deleted them.

He sat at her desk and used her computer.

Chapter Sixty-Six

Russell Garden Mews,
Earls Court, London, UK

Amy woke with a stinking hangover. She reached out from the bed and knocked back the two pain killers and pint of water. She didn't even remember placing them there last night. *Must be getting sensible in my old age.*

She stumbled into the shower and let the hot water roll over her skin for twenty minutes, improving her circulation and easing her headache.

She checked her phone, disappointed no messages awaited her from James. She checked her emails. She found a notification from her dating agency, that she had an admirer.

She'd brought a three-month membership for the dating site, which was about to run out. After an initial flurry of interested admirers, she'd grown bored seeing the same old faces, the same old disappointing dates (who never resembled their photos) and opted not to renew the membership. Her money was best spent elsewhere instead of paying for the privilege of linking up with a bunch of psychos.

With a resigned sigh, she slumped onto her sofa and hit on the link to investigate her new admirer, expecting to feel the usual disappointed response of...*oh my god, no!*

A picture of a dark, ruggedly handsome male popped up on her screen, 'Jack888'. Her mouth dropped open. *Wow, he's gorge.*

Perking up, her attention peaked. She sat on the sofa's edge and ran through his bio. Normally, the self-descriptions beamed full of glowing info about the member, waxing lyrical about their lives and what they had achieved. Most of it bollocks. But Jack had the minimum. His tagline said, "Looking for an Angel."

In his bio, he had 'Ex-Army & Security Services.' She scrolled down, looking for more, but that was it. No hobbies, dreams, first date venues, likes, dislikes, favourite food, music, books, or movies. No hints had been listed on his preferred qualities in a woman or why a woman should choose him. His bio was virtually blank. It intrigued her. She found the scars on his face sexy.

Jack888 had linked her as a favourite, then sent her a message.

"I live in Texas. I've never been east of New York, so we'll probably never meet. Therefore, you are safe with me. I'm just looking for a pen friend to help survive this crazy world. What do you say?"

She stared at the message for a long time. Her fingers hovered over her phone, deciding whether to reply. Her elbow flinched, knocking her hand against the screen, her finger pressing the accept button by accident.

Jack smiled as his nudge worked.

Amy threw the phone on the sofa like a hot coal. *Fuck, fuck, fuck! How did that happen?*

She slowly retrieved her phone and scrolled to Jack's picture. *You are gorgeous.*

What harm could it do? A sexy pen pal. She replied, "Yes, I would like that," and punched the send button.

Again, she found herself chucking the phone onto the sofa as if distancing herself from the madness of it.

Jack leaned against the wall watching her, revelling in her excitement. She adored his picture, scars and all. He was abusing the rules, but he could justify it by saying in order to protect her he needed a way to communicate with her. It would be tricky, but Maggie would find a way. His body buzzed with a revived vigour. At least if he couldn't be with her, he could talk with her and get to know her.

Amy looked at her watch and squealed. Another late start to her day and another excuse she'd have to invent before her boss fired her. *Fuck, fuck, fuck.*

She rushed around the flat like a banshee to finish getting ready. Jack shifted out of her way, arms crossed, smiling, loving every minute, thrilled to be near her.

Using his own image bordered on risky, but Pyke could have added more to his bio. He noted she hadn't recognised his photograph, which proved she had no recollection of her time in the sky or her world-saving escapades. It was safe to communicate with her.

She darted out onto the street and jumped on the number 14 bus to work. He followed and sat beside her on the journey. He gently wiped her hair from her face as the wind caught it, kept her mobile from falling out of her bag, and blocked a cyclist from thundering into her as she crossed the road. *Jeez, how did this woman survive so long?*

Standing arms crossed, watching her step into her office, he realised he was loving every minute of it.

Chapter Sixty-Seven

WTF Creative Management, Cadogan Square,
Knightsbridge, London, UK

Amy hovered over her desk, packing up to go home. She didn't think the day would ever end. The last of her team had already abandoned her. The empty office, apart from her boss in the boardroom on a conference call to the States, carried an uneasiness with all the doors locked.

She stacked empty coffee mugs and drinking glasses she'd gathered from desks, and carried them to the kitchen. The last person to leave at night was responsible for running the dishwasher. Company rules.

She groaned at the lunch debris her lazy co-workers left in the sink and begrudgingly layered the dishwasher racks with their dirty items. Finished, she snapped the machine's door into its locked position and switched it on.

Staring out the kitchen window, she listened to the machine's gurgling and thought of James.

She couldn't believe she hadn't heard from him over the last three days. Why hadn't she heard from him? She'd left him her number, but hadn't thought to get his. She hadn't thought it necessary. Had his behaviour all been a show? Had he just been using her? He'd seemed so keen on her. Keeping herself preoccupied, she spent her days at the office and her evenings messaging her new pen pal, Jack.

The boardroom door opened, her boss paraded down the corridor towards the kitchen and popped his head through the doorway.

"Room for one more?" He shoved his coffee mug forward.

"Yes, sure," she answered, reaching over and accepting the mug from him.

"Err, sir," she said, feeling awkward.

"Yes."

"May I ask about James Smythson?"

"Who?"

"James Smythson, our new client."

"Is he?" He scratched his head. "I've never heard of him."

"I'm sure you have...the guy at the office party the other night."

"Not that I recall."

"He lives in Knightsbridge, Kensington Apartments."

"Doesn't ring any bells. We haven't had any new clients for a few months now."

"Oh, sorry," she mumbled, confused. "Never mind, my mistake."

"Well, no worries. I'm off. Will you lock up?"

"Yeah, sure."

"Have a good weekend, Amy." He walked out, whistling, happy to be going home.

Dumbfounded, Amy stared after him until he was out of sight. *Why did James lie?*

Jack propped himself against the wall, listening. Arms crossed, he watched Amy stare out the window, turning the boss's coffee cup round and round in her hands, shaking her head, muttering.

"What a wanker."

Chapter Sixty-Eight

Kensington Apartments,
Knightsbridge, London, UK

The black taxi pulled up outside the Kensington Apartments and deposited Amy at the curb. She jogged up the apartment steps, prepared to have it out with her one-night-stand and find out why he lied.

She pushed through the main entrance doors and walked across the opulent reception area to the security guard's desk.

"Hello there," she said, aiming her most flattering smile at the guard. He smiled back, a tinge of recognition in his eyes.

"Yes, miss, what can I do for you?"

"May I speak with Mr. Smythson?"

"Who?"

"Mr. Smythson, James Smythson, the tenant on the fifth floor."

"We don't have a Mr. Smythson. I told the other girl as well."

"But I was here the other night with him. He has to be here."

"Maybe he was a guest?" The Guard smiled apologetically. It wouldn't be the first time he'd seen a young lady taken advantage of during his years as a Security Guard. The young girls would get a little tipsy, believe their young men would give them the world, then find out they had been duped. He shook his head with a sigh. "Sorry, dear."

"Who lives in the fifth-floor apartment?"

"No one. It's a show flat."

Amy's heart sank. "Are you sure?"

"I've worked here five years, and in all that time, no one has lived there. I'm sure," he sighed, he'd given many other women the same bad news over the years.

"Sorry to have bothered you."

"Don't worry, miss. It's been a funny old week. I've been bothered left, right, and centre. Seems things are finally back to normal."

"What, with the police?"

He rolled his eyes. "Can you believe it? They've been here for days."

"They were coming in as I left the other morning. What did they want?"

"Haven't you seen the news, miss? About the VIP abuse ring, Doctor Dio Buchananan? He owns the block."

"Oh that, yes." She'd seen a few clips on the news, but didn't know the full details.

"The police have been conducting a search and interrogating residents, but they haven't found anything. They've only just cleared off today. Made a right mess, they did."

"Did you mention another girl?"

"What?"

"You said you told the other girl."

"Oh, yes, the shy one." He pointed outside to a park bench across the street. "She's still there. She doesn't believe Mr. Smythson doesn't live here either. She looks a bit out of it, if you ask me, on drugs or something."

Amy peered through the reception doors to spy on a figure curled up on the park bench all alone, wearing a dark coat and woollen hat, hunched over, rocking rhythmically.

"Sorry to have bothered you."

"No problem. Goodbye, miss. And if I might say, he's a fool to have strung you along. Best you find out now, I say."

Amy forced a grin. "Ahhh, you may be right. He did have bad breath anyway." She half giggled, winking at the guard. If there was any consolation, she had her friend Jack now. She didn't need bollocky James, or whoever he was.

She left the building and took a detour across the road to the bench. The girl raised her head, her gaze half hidden, her features vague. The closer Amy approached, the more nervous the girl became, rocking and visibly trembling beneath her coat.

"Excuse me. Do you mind if I sit here?" Amy asked, using polite, reassuring intonations, demonstrating her nonthreatening intentions.

Silently, the girl scooted to the end of the bench, acting uncomfortable, wrapping her arms around her body as if she needed to protect herself from being touched.

"It's OK," she whispered, her voice weak.

Amy sat with her back erect against the cold bench, her eyes fixated on the apartment building she'd just visited. She took a few sly peeks at the girl, trying to assess her, but her hat prevented seeing her face. The girl trembled; her foot constantly tapped the air. Anxious fingers scratched at her jacket sleeve, as if soothing an itch through the material. She waited a moment to let the girl adjust to her presence.

"Cold out, isn't it?"

The girl's head shifted slightly. Amy caught her taking a quick glance at her, but she still couldn't see her clearly. She didn't answer.

"Have you ever been in that big apartment building?" She'd try a different angle.

The woman started to shake her head but then gave a short nod.

"I don't suppose you know James Smythson?"

"Who?"

"James, the guy who lives in the apartments." She pointed across the road.

The girl sat upright, suddenly interested. She turned to face Amy, both studying each other's faces. Did Amy recognise her from somewhere? The girl's sunken dark eyes and sallow skin outlined an undernourished girl's face.

"Do you know James?" The girl asked, her voice low, her eager eyes staring into Amy's. The longer she stared at her, the more familiar she seemed, but Amy couldn't work out where she'd seen the girl before.

"Yes, and no…I mean, I met him the other night. I wanted to see him again, but he's gone. How do you know him?"

"He helped me find someone. I wanted to talk to him, to warn him."

She looked across at the building. "But he's not here anymore. I don't know what to do next."

"Are you all right? You look a bit out of it."

"I'm on drugs."

Amy gave her a look of distaste.

"No, not those kinds of drugs. I was just released from the hospital… painkillers."

"Oh, I'm sorry. Hope it's nothing serious."

"If you call being abducted by a crazy man serious, then, yes… It's all over the news."

"Oh, my god." The unexpected admission took Amy by surprise. "I'm sorry, so sorry. You weren't involved in that were you... I can't imagine... how awful... how did you..."

"How come I'm alive?" The girl fidgeted again, as if her horrendous ordeal took her back to a place worse than hell. Amy regretted asking the minute she saw the pain in the girl's eyes.

"The police... they came... many police. They rescued me." She wrapped her arms around herself and rocked back and forth in continuous rhythm, silent tears streamed down her face.

Amy reached for a tissue in her purse and gently held it out. She could sense the girl wanted to talk about it, to let it out. She sat and listened.

Once she'd regained some composure, the girl rambled on. "That bastard...they arrested him. Hope he rots in hell. Really, hell is too good for him." The anger spilled forth now. Her face hardened in disgust.

"So, they arrested the perpetrator?" Amy asked, keeping the woman engaged.

"They got the bastard. They got him." Her voice trailed off.

"At least he won't hurt someone else... I mean... now that he's caught."

The girl's eyes raged, the scars of her torment holding her soul captive. "He hurt many, many of us he kept prisoner...forever."

"I'm so sorry." Amy wanted to reach out and put her arm around the girl, but didn't, not sure how her experience would make her react. She'd heard of post traumatic symptoms. She could understand how much easier it was for some people to unload on a total stranger.

"He kept us locked all alone in a small box of a room, barely fed us, did horrible things to us. And I prayed every minute for an angel... someone to find us. And at first I thought I'd died because it seemed so strange that they'd found us. I thought I was in a cloud somewhere with uniformed angels lifting me out of hell. But, it was for real... the police and the bodies they carried out of the cages."

"Bloody hell! How many were there?"

"I don't know exactly... but some didn't make it."

"That's horrifying. Are you going to be okay?"

"No, not really, but I just wanted to see James to tell him."

"What has James got to do with all this?"

"I came to this address, looking for a missing person. I met James, and he was nice to me. He tried to help me find a man that had information on that person. I went to the man, but he turned out to be a psycho, and I got hurt. James needs to know about this man."

"Well, he's not here. You can't stay here all night. Have you a place to stay?"

"Back to the hospital. They'll be looking for me, but I don't want to go back. I can't stand anyone touching me, and they keep prodding me with needles, tests and shit."

Amy pulled her arms closer into her body, glad she hadn't tried to physically comfort the poor girl. For some reason, she felt drawn to this victimized soul. "You're welcome to come stay with me if you wish, just for a short while. We can have a cup of tea. You can get a good night's sleep, then we'll see if we can find James. I can take you back to the hospital when you're ready."

The girl took a moment to take Amy in, and she couldn't blame her. She stared at her, measuring up whether to trust her or not. Finally, she nodded, giving Amy a grateful smile. She stood up and stepped cautiously onto the sidewalk. Amy waved down a taxi.

Jack watched them get into the cab. He tapped his ear and spoke to Pyke.

"What info did you get on Smythson?"

"Hello there, Pyke. How are you, mon petite Chou. How are you managing up there on your own?" replied Pyke, sarcastically.

"Yeah, yeah. How are you, Pyke? Now, what info did you get on Smythson?"

"I see you picked up the dating phone I set up for you. A thank you would be nice."

"Yeah, yeah, for fuck's sake, Pyke. I got the phone, and thank you. Now, could you just answer the bleedin' question?"

"Language... puhlease,"

"Pyke!"

"Is this cos I said I love you, mate?" Pyke asked, pointedly, then broke out in another one of his chuckling spells. "Cos, if it is..."

"For fuck's sake, stop taking the piss and answer the question before I come up there and..."

"OK, OK. Keep your nickers on, mate."

"What info do you have?" he asked, shouting.

"Err.. well, not a lot, to be honest. He isn't on any database. My guess is he's using an alias. There is no Smythson client at Amy's workplace and no Smythson living at the Kensington Apartments address. We have his headshot image taken from the apartment's security CCTV the night he was with Amy. Am putting it through recognition databases to see if we have a hit. Nothing yet, though. He's not known to us or the police."

"Hmmm...OK. I've some good news, sort of. Alice is alive and well...well, not well exactly. She's a bit wobbly, but she's with Amy, going back for a cup of tea and sympathy. They're both trying to track down Smythson."

"Wow! That's great! You've ID'd her? You know it's her?"

"Yep, I clicked some images for you. Check them out. It's definitely her face, and you'll see strands of pink hair sticking out the back of her hat. She looks a bit freaked out, but she's OK. I'll stick with them. Any news from Maggie yet?"

"She's gone a little quiet on me, huddled up with Micael, in meetings. With you all gone, the Unit has been put on hold. I'm sitting here twiddling my thumbs. So, a good time to keep me up to date and use me to find out stuff."

"Is she angry I'm staying down here?"

"I think she understands. She's grateful, and Micael is cool with it. I didn't tell her about your physical contact with Amy or the dating site messaging thing. She won't like that. So, delete all messages and history from the phone every time you use it, OK?"

"Yeah, yeah, I will. You could've fixed me up with a quirky keyboard. I hate these touch phones. My fingers are too big."

"Qwerty."

"What?"

"Qwerty keyboard. It's with a 't' not a 'k'."

"Whatever! Can you keep tabs on Gregori?"

"Not easily. He's not on our system. He moves about underground a lot, but I'll try. He's been put out by us as *wanted*, so I guess he'll stay under the radar. He might not be working alone."

"Mara?"

"I don't know. She hasn't surfaced anywhere. Probably down there with him."

"What's Dio saying?"

"He's playing the 'no comment' card and uncooperative with Police enquiries. He was remanded and pleaded not guilty at the initial court hearing. He'll attend crown court in a few months. I don't expect him to get off with such overwhelming evidence."

"Yeah, but he's a slippery fish. We need to keep an eye on it."

"If Alice is of balanced mind, she will be a crucial witness for the prosecution. A lot of the victims who survived are suffering with mental issues, understandably. It's going to take a lot of therapy to turn it around for them. Meanwhile, they're not fit to attend court and give evidence. This means the burden lies on Alice, which means her life is in danger."

"Fuck."

"Police will probably provide protection and move her to a safe house. These days, safe houses are not that safe. Dio seems to have his fingers in many pies. He has a pretty powerful address book and a lot of blackmail material. Many in authority will do his bidding to stay out of the media limelight. She, and now possibly Amy, are not safe."

"Fuck."

"Yes, fuck."

Chapter Sixty-Nine

Russell Garden Mews,
Earls Court, London, UK

Amy walked fragile Alice up flights of stairs to her apartment, trying not to touch her, whilst gently guiding her hunched body. Alice would flinch at any contact.

Gregori stood at the top of the staircase, observing them.

"Dear, dear, darling daughter, you just can't resist getting into trouble, can you? Like father, like daughter." He leaned against the wall and watched Amy fumble with her keys to open the door. As the girls stepped into the apartment, Gregori dropped through the floor and disappeared.

Amy escorted Alice to the sofa and gently moved pillows out of the way. Alice's visible shivering sent Amy to the linen closet for a blanket. She helped Alice wrap it around her to add warmth. She switched the lights to low, lit a sweet-smelling candle, and put on some soft Ibiza chilled music. She slid behind her kitchen counter to make them both cups of tea.

Amy didn't talk much as she moved around her apartment, understanding her guest's fragile state, her need to adjust to her surroundings and feel safe. She didn't know the extent of her abuse, but whatever it was, the experience freaked her out. Who wouldn't be?

On handing Alice a hot cup of tea, Amy sat at the dining table and signed on to her laptop. The two girls sat in silence, allowing the music and fragrant smells to soothe them.

Alice, cupping her warm drink with both hands, let her head rock back and closed her eyes. For the first time in a long, she felt safe.

Amy tapped various words into the search engine until she homed in on Dio Buchanan and his arrest. Reading about the abuse he'd inflicted on his victims turned Amy's stomach. She looked across at Alice and shook her head. *What a bastard.*

Ping!

A message box opened in the corner of her screen from Jack888. Amy's heart gave a little leap. She opened the message and read.

Jack888: Hi, how are you? Got time to chat?

She winced. Now might not be a good time. She looked across at the sofa to check on her guest. The exhausted, terrified girl snored softly to the music. Amy wondered when she'd last slept without fear.

Amy reached over, removed the cup from between Alice's fingers and placed it on the side table. She tucked the blanket across the exhausted girl's chest and sat back in front of the laptop. *OK, but for just a little bit.*

AngelEyz: Yes, can chat, but not for long. I have a friend here. She's sleeping. When she wakes, I'll have to stop.

Jack888: OK, keep quiet. Don't wake her. What have you been up to?

Jack sat on the chair opposite her, clumsily tapping letters on his phone. He watched her face over the top of the screen, smiling, enjoying the intimacy of reading her expression as she wrote.

AngelEyz: Not a lot. You?

Jack888: I've been reading the British news about a guy called Buchanan. Hope he's nowhere near where you are, that it's nothing to do with you. It's terrible.

Amy squirmed in her chair. *If only he knew.*

AngelEyz: Why would he have anything to do with me? He was in Brighton, on the South Coast. I'm in London, a few hours north. Not even close to me, so no worries.

Jack raised an eyebrow at her little white lie.

Jack888: Good, I just wanted to let you know that I'm in the security business. If you ever need anything or anyone looked at, let me know. It would be a pleasure to help.

AngelEyz: What do you mean?

Jack888: Well, if ever anyone bothers you, you know, an ex or something, I can do a search on them and help you work out what to do. It's part of my job. I'm in the security and protection business.

AngelEyz: You mean, if I gave you a name you could find that person for me?

Jack888: Yes, we have very good search technicians here to source most things.

AngelEyz: Who do you work for?

Jack888: Mainly the government and larger corporations who can afford us.

AngelEyz: Oh, like you're a spy?

Jack888: I'm not very James Bond, I'm afraid.

AngelEyz: No, in your bio pic you look more like Poldark.

Silence.

Jack888: Who?

AngelEyz: Poldark, a television show we have over here.

Jack888: Never heard of it...

AngelEyz: Ahhh, well, check it out if you get a chance. You look like the lead character with your sexy, shaggy hair, mean, moody, complex, stubborn, big on justice thing going on.

Silence.

AngelEyz: It's a compliment!

Jack ran a hand through his hair, trying to tidy it up, like he could see her?

Jack888: Thanks, I think!!

AngelEyz: So, are you a spy?

Jack 888: Not really. It sounds a bit cloak and dagger-like, but it really isn't. Most of the information we use is on the web. Anyone could source it with the right equipment. Everyone and everything is easy to find.

AngelEyz: OK, that's cool.

Jack888: Just saying, if you ever need help.

AngelEyz: Thank you. That's very kind of you. But I'm ok. I know nothing about you. Tell me something.

Jack888: Like what?

AngelEyz: Like where you live, are you married, do you have a girlfriend? Any children, how tall are you, do you have a dog?

Jack888: Whoah...wait a minute. I live in a small town outside Austin, Texas. I'm divorced. I don't have a girlfriend. Well I did, but she just left me. I'm 6'4" and no, I don't have a dog, but I'd love one.

AngelEyz: What would you have?

Jack888: A Saint Bernard.

AngelEyz: Ahhhh! Good choice. Why did your girlfriend leave you?

Jack looked over the laptop at her, aghast. *Straight to the point or what?* Silence.

AngelEyz wrote: Sorry. That's a bit personal. Ignore it.

Jack888: Do you mind if I don't answer that...just yet?

AngelEyz: No, no, sure. It's OK. Sorry. I can be a bit pushy, I know.

Jack nodded in agreement. *How right you are.*

Jack888: What about you? Do you have someone?

Jack eyed her, waiting for her reaction. She hesitated, thinking about her answer. He waited.

AngelEyz: Well, I thought I did. I've only just met him. We spent a night together, and boom, he disappeared. I went to try and find him tonight and instead met another girl looking for him. She's the one sleeping on my sofa.

Jack888: Bummer. Did you like him?

He watched her eyes. She nodded.

AngelEyz: Yeah, I think I did. He seemed nice. I haven't been with someone in a while. I'm not that lucky with men.

Jack888: Well, he was crazy to have left you. You're beautiful.

AngelEyz: Ahhh...thank you.

Jack smiled as she beamed.

AngelEyz: If I'm honest, my bio pic is two years old. I've a few more wrinkles now.

Jack888: Trust me, you're beautiful. ☺

Amy blushed and gave a little happy dance in her seat. *He's so sweet. Thank God, he can't see me now. I'm looking a right mess.*

Jack threw his head back and laughed.

Alice stirred on the sofa and awakened with a start. Jerking upright, her eyes darted around the room, taking everything in.

Angel888 wrote: I have to go. Sorry.

Amy typed quickly and closed the laptop, snapping it shut, leaving Jack888 hanging.

She got up from the table, picked up Alice's tea, and sat down beside her, waiting for her to calm before handing her the cup.

"It's OK Alice. You're safe. He can't get you."

Jack walked out of the room.

Chapter Seventy

The girls chatted until the early hours. Alice became more and more relaxed. She hadn't communicated with anyone else in weeks. Her old self started to come back. Next to Amy's strong determination she felt safe. She told Amy everything.

"I'm supposed to be under armed guard. I hope you don't get in trouble."

"Well, they haven't done a very good job, have they? How did you escape?"

"I don't know. I guess my Guardian Angel helped me," she admitted nervously. "Someone left the security door ajar, so I slipped through. No one saw. I just needed to get away. You don't know who you can trust. Dio was a Doctor, you know. He had a hospital surgery room in his apartment. I never want to see a hospital room again as long as I live. He made me watch a few of his procedures. He was sick. Having those doctors and nurses around me made me want to retch."

"I've a pen pal friend who can find out stuff for us if we want, like where or who James is."

"You can't tell your friend where we are."

"It's OK. He lives on the other side of the world."

"That may be, but you can't trust anyone. What if he has contacts over here?"

"But I've a good feeling about him. I think I can trust him."

Alice yawned, too tired to argue with her.

Amy checked her watch. They'd been talking until midnight.

"Look, let's talk about this in the morning. Get some sleep. Use my bed and I'll sleep on the couch."

Alice looked up to protest, but Amy raised a hand at her.

"Not another word. This is my house, my rules."

She took Alice into the bedroom, showed her the bathroom, and gave her a towel. Alice sat on the bed, bone-tired. Her head rolled to her chest. She started to cry. Amy sat quietly beside her, hesitantly touched her, welcomed Alice's heaving shoulders resting against her. Alice allowed Amy to comfort her until the tears subsided.

"Thank you," snuffled Alice as she kicked off her shoes and pulled off her hat.

Pink hair tumbled to her shoulders. Amy tried to hide her shock upon remembering where she'd seen Alice before.

She was the face in the picture she'd found in James's apartment, the photo lying on the floor. *Why would he have a picture of Alice?*

Curious, she decided she better wait to ask Alice about it when they were more refreshed. She would wait 'til morning. Alice had only just started to relax.

She kissed her on her forehead and left the room.

She needed to find out more about James.

Chapter Seventy-One

A my showered, taking extra precaution to stay quiet. Carefully and quietly, she pulled an old baggy T-shirt over her head and slipped her feet into her faithful tread-worn slippers. Tiptoeing into her compact kitchen, she poured a glass of red wine and sat at her computer. She took a chance Jack888 would still be on his computer and messaged him, ready to take Jack up on his offer.

AngelEyz wrote: Hello, are you there? Please be there.

No answer. She examined the clock, working out the time difference between their time zones. He had to be no more than five or six hours behind her. *So, he should still be awake.*

She tried again.

Hello, Jack888, are you there?

Nothing. She took another sip of her wine.

She'd call Sally for a chat if it weren't so late. Her stomach rumbled. She realised she was starving. Cooking this late made her tired just thinking about it; besides, she didn't want to disturb Alice. Takeaway vendors had all shut down for the night. Her last option? Ice cream—delicious, quiet, and satisfying.

She propped herself against pillows on the sofa, turned the television down low, and tucked into ice cream, her focus glued to a thriller movie. She dipped the spoon, missing the inside of the carton.

Halfway through the movie, boredom set in, the plot was drifting into the mundane. Disappointed, she checked the time again.

"For fuck's sake. What a load of drivel? I'm not wasting another second of my life watching this crap." She grabbed the remote and flicked the television off, blissful silence. She stared into space, contemplating the way her crazy day had unfolded.

Ping!

She sped to the laptop. Her tummy flipped to see Jack888 on the screen. She slid into a chair in front of the screen, tingling with excitement. She couldn't believe how quickly he was getting to her.

Jack888: Hey, beautiful, you OK?

AngelEyz: Send me some pix of you. I want to see more of you.

Jack888: Errr...well I don't have many, but OK.

AngelEyz: And I want to hear your voice. Can you call me?

Silence.

Jack888: Errr...not right now, but I will, if you give me your number.

AngelEyz: And I want you to check out a person for me...well...two people, actually... have you got time to chat? I'm feeling a little frightened right now and can't sleep.

Jack888: Yeah, sure...what are the two names you want searched. And why are you frightened?

AngelEyz: James Smythson, about thirty, lives in Knightsbridge, I think...and a polish girl called Maria Iwanska, about nineteen years old. Her mother is Eva and lives in Wales. I think she may have been in the Doctor Buchanan's house when it was raided.

Jack888: I thought you said you were nowhere near all that shit.

AngelEyz: I did...I'm not...I may have lied, stretched the truth. The girl on my sofa was one of the victims. She seems to be on the run, and I'm scared I'm in the middle of a whole load of trouble.

Jack888: Hell, yeah. OK, we'll start with the names. Talk to me whilst my guys get back to me.

Whilst Jack888 worked at sourcing information, they chatted to kill time, waiting on results to surface. She found it strange sharing things with someone she'd never met in person, but it felt easier than talking to someone she knew, apart from Sally.

Jack888 was sensitive, kind, sexy, protective, funny. She loved chatting with him. It went on for hours; their gentle banter flowed effortlessly back and forth, she felt as if she'd known him forever. Before she knew it, it was 4.00 a.m.

AngelEyz: Oh my god...I have to sleep. I'm knackered.

Jack888: OK, I guess you're going to need it. Alice needs looking after.

Silence.

Jack888: You still there?

Silence.

Jack888: Hello?

Silence.

Jack strode into the room through the wall. His concern turned to smiles as he saw Amy draped over the desk, hugging her open laptop, mouse in hand, snoring.

Jack888 wrote: OK, speak later. Good night, Amy Fox.

Ping!

The sound of the message shocked Amy awake. She squinted at the last few lines of text and slowly typed.

AngelEyz: Nite-nite.

"Night-night, my guardian angel," she whispered as she closed down the laptop and snuggled up on the sofa, pulling the blanket over her tired body.

Jack smiled as she called him her angel; he walked back out through the wall. He had many things to do.

Amy, on the edge of falling asleep, sat bolt upright. *How did he know my name?*

Chapter Seventy-Two

Jack landed on the rooftop of Amy's apartment block. He'd spent the past two hours searching for Gregori, but to no avail.

He sat on the roof tiles, getting his breath back. The morning sun blazed the sky with deep orange and pale blues. Birds skipped from chimneys to tree limbs shading the street. A cool breeze blew his unkempt hair from his face. He closed his eyes and tilted his head up to the sky, taking a moment to enjoy the calm before the city awoke.

He pulled out his phone. She'd wanted to hear his voice. He wondered if it could make calls. He wasn't sure he could bare it.

The small phone made it difficult for his clumsy fingers to operate its functions, but he'd quickly adjusted, proud he could nearly type at a speed equal to hers. He kept his sentences short and succinct to keep up with her. In the beginning, she'd sent several messages to his one. He'd barely had time to answer one question when the next two or three came flying across his screen. She was a speedy typist.

He scrolled through the messages, re-reading them over and over again, smiling at her humour and quick-witted observations.

He tucked the phone inside his pocket, looked up to the skies, and made an announcement.

"I love Amy Fox, and I'm going to get her back."

He stood up, looked down to his feet and let his body drop through the roof into her building.

Chapter Seventy-Three

J ack floated into Amy's sitting room. He stepped through the adjoining wall and peered into her bedroom. Alice lay huddled in the foetal position, gently snoring, enjoying her first uninterrupted night's sleep in weeks.

Happy she was safe, he crept back into the sitting room.

Amy, sprawled across the sofa, had one leg on, one leg off, as she tossed and turned in her dreams.

The morning sun seeped through the gap in the curtains. A white line of light travelled across her carpet, crossed over her shoulder, and settled on her beautiful face. He pulled the curtains tightly closed to prevent the light from disturbing her.

He sat on the edge of the sofa and observed her breathing. Tears streamed down his face. He had to make this work; he couldn't lose her.

He pulled both slippers off her feet and gently lifted her roaming leg off the floor, returning it to the sofa. He retrieved her blanket heaped half on her, half off, and spread it across her body, tenderly tucking the edges under her hips and shoulders.

He knelt on the floor close to her face, swiped stray strands of hair back from her eyes, and leaned down to kiss her forehead goodnight. A small sigh came from her open mouth.

"Jack," she whispered.

He froze, hovering over her face. She lay still, silent. He placed his lips over her eyelids and gave butterfly kisses to her lashes. Her mouth pulled into a silent smile. He loved her smile, her dimples, the lines creasing the corners of her eyes.

He rested his head on her forehead, closed his eyes, and breathed her in. Her smell sent tingles all over his body. What was it about her that turned him on? He took a deep breath and pulled himself up to view her. Still on his knees, he memorized every detail about her. He wanted her, now.

Eyes closed, smiling, she gave a soft groan as her head pushed back into the pillow. Her arms stretched out above her head, her chest and hips pushed up from the sofa, her leg fell to the floor, opening, as if welcoming a lover. She groaned again, pushing her hips up into the air.

"Jack," she whispered, her mouth opening as if in a kiss.

His cock lurched. She was dreaming about him. *Fuck.*

He shouldn't, should he? But they were sort of an item, and she *was* dreaming about him. *Sod it.*

Gently pulling at the blanket, it eased to the floor. She was barelegged, wearing only a baggy T-shirt. He tentatively placed a hand on her chest. She arched her back, willing him on. He trailed his hand across her body. Feeling soft breasts through the T-shirt material, nipples hardening as she lifted her chest to join his touch.

He wove his hand down her body to between her legs and yanked on her outer leg, forcing them wider apart, his eyes gazing up and down her body. She was the most beautiful creature he'd ever seen.

Still on his knees, he lined himself up between her legs, pushing the T-shirt up over her hips, stomach and chest, exposing her body. His cock hardened.

He grabbed the soft skin of her inner thighs and spread them wider. She groaned as her head rocked side to side. Her hips rose, pushing towards him, willing him to touch her. He blew cool air between her legs, across her wet lips, she giggled and shuddered.

"For fuck's sake, Amy, what am I gonna do with you? You are too much." He lowered his mouth between her legs.

Amy whimpered as her back arched and her knees lifted into the air with the exquisite shock of his tongue. She placed her hands on his head, her fingers massaging tousled hair as she pushed his grinding face into her. His mouth drove her crazy.

"Oh my god," she gasped.

He couldn't hold back any longer. He unzipped his trousers, pushed wide hands up under her bottom, grabbed her flesh, and pulled her to the edge of the sofa, lining her up to him. She lifted herself up onto elbows as if trying to see what he was doing.

"Please, please..." she moaned, eyes closed.

He seized her waist and eased her body onto him. She was wet. She slid down his shaft easily with a silent open-mouthed cry. Her head fell back; her eyes rolled with yearning.

He leaned forward, took her head in his hands, held her face close to his and slowly pulled in and out of her.

"I love you, Amy Fox. I always have."

Their lovemaking went on into the early hours, until, exhausted, Jack snuggled up beside her and fell asleep.

Chapter Seventy-Four

A my woke with a start to a darkened room, still on the sofa, but dishevelled and sweaty. *Wow, what a dream!*

Jack888 had visited her, or what she imagined him to look like. She smiled at the memory of him, hugging herself under the blanket, trying to keep hold of the warm squishy feeling, before it wafted away into the ether, to that place where all dreams fade.

She rested her hand against her forehead as reality crept back into her thoughts. She listened for Alice, but no sign could be heard from the bedroom. She checked her watch, shocked to see it was midday. *What the hell? Thank God it's the weekend.*

She snuggled back under the blanket, wallowing for a few minutes more in the lovely tingling feeling of being with Jack888.

The next time she looked at the clock, it said 3.30 p.m. Alice was shaking her shoulders, offering her a cup of tea.

"Wow, Amy, we've slept the day away. Are you ok?"

Alice placed the tea on the floor beside the sofa and plonked herself down on the armchair facing the spread-eagled Amy.

"Yeah, you?" croaked Amy, pulling herself up into a sitting position.

"Yes, thank you. I feel *so* much better. I had a shower and borrowed this dressing gown. I hope you don't mind. I feel bad you're sleeping on the sofa. Was it OK?"

"Oh, no worries. I had a great dream. And last night I chatted with my pen pal friend, Jack, who's looking into Maria and James for us."

Buzz, buzz.

The two girls jumped. The entry doorbell's ring blasted the room. They looked at each other. Jack went to the window and stepped out of it.

"Don't answer it, Amy."

"Hey, it's all right. It's probably a delivery man or the mailman."

"Please don't answer it." Alice pleaded, scared and shaking.

Amy reassured her and wrapped her arms around her, giving a reinforcing embrace.

"Don't worry. Stay there, I'll have a quick look out the window to see if I can make out who it is, OK?"

Buzz, buzz—buzz, buzz.

The sound rang with more insistence. Alice grabbed Amy's hand to pull her back.

"Don't."

"Shhhh, it's OK. They won't see me."

Amy pulled her T-shirt down over her thighs and tiptoed to the edge of the window frame. She pulled back the curtains a fraction and peered down to the street below.

Jack stepped back into the room, his eyes furrowed in thought.

Alice sat with baited breath, waiting to hear who was there.

"It's James... Oh my god, how does he know where I live?"

Brrr, brrr, brrr.

Amy's phone rang, causing the two girls to jump again.

"Oh, for fuck's sake." She picked up the phone and noticed a mobile number she didn't recognise. She looked down into the street again. James paced back and forth in front of the doorstep with his phone pushed against his ear.

"Yes," she answered, as pissed off as she could sound.

Alice put her hands to her face with worry.

Jack, placing his hands on his hips, raised his eyes to the ceiling.

"Amy, it's me, James. I'm outside. Let me in."

"James who?"

"James Smythson. We met last week."

"Who?"

"You know exactly who. Now let me in," he shouted.

"I'm sorry. I don't know who you are. I don't take illicit calls from people I don't know. Goodbye," she said, clicking the phone off and punching the air in satisfaction.

Jack smiled and started to leave the room to follow James.

"Who was it?" asked Alice softly.

"James Smythson. I put the phone down on him."

"OK, and you did that because?"

"He shagged me, and then didn't call me for days. How dare he."

"Maybe he was playing hard to get. I really want to speak with him, Amy. He needs to know about the bastard."

Brrr, brrr. Brrr, brrr.

Her phone rang in her hands, annoyingly.

"What about the fact we don't know who we can trust?"

Brrr, brrr. Brrr, brrr.

"He seems nice. He didn't hurt me. He was trying to help me. And you liked him enough to shag him." Alice pleaded. "What harm can he do with the two of us here?"

Jack shook his head and paced the room.

Brrr, brrr. Brrr, brrr.

"OK, OK," Amy answered, still with a disdainful voice. "Yes?"

Jack threw his arms in the air with frustration.

"I need to speak with you. It's urgent."

"What about?"

"I can't talk over the phone. Let me in. I know Alice is with you. Let me in."

Silence.

"Amy...Amy, let me in. It's life or death."

"For goodness' sake, don't be so dramatic. OK, OK." She marched over to the entry phone and buzzed him in.

Jack tapped his ear. "Pyke, you'd better listen to this. We've got James Smythson at Amy's flat."

The light popped on in Jack's line of sight. Pyke was tuned into what he saw.

Chapter Seventy-Five

"I'm sorry, I didn't manage to get hold of you, Amy. I left a few messages, but I don't understand why you never got back to me."

"No, you didn't. I didn't get any messages."

Jack, watching from the corner of the room, smirked. Pyke tutted, "Did you delete her messages?"

"Might have."

"You lied to me," Amy continued. "You aren't a client, and you don't live at the apartment where we spent the night. Why?"

"I can explain." He turned to Alice. "Are you OK, Alice?"

She nodded, wrapping Amy's dressing gown tightly around her. The two girls sat on the sofa, opposite James, who took the armchair. He felt like he was being interrogated.

"Did you know about Dio Buchananan?"

"Yes."

"Why did you send me to him?"

"I didn't."

"Why did you have a picture of Alice at your apartment?" interrupted Amy.

Alice whipped her head around to look Amy in the eye. She hadn't told her. Amy gave a 'trust me' glance, and placed her hand on Alice's knee to quiet her.

"Look, we haven't got much time. You are in trouble. I am not James. I'm working undercover. We had been trying to catch Dio Buchannan for a long time. I was based at the show flat to gather intelligence on the VIP gang's activities."

Alice and Amy exchanged shocked glances. Did they believe him or was this the worst excuse ever for being a dick?

Jack whispered, "Do you believe him?"

Pyke muttered, "Hmmm, it's possible, I suppose. Our database hasn't brought up anything on his image."

"I don't believe you," smirked Amy. "This is ludicrous."

"Look," he pulled out a Police badge and showed the girls.

"My name is DC Matt Pearson. I work with the Major Crime Team. We've been following this ring for a long time. We were about to nail the bastard when Police swooped on his Brighton address. I'm sorry I didn't stop you going to Brighton. I asked for a marker to be put on you, to be followed, kept safe, but that obviously didn't work. I'm so sorry."

He turned to Amy.

"Once the cops and media were traipsing around his London address, I would have been discovered and our work scuppered, so I had to pull out."

"Why did you tell me you were a new client?"

He gave a slight chuckle and lowered his head, swinging it back and forth in confession mode. "To get into your knickers. I fancied you and didn't want you going back into work. I lied, yes. But hey, you're gorgeous. Can you blame me?" he asked with a shrug.

Jack crossed his arms in a huff, moving a step closer to the man.

"Down, boy," whispered Pyke. "That's not going to help. Let's just listen. I've put his name into the database. Let's see what comes back."

Amy blushed and caught herself. She sat bolt upright, all business, pretending not to enjoy the compliment.

"Look," he said. "I didn't mean to get you involved in this. I was fed up, stuck in that flat for weeks, so I sneaked out to have a drink and act like a normal person. I bumped into you and your office party and joined in. I liked you. I shouldn't have brought you back. I'm sorry."

Amy nodded her acceptance of his apology, grabbed Alice's hand, shrugged her shoulders and asked. "What's next?"

"We've got to get you out of here, now. You don't cross Dio. He'll deal with Alice one way or another. He has loyal associates who'll do his bidding. And now that you're involved, Amy, you'll be on his list."

Amy and Alice exchanged another round of nervous glances. "Where do we go? I can't just get up and leave my apartment, my job, my friends," Amy said.

"I have a car outside to take you to a safe house in Scotland."

"Just like that?" Amy rushed to the window to pull back the blinds and survey the street below. A black people carrier sat parked outside her apartment block. Two men in suits and sunglasses stood guard bedside the vehicle, arms crossed, eyes scanning the street, waiting patiently. She nodded to Alice, who was getting more and more nervous by the minute.

"Pack a bag, the minimum you need, and come with me now," pleaded Matt.

"What about my work?"

"We'll take care of it later."

"How long will we be gone?"

"Until the court case and the threat is over."

Pyke sounded in Jack's ear. "The number plates are fake, but that doesn't mean anything, with these operations. I'm not getting anything for his name. It may be another alias."

"I don't like it," said Jack, watching the girls enter Amy's bedroom.

"Stay with them. I'll do further checks. If they are in danger, it's important they get out of there pronto."

Chapter Seventy-Six

Amy pulled out a suitcase from underneath her bed and randomly tossed articles of clothing into its wide cavity. She gave Alice a change of clothes and a new hat to disguise her memorable hair.

James, or Matt, seemed real enough. She couldn't ignore the few hunks standing outside her apartment. It made sense that a powerful man like Dio would want to get rid of witnesses. It was just a shame she'd gotten mixed up in it.

The girls dressed, joined Matt in the living room, and all three filed out of the flat, jogging down the stairwell to the ground floor. He pulled out a radio and notified his team to have the car doors open. He made the girls wait in the hallway whilst he checked the front door and scanned the street. He then waved them on as they ran out of the building into the waiting people carrier.

Jack stood in the middle of the road watching them drive off at a high speed. He pulled out his phone and started to type Amy a message.

The vehicle drove east towards London City Airport. A motorcycle sped past Jack, driving straight through him. The driver chased after the car, pulled a gun from inside his jacket, took aim at the tyres and fired. The vehicle skidded off the road and slammed into the pillared entrance of a mansion block.

Jack looked up at the noise, he stared shocked, not believing his eyes. Then sped through the air to the smoking vehicle.

The biker pulled up beside the passenger's door, shot through the lock, opened it up, reached in, and fired two shots.

It all happened so fast. Jack arrived at the scene just as the bike raced off into the distance. His cry of "Nooooooo...." bellowed out over the sound of its screeching engine.

He stood at the window, his hands pressed against his head, too shocked to move.

"AMYYYYYY... NOOOOOOO....." his cry could be heard in the heavens.

Pyke tuned into him.

"What's wrong Jack."

Jack couldn't speak. He turned around and around, spinning in the air, screaming Amy's name.

Passers-by pulled bodies from the vehicle as flames started to flicker from beneath the engine. People screamed as the victims were dragged to safety on the tarmac. Amy and Alice's lifeless were bodies stretched out on the ground side by side, blood staining their clothes. Their two male companions sat dazed on the kerb.

A man shouted that he was a doctor. He tore off his coat and jacket, and tried to stifle the flow of blood oozing from the girl's chest. He barked instructions at two women who'd offered to help, giving mouth-to-mouth resuscitation.

Jack spun out of control in the air above, losing his mind, circling and diving like a panicked bird of prey. Feeling helpless, not knowing what to do.

Pyke screamed in his ear to calm down, but Jack wasn't listening. How had he not seen this coming?

The Erthfolk unaware of the cyclone happening above them, carried on fighting for the girls lives. Ambulances, fire crew, and police swarmed upon the scene. Droning sirens echoed through the streets, drowning Jack's cries. More people flooded the street to see if they could help. A few started praying out loud as the Paramedics took over.

Exhausted Jack fell to his knees at Amy's head, begging her not to die and yelling at the doctor to try harder.

He heard laughing, and didn't have to guess who's morbid taunting found entertainment in the scene. Gregori stood beside him, puffing his cigar and blowing spiralling trickles of smoke into Jack's face.

"She's coming with me, Jack, where she belongs...with her father. Get used to it. She's no longer yours."

"But she's done nothing wrong. What have you done? You can't take her. She's mine."

"Blah de blah, dear boy, Blah de bloody blah, do I look bothered?" Gregori rocked his head back and laughed.

Jack lost it. He stood up and threw himself at Gregori. With a loud pained roar he pushed Gregori through the burning car, through a row of houses and into the next street, his hands squeezing at his throat, trying to throttle him.

Pyke shouted at him. "Stop, Jack, stop. You'll be dragged down with him. Stop! He's dead already."

"I don't care. I'll go with her," shrieked Jack.

"You're not invited dear boy," gurgled Gregori, lashing out, trying to squirm free.

As Jack tightened his grip on Gregori's neck, he felt a vice-like hand on his shoulder, pulling him back and tossing Gregori to the ground. It was Micael. His statuesque body dwarfed Jack's. A shining white light surrounded him.

Gregori closed his eyes and shielded his face, unable to look into the light, crying out in pain.

"Jack, come with me. We'll hold her, we'll fight the energy." Micael's deep but soft voice resonated throughout the street.

"He's taking her down, he can't do that, she's done nothing wrong, she hasn't broken the deal... we need more time... I'm gonna kill him," screamed Jack, inconsolable, grabbing at Gregori's neck. Micael raised his hand.

"She needs you. You need to fight for her... and her child."

"What?"

"She's with child. We must hold onto her as she dies and pull her back."

"What child? Who's child?" Dazed, Jack didn't understand.

"We need to go now Jack."

Letting Gregori fall to the ground, Jack followed Micael up over the rooftops. Gregori shouted after them.

"Naive fools, you think you rule the world. But I know that evil is stronger than good. You'll see." He massaged his neck as he raced over the rooftops to follow them.

The crowd circled Amy and Alice, gawking at the sad sight while medics fought to keep them alive.

Micael and Jack knelt either side of Amy's body, placing their hands on her head and shoulders. Gregori hovered nearby, staring at his daughter.

"Fight for her, Jack. Concentrate." Micael whispered.

Jack closed his eyes, resisting the magnetic pull. With all his might, he summoned every last ounce of energy and forced it into her, wrenching her back from the earth. Micael matched Jack's efforts, and together they sparked a red force field glowing around them, burning, spitting, swirling. The noise thunderous, Gregori placed his hands over his ears.

The crowd saw nothing, just two girls lying in the street with gunshot wounds to their chests, pools of blood spreading onto the ground around them, not responding to their paramedics' strenuous efforts to keep them alive.

Micael and Jack started to burn up as they fought to keep her. Crashing thunder deafened their ears as their hands sizzled with pain.

A paramedic finally gave up, whispering to his colleague, "She's gone."

He let her go, wiped his brow and leaned back on his heels.

His colleague replied, "So has this one."

The doctor called it, pronouncing them dead and reciting the time from his digital watch.

Heat and thunder built more and more until a powerful explosion of bright light blasted Jack and Micael off Amy, crashing and spinning them into the sky.

Gregori stared up at them as they left, gave a wave and wry smile, and slid down through the ground.

Everything went deathly silent.

"We couldn't save them," a medic announced aloud, a defeated tone in his voice.

The crowd stepped back, giving the girls space, saying a prayer and mumbling blessings. The other passengers were lifted onto stretchers with cuts and bruises.

Chapter Seventy-Seven

Cloud 9

"It's not your fault. He's a bastard. We just didn't have enough time to work something out," Pyke said, soothing Jack as best he could.

"But why? She did nothing wrong to break the deal. For fucks sake, we save everyone else. Why can't we fucking save our own?" Jack slumped into the sofa.

"I know. But Jack…"

"She did nothing wrong… unless."

"What?"

"Unless." Jack held his face in his hands. "We had sex."

"What?"

"Sex, in her dreams, I made love to her… is that bad?"

"Shit Jack, I am not sure if the Fallen are allowed carnal relations with Erthfolk."

"So it's all my fault… she broke the deal."

"It may not be the reason, you don't know for sure."

Maggie stepped into the office, her shoulders hunched, her eyes red from crying. She walked over to Jack and offered her hand. He took it, stood up, and let her fall into his chest like a child, wrapping his arms around her.

"I'm so sorry, ma'am."

Pyke joined them, circling his two friends in his arms, the three holding each other tightly.

"I let her down. I let you down," Jack whispered.

The doors flung open.

"You SO did, you plonker."

The three looked up to see Amy and Alice standing in the doorway, both beaming with joy.

"Honey, I'm home," Amy smiled. "And I brought my friend with me… let's get back to work."

~~~ The End ~~~

THE DEAL

Thank you for reading *The Deal*, I hope you enjoyed it. I certainly had fun writing it and look forward to *Karma* and *The Calling*, next in *The Fallen Angel Series*.

If you enjoy (adult) psychological thrillers check out *The David Trilogy* on my S C Cunningham Amazon Author page.

Please leave a review if you think worthy, reviews give us Authors courage.

May the Angels and good karma go with you.

Siobhan x

www.sccunningham.com[1] @sccunningham8

---

1. http://www.sccunningham.com

Don't miss out!

Visit the website below and you can sign up to receive emails whenever S C Cunningham publishes a new book. There's no charge and no obligation.

https://books2read.com/r/B-A-ROPG-ANDU

BOOKS 2 READ

Connecting independent readers to independent writers.

Lightning Source UK Ltd.
Milton Keynes UK
UKHW010855080223
416610UK00013B/1078